D0400165

# Fortune Favors the Duke

## KRISTIN VAYDEN

sourcebooks
casablanca

*For my daughters: Women who love others well*
*change the world.*

Copyright © 2022 by Kristin Vayden
Cover and internal design © 2022 by Sourcebooks
Cover illustration by Judy York/Lott Reps

Sourcebooks and the colophon are registered trademarks of Sourcebooks.

All rights reserved. No part of this book may be reproduced in any form or by
any electronic or mechanical means including information storage and retrieval
systems—except in the case of brief quotations embodied in critical articles or
reviews—without permission in writing from its publisher, Sourcebooks.

The characters and events portrayed in this book are fictitious or are used
fictitiously. Apart from well-known historical figures, any similarity to real
persons, living or dead, is purely coincidental and not intended by the author.

Published by Sourcebooks Casablanca, an imprint of Sourcebooks
P.O. Box 4410, Naperville, Illinois 60567-4410
(630) 961-3900
sourcebooks.com

Printed and bound in Canada.
MBP 10 9 8 7 6 5 4 3 2 1

# *Prologue*

QUINTON'S FACE ACHED FROM THE PERPETUAL GRIN HE WORE. There was something utterly vindicating and equally entertaining about watching one's older brother mercilessly badgered by his companions. As the first of his friends to trip the parson's mouse-trap His Grace Avery, the Duke of Wesley, or Wes as he was famil-iarly called, was the recipient of more than his share of jokes and harassment, all in good humor. With the wedding only a week away, Quinton had helped the men assemble a last hurrah of sorts. After all, it was the end of an era.

It wasn't every day a duke married, and as the *ton* had so easily speculated, once His Grace tied the knot, soon the others would follow.

Good Lord, the mamas of the *ton* were probably salivating at the prospect. This particular group was the next generation of power within the House of Lords. All heirs to important titles, there wasn't one who wouldn't have to fight off the debutantes... rather, the eager mamas trying to entangle them with their daughters.

Wesley had resisted the temptation of marriage for nearly a decade, ever since he inherited the dukedom from their late father. But this past season, the usual debutantes had faded into the back-ground upon the presentation of Lady Catherine Greatheart, the season's incomparable and a tempting armful. Theirs had been a whirlwind courtship and was still the on-dit gossip of the *ton*.

Sudden hilarity brought Quin's attention back to the pres-ent. Willowby—rather, the Earl of Willowby—made a show of pretending to clench Wesley's bollocks. The group burst into a new round of laughter at Wes's reaction.

"What about you, Quin? Just enjoying my torment?" Wesley asked, turning to his younger brother.

"Yes, every moment. It's kind of pleasant to have someone else do my dirty work," Quinton replied with a devious tone.

"You always were the wily one of the two of us. You were just quiet so no one suspected it." Wesley rolled his eyes. "Well, we'd best be off if we're to make the hunting lodge before dark. Though I still think this is a daft idea, I'm happy to put my bachelor days behind me."

This statement brought about another round of remarks from his friends.

Wesley turned to Quinton once more. "Are you sure you don't want to come with us?"

"Someone has to be responsible. Plus I have a full day of teaching tomorrow. You'll have more fun without worrying if I'll tell Mother about your bad choices," Quinton replied, folding his arms as he leaned against the library door.

Wesley sent his brother an amused expression. "Because there's so much trouble to be had at a remote hunting lodge."

"First of all, that small castle is not just a hunting lodge." Quinton returned the eye roll. "Second, never underestimate your ability to find trouble. It's a lesson I've learned the hard way."

"Is that so? Why doesn't it surprise me that you're calling it a lesson? Do you ever stop teaching, Professor Errington?"

"No. I had way too much practice being your conscience as a child."

"With that, we'll take our leave." The Duke of Westmore grasped Wesley's arm and tugged him to the door. "Enough," he quipped.

Quinton watched as the men all filed out of the room, giving him firm handshakes and promises to keep an eye on his brother.

As the carriages rolled away, Quinton watched and considered how so much could change yet stay the same.

Growing up, he'd always known there was a difference between him and Wesley. One day, Wesley would be the duke. Oldest sons had a different destiny than those born after; it was an undeniable truth that had forged two sets of friends.

Those who would inherit...

And the younger brothers who would not, and in their turn would have to find their own way.

The world of the *ton* was small, and if a person wasn't known directly, he had at least been heard of. So when Quinton attended Cambridge to study, many faces had aligned with the names he had heard around the dinner table.

Wesley's friends all had younger brothers, similar in age to Quinton. That was all the common ground the group needed, and they quickly fell into easy friendship.

It was those older brothers who now accompanied Wesley to his celebration of the last of his bachelor days.

Quinton walked back into the foyer, directing his steps toward the library. An edge of guilt tormented his mind as he considered that perhaps he should have gone with his brother, but he disregarded the nagging thought. He had a full day of lectures and classes to teach tomorrow.

He'd see his brother when he returned, maybe do something together then, just the two of them.

Yes.

Guilt appeased, he collected his lecture notes and began to study.

Never once considering that tomorrow would be too late.

Because while common sense revealed that life was short, life still always caught folks off guard.

Every. Single. Time.

# One

THE BLOODRED WAX SHONE FROM ITS PLACE ON THE ENVELOPE. Pressing the seal into the pliable form, Quinton took a long and purposeful inhale, resisting the belief that *he* was the Duke of Wesley now.

It had been six months.

Six months since he'd seen his brother's face.

Heard his brother's voice.

He wasn't the only one bearing the inescapable burden of loss.

Every one of his best friends had suffered the same horror. Each one of their mothers had wailed, retiring to her room, refusing to leave for days.

Six months hadn't dampened the pain, just made it possible to keep surviving in the middle of it.

The suffocating pressure was constant. On top of the mourning, Quinton now had the weight of the title of duke and head of his family, the title and heritage bearing down upon him every moment of every day.

He had been content to be a professor of politics and history at Cambridge. He'd loved it, each moment.

But life didn't always turn out the way one expected.

After all, no one had suspected that Wesley and his friends would get *that* drunk, or fail to keep the rug away from the fire. Life had promised that they were young men, with their lives ahead of them…and in a few hours that had all been stolen, reduced to a pile of ash and rubble.

Quinton rose from the desk and walked away, emotionally

leaving the weight behind him. He needed to get out, to get away, but there was no escaping the truth.

He took in the familiar view of his study. He'd miss this place, desperately. Cambridgeshire was his heart's home, but duty called him to London. For a time he had attempted to do both: handle the dukedom and teach. But both the title and his teaching had suffered, forcing his hand. A resignation letter had been dispatched earlier, very reluctantly, to the Fellows at King's College at Cambridge University. It was an abominable time to walk away from the university, with enrollment increasing at such a pace as to outrun Oxford for the first time in the university's history. But there was nothing to do be done for it; he was now the Duke of Wesley and needed to be in London to attend to the matters left behind by his brother.

In thinking of his brother, a wave of grief crested within Quin. Would it be better or worse, returning to London? Leaving one place didn't mean the pain was left behind as well.

As he quit his study, he called to his butler, "Please have the carriage prepared. I'll be out front shortly."

The butler nodded, gave a rather spry bow for his seventy years, and went to arrange Quinton's request.

Bittersweet emotions fought within Quin as he considered his destination. He had spent countless hours in the Cambridge University library. For a brief moment, he had peace of mind. Memories flooded him of a simpler time when books held all the answers and all one needed was time. Quinton straightened his back. His footsteps echoed softly on the polished hardwood floor of the hall as he made his way to the front of the town house.

For a few hours, he would enjoy the peace and quiet of the library and then he would be on his way to London and his waiting mother.

Quin swayed with the movement of the carriage as it bumped over the cobbled stones of the jumble-gut street. His mind wandered as he moved past the scattered colleges throughout Cambridge, each one distinct in its field of study yet unified under the common university. Though he'd made the trek between Cambridge and London many times before, this one had a ring of finality to it that the other trips had lacked. They turned onto Trinity Lane, the ashlar buildings quiet sentinels of knowledge and study, housing ancient tomes of literature and history. The grand old buildings absorbed the twilight as people walked along the street beside them.

The tension melted away as the carriage drew nearer, then came to a stop just before the entrance to the library. Several Fellows nodded in recognition as they glimpsed his opening carriage door and the man within. Quin returned the gesture, feeling at home. In London, the simple social interaction would be far more formal.

"Return in two hours," Quinton instructed as he alighted from the carriage. He lifted his eyes to the tall height of the stone structure. It wasn't as tall as the British Museum, but what it lacked in grandeur it made up for with knowledge.

He took the steps and pressed a hand on the cool wood of the door. The welcoming scent of old dust, history, and ancient artifacts greeted him. His lips turned upward, but the sensation was utterly foreign.

The silence greeted him, his footsteps the only noise except for the delicate flip of pages by a few lingering students. The stone arches wound in circles above his head, directing the eye up to heaven, as if beseeching the Almighty for answers not yet known.

But sought.

Tall wooden bookcases lined the main aisle, each one holding eight shelves divided into three sections, the bookcases bending into an L shape to line the interior wall of the aisle as well. The library was peaceful, beautiful, and inviting for a man who had long preferred the company of books to people.

Quin directed his steps down the main lane till he found a

passage that led to an alcove he'd often used in researching history. Few used it, since it was off the main path, and he'd often enjoyed hours of privacy there. Selecting a modest wooden chair, he drew it out from the desk and took a seat, relaxing. A lamp illuminated the wooden desktop, exposing its grain and the way the finish had faded with use. It was one of the more private areas, tucked behind one of the shelves, where one could seek answers, dive into the depths of some book, and be lost for hours. Scholarly pursuits were simple that way. Have a question? Seek the answer. Read about it, research it if no one had dared to ask it yet, build upon the ideas of others, and grow the pool of ideas and knowledge. It was beautiful, known, and in many ways predictable.

The opposite of life.

The constancy and organization represented by the rows of the library gave a calm to Quin, his ragged soul exhaling the breath that had been held for far too long. Reaching out, he allowed his fingers to slide over the spines of the nearby books, each one unique, an adventure in knowledge of its own.

A book was lovely because one could always skip to the end to find out what happened.

Unlike life, which hit a person like a hammer on glass, shattering from the inside out.

How many hours had he planted himself at this very table as he studied? Closing his eyes, he could almost imagine he was back in time. But unlike with a book, one couldn't just flip a few pages back in life to start over.

It was done, and life moved forward, whether one wished it to or not. In the silence and isolation of the Cambridge University Old Library, Quin gave himself the permission to mourn. It had been necessary to be in control, strong, and collected, because everyone around him was falling to pieces. As a duke, as the head of his family, he didn't have the luxury of losing control, of showing weakness.

Here in the silence, in the isolation that should have felt lonely, Quin found himself finally able to release the bone-deep pain that had held him in chains for the past six months. With every silent tear that rolled down his face, the burden lifted. The pain remained; it was part of him now. It wouldn't ever fully leave; it was his. But the weight was slowly releasing, and as he wiped the salty tears from his eyes, clarity and peace overwhelmed him. The suffocating feeling lifted and in its place came a conviction that come what may, he would survive, and better yet, a determination to thrive in honor of his brother compelled him.

It wasn't a long time that he allowed himself the luxury to mourn, but the cleansing was deep. Quin collected himself. Odd how a library was more comforting than home.

But to him, it made sense. He'd always found books the greatest of friends.

And the ultimate confidants.

Quin pushed away from the table and stood, straightened his shoulders. After replacing the chair back under the table, he moved to leave. A book that hadn't been returned to its proper location caught his eye. Usually, the patrons were finicky about replacing the borrowed books, and when one occasionally forgot, the library staff or other faculty were keen to return it to its proper place. This particular tome had somehow been overlooked, so Quin lifted the book from its resting place, studying the title so that he might put it back where it belonged.

*The Westernization and Civilization of Russia.*

Interested, Quin flipped through the pages of the volume, quickly ascertaining it referred to the time period of Catherine the Great. As he opened the book, he skimmed the pages, quickly finding he agreed with the author's praise of the longest-ruling woman in Russian history. It was a welcome distraction, and finding his seat once more, he gave in to the impulse to read several chapters before he checked his pocket watch, noting that his carriage would be waiting.

He returned the book to its home in the shelves and cast a long-ing last scan at the alcove. Eyes forward, he reminded himself, and made his way back to the center aisle leading to the door. Focusing on what was ahead rather than what he was leaving behind, he pushed on the brass handle and stepped into the waning light.

The barouche sank under his weight, but as the driver took them back out onto the road, Quin could have sworn that he felt two stone lighter.

Grief would do that.

So would the promise of healing.

And he was hopeful that he was on the road to the latter.

# Two

*I beg you take courage; the brave soul can mend even disaster.*

—*Catherine the Great*

LADY CATHERINE GREATHEART STIRRED HER TEA SLOWLY, realizing she wasn't sitting up straight and equally not caring a fig.

"Ducky—"

"Grandmother…" Catherine spoke the word carefully but with a warning edge to her tone.

"I was just going to mention that your sugar cube melted about a minute ago and you're still stirring…" The charming Lady Greatheart arched a brow.

Catherine paused in her stirring, realizing her grandmother was entirely correct. Then with an impish grin, she stirred three more times just because.

"Always pushing. But I must say, it really is part of your charm," her grandmother replied, sipping her tea.

"I find that hard to believe." Catherine lifted her own teacup.

Her grandmother lowered her chin. "Many may say such a thing, but in your case, it is unfortunately the truth."

"Unfortunately?"

"Yes. Because then you won't outgrow it." She gave a slow, disappointed shake to her head, but the corners of her mouth curved in slight amusement.

"And you say this from experience, no doubt," Catherine remarked from just over her teacup as she took a sip.

"Love, where do you think you come by it? Your father? God rest his soul, a more circumspect man never walked the earth." She gave a slight heavenward squint.

"Papa was the most genuine person I know."

"This is true, but the poor man couldn't understand sarcasm unless it was written in Greek."

"At least he was intelligent."

"No arguing there. But I rather think you inherited the best qualities of both your parents. You're brilliant like your father. I'm not sure what I'd do if you weren't inclined toward mathematics. Those ledgers would certainly be the death of me! And your mother, well…she was the beauty, inside and out."

"And you, of course."

"Of course." Lady Greatheart gestured with a flick of her wrist. "Now, what are we doing today? I'm tired of holing up in this estate mourning. I know he was a great man, ducky, but you're young. You have many days ahead of you…and as it turns out, I don't, and I'd like to spend them somewhere other than inside these walls." She sent a dirty look to the nearest wall.

Catherine smirked, then gave in to a small snicker. It was freeing to laugh. There had been little of it since the accident. By now, she should have been married for nearly six months and bearing the title of duchess. But fate had a different plan and nearly shattered her heart in the process.

And the price paid by the families that mourned had been great, was still great. Hadn't she suffered her own share of loss though? She understood better than most the price of moving on without those one loved. At a young age, pneumonia had stolen her mother, only to have her father follow her soon after. Her grandmother said it had been a broken heart that took his life, and Catherine had no reason to think otherwise. It had been a love match of the sincerest variety between the two of them. She had hoped that the match between her and the duke would produce the same kind of relationship.

Her thoughts wandered to Avery, the late duke. So much had been lost that night. Friendship, shared interests, and so many opportunities. Even as she thought the last word, it shamed her because of how it sounded mercenary in intent. But that wasn't the case; her heart had been fully invested with Avery. They had made plans—such plans! As a duchess, her potential to help others would be near limitless. Funding orphanages, assisting the poor, sponsoring the arts…just to name a few. And all of it was reduced to the ashes left by the fire that consumed both her betrothed and the dreams they'd shared. What little she was able to do now was small in comparison to their grand plans. Yet losing Avery… That was by far the most painful.

Catherine didn't delude herself into thinking there was an abundance of forward-thinking men like him, men who would appreciate a woman's keen mind for mathematics and investment. A woman who would appreciate business ventures more than nee-dlepoint. Avery was a rare find, and her heart had immediately known he was her match, but it was for naught. To have everything one ever wanted right at the tip of one's fingers, only to realize it was only ashes. As the gray cinders sifted through, all that was left were a stained heart and hands. Shoulders caving slightly, she released her pent-up frustration.

"Lost in your thoughts again? Someone should give you a map," her grandmother badgered.

"As if you never woolgather," Catherine replied good-naturedly. Through all the loss she had suffered, her grandmother had been there—her pillar, her rock, her constancy and comic relief. There wasn't a more blunt, cheeky, or brazen woman in the *ton*, and Catherine loved her more than anyone else in the world.

"I'm old. People expect it. Besides"—she set her teacup down with a dainty clink—"I look aloof and thoughtful when I wool-gather." She offered a proud sniff.

"I see," Catherine remarked with humor.

"Now then, what shall we do today?" The elderly woman leaned forward with a sparkle of mischief in her gray eyes. "And if you mention anything about ledgers or a new investment opportunity you read about, I'll simply ignore you till you come up with a sensible answer," Lady Greatheart said with a defiant lift of her chin.

Catherine replied with amusement, "But that's ever so much more interesting than the color of the season. And I do have some interesting information—"

"Tut-tut-tut. I said no. And I give you far more freedom than a young lady should have in all those areas. Heaven help me."

"It's served you well. Because of my 'freedom,' as you put it, the estate has grown."

At this, her grandmother gave her a withering glare. "I'm aware, as you remind me every time I tell you to do something more sensible—as per our current situation." She gave a flick of her wrist to prove her point.

Catherine decided to capitulate. "Shopping? It's been a while since we've visited Bond Street," she offered.

"Brilliant. I need a new pair of gloves. Mine seem worn." Her grandmother lifted a perfectly white and delicately gloved hand in the air, frowning as she studied it.

"Nearly threadbare," Catherine said with a cheeky tone.

"I'm glad you agree. We should also stop at the modiste and see about some new dresses for you." Her grandmother paused, then softened her voice. "The season will be here before you know it, ducky. And while you might not be ready now, I do believe that you shouldn't put off moving forward."

Catherine nodded, her eyes downcast as she absorbed her grandmother's meaning. The *marriage mart*, another season... the courting, the flirting. She wasn't sure she could do it. But she didn't have to...yet. It was another four months away. Perhaps by then? She wasn't against the idea of love; the problem was all the unknowns. What if she'd already found her match, and there was no one else for her? What if no one ever measured up? How could she promise to honor another when she constantly compared him to a ghost? It wasn't fair to him or to her.

But she couldn't very well sit in her house for the rest of her life, avoiding potential suitors.

"I'm sorry if I hurt you, ducky. I wasn't trying to be insensitive."

"No, you weren't. You're being sensible. And I understand that," Catherine added quickly, wanting to put her dear grandmother's fears to rest. "It's just… What if I already had my chance at love? What if I have to settle? I don't want to, and that sounds terribly selfish. Also"—Catherine peeked up at her grandmother's dear face, encouraged by the lack of judgment on her expression—"it's so much bloody work, Grandma!"

At this, her grandmother burst into a fit of hilarity. "Good mercy, child, you sound older than me!"

"Do you deny it, though?" Catherine asked with a lilt to her tone, entertained at her grandmother's amusement.

"No. You're right, but I don't think I've ever heard a lady your age mention it, let alone realize it!" Lady Greatheart replied with mirth.

"It is! The flirting, the pandering, the waltzing, the guessing… good Lord." Catherine reclined in her chair, her tone exasperated.

Lady Greatheart lifted a hand to still her granddaughter's words. "The romance, the potential, the what-if, and the flirting with forever, my dear. Look at the beauty rather than the price."

Catherine bit her lip, nodding once. "You are, of course, correct."

"As usual."

Catherine added, "And humble."

"Always."

"Are you quite finished?"

"Not nearly, but I'll let you continue." Her grandmother gave a flourish of her hand.

"How kind," Catherine replied with a smirk. "You win. I'll look at the beauty of the process rather than the effort required. And when…*when* the time comes, I'll put forth an effort. But since that day is not today, we should most certainly have a lovely day outside of these walls."

"I agree wholeheartedly, my dear. I'll have the carriage ready in half an hour."

The fresh breeze cleared the sooty air of Bond Street as Catherine and her grandmother leisurely shopped. They visited the Emporium for Ladies, purchasing several hand creams and a vial of rosewater, and looked in at a milliner's. The day was lovely, even with the chill of the late February air, and seemed to call out to the London *ton*, which meant that several inquiring stares followed Catherine and Lady Greatheart's movements.

"Ignore them, ducky," her grandmother whispered as they strolled in front of a shop.

In the reflection of the window, Catherine watched as a young couple eyed them in passing, then murmured soon after. Heat swelled in her cheeks. Were they questioning her mourning for her fiancé? It had been six months. Her bravery melted like sugar in hot tea, and more than anything, she wished to be home. But as another lady happened by, offering a wave, Catherine's resolve strengthened. She wouldn't let them dictate her future…or her feelings. It was idiotic, really, to live and die by their opinion when it was as fickle as the London rain.

"That's right, dear. Keep your chin up." Her grandmother offered a proud pat to her hand. "Now, what do you think of the gloves in this shop?"

Catherine followed her into the entrance, thankful to be out of the prying view of those on the street. Her grandmother inspected several pairs of gloves, her dainty fingers running over the kid leather.

The proprietress continued to display varieties, and Catherine watched as Lady Greatheart dismissed options, one after another, unsatisfied with the quality, the stitching, or something else equally invisible to Catherine's eye.

"These." Her grandmother pointed to a pair and gave a direct nod. In short work, they were wrapped up. Catherine dispatched the box to their waiting footman as they exited the shop, then carried on down the street.

"I always forget how fiddly you are with your gloves," Catherine badgered.

"It's the first thing a gentleman touches, dear. It's wise to pay attention to details such as these." She lifted her fingers, waggling them in her gloves.

"Ah, is that how you snared Grandfather? Your soft gloved hands?"

At this, her grandmother lowered her tone as if imparting a secret. "No, but it didn't hurt, I'll tell you that." She hid a smirk behind her hand. "Here's the modiste. We should get a head start. Don't want all the good colors and fabrics already spoken for."

The bell tinkled as they entered the shop. "May I help you?" the assistant asked, coming to stand before them.

"Yes, do you have the new fashion plates from Paris? And what are the upcoming colors?"

The lady nodded. "Yes, my lady. Come with me, if you please." She led them to a back room with soft seating, curtains, and mirrors lining the walls. A red-carpeted stool occupied the middle, where ladies would stand and wait for their new dresses to be fitted.

"This year, blossom will be the most requested. I happen to have several shades of its rich rosy pink, if you wish to take a look?"

"Of course," Catherine replied, earning an approving nod from her grandmother.

As the lady left to retrieve the fabric samples, her grandmother leaned over to Catherine. "Such a color will be stunning on you."

"Thank you."

After paging through the fashion book and selecting several bolts of material, they ordered a new wardrobe for the upcoming season. It seemed forever away; yet it would take time to create the types of masterpieces Grandmother had insisted they purchase.

"Apparently, gloves alone won't do the trick for gentlemen?" Catherine remarked as they left the shop, choosing levity even when it still felt like sheer willpower rather than actual emotion.

"Like I said, gloves are the first thing a gentleman touches, but your gown? That's the first thing they see. Keep up, ducky. I'm giving you pearls of wisdom here." Her grandmother elbowed her gently. "Now, are you finished shopping or do you wish for a change of scenery?"

"Don't tell me you're getting tired." Catherine narrowed her eyes.

"I never admit defeat, love. You know this."

"Just making sure."

An exasperated expression formed on her grandmother's face. "How about we have the carriage take us to Hyde Park? It's about the fashionable hour and, love, with all the necks craning to see you, it would be best to just give them an eyeful and then be done with it. Don't you think?"

"No," Catherine replied. "But yes."

"That's my girl."

"Might as well get it over and done with." Catherine grimaced.

"The sooner the better," her grandmother intoned as they found their carriage and were assisted in by the footman.

Hyde Park wasn't far from Bond Street, but the congestion of carriage traffic made it seem much farther. After they arrived, Catherine alighted from the carriage and noted that the weather was holding up. One could never guess with London weather. One moment it could be beautifully sunny, only to have the heavens open the next. The sun broke through the trees, adding warmth, and Catherine stepped forward, waiting for her grandmother.

"It's certainly a busy day today," Lady Greatheart commented, noticing the activity surrounding the park. Rotten Row had quite the congregation of horses milling about and racing by turns. The path that led to the Serpentine was dotted with ladies and gentlemen walking leisurely, and several squirrels raced across the open grass from one tree to the next.

"Where do you wish to go?" Catherine asked.

"Anywhere but here." Lady Greatheart started off toward the Serpentine's path.

At least one of them was decisive. As they meandered down the path, they gave a nod or smile to each person they passed. Most of them were familiar faces, and few seemed judgmental; mostly, the expressions were of pity—which almost seemed worse.

They were rounding a corner when Catherine's breath rushed from her. Coming around the bend was a tall gentleman, which wasn't startling in and of itself, but it was his expression.

Those eyes.

She knew those eyes.

And judging by the way the gentleman froze nearly midstep, he recognized her as well.

"Lady Catherine," he greeted her softly after a lingering pause. He bowed gracefully, taking a full appraisal of her as he did so.

"Quinton… Y-your Grace." Her voice failed her. It was astoundingly difficult, calling him by the title that had belonged to his brother. They were familiar enough; hadn't they almost been family? Surely she should have called him by his first name alone, yet she hesitated and added the title. After all, that familial connection had ended.

His expression clouded, shoulders stiffened, and instinctively she understood how the use of the title must hurt him. Hadn't he lost even more than she? She'd known Avery for a few months, while Quinton had known him lifelong.

He seemed to pause, debating. He took a step closer and spoke. "Please continue to call me Quin. Our association is such that surely it can be possible for you to do so, and I would so much prefer it."

A wave of relief washed over her. "Quin it is."

"Thank you." His eyes shifted to her grandmother. "My apologies, Lady Greatheart."

"No need." Sunlight flashed bright on her glove when she held up a hand as he rose from his bow. "How are you, Quinton?" Lady Greatheart asked, her kind eyes full of sympathy. "It's been an age, and I really must call on your mother as well. It's been too long."

"As well as can be expected," Quin answered, his attention shifting to Catherine. His expression was inquiring, but he didn't voice the words.

Catherine appreciated his restraint. How many had asked her the same question? How many times had she outright lied, or tried to avoid the question? More than she could count. And it was certainly the same for him.

"It's a lovely day, is it not?" she chimed in, neatly changing the subject.

His expression shifted to relief. "It's truly glorious. All the rain seemed eternal."

"Indeed," Catherine agreed, followed by a somewhat awkward pause.

"If you'll excuse me," Quin said after a moment longer.

"Of course. And please give my regards to your mother," Lady Greatheart instructed.

"I will indeed," he said. "Lady Catherine." He nodded to her.

"Quin," Catherine answered softly and then watched as he passed, leaving them halted on the path.

"Well, that was interesting." Her grandmother broke the silence after a moment.

"Yes. It certainly was."

"Quin, hmm?" her grandmother remarked as they started down the path once more.

Catherine wasn't sure if her grandmother was asking or just talking to herself, so she waited, studying her face.

"I think it's time we called on Her Grace the Duchess of Wesley." Her grandmother nodded once for emphasis.

Catherine frowned. "Of course, but…why now?"

But her grandmother had picked up her stride, and if she'd heard the question, she'd chosen not to answer.

Which made Catherine suspicious.

Her dear grandmother was a lot of things, but secretive wasn't one of them. She'd let her keep her thoughts to herself for the moment, for certainly, soon they would overflow in one way or another.

# Three

QUIN DIDN'T REMEMBER THE REST OF THE WALK IN HYDE PARK nor the drive home, his thoughts focused on Lady Catherine. The quiet tick of the clock in his study kept time as his thoughts kept him company, yet he gave his head a decisive shake as his focus landed on the stacks of ledgers that lined the mahogany desk, all awaiting his perusal. Missives from his steward, party invitations, and legal documents all vied for his attention as he continued to transition from professor to duke. He missed the study, the expression in students' eyes when they understood a portion of history or economics that they hadn't known before. The reward of knowledge and growth were like air to him. Yet responsibility was vastly more important and the family legacy now weighed upon his shoulders. He withdrew the ink and began to work.

When the clock struck the hour, Quin paused and took the opportunity to reminisce about the chance meeting earlier with Lady Catherine. To be sure, seeing her had been difficult, and in a moment, he found himself six months in the past, watching his brother court the young woman.

He could find no fault in her; rather, he praised his brother's choice of bride. She was kind, but not overly sensitive. She was entertaining in conversation, without being overly polished. There was an artless beauty to her that spilled over into the room; it had been clear that she and Wes, or Avery, as she addressed him, were fond of each other, which in and of itself would have been a promising start for their marriage.

On several occasions Wes had mentioned Catherine's affinity

for numbers and her keen interest in finance. Quin had openly congratulated him on finding such a rarity among the *ton*, one who also wasn't an utter bluestocking. But now he wondered how Catherine would fare with other potential suitors. It wasn't common for men to appreciate input from women on investments or tallying up ledgers. Wes was a rarity among men as much as she was a rarity among women.

But it was all gone so fast and too soon. He'd been so wrapped up in his own pain that he had all but forgotten about hers. How had she fared these past months? What had become of her? Certainly, she was well cared for. Lady Greatheart was a well-respected and established countess in the *ton*, but to his knowledge, she was Catherine's only family. Assuredly, she had her own demons to face at the loss of such a future as a duchess. But Quin didn't suspect her of putting more value on the title than the man, which almost made it worse. If she had been mercenary in intent, it would have been easy to ignore her loss, but he was certain she had cared far more for Wesley than for his title.

Guilt crept in, reminding him that he wasn't the only one dealing with loss. While he didn't have any responsibility for her, he couldn't help but feel as if he'd shirked some aspect of gentlemanly conduct by not seeing after her in some way, however small. Regardless, there was nothing to be done for it now.

The clock in the hall chimed the hour and pulled him from his thoughts. At the fifth chime, he rose from his chair. His mother had invited him to a dinner party that evening, and he had already procrastinated enough in readying himself for the event. No doubt she had invited several eligible ladies to attend, all hopeful as they would take turns making introductions with the newly titled duke.

It wasn't that he was against marriage, but not now. And certainly not to someone fascinated with his title.

Hell, the title was the part of himself that didn't feel real, and any lady interested in that aspect was least suited for him.

Yet it seemed his title was now the most attractive part.

Quin took the stairs to his chambers. From one nightmare to another, the title seemed to be more of a curse than anything else.

In no time, his valet had readied him for the evening's events, and with a rather trepidatious spirit, he ordered the carriage made ready. It wasn't a long ride to his family home. He could easily make it his primary residence, but something about having his own space called to him, made him keep his bachelor lodgings even when they proved utterly unnecessary.

As he stepped into the carriage, he noted the way the lamps around his door flickered warmly, and he had an impulse to exit the coach and go back inside, consequences from his mother be damned. But he wouldn't do that. More than any other virtue, responsibility weighed heavily upon his shoulders. He had given his word, and by God, he would keep it.

Even if it was just for a bloody dinner party.

Quin allowed his mind to wander as he made the short jaunt to the other side of Mayfair. As his carriage approached, he noted the other carriages lining the drive and wondered if maybe his mother hadn't divulged the full details about her "small party." It wouldn't surprise him.

She had recently been a woman on a mission: find him a wife.

Much against his will, his word, and his vehement arguments to the contrary.

He hoped he was incorrect in his assessment of the party, but he held suspicions. As the carriage rolled to a stop before the entrance, Quin started to plan an escape to the library midparty, just in case it was too stuffy. It was his own home, and if he wished to disappear... Well, that was certainly his prerogative, was it not?

He straightened his jacket as he stepped from the carriage, deeply inhaling the night air. How the hell had Wesley done this—own the title and carry it with such delight? How had he not questioned every smile and suspected every woman of mercenary motives? A new well of respect for his lost brother overflowed.

Quin gave a nod to the footman as he opened the door, the hum of voices immediately filling the air along with the scent of perfume and beeswax from the many candles. He strode through the foyer, his eyes lingering on the stairs that led to the library, silently promising himself to visit there later. A memory of the Cambridge University library washed over him, leaving a wave of longing in its wake. He dismissed the emotion and focused on the flickering candles illuminating the hall. The hum of voices rose in volume as he approached the parlor, and with the escalation of noise, his tension increased as well. Distracting himself, he noted that his mother had redecorated the hall, removing a bust of some relative of importance and replacing it with a crystal vase filled with roses, their scent adding to the perfume of the air.

His movement was nearly silent on the rug that lined the hall, covering the newly polished hardwood floors, but his mother greeted him at the entrance to the parlor as if she'd heard his approach.

"Ah, Quin, how good of you to come." Her hazel eyes danced with some sort of motive.

She had the right intentions, Quin reminded himself, but her application was usually faulty. He steeled himself, taking into account those in attendance.

His suspicions were swiftly validated as he noted several young ladies perched beside their mothers, all eyeing him subtly.

His attention darted back to his mother as he bowed and greeted her. "Mother. I see you've been busy."

"Someone has to be," she quipped. She had the good grace to look abashed. "It's not as bad as you think."

"I find that hard to believe," Quin observed.

"That's because you haven't met everyone yet."

"And I'm sure you're eager to remedy that, aren't you?" Quin challenged.

"It's like you read my mind, darling. Come."

His mother led the way through the parlor, pausing for him to nod to previous acquaintances. Quin tried to linger in speaking with a few, but his mother was dogged in her determination, and by the time they approached Lady Freemon, Quin had accepted his fate of meeting every eligible lady in the room before the dinner began.

"Lady Freemon, allow me to introduce my son, His Grace Quinton Duke of Wesley." Her voice broke ever so slightly over the title.

Truly, if Quin hadn't been waiting for it, or listening for it, he wouldn't have noticed. But it was there, and he felt a kinship with his mother for a moment.

"A pleasure." Quin took his cue and bowed to the lady.

"Your Grace." Lady Freemon gave a curtsy, then turned to the young lady beside her. "And this is my daughter, Miss Amanda Freemon."

"A pleasure." Quin addressed the younger version of her mother.

Dark hair was swept into an intricate design, far more elaborate than a "small dinner party" would require. Her cheeks turned pink at the introduction, and her hazel eyes darted to the floor. It wasn't easy for her to be paraded about, he realized. And in a moment of empathy, he relaxed a bit.

"Thank you for accepting our invitation," he added benevolently.

"We wouldn't have missed it, Your Grace," Lady Freemon assured him quickly.

His mother was already waving, all but shuffling him along to the next lady and daughter.

So it continued for the next quarter hour, though Quin

would have sworn it was much longer than that. As he finished the last introduction, he heard a slight gasp beside him. Curious, he turned to see what had startled the woman. Her focus was on the doorway. He turned his attention in the same direction and froze. Lady Greatheart and Lady Catherine had paused by the door. He felt rather than saw the collective stares of the room upon them and took a step forward to greet them to break the tension. God bless his mother, she'd beaten him to it with a quick step and was already clasping hands with Lady Greatheart, welcoming them.

Lady Catherine's eyes were lowered, as if forcing a calm that didn't react to the interest of the ongoing stares. After a moment, she lifted her eyes to accept his mother's welcome. For a second, he caught her attention. Quin nodded, barely, but to communicate that he understood. That he was sorry. That he saw her and welcomed her too.

Odd how such a simple gesture could communicate so much, but pain—shared pain—had a way of changing a person, changing the way things were seen.

The way people were seen.

He watched her as his mother offered them a seat beside her while they waited for dinner to be served.

When the butler arrived, Quin released a sigh of relief as everyone stood, waiting for him to take his mother's hand and lead the way to the dining room.

He filed through the room and offered his arm to his mother. "Would you do me the honor?"

The Duchess of Wesley inclined her head. "Thank you, but I wish to talk to Lady Catherine for just a moment. Would you escort Lady Greatheart, dear?"

Lady Greatheart was the second-ranking lady, so it made sense, but it was rare that Quin had seen his mother decline his offer. Turning to Lady Greatheart, he offered his arm. "My lady?"

"Ah, it's not every day a handsome devil offers me his arm."

Lady Greatheart smiled, setting her hand on his arm. "Careful, I might not let go." She had a twinkle in her eyes as she looked back at her granddaughter.

Catherine gave a soft giggle that seemed to release some of the tension in her shoulders. "You do that. Enjoy your escort."

"I will. Let's walk slowly, Quin." She paused, then whispered, "It is acceptable for me to call you Quin still?"

Quin couldn't hide his amusement. He was convinced that even if he refused, she'd simply do what she wished, regardless. But it just so happened that he didn't mind her calling him Quin at all. Hadn't he given them leave earlier? "Quin is perfectly acceptable."

"It fits you," she remarked as they made their way into the hall toward the dining hall.

"Thank you. I've always liked my name."

"I wasn't ever content with mine," Lady Greatheart commented distractedly.

"Oh?"

"No. Esmeralda seems too exotic for me. Never fit."

No, exotic she was not; rather, she was a classic Englishwoman, but it was a stately name, and in that respect it did fit her well.

"I beg to differ. It's rather regal."

She studied him. "I never thought of it like that. I like regal. Well, you can call me what you wish. Just don't call me old, yet. I'm close but not close enough to admit it."

He appreciated her candor. "Whatever you wish."

"I like you, Quin. You've been through hell, and you still have your heart and wits about you." She patted his hand.

Quin startled at hearing her rather vulgar word, but her compliment rang all the truer for it.

"Why, thank you." He offered her a roguish smile, hoping to play the part for her.

"Ah, there's that devilish expression. You know, your brother had that very same one."

Her candid words sent a shock of surprise through him. It wasn't often that others mentioned his brother. Usually, it was only in the safe and selective confines of his family that his brother's name was mentioned with anything but a swift and usually awkward condolence following.

"Don't look so shocked. I know it still hurts. As one who knows firsthand how it aches to lose a loved one, I also can tell you from a depth of experience that talking about them helps, even though it hurts. And"—she gave a furtive glance behind them, as if making sure they didn't garner others' attention—"I'd wager that it warms your heart to think that you share something with your brother, carry it with you even though he no longer can." She nodded with emphasis.

Quin turned his attention ahead, not trusting himself to reply at the moment. Unconventional as they were, her words held truth. He did find it comforting to know he shared his brother's smile; it was a piece of Wes that he was able to carry about with him.

"I tend to push too far, or that's what Catherine tells me, so pardon me if I overstepped," she murmured softly.

Quin turned to her then, offering a tone of reassurance. "No, not at all, my lady. Turns out you were right."

"I'll try not to let it go to my head."

They were approaching the dining room, and Quin led her to the proper place beside his mother's, then pulled out the chair for her, waiting for her to be seated.

"Thank you for the lovely chat." He spoke softly.

"The pleasure was all mine." She then turned her attention to his mother, who had just found her seat.

Quin took his place as well, noting the way Lady Greatheart and Lady Catherine engaged his mother in conversation. It had been some time since he'd seen his mother enjoy herself so readily in company, without forcing an engaging nature. He would have expected it to be harder for her to see Wesley's once-betrothed, for that to bring up painful memories, but it seemed to do the opposite; rather, it seemed healing.

For both of them.

Odd.

Maybe the truth wasn't just surviving but finding a new path that hadn't been open before, perhaps one that had been intended for him all along. Death had a way of closing doors but opening others. He only wished he knew which doors were opening and which path he should take.

# Four

*If you feel unhappy, then place yourself above that and act so that your happiness does not get to be dependent on anything.*

—Catherine the Great

CATHERINE COULD FEEL THE ATTENTION OF THE ROOM CENtered on her. Though most of the ladies appeared to be conversing, sipping their soup, or taking a delicate swallow of wine, in truth they were watching her from the corners of their eyes. Their posture was attentive, and if she moved too quickly or spoke too loudly, the facade of their inattention fell and they would glance in her direction. It was distracting at the least, and overwhelmingly stifling at the same time. As if sensing her distress, her grandmother reached under the table and placed a soft hand at her knee, squeezing tightly.

"We had a lovely day today, didn't we, dear?" Her grandmother directed a question to her, and Catherine snapped her focus to the Duchess of Wesley. Nodding first, she then forced her full attention on the woman who once was to be her mother-in-law.

"Yes, it was a fine day, and we took in a bit of sunshine." Catherine was careful to leave out that they had ordered dresses for the season, feeling such a revelation might not be welcome.

"Did you know that blossom is this season's color?" Lady Greatheart interjected into the conversation, causing a flush of heat to creep up Catherine's neck, surely making her cheeks pink.

Leave it to her grandmother to mention the very thing she wished to remain a secret.

"Oh! I had heard, but is it the same weak and watery shade of pink, what was it? Three years ago?" The Duchess of Wesley clucked her tongue. "That color did no one any favors."

"Agreed. And no, this year's is more of a rose pink."

Catherine studied the Duchess of Wesley, noting the way she took the subtle communication of their shopping for the season—meaning potential husband hunting—without a single sign of disapproval or shock.

Was everyone moving on? Wasn't it too quick? Yet at the same time, her fiancé's death felt like a lifetime ago.

She wasn't the same person who had celebrated her engagement with the late Duke of Wesley. Pain changed people, and she was no exception. A warm hand touched hers, pulling her from the deep thoughts.

"Blossom is a lovely color and I do believe will be well suited for you, my dear." The Duchess of Wesley nodded, her expression one of resolve and intention. Her words were heavy with implication, but as she glanced away and squeezed her napkin uncommonly tight, it was clear that the words had also come at a cost.

Didn't everything come with a price?

Catherine nodded. "Thank you, I'm not sure I'm suited for anything at the moment," she added softly.

The Duchess of Wesley gave a single nod; as her eyes lifted, she had understanding in her expression.

Thankfully, Catherine was saved from lingering on what had just been communicated silently between them.

"I was so thankful to receive your kind invitation. You'll have to forgive me for not accepting it sooner," Lady Greatheart remarked.

"It's quite diverting, and with all this rain, it's nice to do something of an amusing nature," the duchess agreed.

"Ah yes, agreed. We said the same to…" Lady Greatheart paused, her brow furrowing.

Catherine regarded her grandmother; it wasn't often she paused midsentence. Lady Greatheart cast a furtive glance to Quin, who was taking a sip of wine.

He set his glass down and happened to meet her wary expression.

"Ahh, you saw my son today." The Duchess of Wesley nodded, the movement garnering Catherine's attention.

Relieved, Catherine released the tension she had been holding. It wasn't often that her grandmother made a faux pas, and when it happened, most just forgave her trespass based on her age or rank. But this time, the gossip would have spun wildly. It was going to be enough that they were attending her former fiancé's dinner party, but if her grandmother had slipped and called Quin by his Christian name, and others had *heard*…the rumor mill would have gone into fits. Such familiarity was unconventional at best. And in society where rumors were traded as currency, it would have been potentially disastrous. On the other hand, calling Quin by his title, to those close to the situation, was painful. And could cause undue pain to the Duchess of Wesley. It was a quagmire of problems no matter how one looked at it. And one couldn't discount the over-eager ears of those at the table, those that were doing their best to seem unconcerned. Catherine knew any interesting news would be all over London by morning.

She forced her attention back to her grandmother, who had jumped on the Duchess of Wesley's words. "Yes, we happened to run into him in Hyde Park."

"So, my son pulled himself away from his lectures and books long enough to take in the air? This is news to me." The Duchess of Wesley gave a pointed expression aimed at her son. "He's not at Cambridge University for the time being, but one would think he were still actively teaching."

Upon hearing her words, Quin smirked. "Ah, I take your advice, and now I'm harassed for it? How does that seem fair?"

"It is not."

"And I'm assuming you care not for such a bias," Quin replied, his amusement growing as he pestered his mother.

"You're correct in your assumption." The Duchess of Wesley bobbed a curt nod, causing a single dimple to wink in her cheek.

It was good, healing even, to see them banter a bit. On the occasions when Catherine had dined with Wesley and his family, it had been clear that they all held a fondness for one another. They were cheeky and smart-witted with a good dose of humor and love underlying their repartee. She wondered how long it had been since they had eased back into their old ways. Probably too long.

"We must have just missed you, Your Grace," Lady Freemon interjected. "We were enjoying the park today as well. It was quite busy."

Catherine watched as Quin directed his attention to Lady Freemon, nodding in response to her statement. "I must confess I was merely using the park as a shortcut, so my amble through it was quite brief. I'm sorry to have missed you, Lady Freemon."

Lady Freemon nodded, accepting his complimentary words, her attention sliding to her daughter beside her as if accepting them as proof of his interest.

Catherine could see the hunger for Quin's title on the faces of those at the table. How had Wesley described it?

It had been a topic of conversation once, long ago...

They had been speaking of titles and family, and he leaned against the stone wall they were walking beside. His blue eyes danced, then they took on a contemplative expression. "Titles, you know... They make the most terrible man desirable and the most desirable man terrible."

She frowned, curious regarding what point he was trying to make.

"Catherine, you are marrying into a title, not the title. There's a difference. Most people don't see that, they just see the title and not the man behind it." He pushed off from the wall and grasped her chin softly. "And that's why I'm thrilled to marry you…not your name, your dowry…you."

The memory flooded Catherine, stealing her air. Everything was too close, too familiar. The walls of the room closed in, inch by inch, as she struggled to take in the oxygen, knowing it was just in her head. An illusion, but her chest was tight. Her hands tingled, her eyes stung, and yet she was frozen, unable to move. Willing her focus to shift, she was able to make eye contact with her grandmother.

Lady Greatheart's eyes widened in alarm, and she quickly made an excuse, grasping Catherine's arm with a fortitude that gave away her grandmother's fear. Catherine leaned into the strength of her grandmother's hold and stood, closing her eyes as the edges of her vision grew dark on the perimeter. Placing one foot in front of another, she followed her grandmother out of the room. As soon as the door closed behind them, Catherine found a nearby bench and all but collapsed.

"Ducky, ducky!" Lady Greatheart whispered loudly, her hands gripping Catherine's chin. "Look at me!"

Catherine obeyed, each inhale labored, still seemingly unproductive.

"Stay with me, ducky. If you swoon now, it will be all over the *ton* tomorrow. Stay with me."

Catherine managed a nod.

"I'm going to find a maid, a footman—someone to get our carriage. Don't. Move." Lady Greatheart's expression was fierce, and again Catherine nodded.

A short breeze let her know that Lady Greatheart had left, no doubt moving as quickly as possible. Catherine leaned back against the wall, inhaling deeply, listening to the sound of her racing heart, willing her body to calm. It was all in her mind.

But damn if it didn't feel like she'd run clear to the Thames and back.

"Are you unwell?" A voice startled her, and she jumped. Green eyes watched her as Quin lowered himself to her eye level. His expression was concerned, but controlled. There wasn't the edge of panic that was in her grandmother's eyes, and it gave her strength.

She gave a weak shake of her head.

"Liar," he accused. "But you're brave. You might not be well right now, but you will be. Don't forget that. Take in the air through your nose, exhale through your mouth. Focus on me. That's it." The words were spoken as a gentle but unyielding command.

Catherine latched onto his words like a lifeline, following his directions and focusing on his calming face.

"Good, feel that? Calm. Let your body take the air. Good." He slowly inhaled through his nose, then exhaled through his mouth, and she matched his cadence, her body relaxing in the rhythm.

"Th-thank you," Catherine managed.

"Shh, it's nothing." He continued breathing with her, and in a few minutes she felt almost normal.

"Good mercy, what was that?" Catherine asked as she closed her eyes for a moment.

"I'm not sure what the technical term is, but my mother calls them the 'can't breathes.'"

Catherine focused on his face, the detail of his features. "Your mother? Does this happen to her?"

"Yes. Not often, but when something is overwhelming…or reminds her of my father, or of my brother…" His focus fell to the floor, his shoulders rounded as if carrying a weight.

"I see. And you? Does this happen to you?" Catherine asked, then thought better of her intrusive question. "Your Grace, forgive me. I shouldn't have asked such a personal question."

"It's Quin, and to answer your question, no. I've never had the 'can't breathes.'" He hitched a shoulder. "But there's always a first time for everything."

"I don't wish this on my worst enemy," Catherine replied. "I dearly hope you never have to endure it."

"So do I." Quin stood abruptly.

Catherine's brow furrowed at his quick movement, and she wondered if maybe she had offended him. But a moment later, she saw her grandmother's winded approach. "Dear heavens, how hard it is to find a footman in this place." And then, as if just realizing Quin's presence, she offered an apology. "My apologies, I was in a panic, but I see that Catherine's come through it. Dear heavens, ducky, don't do that to me again. I thought I was going to lose you and then have to explain the body," she stated with an attempt at humor.

Catherine started to giggle, the loose movement relaxing her further. She turned to Quin, who seemed to have some internal debate on how to take her grandmother's attempt at humor.

"She's joking," Catherine said through her amusement.

"Dear Lord, Quin. Take a joke. I was trying to add levity to the moment. I tend to do that when I'm scared out of my wits. It's better to do that than dissolve into a salty puddle of tears," Lady Greatheart answered.

"I see." Quin nodded, studying Catherine's grandmother as if reassessing her, and then turned to Catherine. "I'll take my leave now that you're in very capable hands."

"I'm not sure about the capable part, but they are most certainly willing," Lady Greatheart remarked.

"Thank you…Quin. I honestly don't know how I would have come through that without you," Catherine said with deep appreciation.

"I have a feeling you would have been fine, but I'm happy to have offered my assistance." And with a jaunty bow, he moved down the hall in the direction of the library.

"Well, shall we go, ducky? I think we've both had enough excitement for one evening."

"That is for certain," Catherine agreed.

When she arrived home, she proceeded to her grandfather's study. It was late, but she wasn't tired enough to sleep, her mind restless. She walked into the large room, its scent taking her back a full decade to when she was a young girl and she'd visited her grandfather as he'd worked on estate business. Books lined one wall, and the other was covered by heavy drapes hiding large windows facing the back courtyard.

The study had remained quite vacant, save for a few times her grandmother used it for sorting through estate matters since all the ledgers were still kept in the room's many cabinets. The aromas of pipe tobacco and peppermint still lingered in the air, and Catherine watched as Brooks directed a footman to start a fire in the long-vacant hearth. Tea was brought in by a maid, and once all was addressed, each exited in turn, leaving her alone in the great room.

It had been a strange night, and she sought the solace of numbers, of finding something absolute and true. She withdrew the ledgers, sifting through them and tracing her fingers over her grandfather's handwriting, then flipping the pages to her own handwriting, a stark contrast, and a legacy that told a story. What had rested upon his shoulders now rested upon hers. Balancing the numbers, directing information, and suggesting options of investment or sale to her grandmother—it was much to take on, but she had loved it. It was a constant in a world that seemed ever so interested in changing. It gave her a steady rhythm when her heart was out of sorts from the evening's events.

It took her mind off the current complications of life and made her calm as she added the sums from one ledger and recorded the total in another, the neat and tidy rows all comforting in their order. After an hour, the sweet ache of fatigue beckoned her to her rooms to find rest. So she tucked the ledgers away and softly padded into the hall.

Her maid quickly helped her undress and slip into a soft muslin night rail, and the soft pull of the brush on her hair lulled her deeper into a relaxed state. When the maid had finished, Catherine excused her and sought the comfort of her bed. The low fire in the grate crackled warmly as Catherine snuggled deep into the soft sheets.

Yet as she was lying in her bed that night, the oddest thing happened.

Rather than seeing Avery's blue gaze in her mind's eye, she saw green.

# Five

"YOUR GRACE, YOUR MOTHER IS WAITING FOR YOU IN THE parlor," his butler notified Quin as he finished adding up the ledger.

"Why in creation is she here?" Quin asked, mostly to himself.

"She didn't say, Your Grace," his butler answered.

"Of course not," Quin replied, then set aside his pen, marked his position in the ledger, and stood. Adjusting his coat, he shrugged it into proper place and then tugged on his cuffs by turns. What was it about one's mother that made all the proper mannerisms come to the forefront? He followed the butler out into the hall and down toward the parlor where his mother waited.

"Ah, Mother, to what do I owe the pleasure?" Quin asked as he walked into the room, taking note that his mother had already requested tea and biscuits be sent in.

"Do I always need a reason to converse with my son?" his mother asked, arching a brow as she took a delicate sip from her teacup.

"No, but I find it's usually the case," Quin answered.

"Tea?"

"Yes, thank you," he replied.

As his mother poured the tea then handed it to him, her expression was a mix of curiosity and concern. "You left quite suddenly last night."

Quin took a sip of the steaming liquid. He'd had a feeling this was the direction the conversation would take. "Indeed. It was a good thing, too. Lady Catherine was having one of your 'can't breathe' fits in the hall," he answered succinctly. Let his mother know that he'd had a valid reason for his exit.

"Dear me." She leaned back, her expression clouded. "Did you help her?"

"Of course, and she came through it quite quickly, but it took a toll. Though I think Lady Greatheart suffered even more than Lady Catherine did."

"I'm glad you offered your assistance. I'm sure they were grateful as well."

"They were, of course."

His mother gave a delicate sniff. "And as for your quick exit, I made proper excuses, so the gossip should be at a minimum," she added, almost as an afterthought.

"Pardon?" Quin nearly choked on his tea.

"The gossip. Surrounding your hasty disappearance after Lady Catherine fled the scene looking quite ill..." His mother started to paint the picture of the scene as it had unfolded.

Good heavens. He had never thought people might misread the situation so badly.

But hearing his mother's interpretation, he saw it clearly.

His brother's former fiancé, feeling ill and leaving, only to have him follow her soon after without any comment...

"What did you say?" Quin asked, stunned by the depth of the realization. This could be dreadfully uncomfortable, especially for Lady Catherine. Hadn't she suffered enough? Hadn't he? Must people always draw conclusions?

"I said you were checking on the welfare of Lady Catherine because of Lady Greatheart's age. When you didn't return, I had a servant come over, told him to leave then return in three minutes and pretend to whisper something to me. He did exactly that, and once he left, I announced that after assisting Lady Greatheart, you sent word that you needed to address some business with the dukedom...so, of course, everyone nodded reverently and carried on with their conversations." She flicked her wrist as if dismissing the whole situation.

Quin nodded. "Do you think people will concoct a story regarding Lady Catherine?"

His mother gave him a disbelieving expression. "Dear, they will always concoct stories. They can be based on fact or fiction, but stories there will be. You need to decide how much stock you'll put in their words."

Quin took a sip of tea. "She doesn't need any more people talking."

His mother paused, studying him for a moment. "No, no, she doesn't." She set her teacup down. "Speaking of Catherine, have you inquired after her?"

Quin studied his teacup, the amber liquid swirling with a slight hint of steam. "No. I wasn't sure it would be…prudent." In truth, he had nearly called upon her twice. There was a…kinship…that he felt with her, and it was comforting, as ironic as it seemed. He had justified his inclination to visit her with several valid arguments, but there was one reason to resist—the talk it could create.

Already he knew the gossip would surround her reappearance into society, both with her visit to Hyde Park and then his mother's party. He didn't want to add to the chatter.

But it seemed he had done that already, unbeknownst to him. If he had realized earlier, he wouldn't have had such persuasive reasons for not calling upon her.

It was for the best, however.

He turned to his mother, her look contemplative as she studied him with a clarity that was unnerving. Damn, when she did that it was like she was reading his thoughts, bloody uncomfortable.

"But you have considered it?"

"Calling upon Lady Greatheart?" he replied carefully.

"It would be the gentlemanly thing to do, you know. After all"— his mother took a delicate sip of tea—"they were almost family."

Leave it to his mother to find the soft spot in his armor—loyalty. Damn it all, but it was the very excuse he needed to do what he wanted to do regardless. At least now he could justify the visit.

"If you insist." He shrugged, putting the weight of the decision on his mother.

As if seeing his angle in the conversation, she hitched a shoulder. "You're quite capable of making your own decisions, dear. I'm simply offering a suggestion."

Quin paused, deciding a different topic of conversation was needed. "So, tell me about Rowles. I recall you mentioning his mother's concern?"

Properly distracted, the Duchess of Wesley dove into some gossip regarding one of his dearest friends.

His Grace Rowles, Duke of Westmore, was one of his oldest friends and in a situation similar to Quin's. Rowles's eldest brother, the former Duke of Westmore, had shared a tragic fate with Quin's brother. Like Quin, Rowles had then inherited his brother's title along with the responsibilities that accompanied it. But unlike Quin's mother, the Duchess of Westmore was not a healthy woman. After the death of her eldest, she had suffered from apoplexy and wasn't quite the same, given to all sorts of wild imaginings. While he loved his mother dearly, Rowles was a deeply rational man and understood what was going on in his mother's broken mind. In many ways, he had lost not only a brother, but his mother too.

"Are you listening to me?" Quin's mother asked sharply.

Quin looked up from the small table holding the tea things. "Pardon? Er, no. I'm afraid not. I was woolgathering."

His mother regarded him with a tip of her head and a knowing stare. "I suppose. Have you seen Rowles recently? How has he been? Ever the professor, I assume he's still giving lectures?"

Quin nodded. "Indeed, much like myself. We can't seem to find a way to let go of our profession."

"You love your profession. There are worse things, dear."

"Indeed. I believe he will be here on Saturday. He's adopted a schedule akin to mine, dividing his time between Cambridge and London."

"Your former life and your new… It seems fitting. After all, our past often helps define our future." She nodded to herself. "With that bit of wisdom, I'll take my leave. Give my affection to Rowles when you see him next."

"I'll be sure to do that." Quin set his teacup down and stood as his mother started toward the door.

"Oh, and I'm hosting a small dinner party this Friday. If Rowles is in town, please let me know so I may invite him. And of course, I expect you to be in attendance." She let her disdain speak for her.

"Of course, Mother."

"And please, as you go to check on Lady Greatheart, remind her of my invitation. I'd love for her to attend as well."

"Is there anything else, Mother? Your list is exceedingly long today."

"No, that will be all," she replied happily. "I'll see you later, dear."

And with that, she took her leave.

Quin watched the door click shut behind her, then exited into the hall as well.

"Ready the carriage, please." At his butler's nod, Quin bounded upstairs to change his ink-stained shirt. With his valet's assistance, he was quickly ready to make the short trip to Lady Greatheart's residence.

As he made his way to the grand white house on Grosvenor Square, a sense of relief filled him. Having his mother mention that Lady Greatheart and her granddaughter had nearly been family had clarified the odd sensation that had been haunting him. Loyalty… He felt a deep sense of loyalty to his brother's betrothed and her family. Once promised the legacy and protection of his brother's name, now they were left without. And while they were well established with both title and fortune, there were some things that a title and money couldn't buy, and an important one of those was family.

Appreciation for his own kin welled within him. Difficult as it had been to walk this journey with them, he was surrounded by friends who had suffered the same loss, along with a beloved mother and kin. Lady Greatheart and Lady Catherine had only each other.

As the carriage came to a halt in front of the Greatheart residence, Quin made a silent vow to watch over the ladies of the house. It was the least he could do for Lady Catherine, and an honor he could do for his brother's memory. *Honor.* The word resonated with him, gave him a peace that had long felt lost. Satisfied with his decision, he hopped from the carriage with a lighter heart and fresh purpose. It settled well with him, and the reasons to keep his distance were forgotten. Gossips be damned. Their words would eventually be proven wrong, and with that, he made his peace.

# Six

*Liberty can only consist in doing that which every One ought to do, and not to be constrained to do that which One ought not to do.*

—*Catherine the Great*

CATHERINE WAS RIDDLED WITH INDECISION. PART OF HER WAS bored to tears being inside; the other part was terrified to move past the safety of the walls surrounding her. Something had to change, and she wasn't sure what it would be.

"If you sigh any more, you might hurt yourself." Lady Greatheart lifted her attention from her needlepoint. "Idle hands, dear. You can always make an effort. Your needlepoint is still awaiting your stitches." Her grandmother nodded to the blue velvet chair where Catherine's floral needlepoint was lying.

"It's so dull."

"Get a sharper needle."

Catherine gave her grandmother a wry expression.

"Oh, ducky, you need to take a moment. You're unhappy inside and you're unhappy outside… You know what that tells me?"

Catherine opened her mouth to answer, but her grandmother responded before she could comment.

"That means it's you. It's not your situation, it is what is taking place within your heart." Lady Greatheart set her needlepoint aside. "I'm not saying you don't have a good reason for feeling as you do, but sometimes it helps to know what the problem is, and in this case it's in your heart."

"How comforting," Catherine replied with veiled sarcasm and moved to the chair to lift her needlepoint. She sat and traced the lines of the embroidery with her fingertips. "I know you're correct, though."

"I usually am."

Catherine gave a soft huff. "Regardless, I'm not sure how to fix it. My focus was all courage and determination the other day, and then as the hours went on, I found that my strength failed me. And then last night… Good Lord, what a disaster. I just lost my wits." She lowered her head, closing her eyes. "It was just so hard, and then add in all those ladies watching me. I could *feel* their attention. It was terrible."

"Oh, ducky, you just noticed it yesterday. You've had that attention for longer than just one evening. Last year at your come-out, there wasn't an eye that didn't follow you in the ballroom."

"Strange how a year can make a difference."

"Exactly, but dear, it's all in the perspective you keep. Last year, it elevated you. You held your head higher, walked with more confidence, and at the same time refused to put too much weight on others' opinions. That's one of the reasons you captured the eye of a duke."

Catherine nodded, her mind drifting back to last summer. A warm sensation filled her chest. "I didn't care what they thought. I mean, I did, but it wasn't—"

"The deciding factor. And nothing's changed, ducky. Just you. And the beauty of it all is that you can amend the way you see it. You can't go back to the way things were, but you can go back to how you once saw the world."

Catherine nodded as she absorbed her grandmother's words.

"Pardon, my lady, but you have a caller." Brooks had entered the parlor with a silver tray. He extended it to Lady Greatheart.

Catherine watched her grandmother's expression shift into a welcoming one. "Well, see him in, Brooks. Oh, and please have tea and biscuits brought up immediately."

"At your service, my lady." The butler bowed and left to execute his mistress's command.

"Who is calling?" Catherine asked, lifting her needle and pulling the thread taut to start a few stitches. One never wanted to appear idle in front of guests.

Lady Greatheart hitched a shoulder and lifted her needlepoint.

A moment before Catherine was going to repeat the question, she heard footsteps in the hall.

Clearly, there was nothing wrong with her grandmother's hearing. Evidently, Lady Greatheart had heard the footsteps before she did.

Catherine made a few quick stitches so that she would appear relaxed and busy, then turned as the butler announced their guest. "My lady, His Grace the Duke of Wesley." Brooks bowed and took his leave.

"Thank you for seeing me, Lady Greatheart." Quin bowed to Catherine's grandmother. "And you, Lady Catherine." He turned his focus to her, his expression edged with concern. "How do you fare today?"

Good Lord, was her life to be one circus of that same litany? She tamped down her rather ungrateful feelings and settled for a nod. "Much improved. Thank you for your assistance last night."

"It was my pleasure," he answered, searching her expression as if to discern whether she was being fully honest. It was unnerving.

She lowered her eyes, hindering any further silent inquiry. "How was the remainder of the party?" Catherine asked after taking another stitch.

"First of all, have a seat, Quin. I've requested tea, and it will be here shortly."

"Thank you, Lady Greatheart." He selected a chair beside the small circular table in the middle of the room and turned his attention back to Catherine. "I left shortly after you made your departure so I'm not entirely sure."

"I see," Catherine replied, her curiosity piqued. "I hope my… behavior didn't distress you."

"Oh, no." He lifted his palms as if to stop that very thought. "Not at all, I was simply ready to make my excuses and took the opportunity."

"I'm relieved to know it," Catherine replied.

"It was quite an eventful evening," Lady Greatheart added, giving a decided sniff.

"Well, I hope you're equal to another social event in your calendar. My mother gave me specific instructions to persuade you to accept her invitation to this Friday's dinner party." He raised a brow at Catherine, then directed his attention to Lady Greatheart.

"When asked with such charm, how could we say anything but yes?" Lady Greatheart replied with approval.

"And here I didn't even try to add any charm. I must be a natural."

"Indeed. I'm sure you have quite the following of ladies with that natural charisma," Lady Greatheart said, arching a brow.

Catherine blushed at her grandmother's brazen statement. It was none of their business.

"While I appreciate your compliment to my character, I'd have to disagree. As I'm sure Catherine can attest, there's a difference between someone being attracted to the man and to the title, and I have no interest in trying to discern either. So I'm abstaining." He gave a curt nod as if punctuating his decision.

"To the great disappointment of many," Lady Greatheart remarked, an impish gleam in her eye.

At this he released his pent-up amusement, his face aglow with enjoyment, revealing a single dimple in his left cheek.

Belatedly, Catherine remembered that Quin was indeed several years younger than Avery. If Avery had been nearly thirty, then Quin must be around seven and twenty?

"That's a pensive expression," Lady Greatheart said playfully to Catherine. "She's been a bit stuffy today."

"Grandmother!" Catherine remarked, shocked. Heat crept up her neck.

"Calm down, ducky. Quin isn't going to think less of you for being stuck in your own mind. Lord knows he's been there too. I'd wager to guess he still is." She jabbed a thumb in his direction and then picked up her needlework.

"I do believe we've both been property humbled," Quin remarked teasingly.

"She has a way of doing that, at inopportune moments."

"The best family always does," he replied.

"As I've heard. I haven't quite the audacity to decide if I agree or not." Catherine shot her grandmother a narrowed glower, even as she couldn't fight her amusement.

At her expression, Quin began to chortle. "Why do I feel as if you two are quite evenly matched?"

"Because you're smarter than you look," Lady Greatheart replied.

At his shocked expression, she added, "And you do look quite smart. Truly, you look the part of a professor. It was meant as compliment."

Quin's brow furrowed as if confused.

"You get used to it, her backward way of complimenting. Her heart is right, but sometimes you just have to remember her age," Catherine replied, arching a brow.

"You're exaggerating, dearie," Lady Greatheart remarked.

Catherine said sweetly, "Just keeping you humble."

Quin shook his head, chuckling at the entertainment before him. "And to think I was concerned about your welfare. I do think I should pity not you but your guests."

"We're lovely hosts," Lady Greatheart countered, and as if on cue, the tea was brought in. "Even my timing is impeccable."

Quin seemed to fully relax. The tight hold of his shoulders had released, and even his expression had softened dramatically. The small lines around his eyes were smoothed away, and his smile was not forced but natural. It was odd. Though he and Avery were very clearly brothers—as was evidenced in several mannerisms and expressions—they were also very different. It was welcome to have an acquaintance, maybe even a potential friendship, with someone who so closely resembled the man she had once loved. It was almost like having a piece of him still, but not quite. Quin and Avery weren't alike enough to confuse the two, by any means. Simply a beloved flavor that was similar.

"Tea?" Lady Greatheart asked as she set aside her needlepoint. Quin nodded. "Please. Two sugars, if you don't mind."

"I had taken you for a purist." She clucked her tongue. "Sugar it is."

"You're awfully cheeky today, Grammy," Catherine chided. "Poor…Quin. Can't a gentleman take his tea as he wishes?"

"Of course, just saying that you can't trust first impressions, that's all." Lady Greatheart handed the china cup into Quin's outstretched hand.

"I can defend my own preferences, Lady Catherine." He shot her a daring look and turned to Lady Greatheart. "You're not the first to be surprised I take anything in my tea, though for the life of me I cannot understand why anyone would care what I do or do not do to my tea."

"It's because you're so serious. People assume you're circumspect and dull. But don't worry." She studied him as she took her seat. "We know the truth."

Catherine was quite diverted by her grandmother's antics.

"And what is that truth, Lady Greatheart?" Quin asked, playing along.

Lady Greatheart took a sip of tea, and Catherine smiled to herself, knowing her grandmother was drawing out the attention. Savoring it. At last she answered.

"That you, Quin, are proper but not circumspect, and you are most certainly not dull. You're quite entertaining in character."

"You say that as if you're surprised."

"I was. But no longer." She raised her cup in a toast.

Quin looked at Catherine with an expression of delighted disbelief. "You have your hands full, don't you?"

"With her? Yes. Always," Catherine replied, amusement on her face.

It was welcome, the sense of lightheartedness. It filled her and felt like warm sunshine on a spring day, a break from the bleakness of winter.

"Tell me, Lady Catherine, do you have any engagements for this afternoon?" Quin asked.

Catherine shook her head, then replied, "Not particularly. Unless you qualify embroidery as a priority."

He grimaced. "I can't say that I do, but I have great respect for those who can make such dainty stitches. What of you, Lady Greatheart?"

"Whatever do you have in mind, Quin? You have quite the captive audience."

Quin grinned at her words, then shrugged. "Nothing too interesting. I just wondered if perhaps you wished to visit the park for a stroll? It's lovely outside and…" He paused, his expression taking on a more serious mien. "I'd rather you not be alone."

Catherine froze, studying his expression and replaying his words in her mind. Suspicious, she leaned forward. "Why is that?" Her words were clipped, even to her own ears, but she wasn't regretful about it.

Quin leaned back, as if her words, or the tone, were surprising. "Because you had a fit of the vapors recently, and I wish to be of service," he answered, affirming her suspicions.

"No, thank you," Catherine replied succinctly, her suspicions confirmed. A swirl of emotion clogged her throat, knowing she wasn't going to react well if he pressed her. She stood and made her excuses, quitting the room before she could say something she couldn't take back or, worse yet, have another bloody breakdown.

She entered the hall and was starting toward the stairs when Quin's voice called out to her. "Lady Catherine."

Taking a deep breath, she turned and watched as he strode nearer purposefully. "My apologies if I said something to upset you."

"It's of no consequence," she replied, careful to keep her chin level.

He eyed her skeptically. "Whenever my mother says something like that, it most certainly means it was of great consequence."

Ire triggered, Catherine took a step toward him, her temper simmering. "Are you saying I'm dishonest?"

"No," he replied, completely cool in demeanor, which only irked her further. "I was saying that maybe you weren't being honest with yourself."

Catherine's mouth dropped open in shock. "Truly."

"Yes. But I don't take you for a woman without courage, so please explain how I offended you so." His voice was level, interested but not irritated.

Catherine contemplated his expression. His green eyes studied her openly, curiosity echoing in his words and demeanor. Very well, she decided. She accepted his calm demeanor almost as a challenge.

She chose her words carefully. Let there be no confusion. "Your Grace..."

He winced at her words, but she continued.

"If I were to offer my friendship to you only to keep you from being isolated and lonely, would that, in truth, be considered friendship? Or merely pity?"

She watched as her words were received, then nodded when

his regard sharpened with understanding. His eyes focused on hers, and he gave a curt nod.

"You think I pity you."

She arched a brow. "Did your words imply anything less?"

"You misunderstood."

"That is possible, but would you have deduced the same if I were to say that to you?" She hitched a shoulder. "And what is worse is that you're one of the only people of my acquaintance whom I'd trust to know how pity is absolutely the devil. Haven't you fought it yourself? The looks, the questions, the way people walk on eggshells around you?" She took a step closer to him, bringing them almost toe to toe. "Just because I had a moment of weakness does not make me weak, Your Grace. It makes me human. I'm able to conquer things that try to break me. The same goes for you. But I did not offer you my assistance because I trust that you are able to overcome as well. I ask only for the same courtesy." She finished, gave one final look, and then turned to ascend the stairs.

She took the stairs carefully, though she wanted to fly up them. It was a harsh conversation, but deep inside she knew the truth of it. Tomorrow she'd likely regret her words, but in that moment, she felt free.

Because in telling someone of her humanity and strength, she believed it herself.

And felt stronger.

# Seven

QUIN CLOSED HIS EYES. THE CARRIAGE SWAYED AS HE LEFT the Greatheart residence. He'd given his excuses to Lady Greatheart and taken his leave, his mind spinning with Catherine's words.

Good Lord, he felt like a beef-witted fool.

So much for good intentions and honor. He'd done nothing but offend, and deeply. And it had all been going so well; it had been one of the most enjoyable conversations of his recent memory, till it all went to hell.

He replayed the conversation in his mind, each point she'd made like an arrow piercing his pride. It stung, her accuracy. But what hit the center of the target had been her final words…

*"Just because I had a moment of weakness does not make me weak, Your Grace. It makes me human."*

He winced at the memory. Because she was correct, and though it hadn't been his intention, he had been acting from pity. Honorable pity, but pity nonetheless. There were few things he hated more than other people's pity.

What a bloody disaster.

He replayed the scenario in his head again, irritated with himself. She had courage, perhaps a touch of daring as well. Even his mother had never confronted him so, and it was sobering, humbling as hell. With clarity and precision, she had put him in his place. And he owed her a great apology.

She'd carried herself with the grace of a queen as she ascended the stairs, and he hadn't been able to pull his attention from her.

Respect had welled within him, and he'd had the distinct impression that she would appreciate such a compliment.

Odd, that. Usually ladies appreciated compliments on their coiffure, dress, or smile. Perhaps the sparkle of their eyes or shape of their lips, or talent on the pianoforte, but he knew instinctively that Catherine would appreciate the compliment of his respect far above all the rest. Maybe that was the best way to apologize. Aside from the simple words, an offering of equality.

At peace with his new revelation, he opened his eyes. The scenery of Mayfair passed by his carriage window, adding to the serenity of the moment. Sunlight filtered through the glass and warmed his fingers. It would have been a good day for a stroll in the park; perhaps next time, with the right motives included. He reflected that it was good to have friends who weren't afraid to be honest. It was a testament to the person's authenticity. And he realized that maybe Catherine wasn't his responsibility to care for. Maybe she was the friend he needed for this season of life.

Maybe somehow she'd need him too. He rapped on the ceiling of the coach and called to the driver, "Please return to the Greatheart residence."

There was no time like the present, and since he had already planned on an afternoon in the ladies' company, he might as well swallow his pride. The carriage paused, then made a sharp turn. Anticipation as well as a healthy dose of trepidation tightened his chest as they reapproached the Greatheart residence. As the carriage came to a halt in the drive, Quin took a fortifying lungful of air and alighted from the vehicle—again. As he ascended the stairs to knock on the door, it opened before he reached it.

"Your Grace." The butler bowed. "How may I assist you? Did you perhaps leave something behind?"

*My pride?* Quin quelled the thought and addressed the butler. "No, but I was hoping I might impose upon Lady Catherine for a moment."

The butler gave a nod, then moved to the side to allow Quin to enter. "If you'll follow me, Your Grace. I'll show you to the green parlor while I announce your presence."

Quin shadowed the man to a different room than he'd been in just prior and took a seat.

After the butler left, Quin's knee bounced restlessly. Irritated with himself, he rose and walked to the window facing the street. He silently rehearsed how he would offer his apology.

"Your Grace." Catherine's voice broke through his thoughts.

Upon turning, he noted her posture—shoulders back. Her expression wasn't angry, but she was certainly bracing herself for something. Curious, he paused to study her before offering a greeting.

Without hesitating further, he stepped forward. "Lady Catherine, thank you for seeing me...again."

She held up a hand as if to stop him from moving closer. "I owe you an apology, Your Grace."

Quin held up his hand to stop her. "You most certainly do not. However, I do owe one to you."

Catherine's lips parted as if to argue, but no words came, and Quin seized the opportunity. Placing his hands behind his back, he changed directions and walked to the left.

"You were right, and I owe you the apology for giving you something I won't accept from others." He turned to her. "I would, rather, like to be your friend, Lady Catherine. A give-and-take on both our parts, no pity involved, simply...equality," he finished.

Catherine studied him, her eyes narrowing as if trying to read between the lines. "Thank you," she replied, her hands twisting as if she was anxious. "However, I still do need to offer my own apology. I should not have attacked your kind offer, for I know you made it with the right heart." She shrugged one shoulder. "You dislike pity as much as I do, so I can deduce that you would not offer it to others knowingly. That much of your character is clear, Your Grace."

"Apology accepted, on one condition," Quin offered with a tentative and hopeful tone.

"And what is that?" Catherine inquired.

"For the love of God, please do not call me 'Your Grace.' It's nearly as bad as pity," he answered honestly.

She paused, then a dimple in her cheek gave away the amusement that danced across her lips a moment later. "Agreed."

"And what of my apology? Is it accepted?" Quin asked.

"Accepted, *Quin*." She emphasized his name, the amusement and approval still evident on her features.

"Brilliant. And what about my offer of friendship? Do you think that might be accepted as well?" he asked, a taunt to his tone.

She sighed dramatically. "If I must. I rather think you'll just force the matter if I don't readily accept it."

"You're learning."

"I try," she returned. "It will be nice to have a friend. One who…knows." She sobered.

"Indeed. My sentiments exactly." He nodded once, then turned to the window. "It's still quite lovely outside. Would you care to take a stroll? Perhaps visit the park?" he offered.

Catherine nodded. "I'd be delighted. Should I ask my grandmother to accompany us?"

"Wouldn't she come regardless?" he asked mischievously.

"Indeed. But it's always nice to be invited."

"A good point," he conceded.

"If you'll excuse me, I'll return in a few minutes." Catherine gave a slight nod of her head and quit the room, presumably to invite her grandmother on their outing.

Quin nodded to himself as a sense of resolution filled him. It was done, the fences mended.

In short order, they were sampling the fresh air. The Greatheart residence was only a short walk from Hyde Park, and the lovely spring weather made each step a delight. Quin assumed a more leisurely gait to accommodate the ladies, not minding the slower pace.

"Thank you for your invitation, Quin," Lady Greatheart commented. "I trust my granddaughter didn't have to insist too much."

"Only mild blackmail was necessary," Quin replied, earning a swat from the older lady.

"Blackmail is always helpful to have in one's arsenal, don't you agree?" Catherine replied, adding to the joking conversation.

"Always," Quin said.

They walked in companionable silence for a few steps, then as the park came into view, Lady Greatheart spoke happily. "It would seem we're not the only ones with this idea. Look! There's the Baroness White! I haven't seen her in an age," she murmured softly to herself. "If you'll excuse me." Without a backward glance, Lady Greatheart abandoned them and headed toward the older baroness.

Quin paused, unsure if Catherine would wish to follow her grandmother's lead or continue on their path to the park.

"She'll catch up later, I'm sure. She won't be out of sight, so we can continue, if you wish?" Catherine offered.

"Certainly," Quin replied, keeping on their way.

As they approached a small archway leading to the park's entrance, Quin noted a familiar form just ahead. He waited a moment to make sure he was certain, then strode forward to see his good friend Collin Morgan, Earl of Penderdale.

"Ho! Old chap, what are you doing in London? I thought you were still in Cambridge!" Quin reached out to grasp his friend's hand as they met under the arch.

Penderdale clasped his friend's hand firmly, delighted. "Some family business required my attention, and it was such a lovely day I couldn't stay inside a moment longer. You know how it is."

"Indeed, I do," Quin replied. "Oh, forgive me. Allow me to introduce Lady Catherine Greatheart." He gestured to Catherine.

Penderdale cast him a look with a curious quirk to his brow that lasted only a moment before he bowed to Catherine. "A pleasure to make your acquaintance again, Lady Catherine. It's been too long," he replied politely.

"Truly, it has been too long, Lord Penderdale," Catherine replied, offering her hand.

The earl accepted it, his attention never shifting from her eyes. "And how are you?"

"Exceptional," he remarked. "But please, call me Morgan. I'm afraid I'm quite accustomed to it rather than my title."

Quin raised an eyebrow but didn't comment. Of all the men affected in the tragedy, Morgan had suffered the largest blow. It had been his twin brother who had passed. The two had been nearly identical in manner and in appearance. They had pulled no shortage of pranks—from leading strings till their last years as students at Cambridge. Quin suspected that they'd often swapped places during key exams as well.

"That's wonderful to hear," Quin said, examining his friend. "How is Lady Joan?"

An indulgent smirk lit up Morgan's expression. "As much trouble as ever. She'll have her season this summer, and Lord help me, I'm not ready for this."

Catherine gave a soft giggle, drawing Quin's attention. "It's even harder on the lady, I assure you."

"While I'm certain that's true, I must say it isn't easy on the guardian either." He shrugged. "I've never had a care for frills or fabrics, but I certainly have less tolerance for them now. However, I now am an authority on the colors of the season and what modiste is in most demand. My sister has educated me, largely against my will."

Catherine tried to imagine it all, finding the idea quite diverting to consider. "It's quite an event."

"That's a kind way to put it."

"I'm sure she values your assistance. You're a generous brother."

Morgan shuffled his feet, clearly unaccustomed to such a compliment. "Your praise is appreciated, but I would be neglectful if I did not take it upon myself to make her season a success. Our mother and father would wish it, and it's an honor to their memory to do it well." He nodded, his expression resolute.

"Certainly, it is," Catherine replied.

"Well, there you are." Lady Greatheart's voice intervened in the conversation, and Quin was thankful for a distraction.

It was always a difficult topic, discussing one's family after any sort of tragedy. Life was never the same, and such a discussion always brought back the feeling of when things were normal and the fact that they no longer were. Sighing, he gave a curt nod to Morgan, conveying that he understood, and then turned his attention to Lady Greatheart. "We didn't wander far, my lady. And we found a friend. Allow me to introduce you to Collin Morgan, Earl of Penderdale."

"Ah, yes. I knew your…well, your father, too, but your grandfather was my contemporary. Handsome fella. You favor him."

Quin watched, biting back a grin as Morgan's eyebrows rose at the turn of the conversation.

"Thank you, Lady Greatheart. He was a good man," Morgan said by way of a reply. He hid his amusement, his lips in a thin line. It took a moment before he sobered and looked to Quin. But not before Quin noted the former struggle.

That was the beauty of friends. One knew them well enough to gather the nuances that made them singular, not just a face but a person.

"What are we discussing?" Lady Greatheart inquired.

Catherine grasped her grandmother's hand. "We were talking about the color of the season. You'd never imagine how knowledgeable Lord Penderdale—er, Morgan—is regarding ladies' fashion."

"Oh?" Lady Greatheart turned to Morgan, her eyes narrowed as if sizing him up.

Morgan shot Catherine a bemused expression. "That's not entirely accurate."

"Oh, I was wondering if you perhaps were one of those fellas who…" She shrugged. "Never mind. I suppose it doesn't matter." She batted her hands as if disregarding the thought.

Quin had a difficult time keeping his entertainment in check as he watched Morgan struggle with an appropriate reply in the presence of polite company, and likely he was considering if Lady Greatheart constituted *polite* society. It was dreadfully amusing.

"So, what color?" Lady Greatheart replied before Morgan could decide how to answer.

"Pardon?" He finally found his voice.

"For this season. Supposedly, you know the best colors. Of course, I know my own opinion, but it never hurts to get a second opinion." Lady Greatheart flicked her wrist, punctuating her question.

Morgan answered quickly, "It is my understanding that blossom is the color of the season, but if I may quote my sister…" He cleared his throat and took on a very serious expression. "'Not the usual color of rose, a lighter color, not enough to be vulgar but with depth to the hue,'" he finished, a proud expression in his eyes as if he'd completed some great challenge.

"I'm impressed," Lady Greatheart remarked, blinking rapidly as if not sure to believe what had just happened.

"It's my pleasure to be of assistance," he replied, then turned to Catherine. "If you wish, my sister has mentioned you with the highest of praise. Might I be so bold as if to ask if she may call on you sometime?" Morgan asked.

Catherine nodded, then answered, "Of course. It would be my pleasure."

"Brilliant," Morgan replied, then leaned forward as if to whisper a secret. "It would be my pleasure, too, for her to have a companion with whom to speak of the season's events."

"I see. You're trying to save yourself the trouble," Catherine challenged playfully.

"You are an astute lady." Morgan nodded. "And so, before you can change your mind, I'll take my leave. It was lovely to see you, Lady Catherine, Lady Greatheart." He bowed to the ladies and then turned to Quin. "I'll see you at White's, I'm sure."

Quin offered his hand in goodbye, then watched as Morgan walked away.

After several steps, Morgan turned, and Quin noted the way his attention flicked from himself to Lady Catherine and then back.

Quin decided that he'd try to find his friend tonight at White's; clearly, there was some curiosity about his presence. He'd set the record straight quickly.

It was a friendship with Lady Catherine.

Nothing more.

It couldn't ever be anything else. Sometimes the past created one's future, shaped it. And his was written in the ashes of the rubble. And while several words were written, Catherine's name wasn't one of them.

# Eight

*A Man ought to form in his own Mind an exact and clear Idea of what Liberty is.*

—*Catherine the Great*

"My lady?"

Catherine blinked several times, stretching her toes as she slowly awoke. It had been a lovely dream, preceded by blissful sleep. Something about the terrible conversation with Quin finding a peaceful resolution and their amble in the park had allowed her a peace she hadn't felt in an age. Sleep had been sweet, both swift and lingering.

"Pardon, but, my lady, please wake." Millard's voice cut through the fog of her thoughts. As her unfocused regard sharpened, she noted her maid's concerned expression. Quickly, she sat up in bed, the pale light of dawn peeking through the window shades.

"Yes? What is it?" Catherine asked, her brow furrowed. It must be some emergency for a servant to awaken her so insistently.

"My lady, it's your grandmother." Millard's voice was trembling as she spoke, and Catherine noted the fear lurking in the maid's eyes.

"Dear God, what is the matter?" Cold dread clenched Catherine's chest. She rose from the bed and rushed to the door. Without waiting for Millard's reply, she darted into the hall and toward her grandmother's rooms.

Millard ran up behind her. "My lady, your dressing gown."

Catherine paused, turning to grab the garment from her

servant's outstretched hands. It took but a moment to slide her arms into the robe and tie it.

Brooks approached just as she finished, his lips in a grim line. "I sent for a doctor as soon as we noticed something amiss, my lady." He spoke softly, his voice hoarse as if holding back.

"Noticed what exactly?" Catherine replied, pushing past him to her grandmother's door.

"The doctor will be here in a few minutes. We sent a servant about a quarter hour ago, and barring any unforeseen circumstances, he should come directly."

"Grammy?" Catherine padded into the room, noting the stillness of her grandmother's form in her bed. Her grandmother was never still, always moving, shifting, restless in the best of ways.

"Grammy?" Catherine called again, this time a little louder.

"D-ducky?" Her grandmother's weak voice sent a chill of foreboding down Catherine's spine.

Determined to be brave, Catherine forced a calm as she approached the bed.

"It's me. Why are you causing such a ruckus? Always after the theatrics, aren't you?" Catherine asked gently, playfully, even as her calm facade froze in place as she laid her hand upon her grandmother's. The coolness of her grandmother's skin pierced her heart.

"You know me. I have a flair for the dramatic," her grandmother whispered, but the usual lilt to her voice was absent; rather, her voice sounded labored, as if each word was heavy.

Words stuck in Catherine's throat. Unable to speak, she tenderly caressed her grandmother's hand.

"I'm not sure, ducky, but I don't feel...well." Her voice was a mere whisper, and she narrowed her eyes. "Strange," she murmured, her focus fading as she closed her eyes.

Desperate to keep her awake, unwilling to consider what could happen if she fell asleep, Catherine squeezed her hand. "What's strange?"

Her grandmother's eyes flittered opened. "Two." Her words were a mere breath.

"Two?"

"Of you," her grandmother said, her body relaxing.

"Grammy?" Catherine touched her shoulder, giving her a careful jiggle.

"Tired."

The words were so soft that Catherine replayed them in her mind to make sure she understood them correctly.

"My lady?" Brooks's voice cut through her focus.

Turning, she noted the entrance of a tall man dressed in a wrinkled black suit.

"Doctor Soffen is here to attend Lady Greatheart."

Catherine nodded, moving to the side to allow the doctor unrestricted access to her grandmother.

"Good morning, Lady Catherine. I'm first going to monitor your grandmother's heart. Your staff notified me of her earlier symptoms."

Catherine nodded numbly, then turned to Brooks, realizing she was still unaware of whatever earlier symptoms had occurred.

Not wanting to distract the doctor from listening to her grandmother's heart, she waited before voicing the questions twisting in her mind.

The doctor nodded to himself, then leaned over to open the large black bag beside him. Placing the listening instrument back within the bag, he placed his hands on her grandmother's palms, then forehead, silently listening to her rhythmic inhale and exhale.

"Has she woken up since you've been in here?" the doctor asked.

Catherine nodded. "Yes, she was talking a moment ago."

"What did she say?" he inquired, his focus on her grandmother as he continued to study her.

"One thing I found odd was that she struggled to focus on me, and when she did, she said it was strange, but there were two of me," Catherine explained, her heart pounding harder as the doctor paused his study of her grandmother and met her gaze with a frank one of his own.

"Two, as in she was seeing double, my lady?" he questioned.

"That's what it sounded like," Catherine clarified.

He gave a solid nod and then stepped back from the bed. "May I have a private word with you, Lady Catherine?"

For the first time, Catherine noted the several servants and Brooks who were hovering by the door, clearly concerned. Two maids curtsied and left. Brooks gave a curt nod and ushered the rest from the door and closed it with a soft click.

Catherine turned to the doctor, as she mentally prepared for whatever news the man was about to give; she was certain it wasn't the kind she'd wish to hear.

"Lady Catherine, it would seem your grandmother suffered a stroke. I'm not sure the extent of the damage or injury, but time will tell. Let her rest, and I'll come back in the afternoon. There isn't much I can do at the moment. We simply need to wait."

"Wait?" Catherine repeated. "You can do nothing?"

"If I do the wrong thing, it could make her worse," the doctor said softly, sympathetically. "The fact that she is seeing double means her vision is affected, and we aren't sure what that means. But I would spend time with her, and if she becomes conscious, perhaps say your goodbyes, because usually with the kind of stroke that affects vision, there is less chance of recovery. I'm sorry." He nodded, then reached for his bag. As he walked toward the door, he turned back. "I'll return around four."

Catherine watched his departure wordlessly, hopelessness filling her.

As she turned back to her grandmother's sleeping form, loneliness crept around her like a fog, closing in, threatening to devour her.

Hadn't she lost enough already?

Now her grandmother too?

How much was too much before it broke her?

And what would happen if it did?

Turning back, her entire being was attuned to the small form of her grandmother beneath the bedclothes. The rise and fall of her chest gave Catherine a glimmer of hope, but it wasn't enough to overwhelm the anxiety that coursed through her.

"Whatever am I going to do if something happens to you?" Catherine murmured softly, a warm tear spilling down her cheek. Nearing her grandmother's sleeping form, she placed her hand upon the weathered one, squeezing tenderly. Why was it that life only seemed short when one was facing the finality of it? But no, she wouldn't dwell on such thoughts.

"Fight, Grammy. Don't get this get the better of you. Sleep and fight," she said, her own resolve willing the words over to her grandmother.

A knock sounded at the door. "Yes?" Catherine turned to the opening door.

"Pardon, my lady." Brooks stepped into the room softly. "But I or any one of the servants are happy to sit with Lady Greatheart while you dress. We will be sure to notify you if there is any change."

Catherine frowned, then looked down at her attire, realizing she still wore her dressing robe over her nightrail. Nodding, she gave Brooks a grateful look. "Thank you, but instead please send Millard in with my things, and I'll change in here. I don't want to leave my grandmother."

Brooks nodded and disappeared through the door, closing it softly.

Catherine turned back to her grandmother, memorizing every line of her face and the posture of her body, just to ensure that if there were any change, she'd notice it readily. Four in the afternoon seemed an eternity away, and much could happen. But one thing was certain.

Whatever happened, her grandmother wouldn't face it alone.

Catherine would see to that.

# Nine

"Odd, but I thought you mentioned that Lady Greatheart and her granddaughter planned to attend the dinner party," the Duchess of Wesley said by way of greeting as she walked into her late husband's study.

Quin had been reviewing documents and wasn't paying much mind to his mother's entrance or words.

"Pardon?" He lifted a piece of paper and studied the scrawled writing. His eyes narrowed in an attempt to decipher the wording.

"Are you paying attention this time?" his mother asked with an annoyed tone.

Quin set the paper down, made a quick note, and then folded his hands over the desk and leaned forward, a taunting smirk on his lips.

"If only you were always so attentive," his mother quipped. "I was saying you mentioned that Lady Greatheart and Catherine were coming tonight, and I have received no acceptance of my invitation. It's not like them to say one thing and do another." She waved a hand dismissively.

Quin released a pent-up breath. "I have no idea, Mother. They said they plan to attend. Something might have come up. I'd not worry." He turned his attention back to the papers.

When his mother didn't move to leave, he looked up from his work. "Was there something else?"

"My, you're testy today," the Duchess of Wesley remarked, then took a few steps forward, lowering her voice. "I heard something and, well, I think you should perhaps check on Lady Greatheart."

Quin frowned. "And what did the gossipmongers have to say this time? I can assure you I will not care for it."

The Duchess of Wesley glanced behind her to the open door, then turned back to her son. "The doctor was summoned. And no one has seen either lady since," she whispered.

Quin nodded. "If you're concerned, why not call upon them yourself?"

"I did," the Duchess of Wesley replied, surprising Quin.

"You did? When?" Curious, Quin set the papers back in place and leaned forward, this time actually interested.

"As soon as I heard the news, I went. Their butler was very kind but refused me entry. Odd, don't you think?" She raised her eyebrows meaningfully.

"Perhaps they weren't at home," Quin replied, shrugging.

"No one has seen them!" his mother repeated.

Losing interest, Quin retrieved the papers for the third time. "Maybe they aren't taking callers. There's a plethora of valid reasons," he replied absentmindedly.

The Duchess of Wesley laid her hands on the desk. "I want you to check in with them. You've established some sort of friendship with them, haven't you? If something is amiss with Lady Greatheart, why..." She waited till Quin looked up. "Lady Catherine has no one else."

Quin tapped his finger on the desk. "Very well. I'll call on them this afternoon when I finish." He gestured to the table.

"Thank you," his mother intoned, relaxing her anxious posture. "It's just that, with all that Lady Catherine has endured, it would be a pity for her to be alone."

"I understand. You've communicated very clearly," Quin remarked, his eyes still on the papers.

"I'll leave you to your work." And with a swish of fabric, his mother quit the room, leaving silence in her wake.

Quin set the papers down again. Bloody hell, he couldn't focus.

He'd already been struggling before his mother came in, and now trying to concentrate was utterly useless. It had been a few days since he'd seen Lady Catherine and Lady Greatheart for their stroll in the park, and he had fought the inclination to visit them since. But he'd kept his distance; no reason for people to draw incorrect conclusions. It was safer, better for him to keep some space lest the *ton* get the wrong idea regarding his intentions.

Leave it to his mother to find him another valid excuse to do that which he already wished to do. She was becoming quite helpful— though he'd never tell her. He set the papers aside and rose from the desk. The tall grandfather clock showed three in the afternoon, a perfectly acceptable time to make a social call. So he abandoned the study and headed for the foyer to call for his carriage.

Not long after, he studied the entrance of the Greatheart house. He took the stone steps two at a time, then halted to knock at the door.

There was a short pause before the door opened. "Your Grace, how may I be of service?" the Greatheart butler inquired, his expression unreadable.

"Good day. I was…" Quin paused, remembering his mother's earlier attempt to gain entrance and quickly changed his plan. "Just accepting Lady Catherine's invitation."

It was a bloody lie.

A terribly executed one at that. But, holding his position, he met the butler's stare and waited.

"I'll escort you to the parlor, of course, Your Grace." A slight narrowing of the butler's eyes indicated that perhaps he didn't fully believe Quin. But wearing the title of duke had its benefits, one of them being that no one would ever accuse him of lying.

Even when he clearly was.

"Thank you." Quin followed him down the hall, noting the slight changes since he'd been shown to the same parlor several days prior. The servants moved about softly, quietly, as if trying to be silent. The usual bustle of a well-run household was subdued, and with foreboding, he took a seat in the parlor to wait.

Wondering if Catherine would see him.

Or if he'd be lied to, just like he'd lied to gain entrance.

Not that he had any moral ground to stand on, but he rather hoped she would trust him enough to tell him the truth, difficult as it might be.

As he waited, the silence was grating on his nerves. Tea was brought in, which he took as a good sign. Surely, if he was to be turned away, they wouldn't be bringing in biscuits. After a good quarter hour of waiting—and a few biscuits later—the door to the parlor opened. Quin had taken a seat, but abruptly stood when he heard the turn of the doorknob. Catherine entered, and immediately he could see something was wrong. Her usually glowing countenance was lined with tension, and there was none of her usual warmth.

"Good afternoon," she greeted him. "Please forgive my tardiness."

Quin nodded, unsure how to continue. The candid part of him wished to inquire immediately what was amiss, but propriety dictated he wait for her to divulge the information, if she wished.

"It's of no consequence," he answered, studying her.

As she moved farther into the room, he noted that purplish half circles shaded her eyes, as if she hadn't slept or at least slept well in a while. The usual easy manner with which she carried herself was absent, and he missed the sunshine that usually accompanied her.

"Brooks mentioned that I'd invited you—which we both know I did not. So I'm assuming that somehow you've heard the news." She took a deep inhale of air, as if fortifying herself.

"My mother mentioned that Lady Greatheart had requested a doctor, and we were both concerned for each of you," Quin replied, then waited to hear how much information she wished to convey. He'd long ago learned that silence was the best kind of persuasion.

"That much is true. I see the gossip moves as quickly as it always has." A moment passed as she took a seat across from where he stood, waiting. When she sat, he followed suit and leaned forward, intent on her next words.

"My grandmother had a spell after our outing. The doctor was summoned, and we're still waiting..." She paused, then continued, "We're waiting for improvement of her condition."

Quin nodded. "Did the doctor say what he thought was ailing Lady Greatheart?" he inquired.

"A stroke," she answered softly. "So far she hasn't worsened, which is good, but neither has she improved, which isn't." Keeping her eyes downcast, she served herself tea, stirring the sugar in delicately, as if thankful for something to keep her hands busy.

"Catherine, is there anything that I or my family can do to be of assistance?" he asked, watching as she took a sip of the steaming liquid.

She set the teacup back in the saucer, where it made a soft clinking sound. "I thank you for the kind offer. But I've already been in contact with my grandmother's solicitor, upon the suggestion of the doctor. I'll be meeting with him later this afternoon," she finished.

Quin nodded. "May I accompany you?" he asked.

Catherine glanced up abruptly, her eyes studying him. "Pardon?"

Quin treaded carefully, knowing it would be easy for his intentions to be misread. "You're a very intelligent and capable woman, Catherine. But sometimes it helps to have another set of ears when dealing with such information. I speak from experience," he added meaningfully.

She nodded. "You're right, of course. But I couldn't ask it of you. It's not your responsibility."

"You didn't ask. I offered, and it would be my pleasure to be of assistance," Quin stated, hoping she'd accept his offer. Solicitors were curious folk and tended to speak in little better than circles. He'd dealt with his share of them after his brother passed and didn't look forward to any of those meetings.

"Then I accept your kind offer," Catherine responded. "If you're sure you don't have any prior engagements for this afternoon."

"None," Quin answered swiftly.

"Then I'll excuse myself so I can be ready. The solicitor will arrive in about a half hour."

"I'll await your return." Quin nodded, watching as she left, her shoulders back and head high. The weight of the world had settled upon those delicate shoulders, but she didn't bear the weight with resentment, just faced the difficult road ahead with dignity. He respected that. It was bloody hard to face indecision and not let it conquer the spirit.

Helping himself to another biscuit and more tea, he awaited her return, considering all the legalities that lay before her. Hoping that the road ahead was easier than the one behind her.

# Ten

*I am one of the people who love the why of things.*

—*Catherine the Great*

As much as it grated on her pride, Catherine was thankful that Quin had volunteered to accompany her to the meeting with the solicitor. With a reluctant sigh, she studied herself in the mirror, thankful for a chance to collect herself before forcing the calm facade that would be necessary in a few moments. She'd push aside her emotions, study the facts, become a student of them, and move forward; that was her only option until her grandmother healed.

And she would heal.

She would gain her strength, her wit, her courage and rise above whatever illness harmed her and held her captive for the moment. It wasn't stronger than she was, and eventually, it would lose.

It had to.

Quin was waiting, and as she peeked at the clock near the window in her room, Catherine noted the time. The solicitor would arrive soon, and it would be unpardonably rude to make him wait. She released the tension in her chest in a long exhale. Striding through her door, she turned left and headed to her grandmother's rooms rather than taking the hall that led to the stairs.

As she neared, a servant rose from her seat just outside the door. "My lady." The woman curtsied.

"Any change?" Catherine inquired.

"None, my lady. She's sleeping. I was able to coax her to take a bit of broth about an hour ago. Do you wish me to check on her?"

"No need. I'll see to her myself," Catherine said.

She twisted the knob to the door slowly, keeping the mechanism as quiet as possible. Tiptoeing into the room, she noted her grandmother's sleeping form, and the sweet sound of her breath gave Catherine a wave of relief. The witty woman with a heart bigger than the continent was far too still, too silent, and Catherine fought tears.

"Fight, Grammy. You're strong. Don't let it win," Catherine said, the words like a prayer. Lightly tracing her grandmother's hand, she lifted her fingertips to her lips, kissed them, and placed her fingers back on her grandmother's, baptizing her with the kiss.

"I'll be back soon," Catherine promised the silence and then retreated to the door.

"Any change?" the maid asked, her voice eternally hopeful.

Catherine gave a mournful frown. "She's sleeping peacefully."

At the maid's nod, Catherine made her way to the stairs. It was time.

As she entered the parlor where Quin was sitting, she offered an apology for his wait. They had forged a unique friendship, and it was still uncharted territory for her. He owed her nothing, yet he had offered his assistance, his friendship. He was harder to read than his brother. Avery had been, in many ways, predictable. His easy manner and candor in life had been consistent, and his opinions and views could easily be known by reading his face. He'd been open, while Quin was far more closed in countenance. While Avery had engaged in conversation for hours on end, she intuitively knew that Quin was a man of many fewer words—but those words were well placed, intelligent, and filled with purpose.

"Thank you for waiting," Catherine offered, studying the tea things.

Brooks or another servant had seen to refreshing the pot and adding another plate of biscuits.

"It was nothing," Quin replied. "If I may be so bold, what exactly is the solicitor planning to explain?" He had risen when Catherine entered, and as she took a seat, he sat as well. "You're of age, so everything should be straightforward, I'd imagine."

Catherine nodded. "I'm my grandmother's sole heir, which does serve to make things less complicated, but as I'm a mere female, in circumstances like these, a trustee oversees the estate for me." Catherine struggled to keep the irritation from her words. It was how things were done, but that didn't mean she had to like it. "My cousin, Lord Bircham, was delegated by my grandmother decades ago, should this ever happen. But the gentleman passed away, leaving the responsibility and title to his son."

"I see. Do you know him?" Quin asked, his green eyes intent on her. They flashed with intelligence.

"No, I believe I met him once when I was much younger, but I can't rightly remember. He has a small estate in Cambridge," Catherine answered.

Quin shifted in his seat; the name sounded familiar. And being from Cambridgeshire, it was likely he'd at least heard of him. "Is he married?"

Catherine's heart pinched, certain where his line of thought was leading him. "No."

"I see."

And she was certain he did, just as she had *seen* as well when she'd discovered the connection. Would this Lord Bircham wish to try to take advantage of his position and pressure her to marry *him*? It was possible, but she hoped irrelevant to the circumstance. Unfortunately, only time would tell.

The silence stretched for a moment before Brooks entered the parlor, announcing the solicitor's arrival.

Catherine stood and walked toward the small-framed man

with spectacles. He bowed to her. "Lady Catherine, thank you for seeing me."

"Of course, Mr. Sheffield. And may I introduce"—Catherine turned and gestured to Quin—"His Grace, the Duke of Wesley." The words felt odd in her mouth, but not bitter, just thick and uncomfortable. By the stiff nature of Quin's shoulders, he felt the same.

"An honor, Your Grace." Mr. Sheffield bowed.

"Please, sit. Can I offer you tea?" Catherine asked, being the proper hostess.

"No, I thank you," the solicitor replied, taking a seat in a wooden chair. He set a satchel beside him, then folded his hands as he leaned forward to face Catherine. "First, may I give my sincerest regards. I pray fervently for the recovery of Lady Greatheart."

"Thank you," Catherine accepted, but her emotions were tamped down in her chest. Wanting a clear head for this, she refused to give the fickle feelings any room in her mind.

"And as I'm sure you're aware, this is mere formality. However, given the age and situation of Lady Greatheart, I find it prudent to outline the procedures should we need to make any decisions later on. Given her current prognosis from the doctor, I feel it's in your best interest and the best interest of the estate to be prepared for any potential future outcome."

"I understand," Catherine remarked.

From the corner of her eye, she noted the way Quin leaned forward, listening intently. A flood of gratitude filled her at his gracious offer to stay, to listen. She would have done it alone, survived and surely done fine—but it was better, comforting and a relief to have another person hear the words, interpret them, find the pieces she might somehow miss.

"Your grandmother's estate is very clearly outlined, there is little to discuss." Mr. Sheffield pulled out several papers, laid them on his lap, and thumbed through them. Brow furrowed, he selected a single sheet from the stack and silently read through it. Nodding to himself, he turned his eyes upward. "You're of age, so you won't be a ward of a relative or placed under guardianship. However, there is the matter of the estate's trustee." He paused.

Catherine nodded. "What exactly does 'trustee' mean?" Though she was certain of the generalities, she wanted to know all the details. Knowledge was power, and she wasn't going into this blind. Not if she could help it.

The solicitor set the pages down and folded his hands. "It's not common practice to have a young, unmarried lady as the sole heir and regulator of a large estate, of which I'm sure you're aware. Until you marry, the trustee of the estate will make legal and financial decisions with your best interests in mind."

"Which means?" Catherine inquired further. In this case, ignorance was not bliss.

"Which means that while you will not answer directly to him as guardian, he will have discretion and stewardship of the Greatheart estate for the time being."

"But that's not set in stone," Quin interjected.

The solicitor turned to him. "No, but it's the usual practice."

"But only until I marry," Catherine stated, choosing her words intentionally. Not *if*, but *when*. And all this was hypothetical anyway; her grandmother was going to heal, grow strong once more, and terrorize them all.

But a small voice whispered, *"What if?"* silencing all the brave words she heart-whispered to her head.

The solicitor was answering her question. "Yes. It's only until you marry. Then, of course, your husband will have control of your estate."

It grated on her, reminded her that she still held the weaker cards in the game. It also reminded her that marriage couldn't be forced or taken lightly. Whoever she married would have control of her estate—for better or worse. She had never wanted to marry for anything but love, but now that seemed most important.

The concept of love in a marriage took on a whole new meaning. The estate's management had been her responsibility. Catherine had happily dived into the ledgers, spending hours poring over the figures. Now, she was powerless and could only watch as it was handed over to someone whom she didn't know and consequently didn't trust. To think that all her effort in managing the estate would be for naught and now at the mercy of someone she hardly knew was unpardonable. But she had little choice in the matter.

Life was never fair.

And she had never felt its unfairness more than now.

# Eleven

"WHAT'S HIS NAME?" QUIN ASKED CATHERINE WHEN THE solicitor had finally left.

"The solicitor?" Catherine asked, her brow furrowed.

"No." Quin waved a hand, his thoughts clearly outrunning his mouth. "Your cousin, the trustee."

"Lord Bircham," she answered. "I don't think he visits London often, but you might know him."

"The name sounds familiar, but I plan to find out more about him before this goes any further." He rose. "I don't think it wise to leave any angle unstudied."

"Why does that not surprise me?" Catherine remarked, her tone taking on a lighter lilt.

Relief pulsed through him at the sound of her teasing tone. She was stronger than most would give her credit for, and he appreciated that about her character.

"Is that a compliment?"

"As close as I'll hand out today," she returned.

"I'll take it as a compliment then. Do you have any questions? I thought the solicitor explained things well enough," he said, continuing to study her and trying to read if she truly was as well as she claimed.

Catherine hesitated. "Yes, well, I rather dislike the idea of having my estate handled by someone else, but aside from that, it's as I assumed."

"That part is the pity," Quin remarked. "But it is only for the interim." He didn't mention the stipulation of marriage; he wasn't sure if that would bring back the pain of his brother's loss for her, or if it would bring it to the surface for him as well.

She gave him a wry expression. "Much can happen in the interim."

"The courts won't give your cousin complete rein. He'll be held responsible for his stewardship." Quin tried to put her suspicions to rest.

"It's more than just the stewardship. I've been managing the estate for several years now. To think of someone else interfering is rather unwelcome." She shrugged. "You'll have to excuse my lack of faith in humanity when money is involved." She paused, wincing. "That wasn't very fair of me. I apologize," she added after a moment.

"No, I can understand your sentiment. I share it, even. Don't apologize."

"Thank you," she said softly, "for staying."

Quin lifted his hand to halt her words. "It was nothing."

"It was for me, so thank you." Catherine extended her hand.

Quin smiled and took it, giving her fingers a gentle squeeze. The scent of rosewater clung to her skin, and her gloves were impeccably soft and creamy. Odd, he'd never noticed a woman's gloves before.

He released her hand reluctantly. She wouldn't appreciate his sympathy. But whatever was stirring in him didn't feel like sympathy. Maybe it was empathy, or just raw knowledge of the pain she was working through. Regardless, it made him edgy. It made him want to leave and stay at the same time. Choosing the first over the latter, he offered his excuses and a promise to call upon her again in the near future before quitting the room.

During his carriage ride to his lodgings, he made plans.

As a professor, he was used to finding the devil in the details. This was one circumstance that was certainly filled with possible snares, and he didn't want Catherine surprised by any of them, not if he could be of help. As he rode to his house, he searched his memory for the name of her cousin, recalling every detail he could find. Lord Bircham didn't have the reputation of a gambler or womanizer; rather, he was known to be eccentric, keeping mostly to his estate in Cambridge. Quin wasn't sure he would be a bad candidate for overseeing the Greatheart estate. He could think of far worse men, but that didn't mean Lord Bircham didn't have secrets, and Quin wasn't about to let those secrets make Lady Greatheart or Catherine's lives any more difficult.

They had suffered enough.

And now Catherine was facing that future alone, save for her grandmother's silent company. Upon arriving at home, he strode directly to his small study. The flickering candlelight leaned as he walked past briskly, casting quavering shadows before stilling once more. The soft scrape of his drawer opening was the only sound in the room as he withdrew a piece of parchment. He scribbled a message on the parchment, the goose-feather quill scraping along the paper with every flick of his wrist as he wrote. Succinctly, he notified his staff in Cambridge that he'd be arriving in a few days' time. After signing his name, then sealing the folded linen woven paper with bloodred wax and his stamp, he called for his butler.

The butler bowed as he entered the room, and Quin lifted the missive from his position behind the wide desk. "Please have this dispatched to Cambridge."

"Of course, Your Grace." His butler took the letter and disappeared into the darkened hallway.

Quin tapped his finger on a closed book upon the desk, the hollow noise punctuating his thoughts. He'd keep his plans with Lady Catherine for the next day, but then he'd inform her that he was departing on the following one—for Cambridge. She was quick to catch on to nuances of conversation and would likely see his intention for traveling there, but he didn't need to confirm her suspicions. It would do no harm to dig around a bit, make sure that

Lord Bircham was exactly who he was reputed to be, and if not, he could weigh his options from there. Catherine couldn't travel to Cambridge at such a time, not with her grandmother ailing. So it was an easy decision and left him feeling at rest, knowing he had a plan and that it was solid in nature. He doubted even his mother could find fault in it.

Which only served to remind him that he was to report back to his mother, to give her the news of Lady Greatheart. He doubted that would be offensive to Catherine, since she knew the gossip had made the rounds. Regardless, it would be good for his mother to check in on them both in his absence. For all his mother's faults, lack of compassion wasn't one of them. She would be a comforting friend at such a time as this.

Mind made up, Quin rose from his desk and scanned the large clock. It was the dinner hour as he made the choice to depart once more, only this time for his family home. Might as well communicate the details now; it would save him the trouble tomorrow, and honestly, he'd been running around London all day. Why deviate now? Maybe then he'd be able to focus on the ledgers he'd failed so miserably to study earlier. With his mind clear, surely it would all make sense.

Life was like that.

Indecision always made life out of focus, but with a sharp decision, a clear direction, everything came into focus. As with the fog burning away from the heat of the sunshine in spring, the world looked new, fresh, solid.

# Twelve

*There is nothing, it seems to me, so difficult as to escape from than that which is essentially agreeable.*

—Catherine the Great

CATHERINE STUDIED THE SKY FROM WITHIN QUIN'S CURRICLE as they swayed with the rhythm of the finely sprung conveyance.

"Was I misleading you?" Quin asked, pulling her attention from the blue sky.

She narrowed her eyes playfully. "No. Though you're irritating to make me admit it."

He chuckled, the sound warm to her ears. "Oh? I'm irritating now, am I?"

"Yes." She arched a brow.

"How many days has it been since you left your house?" Quin asked, his expression questioning, his green eyes sparkling with triumph, knowing where his question would lead—to his being confirmed correct.

"You're insufferable," Catherine remarked, but her lips pulled at the corners in amusement. His arm brushed against hers as he snapped the ribbons. The innocent touch sent tingles along her skin, and in response, her heart skipped.

"I've been called worse."

She turned to him. "It is hard to imagine. You're polite to a fault, in every way a gentleman. I find it hard to believe you being called anything less." She studied him curiously. His eyes crinkled slightly at the edges as he grinned, and she found it awfully endearing.

"I do not know if that was a compliment. Your words are kind, but your tone seems skeptical," he pondered, leaning against the corner of the curricle, studying her.

His look was engaging, and his manner always set her at ease. In a world that held so much uncertainty, it was a welcome constant.

"I just can't see you getting in trouble." She shrugged. "And I fancy you will say that you can't imagine me staying *out* of it," she joked.

"You said it, not me," he remarked. "And I've been in more than my share of mischief. Remember? I'm the younger brother," he said, his eyes clouding.

"Ah, well, you have me at a disadvantage. I never had siblings, so the dynamic isn't one that I'm familiar with."

His smile displayed straight white teeth with a slight gap in the very front. "Imagine being able to irritate an older version of yourself just by following him around and copying his every move."

She groaned. "It must be terrible for the elder sibling, but at least you were never lonely."

"This much is true," he conceded. "But trouble abounds. That is the point I'm trying to make."

"Since I can't refute your point, I'll have to assume you are correct."

His brows lifted. "I'm not sure what to do with such a victory," he said. "You're usually much more difficult to convince."

She sniffed dramatically. "I like to think I'm humble enough to admit when I'm wrong, or otherwise."

"Indeed," was all he said in reply. His expression relaxed, his usual astute expression peaceful, and she had a quick vision of him running around as a boy, chasing things, carefree and without the weight he usually bore on his countenance. But life had a way of changing one. While he'd lost some of that weightlessness, he'd likely gained perspective and wisdom.

She knew she certainly had.

Which was why she'd not protested too much when he'd invited her out for a ride. And he had made a solid point: she hadn't left the house in several days. After she checked on her grandmother and had been certain that an hour or so from her bedside wouldn't see much alteration, Catherine had switched into a day dress and made her way to the front of the house.

The light of the sunshine filled her soul, warming her lap and the gloves on her fingers. She closed her eyes, soaking up the rays.

"Has there been any improvement?" Quin asked, his words piercing her thoughts.

She answered without opening her eyes. "No. She sleeps more than not, and when she wakes, she only whispers softly." Catherine opened her eyes.

"I see. I'm sorry for that."

"As am I, but time will hopefully bring healing."

"Indeed." His clothing whispered against the red brocade upholstery as he shifted on the seat. "I'll be departing tomorrow for Cambridge."

"Cambridge," she repeated.

"Yes." He nodded, not giving further details.

His comings and goings weren't her business, but—would he go there simply to check up on her cousin? She weighed the idea, testing its possibility. Regardless, it didn't matter. But if he did find some information, he'd surely share it, wouldn't he?

"Do you miss teaching?" she asked, belatedly realizing that he was likely going back to Cambridge to participate in something at the university rather than anything to do with her affairs. Scolding herself, she widened her world view beyond herself and her own problems.

"Yes and no." Quin's shoulders relaxed, and then he answered her query. "The students can be...unruly at times. But I love the material. History and politics go hand in hand. Naturally the field is varied and constantly shifts, making it an ever-growing study." His green eyes flashed with delight at he spoke about it, conveying his true love for scholarly pursuits.

Did she feel passionate about something like that? Enough to dwell on its subject matter day and night till she understood it? She frowned, unable to think of anything in particular that captured her so. She enjoyed mathematics and managing the estate, but that wasn't what she fancied most. Her thoughts flickered back to her plans with Avery. Philanthropy: to benefit the arts, to assist the poor, to do more than just work on her ledgers and count money—but to do something with it that made a difference.

"History isn't the most exciting subject matter to most," he said, studying her. Had he interpreted her frown as disinterest?

"I think anything can be fascinating if you are passionate about it." The curricle hit a rut, and Catherine gripped the side. Quin's hand had grazed hers when they'd hit the rut, sending shivers through her. "And to have such an inclination to study something as you have is commendable," she complimented him, swallowing hard as she fought the temptation to feel his touch once more, even fleetingly.

His green eyes held a wealth of intelligence, adding a becoming light to his face. Catherine was unsure how she had missed that before. Her hands tingled, her fingers twitched as if wishing to tip his chin ever so slightly upward to get a fuller view of his countenance, to study that keen awareness in his eyes. His chin arched gracefully to his lips, drawing the eye of the beholder to the masculine beauty of them.

He inclined his head.

Abruptly, she realized she'd been staring. Clenching her hands into fists, she took a long, calming inhale through her nose before speaking. "How long will you be staying in Cambridge?"

"A week. And I would expect my mother will be calling

upon you during that time. She's been asking how you and Lady Greatheart are faring."

"That is very kind of her."

They fell into companionable silence, and Catherine studied him from the corner of her eye. Usually the impulse to fill the void in a conversation was overwhelming, but with him it seemed natural, as if they had chosen to enjoy the quiet rather than run out of things to speak about.

"Promise me something?" he murmured softly.

Catherine turned to him, but his attention was ahead on the road. She waited, watching, using the moments to study him once more. Something swirled in her belly, hinting at attraction.

He turned to her, arching a brow.

Forcing herself to meet his regard unabashedly, she raised her own brow as she answered. "I'm not promising anything till I know what you're asking."

He spoke in a wry tone. "Very well. Just promise me you'll not sequester yourself in your rooms and parlors while I'm gone."

"I wasn't—"

"Be that as it *may*," he interrupted, "just promise me."

Catherine narrowed her eyes, then answered, "Very well."

"See? Was that so difficult?"

"Yes," she replied.

He rolled his eyes. "Only because you made it that way," he retorted.

She bit her lip to keep from smiling too widely. "I would never do that…"

"Clearly."

She giggled softly, the relaxing nature shifting something in her heart, releasing some of the tension she'd been carrying.

"Promise me something?" she asked him, using his words.

He bent forward. "Yes."

"Yes you're listening, or yes you promise?"

"Yes." He shrugged.

She resisted the urge to roll her eyes. "Smile more."

He frowned at her. "I do."

"Like you are right now." She narrowed her eyes playfully.

He relaxed his frown and forced a wide toothy grimace.

She grimaced back. "Not like that."

"I'm a very jolly person." He waved his hand dismissively.

"Just like I'm the social butterfly right now."

He studied her then. "Do I honestly not appear happy?"

"Happy is different, Quin. You should know this," she continued. "Happy is a state of heart. A smile is just the overflow from it. Sometimes our happiness isn't quite enough to overflow onto our faces. But when it does, it's a good thing. So don't be afraid to let it overflow, Quin. It looks nice on you." A rush of heat swept up her neck, and she turned her attention to the passing scenery once more.

"Then I promise," he answered, and to her great relief, they'd arrived back at her home. He reined in the matched bay horses, then disembarked swiftly and held out his hand to assist her.

"Good," she answered, taking his offer of assistance as she alighted from the curricle. Her eyes followed him as he placed a tender kiss on her hand, then stepped back into the driver's seat and snapped the ribbons.

As Quin drove away, Catherine forced her attention to the house before her, to her grandmother waiting within. She wasn't just talking to Quin about smiling; it was something she needed to hear—to practice herself.

They had both been through much.

Still enduring.

Happiness seemed dear.

Fleeting.

But maybe, if they both fought for it, it could be found once more.

# Thirteen

IT WAS HER EYES, THE HAZEL HUE THAT HID NOTHING OF HER emotions, that scorched right through him. Desire swirled in those depths, warm and welcoming as she held out a hand that grasped his in a familiar touch, sending a wave of need through his body.

She sucked her lower lip between her teeth as she drew him toward her, walking backwards down the hall. He followed, giving the slightest resistance to her pull only to prolong the game. As if understanding what he was about, she gave him a scolding expression and paused in her efforts. Changing tactics, she meaningfully closed the distance between them and rose onto her toes, hovering a whisper away from his lips. Good Lord, the heat from her proximity was a siren call his body would follow to the ends of the earth.

"Quin…" She drew out his name, caressing the word with her tone, her mouth, her lips till it felt like a touch. "Do you want to play out here…or in there?" She looked behind them to the slightly open door.

"Always so impatient," he answered softly, then leaned forward to steal a kiss.

She withdrew, taunting him flirtatiously.

"Now who is being evasive?" he asked, taking a step toward her.

She backed up again.

Quin maneuvered to the left slightly so her next step would bring her closer to the hall wall, and in a moment, her back was pressed against it. Bracing his hands on the wall on either side of her face, he caged her in.

"Am I a prisoner?"

"I rather think I'm the one who's captive," he replied, his attention lingering on her mouth—the perfect bow of her upper lip, the contrast of her plump lower lip—begging to be kissed. "I'm utterly bewitched," he confessed, then tasted the pleasure of her soft kiss.

His body ached with the sweetness of her flavor. The instinctive, primal need to taste more, press further, lose himself in her affection was nearly overwhelming.

She shuddered under his touch as he moved his hand to trace along the delicate skin of her throat till he could arch his fingers into her soft hair, the pins scattering to the floor.

He drew back, using a force of will that could only be exerted with the knowledge that it was temporary, and he lifted her into his arms. A man on a mission, he carried her to his room before the dream faded to light.

Gasping, Quin sat up in bed, his heart pounding. He covered his face with his hands, struggling to regain his wits. Lowering his hands, he focused on the window, then his bed. The light of dawn weakly illuminated the rumpled covers and the fact that he was very much alone.

He had never had such a dream before.

He had the urge to search the covers to make sure he really had dreamed it. It had been so blasted real. He took an irritated snort as he thought back to the dream, then froze. He'd been so startled that it hadn't been real—that he hadn't truly considered what he'd been doing.

Or with whom.

Bloody hell, he'd been kissing Catherine. And not in a casual fashion. He'd possessed her...yet been captive as well. The tension, passion, and love—there could be no other name for it—was so real and strangely comfortable, as if it were not the first kiss but the millionth.

And instinctively, he knew that the ten-millionth kiss would be just as powerful as the first.

He didn't regret any part, and the dream had been so authentic. Which was worse. Wouldn't an honorable man experience guilt over such a provoking dream about an innocent? Perhaps he wasn't as honorable as he perceived himself to be, which was equally disturbing.

Heavens, it had felt more real than the last kiss he could remember.

If that was even possible.

She'd said his name, though of course it was *his* dream. He supposed that the dreamer had such powers, to make people do impossible things. She could have bloody well flown if he'd wished it in his dream. But it unnerved him how normal their actions had felt in his dream.

As if it was usual, that kind of earth-shattering passion, that kind of love.

He couldn't go there. Not with her. Anyone but her. He resolved to push it from his mind and rose from his bed. For once, rather than fighting the reasons to visit her, he was thrilled to be leaving London. He couldn't face her, not yet. Not when the dream had been so real. Not when he wanted it so badly. Did she dream at night about his brother?

Quin's blood ran cold, a stark, frigid chill that iced his veins compared to the way his blood had boiled only moments ago. In all the years of his brother's life, he had never been jealous. Not of his title, his honor, his bride.

Till now.

And it terrified him. Because how could one compete with the dead? It was impossible. Not that he was going to enter into any competition for Catherine's heart. It was preposterous. But that dream... It haunted him.

As he readied himself for the day, broke his fast, and then called for his carriage, the dream lingered, whispering memories to him of what had never actually happened. But felt like it had. His body still tingled. His lips still felt hers. And he bloody well remembered the way his name sounded on her lips. He wanted to hear it again.

Desperately.

With enough power that he fled in the opposite direction, to Cambridge. With each village he passed, he released some tension. But it was only a temporary fix. Because he'd return to London. And he'd see her. He wasn't sure he could prepare for such a thing. To be unchanged. And for her to be blissfully unaware. But she had to be. It couldn't change, the friendship. So with a cold grip on his emotions, he forced them into submission as he put distance between him and London. Praying that seven days could cool a body as fevered as his. And a heart that clearly had no scruples for what was honorable. Perspective, he would drink it in. Remind himself that he might not be the one who roamed her dreams.

Time passed quickly, and though it would be a long day in the carriage if he were to travel from London to Cambridge in one day, he was more than happy to gain the distance needed for a clear head.

The coach stopped at a small inn near Hertford, the halfway point. The stay was shortened by the opening of the skies, and not wanting to travel longer than necessary on an excessively muddy road, Quin had ordered his coachman to leave directly.

The rain pelted the carriage roof and blurred the windows of the vehicle, leaving Quin without distraction. The final three and a half hours passed slowly, his thoughts plaguing him.

When the carriage came to a final halt before his Cambridge lodgings, he nearly sang with relief. His body was coiled with tension like a spring tightened far too much. He stepped from the carriage and released the pent-up breath that had been building in his chest.

Quin studied the large stone building, which was simpler than his London home. It was an older one that carried on for the length of an entire block. Every few feet, a new set of steps reached for another door, another home for one of his neighbors. The stone was a cold gray, not nearly as charcoal black as the edifices in London, but then again the coal smoke wasn't as thick in Cambridge so the buildings weren't nearly as stained.

He had a fleeting thought that reminded him of the red-colored stone buildings in Edinburgh, Scotland. One year he had given a guest lecture at the University of Edinburgh, and he'd noted the crimson structures. Because Edinburgh had used the red stone for its buildings, the coal smoke had been far more noticeable, and entire buildings were streaked with black with only the lower levels the reddish hue that they had originally held.

Avoiding his thoughts, he strode up to his front door, taking the five steps in quick succession. Before he reached the door, it was opened by his butler in Cambridge.

"Your Grace." The man bowed, opening the door wide.

Quin nodded, then handed him his hat. Drinking in the sight of his Cambridge residence, Quin felt a sense of peace rest on his tense spirit like a balm. While London was his childhood home, Cambridge was where he had found himself. Where he'd grown from a boy to a man, and there was a sense of pride and strength that came from that. The fears, the tension and uncertainty that had followed him from London held no power here and, as if sensing it, melted away.

He took the hall down to his study.

"Shall I have tea brought in?" the butler inquired.

"Yes, thank you," Quin replied.

"It shall be brought directly."

Quin nodded but was already to his study door. The room beckoned him to enter, a crackling fire glowing in the hearth. He withdrew a few books of study and set to work. Tea was brought in. Then biscuits. The solitude was his companion, and he didn't realize how much he'd missed it. The quiet.

He spent the next hour and a half sorting through the scholarly accumulation before he decided to tackle the reason he'd come to Cambridge.

He slid open the drawer to his right and withdrew a fresh sheet of paper. In short order, he scribbled a few questions and signed his name, then withdrew the Duke of Wesley seal, watching as the bloodred wax hardened with the stamp.

He called out, knowing the butler wasn't far. After all, it was a much smaller residence than his London home.

In a few moments, the butler entered the study.

"Please dispatch this to Morgan." He didn't use his friend's full title; they'd known each other since long before the titles mattered.

The butler nodded and took the letter.

Morgan worked for the War Office and was excellent at finding information. With him returning to Cambridge, the timing was good. If anyone could find out information about Lord Bircham, it was he.

"Will there be anything else?" the butler asked.

Quin shook his head, feeling the fatigue from the trip catching up with him. "No, that will be all. And I'll take supper in here."

The butler nodded.

Quin watched as the man left, closing the study door with a soft click. The sound of the fire crackling lured him into a sense of peace, and he soaked up the glory of a quiet evening at home. Here the ghosts of London wouldn't haunt him. One way or another. Or so he hoped. He'd find out when he fell asleep, and he wasn't sure if he hoped his dreams would be haunted or not.

# Fourteen

*To tempt, and to be tempted, are things very nearly allied...*

—Catherine the Great

CATHERINE COULD NOT SLEEP. IN FACT, WHEN SHE CLOSED HER eyes, it was as if she became more awake.

She rose from bed and padded over to her chair by the low-burning fire. There hadn't been much change to her grandmother's condition, and if she didn't improve, the solicitor would likely recommend that Lord Bircham be contacted.

How she hated that he could hold any power over her future! Someone she didn't know, who hadn't any understanding of her or her grandmother, was to be given power over an estate he didn't earn or inherit, all because he was a male relative.

It was bloody well infuriating.

And she wasn't going to sit back and let it happen.

No.

She'd fought through too much pain, survived too much to allow her future to be dictated to her. This was her family, her estate, her future, and she was going to have a say in it, come what may.

But she needed information.

Who was this Lord Bircham? She had only met him once, and it was so long ago. The fire burned lower in the grate as she watched the embers stir and flare, her thoughts swirling. Who would be the best informant? She could have—should have—asked Quin, but he had done so much already. She didn't want to rely on him, not for this, though she did have the sneaking suspicion he wasn't asking for permission, simply going and finding information regardless.

If so, all the better. But she wasn't going to wait for him.

She wished there was some random gossip she could uncover—it would be the easiest way to find out information—and as soon as she thought of that, a plan formed in her mind.

Who else knew everything except for the ladies of the *ton*? If there was a scandal, or rumor of one, they would know.

What she needed was someone she could trust, who wouldn't turn her situation into new gossip, someone who would just give information, not take it. Lord Penderdale—Morgan—had mentioned his younger sister was debuting this season; Joan was her name. Perhaps she would know something? Yet as she considered it, Catherine disregarded the idea.

She needed someone who had listened to the gossip for years, who would know the older scandals, or lack thereof.

Relief flowed through her and she smiled as she thought of a name.

Yes, it was perfect.

And trustworthy.

A sense of peace eased her anxious mind as she started to work out the details. The desk was a short walk from her place near the fire, and with a few steps, she was sitting before a leaf of paper and writing a quick note.

*Your Grace,*
    *It would be my sincerest honor to have you over for tea. Would today be acceptable?*

                                        *Yours,*
                                        *Catherine Greatheart*

Catherine sealed the message and set it just to the side of her desk, awaiting dawn. With a plan formed, she returned to bed, hope filling her heart, and finally fell asleep.

When she awoke, the sunlight was already brightly streaming through her bedroom window. It took only a moment for her to remember her plans from earlier, and with a determination she hadn't felt in some time, she rose from bed and slipped the letter from her desk. Ringing for her maid, she swept her hair to the side and over her shoulder, pondering the other aspects of her plan that she would need to put into motion today.

As she caught a glimpse of herself in the mirror, she paused. Her grandmother would be proud of her progress, taking control— and doing it regardless of the fear that could easily consume her.

Fear of the unknown.

She nodded to her reflection, determination patching all the leftover cracks that hadn't been filled before. The door opened, and Millard entered, offering a quick curtsy.

"Good morning. Please have this dispatched to the Duchess of Wesley's residence."

Millard took the note. "Shall I have the messenger wait for a reply?"

Catherine thought for a moment. "No." She was quite certain the Duchess of Wesley would accept the invitation; Quin had already implied she was planning to visit anyway.

"Right away, my lady." Millard left to give the message to the servant who would deliver it, leaving Catherine with her thoughts once more.

She looked at the clock on the mantel over the fireplace and noted she had a lot of time before she could expect the duchess.

Perfect.

When Millard returned, Catherine put on a lovely day dress. She was going shopping—and not just for clothes, but for everything else that could land her the most important piece of her plan.

A husband.

The season would start soon, and she needed the dresses they'd already ordered to be ready, but with a few changes. She wasn't a debutante anymore. But neither was she a widow. However, there was a thin line between the two that allowed for some freedom in her choices in clothing. She wasn't going to sit by idly, waiting for someone to win her heart. No. She had done that and lost nearly everything.

The morning light illuminated her desk as she approached, her need to write a list burning inside her. Something to keep her focused. Something to keep her from settling for less. She inked the pen and hovered over the paper.

*Husband requirements:*

- *Rich—no fortune hunters*
- *Not belittling of women in business ventures*
- *Interested in supporting the arts*
- *Established*
- *No gambling history*
- *Kind to his mother/sisters*

She studied the list and frowned. That was pretty much every other lady's list; there wasn't anything unique about it. She doubted anyone wanted a gambling and abusive man—but she needed, *wanted* something more than she could articulate.

Love?

Of course, but she wasn't going to hold out for it. She'd had it once, or close enough. She wanted…

The word hit her with a solid thump in her chest, setting her heart to pounding. A partnership. Not a legal obligation. Not a man to officiate her life. Someone to walk beside her, to listen to her. Heavens, was that asking too much? To have a husband who could take advice from a woman? She grimaced. It shouldn't be asking too much, but she wondered if maybe it was still difficult to find in a London ballroom. Perhaps she needed more from the Duchess of Wesley than merely information on her cousin. Maybe she needed information on other things too. Other people.

Could she do it? Take that step? Did she dare ask her almost-mother-in-law about other men? Did she have anyone else to ask? No. She didn't. So, with a bit of a hysterical chuckle, she realized she was going to do the unthinkable. Ask the woman who was going to be her mother-in-law for help on finding a husband.

Good Lord.

She was either making a brilliant plan or a fatal error. And the worst part was that she wouldn't know till later. She'd need to wrestle with the decision for hours yet, if not days.

But if it worked…

The hope of that echoed through her, filling her and pushing back the fear. The risk was far outweighed by the reward. And right now she needed an ally. She only hoped she'd made the right decision in who.

# Fifteen

"Interesting note you sent." Morgan waved it in the air as he strode into Quin's study.

Quin set the newspaper down, folding his hands as he greeted his friend. "Good day to you as well."

"Good day." Morgan arched a brow. "I knew there was something going on when I saw you two." He waggled his brows as he approached the desk.

Quin frowned at his friend's words. "What do you mean?"

Morgan shrugged. "You and Lady Catherine. You were quite cozy in the park."

Quin stiffened in his chair. "I'm not sure what you're insinuating." Thankfully, he hadn't dreamed anything exceptional last night, merely a blur of color he couldn't remember when he awoke. But the dream of Catherine wasn't so far in the past that he didn't recollect it with stunning clarity. As soon as Morgan's words implied some attachment to Catherine, Quin's body tensed.

"Fine, whatever you wish to deny is your choice, but at least explain this." He set the letter on the desk and tucked his hands in his pockets.

Quin chose not to pursue the first line of conversation and nodded toward the letter. "I need information. It's just that simple."

"On Bircham. Why?" Morgan shifted, then sat down in the chair across from Quin's desk.

Quin proceeded to explain the situation to his friend, careful to convey an almost professional interest in Catherine's circumstance.

Bloody hell, he even sounded stuffy to his own ears.

As if sensing the care with which Quin spoke, Morgan leaned back in his chair, regarding his friend with a pensive expression. "Very well."

Quin released the tension in his shoulders and relaxed slightly. "So you'll look into it?"

Morgan nodded. "Yes, it won't be difficult." He continued to study his comrade.

Quin's skin itched at the way his friend regarded him. "Is there something more?"

Morgan frowned. "Just thinking."

"About?" Quin asked, his patience wearing thin.

Morgan picked a piece of lint off his coat sleeve and shrugged. "It sounds like she needs a husband."

Quin clenched his jaw. "Yes, but she doesn't need to run head-long into marriage just to avoid whatever character her cousin is. For all we know, he's an upstanding countryman. This might all be for naught."

At this, Morgan looked up, his expression amused. "Countryman?"

Quin waved his hand. "You know what I mean."

"Damn, Quin. You're old. No wonder you aren't interested." Morgan stood, adjusting his coat.

"Interested?" Quin repeated before he thought better of the word. No need to open that conversation. "Never mind."

"That's what I thought." Morgan gave a bemused leer and nodded. "I'll let you know what I find out."

Quin's hands clenched into fists at the knowing expression on his friend's face. Bastard. But rather than fall into Morgan's verbal trap, he nodded. "Thank you."

"Ever the gentleman… I'm sure that will serve you well," Morgan said just before he quit the room. Leaving the words hanging in the air. Leaving Quin to wonder just what his friend had meant by such a thing. He *was* a gentleman. So was Morgan, and their friend Rowles… But there was something in his words that made Quin pause, wondering if maybe there was a time and place for gentlemanly behavior.

And a time and place to be without it.

But he disregarded the words, choosing to ignore whatever implication his friend had left in the room. He had more important things to do. While Morgan was investigating Lord Bircham, Quin was going to do his own investigating.

One could never be too cautious.

But first he was going to take a much-needed trip to the university.

It had been a few months, and he wanted to address the fact that he wasn't going to be teaching for the next year or so. He'd said as much in his resignation letter. The university had been exceedingly kind, explaining they would welcome him back whenever he was able to teach once more.

A wave of disappointment flowed through him, and he wished his life could be different. He had tried to do both—handle the dukedom and teach—but one or the other suffered for his efforts. And that wasn't fair to his family or his students. He'd had to make a choice.

Rather, life had made it for him.

He opted to walk to the university rather than ride in his carriage, giving him time before he had to say goodbye for now. The butler followed Quin to the door, offering a black umbrella. "Just in case, Your Grace."

Quin took the long wooden handle and nodded his thanks. As he stepped through the open door, the cloud-filtered sunlight illuminated the street before him. Taking the steps one by one, he tucked the umbrella under his arm and started down Canterbury Street. Few were out walking, and even fewer carriages rolled by as he passed through the neighborhood. Turning onto the main road, he noticed the traffic increased, and he shifted the umbrella from under his arm to use as a cane as he made his way through the people toward the city center. The narrow medieval streets fanned out from the larger thoroughfares, all filing into the main hub of Cambridge where the colleges could be found.

Cambridge was a unique town in many ways, but its university was the main attraction for most. With over thirty colleges, it was spread out through the city center, each building housing a different discipline in education. As Quin approached Castle Street, he took a few side streets to intersect with Queen's Road. He allowed the sweet serenity of the large green courts in front of the colleges to relax him. It was a soothing sight, and he welcomed the familiarity of it all. How many times had he made the same walk, ambling through the streets, taking in the scenes? How much longer till he could resume?

But that wasn't to be, not for now. He passed a small side street from Queen's Road, passing several colleges as he made his way toward the library. As he passed, he could almost smell the history, and memories of studying in the sacred halls filled him with longing.

Pushing onward, he paused in front of the library, its knowledge and respite calling to him. He could lose himself in there, and maybe find the piece that seemed missing from his heart as well. It wasn't likely, a dark whisper suggested, for the missing piece was back in London. He silenced the traitorous thought. So much of life was what one chose to focus on.

He kept reminding himself of that truth.

With a reluctant pace, he walked up the long path to the entrance of the building and murmured a prayer that he'd return soon.

Saying hello rather than goodbye again.

# Sixteen

*I may be kindly, I am ordinarily gentle, but in my line of business I am obliged to will terribly what I will at all.*

—Catherine the Great

CATHERINE WAS PLEASED WITH THE ADJUSTMENT SHE'D MADE to the dresses she had ordered with her grandmother. Longing spread through her. How she wished her grandmother were with her now!

She had asked the modiste to alter the cut of several gowns to something not too scandalous but definitely flirtatious. And for the first time, she wished she was a widow, to have lost a husband rather than a fiancé. As terrible as it sounded, that would have been much easier to navigate. As a widow, she would have control over her estate, her life, and her future. But that wasn't to be, and she was also glad that she hadn't suffered that deep a loss. It was hard enough to have lost Avery as her betrothed; part of her heart whispered it would have been far worse if he had been her husband.

And at least she had one aspect that could work in her favor, that couldn't be taken from her. She had to give it: her virginity. It was a priceless commodity.

She dislodged the heavy thoughts and took the stairs to her rooms, instructing the footman to deposit her packages where her maid could unpack them.

She tugged off her gloves, slipping them off her fingers as she halted by her grandmother's door. With a gentle twist, she turned the knob and moved silently into the darkened room. The maid who was attending her grandmother stood at her entrance, but Catherine waved her off silently, and the woman went back to her darning in the chair beside her grandmother.

A slight breeze shifted the curtains on the other end of the room, and the clean scent of early spring wafted on the air. It wasn't cold weather, so Catherine was thankful her grandmother could enjoy the bit of freshness, even if she wasn't awake enough to realize it.

"Grammy?" Catherine said, placing a hand on her grandmother's. Thankfully, it was warm, not the awful chill that had greeted her that first morning. Certainly, that was a good indication that her body was healing? Maybe? Catherine wasn't sure anymore. Hope hadn't helped yet, and she wasn't sure it ever would. But as long as her grandmother drew breath she would be nearby, giving her love.

"It's a lovely day today. You'd be eager to be out and about, I'm sure. I went shopping," Catherine said, taking a seat in the chair beside her grandmother. "I made some adjustments to the gowns, and I think you'll approve." She said the latter to herself, imagining her grandmother's reactions.

She traced the lines of her grandmother's fingers and continued. "I'm meeting the Duchess of Wesley today…" She waited, watching for any reaction in her grandmother's expression. At times, her eyes had fluttered as if she'd heard the words. No such reaction today. Catherine continued, "I'm going to ask for her help. I need some information, and I think she's the one I can trust. I guess we'll find out the hard way if I'm right," she added, again mostly to herself.

"Anyway, I miss you." Her voice trembled. "I really miss you. Keep fighting, Grammy. Be strong." She bent and kissed her grandmother's cheek, closing her eyes and willing her own strength into her grandmother's frail form. "I'll be back later to tell you how everything went."

As she was standing from the bed, her grandmother's hand twitched. Catherine paused and hazarded a look from the delicate hand to her grandmother's face.

Her eyelids opened for a moment, then slid closed, but her lips formed a single syllable.

"Love."

Tears sprang to Catherine's eyes as she hastily sat back down beside her grandmother and gently squeezed her hand. "I love you so much." The tears flowed swiftly, and Catherine reached up to touch her grandmother's face. "Rest, but thank you. I needed that, to see that you're fighting. Grammy...I just need you to overcome whatever this is," Catherine said as she gently wiped the tears from her eyes.

Grasping her grandmother's hand once more, she was relieved to feel a slight squeeze, giving hope to her heart. When her grandmother's hand relaxed, Catherine noted the way her chest rose and fell softly with sleep. Rising once more, she padded from the room and spoke with the maid about her grandmother's reactions.

Tears welled within the maid's eyes as well. "Should I call back the doctor, my lady?"

Catherine paused. "No, she's doing exactly what she needs to. She's resting and fighting. He said she'd come from it on her own. There's nothing more he can do..."

"I see. I'll remain by her side, my lady."

Catherine nodded. "And please come and notify me if she awakens again."

"Yes, my lady."

Catherine cast a loving look back to her grandmother's sleeping form as the maid went to sit beside her in a nearby chair. Tears threatened, but they were tears of joy—of relief, which was a welcome change from the tears of pain and loss she'd cried far too often during the past year.

She walked the short distance to her rooms to prepare for her upcoming conversation with the Duchess of Wesley.

As she changed her dress, she practiced the questions in her mind, trying to find the best way to ask everything. In short order, she was ready and taking the stairs to the parlor.

The Duchess of Wesley was prompt, arriving the moment the clock struck four. Brooks announced her, and Catherine stood quickly as she entered the room.

"Your Grace, thank you for accepting my invitation."

"Of course!" The Duchess of Wesley gave a warm expression at Catherine's words. "I was all too happy to receive it. Tell me, how is your grandmother?"

Catherine gestured to a chair, and the duchess took a seat on a wing-backed one near the small circular table before them.

Catherine sat down across from her guest and answered the question. "Much the same. I assume your son told you what transpired?"

"Yes. Poor thing. I hate that this happened to her." The Duchess of Wesley clucked her tongue. "And the doctor has been in consistently?"

"Yes. Every other day," Catherine replied, shifting a little. She wasn't sure how to start the conversation and yet was impatient to begin.

A maid entered with a tea tray and set it on the table between them. The hot steam swirled from the cups as Catherine poured. As she handed a cup to the Duchess of Wesley, she gathered her courage. "I was wondering, my lady, if you have ever heard of Lord Bircham. He's from Cambridgeshire."

Catherine watched the Duchess of Wesley's expression narrow as she tilted her head to the side. "Bircham."

"Yes." Catherine hoped she wasn't overstepping; she needed an ally now more than ever.

"Isn't he... Yes. I remember him." She nodded, her expression illuminating with a memory. "He's about the age of my son—Quinton—though I'm not sure they went to Eton together. Odd, that." She frowned. "But as far as I know, he hasn't come to London in some time, and he is unmarried." She studied Catherine. "Why do you ask?"

It was truly now or never. "Your Grace, may I trust you with some information?"

The Duchess of Wesley gave a decisive nod of her head, her stare fixing on Catherine.

"Because of my grandmother's condition, our solicitor will be contacting Lord Bircham. He's the trustee of the estate..." She let her voice trail off, allowing the Duchess of Wesley to put together the pieces.

"I see," she replied with an understanding tone. "And you want to make sure he's not a wastrel."

"Exactly."

The Duchess of Wesley frowned. "Cambridge, you say?"

"Yes," Catherine replied, taking a sip of her tea.

"Hmm, interesting" was the response.

When her guest didn't elaborate further, Catherine moved forward with her questions.

"And I'm sure you can see what a position this puts me in."

The Duchess of Wesley took a sip of her tea, pausing before answering. "You need a husband."

Catherine froze, only listened to her heartbeat as she carefully gauged the Duchess of Wesley's reaction. Would she be hurt? Offended? Good Lord, she couldn't offend such a powerful person in the *ton*.

"Well, you do." The Duchess of Wesley gave a shrug. "Don't look so terrified."

Catherine found her voice. "Yes, well, but I don't wish to offend—"

"Pish, dear. You'll have to do worse than that to offend me." The duchess speared her with a calculating stare. "Not that you should take that as a challenge." She waved her hand in the air dismissively. "I think you're wise to look ahead, and I'll help you."

Catherine swallowed, not quite believing her ears.

"That is what you want, is it not?" the Duchess of Wesley added when Catherine didn't reply.

"Y-yes, please. I find I'm quite…"

"Lost?" the Duchess of Wesley finished for her. "Of course you are, and I'm the right person to ask. I have the connections you need, and there's already an established connection between you and my family." She flicked her fingers as if it was simply common sense, not a plan born painstakingly in the middle of the night.

"Thank you." Catherine nearly crumpled with the relief that flowed through her.

"Well, shall we start, then?" the Duchess of Wesley asked, her eyes dancing with anticipation. "I don't have any daughters, so you'll have to excuse my eagerness. This should be fun."

"For you, maybe," Catherine grumbled, but a laugh escaped her lips. "I can't say I'm looking forward to it."

"You will. By the end of all this, you'll look back and see it wasn't as bad as you thought. Now, do you have anyone in mind?" the Duchess of Wesley asked, her attention dropping to her teacup, hiding whatever expression was in her eyes.

Catherine's brow furrowed, and then she answered, "No. And I wish you to know there isn't anyone in my heart since Avery."

The Duchess of Wesley nodded. "I trust that, but—" She paused a moment. "But my eldest is no longer here, and we must move forward. You included."

Catherine didn't know what to say, how to react to such a gift from someone who'd suffered even more than she did at the loss of Wesley. Words weren't enough. "I have no words to express—"

"You don't need any. Now. Have you been to the modiste? I think I remember you mentioning it..."

Catherine went on to describe the dresses, quickly gaining approval of the colors and styles. The duchess wasted no time in diving into thoughts of potential suitors, and before long she had created a list.

One name was missing that Catherine had hoped the duchess wouldn't mention.

Quin.

Because while he was a good friend, some lines couldn't be crossed.

Could they?

# Seventeen

MORGAN RETURNED TO QUIN'S CAMBRIDGE HOME THE NEXT day, his expression aglow with knowledge. Quin knew his friend had something of interest to share by the way his eyebrows arched as he entered Quin's study unannounced.

"You'll want to hear this without delay," Morgan said.

Quin gestured to a chair. "It's a bit early for brandy, but..." His voice trailed off as he turned his focus to the sideboard. His nerves were already tight; the offer of brandy wasn't simply a kind gesture for his friend's sake.

"Pour" was all Morgan said.

Quin was amused. He stood and strode over to the sideboard, withdrew a decanter of fine brandy, and poured two snifters. He took a sip and then offered the other snifter to his friend.

"Out with it," Quin requested.

Morgan took a long sip, his eyes closed in appreciation, then leaned forward. "I went to great lengths to make sure my information is correct, mind you."

Quin waved his hand, having assumed as much already.

"If he's a scoundrel, he's done a bang-up job of hiding his tracks. As you said so eloquently earlier, he's an 'upstanding citizen.'"

Quin listened intently, not sure why this information didn't sit well. He took another sip, then returned to his seat behind his desk as he waited for his friend to continue.

"And he's unmarried," Morgan added, his expression calculating.

Quin resisted the urge to squirm under his friend's scrutiny.

"Is that so?"

"Yes."

"I see. And he's titled… He might be a good option for Catherine," Quin said, mostly because he was assuming it was the last thing Morgan expected from him.

Morgan shrugged a shoulder. "I'm glad you see it that way. I suggest you recommend it to her when you see her." He leaned back, his stare unwavering, as if calling his friend's bluff.

"I don't feel I'm in a position to recommend suitors, but if she asks, I'll give her your opinion," Quin replied, keeping his focus on Morgan, not willing to fold.

"Brilliant," Morgan replied, his word at odds with the focus of his expression.

"Thank you." Quin lifted his brandy to salute his friend's efforts. "I appreciate you looking into it."

"It's the least I can do for her. But I feel I should mention one thing." Morgan took a sip of his brandy, stretching out the moment.

Quin waited for his friend to continue.

Morgan took another sip, and Quin damned his comrade's flair for the dramatic.

"What is it?" Quin bit out, his patience wearing thin.

"Oh? You're interested now?" Morgan asked, clearly amused to have pestered his friend to the point of breaking through his calm facade.

"Well?"

"Well what?" Morgan stared at Quin, his expression innocent.

"You're a pain in the ass."

"Ahh, compliments." Morgan lifted his glass in a mock toast. "All I was going to say is this… You're a bloody idiot if you don't look in the mirror and tell the person you see in the reflection to offer for Catherine. I'm not blind, and I'm not an idiot. But apparently you are, and you need to chase after her before it's too late." Morgan leaned back in his chair and lifted his hands. "That is all."

It was Quin's turn to frown and give an innocent expression. "I'm not the one for her."

"Ah, there it is." Morgan lifted his glass in salute. "You don't see it yet, fine. But you will…and I'll be watching and be the first to offer my congratulations and 'I told you so.' I only hope you're not too late."

"Thank you for your helpful insight," Quin replied with sarcasm. "But I wouldn't hold too high of expectations."

"I won't, but I'll surely enjoy it nonetheless," Morgan boasted. "Now, I'll take my leave. I need to finish a few things before I head back to London. Joan has a ball this Friday she wishes to attend."

"How is that going?"

"Good… At least as well as can be expected. We'll see as the season progresses. You might have to act as my second if any unsavory character offers for her and won't be hinted away. I'm too pretty for prison, and I'm hot-tempered enough to accept a challenge."

Quin chuckled. "If it comes to pistols at dawn, I'll be sure to tie you to a chair."

"It might take more than a chair."

"I'll do what I must."

"Besides, pistols at dawn are so overdone. I hope I'd have better taste in taking extreme action than that… Knife in the heart, you know, something spectacular."

"You've been working for the War Office too long. You've become bloodthirsty."

"No, my tolerance for pretense has disappeared." Morgan rolled his eyes. "Like what I'm dealing with now." He shot his friend a glare. "Regardless, I doubt it will come to that. I'm sure I'll see you in London."

"Yes, I'll leave here Wednesday, so I'll be back in town a few days from now. My mother wrote with details of the next few events she will be hosting and requested my presence. I can't delay now."

Morgan joked, "Best of luck with that."

"Thank you. Though I think you're in need of more luck than I…" Quin offered.

"That's fair. Well then, until later, chap."

"Good day, Morgan."

As soon as Morgan left, Quin withdrew the letter from his mother he had been reading before his friend arrived. Within a moment, he found the place where he'd left off.

His mind spun as he read then reread the words.

> *I wanted you to know before you returned that I've taken Catherine Greatheart under my wing. She will be in attendance for the upcoming events, and I need you to keep an eye on her as we've invited several gentlemen who are of interest. While all the men we've selected are of sterling reputation, I don't wish to be naive. If you have any knowledge of these men's reputations, please let me know promptly.*

Quin paused, his contemplation shifting to the fire in the hearth, unseeing. This was a surprise, to say the least. Never would he have expected this kind of involvement from his mother.

He turned back to the letter, studying the names listed.

Two names were friends of his; one had an old and established title and an impeccable reputation. It was the last name that gave him pause.

It was his.

He read it again, trying to figure out what his mother was doing. His name was the last name that should be listed. Catherine had been betrothed to his brother, for heaven's sake.

If she showed any interest in him, it would be assumed she was only after the title. While Quin knew better, society would see a mercenary intention. She hadn't acquired the title with his brother, so she was going after him next.

It made him sick to think of it, for people to see her that way—so heartless, and completely inaccurate.

He set the letter down, thinking over the implications. And as he thought it over, he realized that he'd never once considered the other names.

But disregarded them immediately.

The only name he'd considered was his own, which scared the hell out of him.

Because he was going to London in a few days—seeing Catherine in a few days.

He had some choices to make.

And he felt entirely unable to make them.

But such was life...

It forced the choice when you least wished to make it.

# *Eighteen*

*It is better to inspire a reform than to enforce it.*

—*Catherine the Great*

WHEN WEDNESDAY ARRIVED, CATHERINE COULD SCARCELY believe the flurry of the past week. So much had happened, and so much had changed. The Duchess of Wesley had done more than expected, and she was a regular visitor to the Greatheart residence. Catherine learned her opinions on fashion were excellent, and they made a few slight changes to her already-altered gowns, preparing for the Wednesday evening party.

The Duchess of Wesley was hosting, and if that weren't enough, she had come up with a list of names of suitable husbands.

It was truly too much, and Catherine had tried to keep the tears walled up behind her lashes when the Duchess of Wesley handed her the note. It was a sacrifice for her to do such a thing, to offer someone to whom she had no obligation the greatest gift of all.

Hope.

Catherine had scanned the listed names, then focused on the few she recognized.

*Lord Stuarthall*
*Baron Hightow*
*the Duke of Westmore*
*Lord Partore*

She trusted the Duchess of Wesley's judgment. If she'd listed the names, then they needed to be seriously considered. And as

Catherine readied herself for the evening, she thought over the gentlemen suggested. But it plagued her that one name was missing, because she was equally torn between wishing it were there and being relieved it was not. *Quin.* It would have put them all in an awkward position, but she couldn't help but wonder if there was something the duchess wasn't saying. Maybe she didn't want her to consider Quin at all—not that she was. It was just… Well, she was overthinking it. Nothing was meant by the omission, she was sure, but Catherine kept thinking his name, seeing his face… and she wasn't sure what that meant.

She'd missed his company, his perspective on things, and the strength with which he moved through problems, not seeing them as obstacles but rather challenges to think around, to solve. She'd grown to appreciate that perspective, adopted it in many ways herself. He'd only been gone a little over a week, and she had felt his absence.

But that would be true for any friend, wouldn't it?

Pushing her confusing thoughts aside, she focused on preparing for the evening. She'd selected a blossom-colored evening dress. The neckline was only a quarter inch lower than usual. The color brought out the gold flecks in her hazel eyes, or so the Duchess of Wesley had said when she'd had it fitted earlier this week, checking the latest adjustments they'd made. The fine muslin hung in smooth arcs, with the tuck of the empire waist giving a fairylike impression to the gown. It was beautiful, and Catherine felt she made a striking appearance.

Millard worked tirelessly pinning her golden curls into loops and braids that crossed each other in an intricate design, and by the time the maid was finished, Catherine wondered if she was overdressed for a dinner party.

As she studied her reflection, taking in every nuance of her attire and coiffure, she reminded herself it wasn't just a party. It was an introduction. A beginning. The beginning set the stage for the rest of the story, and Catherine was going to make sure her story was one worth the telling.

As the clock in the hall chimed, she made her way to her grandmother's room. "Grammy," Catherine murmured, "I'll be back later, and I'll be sure to tell you all the details tomorrow. I promise." She leaned down and placed a soft kiss on her grandmother's forehead.

Recently, her grandmother had started to respond more, feeding Catherine's hope for her eventual recovery. But as she noted her grandmother's closed eyes, she realized this wasn't one of those moments of conversation.

The slow rise and fall of her chest was the only response to Catherine's words, and with a loving pat to her grandmother's hand, Catherine walked back into the hall. She straightened her shoulders. It was time.

The carriage was waiting out front, and as the footman helped her take the two steps in, she pulled in the trailing muslin of her gown and tucked it beside her, careful not to wrinkle it. The driver started on their way, and Catherine closed her eyes, savoring the comforting sway of the carriage as it carried her along.

The conveyance soon slowed and came to a stop in front of the Wesley town house. Catherine had arrived early, at the instruction of the Duchess of Wesley, but it looked as if several others had decided upon the same idea. As she alighted from the carriage, she smoothed her dress and took the steps toward the large gray door surrounded by windows glimmering with candles winking through the panes.

The butler opened the door before she took the last step, and she said her thanks.

"Lady Catherine." The older man nodded, gesturing for her to enter. "Her Grace is expecting you in the parlor. If you'll follow me."

Catherine thanked him and trailed behind as he traveled down the hall. It hadn't been so long ago that she'd been here with her grandmother for the Duchess of Wesley's dinner party, but it felt like a lifetime. So much had changed. Yet even before that, it had seemed like a lifetime since she'd said goodbye to Avery, since they all had said that final goodbye. The butler turned and opened a double door, allowing light to spill into the hall.

"Lady Catherine Greatheart," he announced as she walked into the parlor. Immediately, she saw the Duchess of Wesley, who had risen from her place on the sofa and was striding forward to welcome her.

"My dear, that dress is even lovelier than I remember." The Duchess of Wesley took her hands and squeezed them in greeting.

"Thank you," Catherine replied, then took in the rest of the room. They weren't alone, and a pair of green eyes caught her attention.

Quin.

He was standing beside a tall table, his posture relaxed as he offered her a welcoming grin. Like a warm bath, it relaxed her tight nerves and gave her a dose of the welcome familiar. "Good evening."

He raised his glass. "Good evening to you too."

"I didn't realize you had returned from Cambridge," she said welcomingly.

"Just today. My mother had important business." He gestured to the room.

"I see," Catherine replied, scanning the room. The butler announced another person, and Catherine turned at the mention of his name.

"His Grace the Duke of Westmore."

"Rowles!" The Duchess of Wesley moved past her to welcome the gentleman. Catherine turned, studying the man who was on the list of the Duchess of Wesley's gentlemen of interest. He was taller than Quin, and far leaner in build, almost slight. His blond hair waved over his forehead in the latest fashion, and blue eyes met hers with a flare of appreciation. Mischief danced in those cool depths; it was an interesting revelation.

The Duchess of Wesley made the introductions.

"Come, Rowles. I don't think you've met my dear friend, Lady Catherine Greatheart."

"A pleasure." He bent in a bow and took Catherine's hand. His voice was deeper than she'd expected, in contrast to his size. A baritone if he were to sing, she suspected.

"A pleasure, Your Grace," Catherine replied, unable to hide the fullness of her smile. So much for being coy.

"Rowles." Quin's voice interrupted Catherine's thoughts, and she turned to him as he approached their small circle. "It's been too long. How are you?"

Quin spoke with the familiarity of an old friend, and Catherine wondered at the history of the two. And furthermore, had the Duchess of Wesley made a list of suitable gentlemen based on Quin's friends? That would certainly be an interesting twist.

"Doing well! I hear from Morgan that you've just returned from Cambridge." He shrugged good-naturedly.

Catherine watched as Quin's eyes narrowed.

"Morgan, eh? He's certainly been busy." His eyes flickered to her, then back. He looked as if he wished to say something more, then thought better of it. "It's good to see you. Claret?" Quin lifted his glass at the query.

The Duke of Westmore nodded, and the two gentlemen walked toward the sideboard.

"I've known him since he was a boy. Good man, good family." The Duchess of Wesley murmured so softly Catherine had to concentrate to hear her. "His mother is unwell, but he keeps his spirits up."

Catherine nodded to signal she'd heard. They had something in common then—an ailing loved one. She compared him to Quin, then realized what she was doing and turned her attention elsewhere.

The evening continued in much the same fashion, with the gentlemen on the list arriving one by one, to be introduced to her and then taken away by Quin so that the Duchess of Wesley could give her a few details.

It was a smooth process, and Catherine wondered how much Quin was aware that he played such a part in the whole orchestration.

Was he privy to the whole plan? If so, how did he feel about it? Did he encourage it? The thought went against the grain, and she pushed aside her unease. Why did it matter if he assisted? He was a friend, was he not?

Yet as the evening came to an end and the events began to swirl together, Catherine considered one truth.

In the middle of all of it, the only time she'd been at rest was when Quin was near.

That made sense if he were her friend, but a part of her heart hinted that it could mean more.

So much more.

## Nineteen

QUIN TASTED BLOOD AND REALIZED HE'D BEEN BITING HIS tongue. His focus had been on keeping a calm exterior, but his plans had nearly failed the moment Catherine walked into his mother's parlor. He drank her in like exquisite French brandy, complete with the warming sensation from the inside out.

The color of her gown highlighted the gold hue of her hair, braided and tucked up to draw a gentleman's eye to the curve of her neck and lower.

*Good Lord.* Her neckline was walking a thin line between scandalous and innocent, leaving the admirer in a state of torment because it hid and hinted at the same time.

As if the temptation wasn't enough, the thin fabric clung to every valley and swell of her curves, playing hide-and-seek with the onlooker. It left him to study every fold to see if the slightest shift would make the fabric cling to skin.

He tore his attention away and felt his mother's focus shift to him before he turned to her. She'd obviously noticed his assessment of Catherine; he only hoped his expression hadn't betrayed the depth of his appreciation. His mother turned her attention to welcoming her. He watched as Catherine's shoulders relaxed at his mother's greeting, as if starting to unwind from some earlier tension.

The greeting completed, he watched as Catherine scanned the room, pausing when her eyes met his. A familiar warmth lit her features, and he tried to tamp down his delight that her beautiful upturned lips were for him alone. They were friends.

Nothing more.

But certainly nothing less.

He met her attentive regard, welcoming her, enjoying the moment that made the rest of the room fade.

But only for a moment, since Rowles was announced next, and judging by the way Catherine's attention was immediately arrested, Quin realized she recognized the name his mother had listed.

*Damn it.* He'd known it wouldn't be comfortable, but the stab of resentment against his friend's entrance surprised him.

Rowles had no idea what was going on.

But Catherine did. The understanding struck Quin deep in the chest, stealing his breath. His mother made the introductions, and before Quin could change his mind, he was striding toward the small group. Then, of course, Morgan's name had to be mentioned. Quin couldn't believe his friend had overstepped in such a way. Bastard, he was truly becoming a bother. He couldn't just leave well enough alone, could he? Simply had to let their friend know that something was afoot. There was truly no privacy among friends.

Quin had nearly rolled his eyes at the implication, but then steeled himself against the impolite gesture and instead offered Rowles claret, which served two purposes. One, it would refill his own glass, and based on current events he needed to take the edge off his own intensity. And two, it would remove Rowles from Catherine's proximity. It was a brilliant plan. Until the other gentlemen were announced. And introduced, soliciting smiles from Catherine as they engaged her in conversation. It was enough to make a saint swear. Quin had fallen into a routine, offering each gentleman claret after the initial introduction simply to get him away from Catherine, to no avail.

His mother had superbly made sure that each one had adequate time with Catherine throughout the evening, and it took all of Quin's self-control to maintain a passive expression. During dinner, Quin was seated beside his mother, which put him farthest from Catherine, who was seated beside Rowles. Every attention she gave his friend set Quin more on edge. When dinner ended, the gentlemen adjourned to the parlor while the ladies all joined together in a separate parlor for their own purposes.

"You want to tell me what Morgan was referring to?" Rowles asked from beside him just as Quin took a sip of brandy. He wasn't one to overindulge in liquor, but tonight had him drinking more than usual.

"No," Quin replied tightly.

"Helpful." Rowles paused as if considering his next words. "I didn't realize your mother was so…involved with Lady Catherine's social life."

Quin regarded his friend. "That's a delicate way to say it."

"I am a gentleman, after all."

"I know," Quin answered.

And it was true. Of all the men his mother had listed, Rowles was the best of the lot. Kind, attentive, and loyal, he would make any lady a fine husband. Which made it all worse, because there was truly no fault to be found in him.

It would be so much easier if Quin could just blame the whole lot of them and justify chasing all the men out the door. But he couldn't. He hadn't any moral high ground to stand upon.

The gentlemen started filing out toward the other parlor to join the ladies, and Quin followed wordlessly. As he took up a new position in the room, he chose a vantage point where he could see Catherine. He lifted a book from the nearby shelf and pretended to examine it.

"Are you sure you don't want to tell me what Morgan meant in his letter?"

Quin nearly jumped. He hadn't heard Rowles's approach since he was keeping an eye—while trying to appear as if he weren't keeping an eye—on Catherine and her suitors over the edge of the book he was holding. Giving a glare to his friend, he held the bridge of his nose.

"Good Lord, man. What is the matter?" Rowles shot him a concerned expression, then followed to where his focus had been a moment before. "Oh."

Quin aimed another glare at his friend. "What do you mean, 'Oh'?"

Rowles quirked the corners of his mouth as if trying to suppress his reaction. "Nothing. Absolutely nothing." He failed at suppressing that reaction and opted for turning away. "Interesting."

"What is so bloody interesting? You're as bad as Morgan," Quin grumbled, his attention flickering to Catherine at the sound of her laughter, then away.

"I had no idea, but it makes sense now." Rowles nodded, regarding his friend with a knowing expression.

"I don't want to know."

"Very well." Rowles snickered, giving Quin a sidelong stare and then turning to face him fully, studying him.

"I can't," Quin replied after a few moments of his comrade's quiet scrutiny.

"Why?" Rowles asked without judgment in his air, just open curiosity.

Quin turned to him, arching a brow and giving a wry twist to his lips. "She was betrothed to my brother, Rowles." He whispered so softly he barely heard the words himself.

"And?"

"And…I'm not Wes." He shrugged. "I never will be. But I'll always remind her of him, and that's too much. For both of us," he finished.

Rowles nodded.

Quin closed his eyes, paused, then opened them again and

spoke. "I'm going to take my leave. It was good to see you, even if you do annoy the hell out of me." He offered his hand.

Rowles took it, then cocked his head to the side. "You're wrong, you know. You're not Wes, that's true. But that's not what's stopping you. The biggest barrier is fear. And that, my friend, is a poor reason not to try." Rowles arched a brow. "Good night."

Without a further word, Quin watched as his friend moved through the dwindling crowd toward Catherine and said something that caused her to look in his direction.

He couldn't help the way Rowles's words rang in his ears. Only to have his own convictions pour water on the glowing embers. It wasn't meant to be. No matter what they said. With a slight bow in Catherine's direction, he said goodbye to his mother and took his leave.

The quiet of the carriage contrasted with the way Quin's mind and heart warred with each other. After he arrived at home, he made his way to his rooms to get some rest. And no sooner had his eyes closed than the dreams started.

It was as if since his heart knew it was fighting a losing battle, he conjured up the visions in fantasy to make up for the loss in reality.

The dreams were of her looking at him, the feel of her kiss—

Quin awoke abruptly, his heart racing even from dreaming about that simple contact. The need for more overpowered him, and he rose from bed and strode to the window. The dark evening hid the view as he leaned his head against the cool glass, feeling its chill through his fevered body.

"It's just a dream." His voice was hoarse from sleep. The low embers in the fireplace illuminated enough to allow him a clear view of the path back to his bed. He sat on the soft mattress and slowly lay down. The canopy above him grew blurry as sleep called.

The fragrance of her skin beckoned to him, and he gently slipped the silky weight of her hair from her shoulder and inhaled deeply. Lavender and lemon flooded his senses as he traced his nose along the sensual curve between her shoulder and neck, his body responding as she shifted closer.

"Quin."

Her voice was husky with sleep, but warm and enticing, stirring his blood. He reached around her soft form, his hand caressing the front of her hip, and drew her back into the circle of his waiting arms, nipping at her neck as he gently pulled her near.

In a flash, he was holding nothing but air. He stared at the night, gathering his wits as his mind spun. The orange light from the embers filled the darkness, giving a sharp dose of reality to the fantasy that had lived only moments before. He could feel the heat of her body. Hear the sound of her voice saying his name. It had only been a dream.

Again.

This had to stop, but it wasn't as if he was doing it all on purpose or could somehow make it end. He did the only thing he knew would stop the dreams. He stayed awake, wondering how many sleepless nights it would take to cleanse him from the dreams that haunted him in the dark.

# Twenty

*All this is only for the mice and myself to admire!*

—*Catherine the Great*

CATHERINE HALF EXPECTED QUIN TO VISIT THE DAY AFTER the party at the Duchess of Wesley's. She hadn't had much conversation with him since he'd returned from Cambridge and she missed that aspect of their friendship.

The Duchess of Wesley called on her a few days later and they made further plans for the upcoming parties, with special attention to ones that would start leading into the London season just around the corner. Catherine was tempted to ask after Quin but hesitated, not wanting her query to be mistaken as interest.

It was the beginning of a new week when she received an invitation to the Wesley house for tea. She accepted readily and at the appointed time arrived for a visit with the Duchess of Wesley. It had been nearly a week since she'd been at the dinner party where she'd met all the gentlemen the Duchess of Wesley had invited. The parlor where they had all adjourned after dinner was the same that she was led to for afternoon tea. As she followed the butler into the spacious room, she was greeted by the duchess.

"Good afternoon!"

"Good afternoon," Catherine returned. She noted that no one else was present for tea and took a seat when the Duchess of Wesley gestured to the sofa.

"Thank you for joining me today. Now, you accepted Lady Winstead's invitation, did you not?"

Catherine dove into conversation and planning with the Duchess of Wesley, as was their custom when together. But when their plans were established, Catherine made a request.

"Would it be unpardonable for me to ask to borrow a few books from your library, Your Grace? I've read most of the ones I find interesting from my own."

The duchess nodded as she set her teacup in the saucer. "Of course. I'll take you there directly. In fact, make yourself at home and read for a while, if it suits you. No one uses the library save Quin, and I don't think he's visited it for some time." Her brow pinched at the mention of her son's name, and Catherine wondered why.

"Thank you," she responded and, following the Duchess of Wesley's lead, stood and trailed her into the corridor.

"It's just down this hall, the double doors on the right." The Duchess of Wesley motioned as she spoke over her shoulder. When the duchess turned the brass knobs, the heavy wooden doors opened wide.

The first things Catherine noticed were the large windows that filtered sunlight onto the rows of books lining the walls. The room was much larger than her own library.

She gloried at the possibilities of endless reading. "Thank you," she murmured.

"My pleasure. If you need anything, ring for a maid. I'll come and check on you later." With a gracious nod, the Duchess of Wesley departed from the library and went into the hall, leaving the doors wide open.

Catherine studied the rows of shelving, wondering about the order in which the books were placed. The wall to her left was nearest, and she walked over to peruse the titles. Her fingers traced the leather bindings as she walked by, reading them in the beautiful sunlight. At the end of one row, she moved on to the next, which took her toward the back of the library. As she ended the last row, she turned to the shelves on the opposite wall and paused, hearing a soft noise.

Tipping her head in the direction of the sound, she frowned and walked forward, past a half shelf of a bookcase and into a small sitting area where she found the source of the noise.

A warmth spread within her heart at the sight of Quin's sleeping form sprawled across a sofa, his long legs bent over the arm of it. She covered her mouth to muffle her amusement. An errant thought flashed through her mind as she wondered how his hair would feel as she smoothed it back from his face, or if her glove would hinder any sensation. Yet she sobered when she noted the dark rings under his eyes, as if he hadn't been resting well—or at all. His skin was paler, too, as if he was exhausted. She tiptoed away, not wishing to awaken him.

What had caused him to be so wearied? What kept him awake at night? Tenderness filled her at the thought of some burden weighing on his chest, causing such anxiety for him. Maybe that was why the duchess's expression had been so concerned at the mention of Quin's name.

She wouldn't wake him. Let him sleep.

The shelves of books beckoned to her, and she returned to peruse the titles, selecting four to take home with her. She chose a chair on the opposite side of the room from Quin's sleeping form and set to reading with the knowledge that having Quin nearby somehow set her further at ease. Her finger skipped over the page as she tried to turn it. Frustrated, she set down the book and slipped off her gloves, setting them aside before lifting the book once more. The page turned effortlessly, and she lost herself in the words.

She was finishing the fourth chapter in the first book, *The Mystery of the Scottish Moors*, when the duchess walked in. Upon seeing Catherine reading, she asked, "Did you find what you were searching for?"

"Yes," Catherine replied in a subdued tone. "If it's acceptable, I'd like to borrow these."

The duchess waved her off as she pointed to the books. "Of course, and take more if you wish. I'll send a footman to collect the books in a while and place them in your carriage. Now, if I could only find my son as easily as you found your books." The duchess's lips twisted ruefully. "He must have departed earlier. It is of no consequence." She dismissed any reply with a flick of her wrist and left the room. Catherine almost called her back to let her know just where her son was...but hesitated.

Maybe Quin had selected the library because he assumed no one would find him here.

If so, he probably didn't want his mother to discover him asleep. She'd likely have the same questions Catherine had and would demand the answers Catherine had no right to ask.

As the library fell into silence once more, Catherine stood and quietly made her way back to where Quin slept. As she came around a corner, she watched as his chest rose and fell with a peaceful rhythm. Should she wake him? She turned to the large clock guarding the doorway; it was late in the afternoon. No telling how long he'd been asleep. But if he had any prayer of sleeping this evening, he probably should awaken.

Or so she told herself as she stepped forward. She knelt beside the sofa. Tipping her head to get a better perspective of his face, she studied him. He was so peaceful in sleep; the pensive expression that would filter across his face was absent, and he looked younger, even though he was still several years older than her. Without thinking, she brushed away a wayward curl that had fallen over his forehead, her fingers grazing his skin ever so lightly, but the touch sent a shock through her, causing her to gasp.

Quin's eyes opened, and he blinked several times before his eyes focused on hers.

"Quin?" she said softly, her voice foreign to her own ears.

His expression sharpened, not with the awareness that usually followed waking up, but with a tenderness that was deeply familiar, as if he'd been waking up to the sound of her voice for months—years.

It warmed her, filled her with something she'd forgotten and never named. It reached in, wrapping itself tightly around her. Heartbeat stuttering, she was reminded of the way she felt when she had first been kissed by Avery, just after their engagement. The breathlessness, the anticipation, the desire: she had forgotten how it felt to have that connection, that vulnerability with someone.

"Catherine?" He said her name like a prayer, his soul drinking her in.

Without realizing it, she moved her hand to cup his jawline, the million sensations of his skin's texture and his slight stubble swirling in her mind and captivating her with that simple touch. She lowered her attention to his lips, unable to look away. She'd never initiated a kiss, but his lips were too great a temptation, and she leaned forward, unable to stop the compromising movement.

As if impatient with her hesitant movement, Quin surged toward her and captured her lips. She had anticipated a soft, tender kiss, but she was wrong. His lips covered hers with a demand that left her senseless and hungry. This was no simple meeting of the lips. This was a devouring, and she leaned into it, craving the desire she tasted there. The kiss apparently wasn't enough for him, and his hands arched over her shoulders and pulled her closer, wrapping around her back and holding her captive as he continued to ravage her lips.

Never had she experienced such a kiss. It was new, exhilarating, and awakened something within her she hadn't known lay in wait. His tongue was wicked, branding her from the inside out as he danced around her lips, playing coy with her own tentative tongue and teaching her with every seductive stroke. His teeth gently nipped at her, playfully drawing her in, making it more than just passion, making it a seductive game that she wanted to play.

Then abruptly he pulled back, his expression wide and alert.

Catherine tried to gather her wits about her at the sudden end of the passionate exchange. He still held her, but his movements had frozen, much like the hold he had on her back.

His eyes narrowed and he inclined his head.

"Dear merciful heavens," he said, then released her, slowly inching away.

She felt the distance like a wash of cold water, a chilling premonition warning her from the inside out. What had they done?

"Am I really awake, then?" he asked.

What an odd question.

Catherine tilted her chin and frowned. Did he think this all a dream? Who did he kiss like that while dreaming? Jealousy flowed through her veins at the thought of some mysterious rival for his affection.

Belatedly, she realized what that meant for her own emotions.

He was watching her as if expecting an answer.

She nodded. "Are your dreams so real?" she asked, a little irritated at his horrified expression.

"Bloody hell." The words rushed out of him.

"Pardon?" Catherine replied, trying not to feel insulted, but honestly, who kissed a lady like that and then swore when he realized his actions?

"I… That is—Excuse me." Quin stood and rubbed his hand down his face. "Catherine, I'm so sorry. That was…unpardonable." His eyes fixed on the floor as the words tumbled out.

Catherine stood then, pushing back her irritation and hurt, and debated on the best course of action.

With a feeling rooted in mischief, she formulated a plan.

As Quin's stare lingered on the carpet, clearly tormented, Catherine closed the distance between them. Propriety be damned, what was done was already done. Now she would savor the moment, the touch and feel of him. A shiver of deep anticipation rocked through her.

His regard met hers, and as her cheeks heated with her forward manner, she leaned up on her tiptoes, grasped his shoulders for balance, and kissed him, ever so softly. It was an invitation, an open door that he could walk through should he wish. His lips were soft, embracing hers for a moment, yet hesitant, as if unsure he was truly awake or still dreaming. She withdrew slightly, speaking softly against his warm lips.

"Every dream should have a happy ending. Don't ruin this for me either." She lingered there, hovering, waiting for him to answer her, to make a decision—though the decision was made for them. They had kissed; she was as compromised as if he'd bedded her. But honor and desire didn't necessarily mean the same thing, so she waited to see what lay in his heart.

And answer her he did.

He closed the distance, but unlike the first kiss that melted her from the inside out, this was tentative, searching, and hopeful. It ended far sooner than she would have liked, but she met his contemplative regard with a shy smile of pleased wonder. As if unable to resist touching her, he leaned forward, placing a tender kiss on her forehead. His breath was warm on her skin; the scent of peppermint and clove laced the air, inviting her to move closer.

"I—" He lifted her chin up to meet his eyes, the green depths of his eyes beckoning her. His thumb rubbed over her lower lip, the heat of his touch creating a wave of tenderness and desire swirling through her belly. There was no hesitation when he covered her lips with his own, just a deliberate, mutual need to touch, to communicate what words could not.

He made love to her mouth, torturing her with a taste of the pleasure she'd never experienced but desperately wanted. But honor would bind him, she knew.

And as she considered it, lost herself in his kiss, she realized that she knew Quin well, inside and out. The kiss was natural, a fork in the road of their blossoming friendship that she should have seen coming.

His lips bent upward against hers as he drew away, resting his forehead against hers. The quickness of his breath was echoed in her own rapid heartbeat.

"I cannot tell you how many times I've wished to do this." As if proving his point, he captured her lips once more, searing them with his affectionate kiss.

He withdrew as she leaned in, chasing his kiss, then allowed himself to be quickly caught, meeting her with joyful enthusiasm.

She withdrew slightly, her lips warm and swollen from his tender assault. "I was a bit forward."

"Thank God," he muttered and kissed her once, as if punctuating his prayer. "I wasn't sure my pursuit would be welcome, or if even proper—"

"I rather think propriety has escaped us for the moment," she interrupted with a disbelieving tone.

He laughed, rich and deep and alluring against her neck as he placed a lingering kiss just below her ear. His breath tickled her sensitive skin, sending shivers of need through her blood. Warm hands enveloped hers, reminding her of the absent gloves. The sensation of his skin caressing hers nearly left her as impacted as the kiss.

"It would seem so. But I'm finding it rather difficult to be properly chastised about it." He squeezed her hand, then glanced down as if realizing her fingers were bare. Lifting a hand, he kissed it tenderly, his focus never shifting from hers. Goose bumps erupted on her arm, sending delicious shivers up her back and inducing a craving for more.

"I as well," she answered.

He lowered her hand and tugged her closer, his lips hovering above hers. Her thoughts were immediately lost among the millions of blissful sensations his kisses along her jawline sent through her. He paused, and her body immediately missed his artful seduction of her neck.

Her eyes flickered open and met his, her senses sharpening as she noted the clear intent in his expression. She could see it, the honor rising to the surface above the desire. Quin couldn't ignore it for long. He was too loyal, too much the gentleman to not make things right.

It was one of the many things she adored about him.

His green eyes were fixed on hers as he grasped her hands. "I promise I'll do a proper job of this later, but for now, you can rest assured I'll make this right, Catherine." His thumbs caressed her wrist as he leaned forward and kissed her forehead gently. "Be mine?" The question lingered on her skin.

She inhaled the delightful scent of him, memorizing the moment. In truth, they didn't have much of an option. Society would demand he make good on his actions, but this wasn't a clandestine affair.

This was a friend who had somehow become so much more.

"Yes, Quin." She vowed the words with all her heart, arching up on her tiptoes to seal the promise with a kiss. He met her halfway, his hands releasing hers to trail up her arms, grasp her shoulders, and pull her in tight as he deepened the exchange, branding her with his honor.

A sound from the door alerted them to an intruder on their private moment. Catherine took a step back just as Quin did, placing a proper amount of space between them, though if one looked closely, she was quite certain there was nothing proper about the way she looked at Quin.

Catherine turned to the footman, gesturing toward the long-forgotten pile of books she wished to borrow and the discarded gloves beside it. It seemed like a lifetime ago, those few moments prior to that kiss that changed everything.

"I'll call on you tomorrow." Quin's promise hung in the air, his expression conveying far more than those five words could contain.

"I'll look forward to it," Catherine replied, the air thick with promises as she retrieved her gloves. As she slipped them on, her fingers tingled with memories of Quin's skin and the thick fabric of his coat. She swallowed the impulse to relive those precious memories and followed the footman out the door. Her lips tingling from Quin's kiss, she glanced back for one final look, her heart thundering at the fierce adoration on his face.

That expression haunted her deliciously all the way home.

# Twenty-one

QUIN NEARLY FELL BACK ONTO THE SOFA, HIS LEGS NO LONGER willing to support his weight under the power of the shock that he'd just endured.

Good Lord, he'd kissed Catherine.

And holy hell, she'd kissed him back.

He had been resting so peacefully, his mind completely vacant for the first time in days. Sleep had captured him and wasn't tormenting him with feverish dreams. Then just when he thought he'd finally escaped, he'd seen Catherine. Her expression had been one of wonder, awakening, and tenderness. Her eyes had roamed his features with such affection, and then she'd said his name— like in all his dreams.

He hadn't even thought to consider if it was real; he'd just assumed he was still asleep. As with all his other dreams, he'd wanted it to be real. With a desperation that leaked through, he'd closed the distance and kissed her. More than that—he'd devoured her. It had been such acute torture in the past week to watch her from a distance, knowing she was out of reach and yet so close. His control had snapped in that moment, and he'd needed her, plain and simple, raw and unrelenting.

So he'd kissed her with abandon, without reservation, and hadn't even questioned it when her kiss hadn't been as skilled as in his dreams. It was all the dearer because of it. But reality had washed over him like freezing water from the Thames.

He hadn't been dreaming.

*What have I done?* The thought had flickered through his mind a moment before the only solution came to rescue his tortured soul. He would marry her; there was no other option. Compromising her wasn't exactly the kind of proposal a woman dreamed of, that was for certain. But he would make it right; he'd ask in the way she deserved—later. So he'd assured her of his intentions, and he'd leave the more romantic notions for later when he could plan and do justice to his affection for her.

He wiped a hand down his face, unseeing as his mind continued to spin.

"Quin?" His mother's voice shattered his fragmented thoughts further, and he turned to the sound of her voice, immediately thankful she was at the doorway, far enough away not to see his surely tormented expression clearly.

"Yes?" He cleared his throat, feigning some semblance of normalcy while his mind was still suffering from shock and rolling through the consequences of his actions.

All the while his body demanded more of Catherine's kiss.

His mother started toward him, and Quin straightened his coat, certain he didn't look even as presentable as he felt—which wasn't much. After all, he'd been asleep on the sofa for heaven knew how long.

"Where have you been? I thought you'd left hours ago." Nearer now, she studied him, cocking her head to the side as a mother did when studying a wayward child.

"I…" Quin thought quickly. *Ah hell, no way now but through it.* "I had fallen asleep, if you must know." He shrugged, playing off the words as casual.

"Oh." She regarded him steadily, her expression schooled. "I'm glad you did. You've been awfully pale. I was concerned that perhaps you'd been ill in Cambridge." She clucked her tongue. "Oh well, nothing a good rest won't fix." She stilled and creased her forehead. "Catherine must not have seen you. She was here gathering books to borrow." She tapped her finger on her lips. "You always were a sound and quiet sleeper. I doubt I would have found you if you hadn't stood up. It's quite a large library, after all."

"Indeed," Quin replied, at a loss. Let his mother draw her own conclusions; it would be far safer that way.

"Regardless, I was letting you know that you received a message from your friend Morgan. He delivered it here for some reason rather than to your residence, so I wanted you to take it before you left."

Quin nodded. "Thank you. Is it in the study?"

"Yes."

"Very good, I'll take a look at it right away."

The Duchess of Wesley nodded, her brow furrowing. "Did… That is, you received my letter I sent to Cambridge…"

Quin clenched his jaw. Yes, he remembered that letter. The damn thing hadn't been far from his mind since receiving it. "Yes."

She arched a brow and waited, then apparently reaching the end of her patience, spoke. "Well?"

"Well, what?" Quin replied, albeit a bit harshly.

"Do you have any information I should know about?" Her words were innocuous enough, but Quin heard all the questions between the lines. *Did the gentlemen I selected pass muster? Are they good men?* And, most importantly, *are you interested in her too?*

Quin stared at the rug on the floor. "I have nothing to communicate yet." It wasn't time. Everything was too fresh, and for the moment, nothing was settled between him and Catherine. He'd wait to include his mother in the news.

He looked up then, meeting her regard with a frank one of his own.

"I see." She smoothed her skirt and turned toward the door. "Very well, thank you. I'll see you tomorrow for the Winstead ball?"

"Of course," he quickly agreed, anything to escape and find a moment's peace. He had much to think about, even more that required careful planning.

"Very well," she replied and took her leave.

Quin released the air he'd been holding tightly in his chest and rubbed the back of his neck with his hand. First things first. He waited a few moments, then exited the library as well, turning right and down the hall to take refuge in the study.

He closed the door and helped himself to a snifter of brandy before looking for the letter from Morgan. Just as his mother said, it was waiting on the desk. He withdrew the silver letter opener and sliced through the seal.

As he read the missive, his brow furrowed. *This complicates matters immensely*, he thought.

The letter from Morgan was short and directly to the point. Lord Bircham was on his way to London, presumably to meet with Lady Catherine Greatheart.

It wasn't completely unexpected, but it could mean a lot of things. One thing for sure: the solicitor for the Greatheart estate was moving forward with having Lord Bircham take over stewardship.

Which meant he would meet Catherine. Which also meant that Catherine would be, in some fashion, at his mercy for the time being. While Quin was thankful that there wasn't a thick fog of gossip surrounding Lord Bircham, he didn't know the man and therefore didn't trust him. Especially with something as precious as Catherine's future. Action needed to be taken, but it wasn't his place to take it. He could offer advice, but now, given the events of this afternoon, he couldn't even pretend objectivity.

It was a bloody mess. He only hoped the situation wasn't as bad as it could be. Perhaps everything would turn out all right. Maybe all his concern was for naught. But he wasn't placing his bet on it. He'd learned to expect the unexpected, and Catherine certainly fell into that category. Unfortunately.

He'd call on her in the morning. No, he couldn't. Propriety had been bent enough with her grandmother unable to chaperone. He had to be extra cautious. There was no need to take risks with her reputation, especially since he'd nearly done more than compromise her in the library this afternoon.

He tapped his chin, thinking. He'd…invite her here, to his family estate. No talk could start over her visiting the Duchess of Wesley, and if Quin *happened* to be there, all the better. But that meant he'd have to inform his mother, who would in turn have many questions.

All of which he didn't particularly wish to answer.

But there was nothing else to be done. He needed to clear the air about today, and he needed to remind Catherine that she wasn't alone for whatever the future held, especially with Bircham's imminent arrival.

His plan wasn't ideal, but it was better than nothing. So with a final swallow of the remainder of his brandy, he left his study in search of his mother.

Catherine had found in her a worthy ally.

Perhaps it was time for him to do the same.

# Twenty-two

*I cannot live one day without love.*

—*Catherine the Great*

CATHERINE BIT HER LIP AS SHE READ THE LETTER FROM HER solicitor. Lord Bircham was en route to London, which meant she was to meet him soon.

Lord Bircham: the man who would have stewardship of her estate while her grandmother walked the line between here and heaven.

Catherine inhaled deeply, then closed her eyes. The unknown... it was so overwhelming. Just when she'd had a moment of delight, something that consumed all her thoughts, this happened, threatening to steal the joy she'd found.

She pushed the letter from her and then decided that wasn't enough. She grabbed it and stuffed it in a drawer and walked away, as if the distance would make it less powerful in her mind.

Her attention wandered for a distraction, and it landed on the neat little pile of books she'd borrowed from the Duchess of Wesley's library. In doing so, she found the joy she'd nearly abandoned.

Quin.

She gave a disbelieving touch to her lips, tracing them, imagining. Reliving it. It wasn't as if she'd never been kissed. Wesley had kissed her several times. But it had always been measured, careful, as if he might break her. But Quin...Quin had kissed her without reservation.

And she hadn't broken like some glass doll. Rather, she'd felt stronger, as if she rose to the occasion and met him there.

She walked over to the pile of books and lifted one; she slid a finger down the edge of the binding and flipped it over to find her place.

That she felt something for him was true, but she wouldn't force him into action simply because of her own emotions. She decided it was best to follow his lead. See where it took them. After all, he was certainly capable of offering for her himself, regardless of the gossip that would likely surround them. She shuddered at the thought. It would be worth it. Surely, he'd be in attendance at Lady Winstead's ball. Maybe he'd ask her for a dance. Maybe a waltz?

She soaked up the thought, then settled down with the book, intent on enjoying a few hours of reading.

She was only three pages in when Brooks knocked on the parlor door. "My lady, there is a gentleman to see you. I told him you were not taking callers, but he insisted I give you his card." Brooks held out the silver tray; a small square of parchment rested there with a name printed on it.

Percival Armstrong, Baron Bircham

Well, that hadn't taken long. Lord Bircham must have made her his first visit in London. Odd.

Catherine frowned at the slip of a card. "Even if he is my cousin, I cannot see him without a proper chaperone."

She returned to her book. It wasn't as if she hadn't broken propriety before, but she wasn't about to bend the rules for the person who was likely intent on enforcing all of them for her.

"He has a lady with him."

Catherine nodded, then hesitated. "Show them in."

It was better to get this out of the way. She could study him, get a first impression that might serve her well later. If he was this impatient to meet her, that could work in her favor. He was likely tired from his trip, and his demeanor could be less protected, revealing more of the man within.

Brooks paused, his salt-and-pepper brows knitted. The parting of his lips let her know he wanted to question her words, but Catherine gave a decisive nod.

"I'll be waiting right outside the door, my lady." Brooks gave her a level stare. "With a few footmen."

"I'm sure it won't be necessary...but it will put my mind at ease. Thank you."

Brooks nodded.

"And please have tea sent up as well."

"Of course, my lady."

Brooks hesitated, then bowed and took his leave. Catherine stood up, smoothed her skirts, and placed the book she'd been reading on top of the tidy pile. She cleared her throat just for good measure.

The sound of footsteps filtered down the hall, and she studied the door, waiting. A strand of hair tickled her cheek and she tucked it behind her ear, lifting her chin. As she waited, her mind spun with irritation that this man, unknown to her, was being given more power than she over her own estate. It was maddening, but there wasn't much she could do about it.

The footsteps closed in, and she prayed he was as good as his reputation suggested. Perhaps then it wouldn't be so bad?

Brooks entered first, stepping aside for a man with a much smaller frame. Dusty blond hair curled over a wide forehead, and shrewd eyes studied her unreservedly as she met the cool regard of Lord Bircham. He carried a long black and silver cane, its embellished head clearly designed to be decorative. He paused just past the threshold and took his focus from Catherine, regarding the room as if taking in its worth. Nodding in what seemed like approval, he continued into the room and gave a snap of a bow to her.

"Lady Catherine Greatheart, it is my pleasure to make your acquaintance. I am Lord Bircham, your cousin and the estate's trustee." He regarded her coolly, waiting.

"A pleasure," Catherine lied.

"Allow me to introduce you to Mrs. Burke. She will be your chaperone since your grandmother is unable to perform that duty currently." He gestured behind himself, just as a woman entered the room.

A thousand words of description flowed through Catherine's mind, but the one that fit the woman was obvious: harsh. Hard lines made up the contours of her face, flowing down to the slim and pointy frame of her body garbed in widow's weeds. Her eyes held no delight as she nodded to acknowledge being introduced, then came to stand behind Lord Bircham.

Had the situation been less tense, Catherine would have seen it with amusement. Mrs. Burke towered over Lord Bircham, easily seeing over his head, yet her frame was so slight. Catherine mused that if she were to stand directly in front of the two, it would look as if Lord Bircham had two heads, one right above the other. She bit her lip to keep from smiling at her own whimsy.

"Mrs. Burke, this is your charge, Lady Catherine." Lord Bircham stood to the side as he led the introductions.

"A pleasure," Catherine began.

"I would think so." Lady Burke sniffed and then turned her attention to the room, her eyes narrowing as if already finding fault.

Catherine bit her tongue against a retort and decided to rise above Mrs. Burke's distinct lack of breeding. "Will you sit? I've ordered tea."

"Thank you, but I won't be staying long." Lord Bircham dusted his sleeve of imaginary dust. "It was imperative that you had a proper chaperone, so I wanted to make arrangements for Mrs. Burke to take up residence here. I will continue on to my lodgings and return tomorrow with Mr. Sheffield to go over any legal information."

"I see." Catherine unclenched her jaw. "I assure you I have been quite sufficiently chaperoned." She offered a smile sweetly, hoping to overlay the clipped quality of her words. "The Duchess of Wesley has been personally overseeing my social calendar and performing chaperone duties in the interim." A surge of self-satisfaction filled Catherine at the impressed expression that lifted Lord Bircham's eyebrows at the mention of the duchess's name.

Let him know she was not in the least bit waiting for his counsel or assistance.

"I see. Well, now you have a chaperone and companion at your home." He shrugged as if his plans were still superior.

Catherine stifled. No need to make enemies…yet.

"I'll be happy to offer my hospitality to Mrs. Burke for the time being."

"Yes, well, it is, after all, in your best interest." Lord Bircham arched a brow as if scolding her.

Catherine bit her tongue.

"If there's nothing else, I'll be here for our four o'clock appointment on the morrow."

"Very well, until then," Catherine replied, nodding. He gave a final bow, tipped his hat to Lady Burke, and then took his leave.

Brooks stepped from the side of the door immediately, because he'd likely been waiting there and listening to their conversation. A flood of gratitude filled Catherine at the protective interest displayed by her staff as a footman also stood from the side and helped escort Lord Bircham to the door.

"Your staff is impertinent," Mrs. Burke spoke into the silence.

Catherine turned to her, frowning. Her first reaction was to ask her to repeat her rude remark, but then Catherine decided she didn't care what the lady thought. "They are protective, which is exactly as they should be."

Catherine lowered her chin, leveling a stare at Mrs. Burke that dared her to question that protectiveness. It was a veiled threat if Catherine had ever used one, but she wasn't in the mood to play games. Let Mrs. Burke know which way the wind blew and use caution.

As if understanding the underlying message, the older woman sniffed and stuck her nose in the air, unperturbed. "If you'll be so kind as to show me to my accommodations?" Her words were more polite than her tone.

"Our housekeeper wasn't planning on guests," Catherine started. "But my staff is unparalleled. I'm sure your rooms will be ready shortly. No doubt Brooks has already notified our staff of the change in plans."

"Well, it's not your place to question your guardian's instructions."

At this, Catherine whirled around to face the woman fully and, after striding toward her, stopped only a foot away. Keeping her voice level, she answered the woman's faulty statement. "I'm of age, Mrs. Burke. And as such am under no guardian. My *estate* is under care. I am not the property of said estate, and it would be well for you to remember that. As it seems you're in a mood to quarrel, please inform me when the inclination passes."

Mrs. Burke gave a small nod, but her stare was flint. "Of course."

"And you are to address me as 'my lady.'" Catherine pushed the propriety that had been hoisted upon her with Mrs. Burke's arrival.

"My lady." Mrs. Burke all but sneered the words.

Catherine took a step back, nodded her approval—which she hoped irritated the woman further—and then relaxed when a maid arrived with the tea service.

"I'll be retiring to my room to read. Enjoy your tea. I'll have the housekeeper take you to your rooms when they are ready. I bid you good day." Catherine took her leave then, not waiting for Mrs. Burke's permission or questions.

It was her house.

Her home.

No one, and that meant *no one* was going to tell her how to run it.

Or place demands on her life.

She wasn't sure when it had taken place, but she'd reached the end of her rope.

Something had to give.

And it wasn't going to be her.

# Twenty-three

QUIN WASN'T SURE WHAT HE WAS EXPECTING AFTER KISSING Catherine—twice—but he surely wasn't expecting the beak-nosed widow staring at him from across the parlor. If a gnarled old tree had a face, it would have looked like his new acquaintance, Mrs. Burke. He lowered his eyes to the teacup before him, trying to ignore her hard stare which had been on him unblinkingly since his arrival five minutes prior.

Initially, he'd planned to invite Catherine to his family house under the guise of his mother's invitation. But when he'd asked his mother—a situation that had raised an eyebrow since his earlier denial of any interest—she had informed him of Catherine's recent communication.

She'd been given a chaperone: an old crone by the name of Mrs. Burke.

Quin sipped his tea. It wasn't as if he didn't believe Catherine's description of the woman as an old crone; he'd just...well, had never seen such a real example of it. Till now. If only the damn woman would stop staring a hole through him as if he were on trial.

The sound of footsteps echoed in the hall, and Quin exhaled with relief. Ignoring the chaperone, he stood at Lady Catherine's entrance. Her warm presence melted his tension and filled him with a new feeling that was decidedly more welcome.

"Good day," he murmured, taking her hand and drawing her a few inches closer. The scent of rosewater filled his senses, and he allowed himself the pleasure of taking an extra moment to hold her hand before releasing it.

"Good day to you as well." Catherine's voice welcomed him, and he couldn't help the approval that spread across his features in response.

"I assume your mother has communicated the pertinent information?" Catherine asked, her eyes darting behind him, and then back.

"Your use of adjectives was impressive."

"Not only fanciful, I hope?" she flirted.

"Just accurate."

"Lovely." Catherine made her way to the sofa.

Quin returned to his seat as well but was quite at a loss for how to have a private conversation in a public venue. He was aware that other gentlemen had mastered the art of innuendo and allegory, but he was a professor, a student of clarity and facts.

"How is your mother?" Catherine asked, serving herself tea.

"Scheming for your arrival tonight."

Though he had his own plans.

"Sounds about right." She blew across the cup, drawing his eye to the way her lips made a soft O. The color of her lips heightened, and he licked his in response, the flavor of their kiss filling his recall. He tore his stare away, not wanting to lose his wits over a bloody cup of tea.

"I hear you've met the trustee of your estate?" he asked, staying on a safer topic.

Quin kept his expression impassive as Catherine all but scoffed into her teacup. With any luck, Mrs. Burke wouldn't have heard the soft sound. He certainly wouldn't give away Catherine's expression by mirroring it.

"Yes," Catherine replied, arching a brow. "It's amazing how one meeting can teach you so much about a person."

Quin nodded. "There's a reason first impressions are important."

"Indeed." She sipped her tea. "How is the weather?"

Quin frowned at the quick change of subject. "It's quite fine."

"I feel like it's been an age since I've had a decent walk through the park…" Catherine lowered her chin and speared him with a pleading expression.

"Allow me to remedy that immediately." Quin quickly understood and rose, offering his arm.

"Delightful! I can't think of anything I'd love more." She beamed at him, and Quin held back a chuckle at the manner in which she was playing the game. Minding propriety was imperative, and Catherine understood the need to maintain good standing before her trustee's delegate.

And Quin did too. He led her from the parlor and out the door into the bright sunshine, thinking, *Let the games begin.* It certainly wouldn't be the last time he'd need to read the cues, and he was determined that if Catherine needed an ally…

It would be he.

Mrs. Burke trailed them as they rounded the bend toward Hyde Park. Quin could hear her footsteps and knew she was near enough to be proper, but perhaps not near enough to overhear their conversation.

Quin leaned toward Catherine, guiding her closer by drawing in the arm which she held as they walked. His body relaxed at having her close, as if finally at peace. Her eyes darted to his at his subtle movement, locking in, stealing his breath momentarily. How could a mere look move him so? Her hand tightened on his arm as a blush stole across her features. Quin memorized the hue of her tinted cheeks, the glow of her intelligent eyes and marveled. Struggling to keep his tone light, he leaned in slightly as if about to impart a great secret.

Her eyes danced with merriment as she followed suit, waiting.

"Any particulars you wish to impart?" he asked in a low voice.

Catherine turned back to him. "Nothing that I should say as a lady."

Quin's brows arched in surprise before he let out a snigger. "And why am I not surprised? I promise not to think less of you for your frankness."

"Why, thank you," she said graciously. "Honestly, it's more that my own anger at the situation has made me ungracious and cross. Of course, that Mrs. Burke haunts me like a shadow hasn't improved my disposition." Her tone turned impatient.

"I don't blame you for that. I trust a saint would be found ungracious in such a situation. She certainly doesn't seem to possess a warm personality."

"Blizzards have more warmth," Catherine retorted.

Quin bit back his amusement at her apt statement. "If I may inquire, when do you meet with your solicitor and cousin?"

Catherine's grip tightened on his arm as her attention flickered to the ground, betraying her tension at the prospect. "This afternoon. As much as I am dreading it, I'm also thankful for the clarification it will afford."

Quin nodded, his thoughts inward. "Do you wish me to stay?"

Catherine answered, "I appreciate the offer, but I think it would be best for me to be alone this time." She squared her shoulders as she spoke. "I have considered every angle, and I feel that Lord Bircham will be less on guard if he feels he is in control. I wish to uncover as much about the man's character as possible, and that won't happen if he's trying to impress a duke." She gave him an apologetic expression.

"I'm growing more accustomed to the title," Quin confided. "It doesn't make it easier, but I've made peace with it."

Catherine regarded him with an expression that held both warmth and understanding. "That pleases me to hear."

Quin gave a nod of approval, then turned his focus to the path before them, leading the way through a side gate of the park's entrance. He had a question on his mind and it was the perfect opening to risk it, but he hesitated, not wanting to press too hard.

It was a delicate balance that he wasn't sure how to maintain or cultivate into something more. It was uncharted territory for him. And with so many aspects of his life, when faced with a problem, he studied, researched, tried different solutions, and proceeded.

Not so with this, with her. It was all risk and reward—or so he hoped.

Formulating the question in his mind, he turned to Catherine. "And how are you? As I said, with time, peace has overcome the initial resistance I had. Is it the same for you?" Quin studied her face for an answer before she voiced it. Had his heart not been so deeply invested in hers, the question wouldn't have been as difficult to voice. But as it was, his heart was in his throat, and he watched her reaction before her words answered his.

Her brow furrowed slightly, and she paused as if carefully considering her words. "In a way, yes. Time doesn't heal wounds but allows you to adapt to them in a manner. Does that make sense? And it has become easier, in large part thanks to you."

She turned away, but Quin noted the heightened color in her cheeks, a fetching pink that trailed down her neck and drew his eye lower than he'd ventured to look before.

He struggled to compose himself while also enjoying the delight her words gave him and the hope therein. But it wasn't her actual words as much as her reaction. She peeked up at him then, and Quin allowed himself the pleasure of holding her regard. What was it about a look that could speak far more than a word? Or even several words? In those precious moments, he felt her tenderness like a kiss, and he hoped his expression displayed the same affection.

A grumbling voice interrupted the moment, and Quin chuckled as Catherine covered her mouth with a gloved hand in an attempt to hide her reaction. Apparently, they were boring Mrs. Burke who was mumbling to herself about something or other.

"A lovely day." Quin broke the silence, choosing a topic Mrs.

Burke couldn't find offensive. She'd picked up her pace, or perhaps they had slowed theirs. He couldn't tell or remember; he'd been too lost in the moment.

Regardless, a quick peep behind assured him that she could easily overhear their conversation now, so it was safer to pick a topic that couldn't be reported as scandalous to Lord Bircham.

"Indeed, it is," Catherine replied, biting her lip to keep from smiling too broadly, and Quin was thankful to know such nuances about her.

Knowing such things was just the beginning of his education.

Because he'd always loved learning, and he was determined that studying Catherine Greatheart was going to be the most enthralling project he'd ever undertaken.

# Twenty-four

*Do not worry about things you cannot alter.*

—Catherine the Great

THE AFTERNOON DREW NEAR, AND CATHERINE STOPPED BY her grandmother's rooms before going downstairs to the parlor to await the arrival of Lord Bircham and the solicitor.

A slight breeze made the curtains dance as she walked into her grandmother's bedchamber. A welcome sight lifted her spirits as Lady Greatheart was sitting up, taking sips of broth from her maid.

"Awake?" Catherine asked softly.

Lady Greatheart had slowly been regaining some strength, but it was so intermittent that Catherine had held her hope in check.

Lady Greatheart opened her eyes then, squinting. Her vision still was doubling, and it created the most terrible headaches that left her with the need to sleep the day away.

"She's been awake longer this time," the maid replied softly, lifting the spoon to Lady Greatheart's lips.

Lady Greatheart took the broth and swallowed, closing her eyes. "I'll just keep my eyes closed if you don't mind."

"Whatever feels best," Catherine was quick to answer, thankful her grandmother had spoken at all.

"And no more laudanum." Lady Greatheart's next words were little more than a whimper.

Catherine turned to the maid, giving her a questioning look. Laudanum was the only thing that helped with the headaches.

"Are you sure?" Catherine asked, coming closer and sitting on the bed beside her beloved grandmother.

*"Yes."* Her lips formed the word, but she had no voice. She paused and tried again. "Yes."

Catherine turned to the maid. "Very well, but have it near in case she asks for it."

"Of course, my lady."

"Enough," Lady Greatheart replied then, turning her head away when the maid offered the spoon again.

"One more bite, my lady?" the maid encouraged.

Lady Greatheart gave a sigh, took the final spoonful, then swallowed.

"Sleep."

Catherine helped her grandmother settle back into the bed, her tiny frame growing smaller with time and inactivity. Whispering a prayer over her grandmother, Catherine watched as she quickly fell asleep.

"Her coloring is good, my lady. She's improving, just…slowly."

Catherine turned to the maid and nodded. "Please inform me if she awakens."

"Of course."

Catherine kissed her fingers and placed the kiss on her grandmother's forehead, lingering there as she caressed her features with her gaze. "I love you."

She quit the room and slowly walked down the hall toward the stairs that would lead to the parlor where so many questions and answers would be found.

As she made her way to the meeting, she sent a maid to fetch tea. The gentlemen would be arriving soon, and she was certain Mrs. Burke would be in attendance as well, if not already waiting in the parlor.

When she crossed the threshold, her assumptions were proven correct as Mrs. Burke waited for her, needlepoint in hand, with a sour welcome.

"Good afternoon." Her expression belied the welcome.

"Indeed," Catherine replied, then took a seat near the table where the tea tray would shortly be set out.

She thought back through the questions she wished to have answered, and no sooner had she run through the list than Brooks announced the arrival of Lord Bircham.

In much the same style as the previous day, Lord Bircham walked into the room with purpose, his cane in hand. His attention found Mrs. Burke, and he nodded. He then turned to Catherine. "Good day." He bowed.

"Good day," Catherine replied. "Will you sit?" She gestured to the chair across from her.

He gave another nod and took the directed seat. She'd tried to be strategic in her placement of the gentlemen, wanting to see them without having to turn her head too much one way or the other, allowing her to see the expression of one while the other talked. It might be nothing, but she didn't want to miss something.

The tea was brought in, and as she was pouring for Lord Bircham, the solicitor was announced.

"Ah, welcome." Lord Bircham stood, offering the man a handshake.

In turn, the solicitor bowed to her and took the seat Catherine offered.

Situated, Catherine presented tea to the solicitor and then served herself, thankful her hands didn't tremble.

"Shall we begin?" Lord Bircham asked, rubbing his hands together.

The solicitor withdrew a leather-bound folder and adjusted his spectacles. "Of course." He sorted through several documents and then squinted up to meet Catherine's waiting expression.

"Lady Catherine, before your grandfather's death, he named Lord Bircham as the trustee of the estate, since he was the closest relative at the time. Since then the senior Lord Bircham has passed as well, leaving his son as trustee."

The solicitor gestured to Lord Bircham, who inclined his head.

"You'll find I am very thorough in the details, and I wish you to have full understanding," the solicitor said to her.

"Thank you."

"Please continue," Lord Bircham requested.

The solicitor nodded. "In the event of your grandmother's spell, Lord Bircham is to oversee the estate until such time as you are married, and then your husband will take over, or until Lady Greatheart's health is improved to the point she is able to oversee the estate herself."

"I see," Catherine replied, thankful that so far there weren't any unexpected details.

"Very good. Now, as the trustee of the estate, Lord Bircham is to oversee the estate's financial details, current investments, and the properties therein. He is also to ensure you have access to the funds necessary for your season and other needs."

Catherine frowned. "So I won't have direct access?"

"No," Lord Bircham answered, his tone amused as if such an idea were absurd.

The solicitor turned to him, his expression scolding, and then turned back to Catherine. "You won't have direct access, but as long as you are not asking for something excessive or out of the ordinary, Lord Bircham doesn't have the right of refusal." The solicitor speared the man with a warning glare.

Lord Bircham gave an expression that was the equivalent of a shrug of indifference.

Catherine nodded. "What avenues do I take to acquire funds?"

Lord Bircham opened his mouth, but the solicitor was quicker. "You can come through me or directly to Lord Bircham. However, I don't see any issues, my lady. Currently, all your needs are met, and any bills from shops, et cetera, will be handled as usual."

Catherine pursed her lips as she thought over the solicitor's words. It would be quite a change, the overseeing of her estate management, rather the fact that Lord Bircham now oversaw it. It was a frustrating notion; while no one knew she had been managing it, no one had interfered. Now that her grandmother was ill, it was assumed she needed assistance, though no one even thought to ask if she wished for it.

"Do you have any other questions before I proceed?" he asked, regarding her over the rim of his spectacles.

"No, please continue." Catherine folded her hands in her lap and waited.

The solicitor shuffled the papers till he found the one for which he was searching. "I see that Lord Bircham has supplied a chaperone for the time being, which is certainly a helpful assistance. There are a few other details, but I'm sure you won't find a vast difference in the way everything operates as far as your estate is concerned, Lady Catherine. I assure you whatever adjustments necessary will be made as smoothly and quickly as possible, and you should feel very little change."

"That is very good to hear," Catherine replied, resisting the urge to spear Lord Bircham with a steady look. So far, she'd already felt the difference; it wasn't as seamless as the solicitor had said. But there wasn't anything she could do for now.

"If I may?" Lord Bircham's voice interrupted her speculations. The solicitor nodded.

"Lady Catherine, I wish to assure you that every effort has been made on my part to see your new arrangements are satisfactory, and should you have any questions, I'm happy to answer any inquiry."

Catherine flicked her attention from Lord Bircham to the solicitor. "While I appreciate this, I believe I will address my inquiries to my solicitor."

Lord Bircham's expression darkened, as if surprised and offended by her rejection of his assistance.

Sensing she was making more of an enemy than she had before, she quickly amended her words. "I wouldn't want to trouble you. After all, you are not compensated for your goodwill."

Lord Bircham nodded but didn't seem convinced by her placating words.

The solicitor addressed her. "I'm at your disposal, Lady Catherine." He closed his leather-bound case and stood. "Lord Bircham signed the necessary papers yesterday, and so all is in order now that you're aware of the details. As always, I'm happy to be of assistance, should you have questions. If that is all, I'll take my leave."

"Thank you." Catherine stood as well, walking the man toward the exit and feeling the watchful expression of Mrs. Burke on her back as she did so.

As the solicitor left, Catherine turned to Lord Bircham. "Was there anything else, my lord?"

Lord Bircham lifted his teacup and took a slow sip. "Not at the moment. However, I think it prudent that we get to know one another. Will you sit?"

Catherine took her seat again, suspicion welling within her. "Very well."

Lord Bircham gave her a wan sneer. "I don't want you to be concerned. I'm sure that your feminine mind is surely spinning with anxiety, and there's no need for a brave face any longer. I'm here to care for your needs."

Catherine frowned, regarding him before answering. "I assure you I'm quite well, and my *feminine mind*, as you put it, is very much stronger than you are willing to credit."

"I see. Well, when that frail wall you've built comes crashing down, I'll be here to assist you. Women are such delicate creatures." He said the last words over her head as his expression sought Mrs. Burke.

Catherine silently scoffed at his words. While she was anything but frail and weak-minded, she was certain that Mrs. Burke wasn't exactly a wilting flower either.

She turned to gauge the widow's reaction, but to her surprise, she nodded as if in full agreement.

She was surrounded by misogynists.

At least it was out in the open. "Is there anything else you need, Lord Bircham?"

Lord Bircham covered his heart with a hand. "No, are you so ready to be rid of me? I find your lack of hospitality disconcerting. I'm sure your grandmother wouldn't approve." He tsked his tongue.

At this, Catherine couldn't hold back the laughter that bubbled from her chest. "My grandmother?" she repeated, then checked herself, gaining control of her emotions once more.

"Yes." Lord Bircham nodded, but his brow furrowed with confusion.

"Did you ever meet my grandmother, Lord Bircham?" she couldn't help but ask.

He glowered. "No, I never had the pleasure."

She nodded. "Then allow me to acquaint you with my very prim and circumspect grandmother. Because if you have met me, you have met the milder version of the original," she said in a fierce tone. It was the truth, and it resonated in her like nothing had this day.

She had her grandmother's strength. Her resolve. Her passion. Her dedication to family. Her tenacity. Her frankness. And damn it all, she had her wit.

Lord Bircham's expression was disapproving, but he didn't comment.

Perhaps he was smarter than he let on.

"Speaking of my grandmother, I must now look in on her, so if you'll excuse me?" She gestured toward the door, which was indeed on the edge of being rude, but it was the most she could manage at the moment.

"I understand." Lord Bircham stood. "I'll see you on the morrow, then."

Catherine paused. "On the morrow?"

He nodded. "When signing the papers as the trustee of your estate, I was given its financials, and I must say it's quite lacking in diversification. I'd like to discuss some ways we can remedy that. I'll see you tomorrow to go over the particulars and gain your signature on several investments." He took his cane and quit the room, Catherine's narrowed regard following his retreat.

"You'd be wise to listen to his counsel." Mrs. Burke interrupted Catherine's thoughts.

"Thank you for your unsolicited advice, but I have others to consult, and if ever I need advice from you, rest assured I'll ask you before you need to volunteer it." Catherine peeked over her shoulder and then left in a swish of muslin.

It was a good thing the ball was tonight.

Lord Bircham had said they needed diversification...

She immediately made a mental list of the recent possible investment opportunities she'd been unable to discuss with her grandmother. Perhaps this was more of an opportunity than a misfortune. She'd take the first chance to talk with Quin at the ball. As she walked up the stairs to check on her grandmother, a wave of gratitude filled her. It had been rare to find a man who appreciated a woman with a keen mind, and it had been a miracle to find another. Quin was certainly her miracle.

# Twenty-five

QUIN RESISTED THE URGE TO TUG ON HIS CRAVAT. HIS VALET had taken extra care with his evening kit, but that also meant the wicked neckcloth was far stiffer and tighter than usual.

Blast it all.

He'd arrived fashionably late to the Winstead ball, preferring to wait in his own study rather than in a crowded ballroom for Catherine's arrival. Each year at the beginning of the season, the Earl of Winstead—rather his wife—threw a smashing ball where everyone of the prestigious *ton* would be in attendance. It was where the London elite began the gossip mills for the season, and where the competition among the ladies was evaluated and the bachelors sorted in order of desirability.

It quite reminded him of a market, but much cleaner.

Quin gave a wide berth to a circle of young ladies, all shadowed by their mamas. The collective focus of the group followed him till he disappeared into the crowd; he could feel it.

He wasn't sure what was worse—that he was regarded as the bachelor of the season, or that soon people would be speculating about his interest in Catherine.

Because, devil take it, he was going to waltz with her.

That was if he could find her in the sea of humanity. Taller than most, he usually could see over the crowd with some ease, but Lady Winstead had decorated the ballroom with several sculptures and trees, giving an ethereal feel to the room but also inhibiting his view.

He rounded a statue that was a replica of Venus, only much

smaller, and scanned the crowd. To his left, he caught a glimpse of his mother, and beside her he found his target. Catherine was murmuring something, her lips hinting at a grin as she spoke quietly to his mother.

The Duchess of Wesley held up her fan, but Quin could see by his mother's expression that though her mouth was covered by the fan, she was charmed at whatever Catherine had said.

He scanned the room, searching for the best method to find his way to them. He meandered around a group of gentlemen talking, passed them before he heard his name.

"Quin!"

Pausing, he turned to see Morgan's welcoming presence. "Well, it looks like they're inviting everyone these days." He clapped his friend's back.

"I was just thinking the same thing when I saw you," Morgan replied with dry humor. "How goes it?"

"Good, good. Just heading over to see my mother," Quin replied, then speared his friend with a meaningful stare.

Morgan paused, then shifted his focus to behind Quin's back, toward where the Duchess of Wesley stood some few yards away.

Quin noted the way Morgan's expression widened, then turned back to him. "Looks like someone lit a fire under you finally."

"Perhaps." Quin nodded, thankful for the subtle understanding that had passed between them. As much as it was a bother to have friends who knew you so well, it was also a boon when you wished to communicate something without including others in the details.

"Best of luck with that."

"I'm certain I'm going to need it."

"Conceivably, but I'd move quick. Rumors have started to spread that she's partaking in the season, if you gather my meaning." Morgan lowered his tone, then stole a look behind him to the group of gentlemen still conversing between themselves.

"I see. I suppose I expected as much."

"But you have a leg up, don't you, old man?" Morgan winked.

"I should think so," Quin replied, unable to hide his self-satisfaction.

Morgan lowered his chin. "Perhaps more than a head start then. Well, I must say I'm proud of you. I'll not detain you further. Oh, but I have one request. Can you please ask Joan for a dance? I would like to know that she has at least one person I can trust on her dance card."

Quin nodded. "It would be my pleasure. I'll ask her directly after I take care of one matter."

"Brilliant. Thank you and good luck." Morgan winked again, patted his friend on the shoulder, and turned back to the others.

Quin continued on his way toward where Catherine waited. As he approached, his mother welcomed him with a wave of her fingers. "Finally. I was beginning to think you'd forgotten."

Quin kissed her hand and bowed. "Forget? Never," he replied and then turned to Catherine. "Good evening." He grasped her hand and, bowing over it, gave a tender kiss to her gloved wrist. The scent of roses teased his senses, and he lingered just a moment to enjoy the torment. Releasing her hand, he met her amused expression, just before her cheeks bloomed with color and she averted her eyes.

"Holding court, I see." Quin moved to stand beside her. He studied the gentlemen who lingered near, waiting for an introduction or an opportunity to speak with her. Quin was thankful for the presence of his mother, who tended to make an eager buck think twice about approaching the beauty beside her.

"About as much as you were." Catherine turned to him, arching a brow. "You certainly were attracting attention."

"Watching me?" Quin asked, baiting her.

"When half the *ton*'s scrutiny shifts to a particular person, it's hard to ignore," she replied with a joking lilt to her tone.

"It wasn't that bad."

Catherine scoffed playfully. "You didn't see the half of it. I almost sent your mother to your rescue, but she wouldn't abandon me. I think she likes me more."

"While I'd love to refute your claim"—he leaned toward her ear, murmuring—"I think you're correct."

He noted the way she shivered slightly at his words, as if his nearness was as electric to her as it was to him.

"I won't put you through the torture of finding out the truth. I'll let you keep your hope," Catherine said after a moment.

"Dance with me?" he asked softly, pleadingly, and hopefully seductively.

Catherine looked at him, her eyes meeting his with a clarity and depth that left his heart pounding. "Now?"

Quin studied her. "As much as my impatience wishes me to say yes, I'd much rather you save me the supper waltz."

Catherine nodded. "Done."

"Thank you," Quin replied, his entire being focused on her as if she were the center of the world…his world. "And if you find yourself another disengaged dance, I'd be happy to help you fill it."

Catherine's eyes narrowed slightly. "And you're prepared for the talk that will certainly ensue? Two dances, are you sure you wish that?"

It was all but stating his intentions publicly and open for speculation. There would be talk with one dance, since it was a waltz. The combination of two dances was an announcement and acknowledged as confirmation of whatever gossip could not validate.

"I find the reward is worth the risk." He winked daringly to her. "Don't you think?"

Catherine bit her lip, but her approval glowed in her expression. "And who says I have a disengaged dance to offer you?" she challenged.

"You find me overconfident?"

"If you are overconfident, then I am forward. And I've been called worse."

"I find your forward manner refreshing." His eyes darted to her lips, then back to her eyes. "So…do you?"

Catherine faltered, as if breaking a spell. "Do I?"

Perhaps he wasn't the only one so deeply affected. "Have a disengaged dance?"

Understanding dawned in her expression. "You mean, another one?"

"Yes," Quin replied.

"Well, your dear friend Morgan asked me just five minutes before you, and he took my last one, minus the waltz. It turns out I forgot I had that one available…" She looked down as if slightly embarrassed.

"Ah, so you were saving it for me? How thoughtful."

"I didn't say that."

"You implied it, and I'm taking that as a confession," Quin said charmingly. "And hang Morgan, he'll not be offended if you slight him for me."

Catherine gave him a dubious expression. "Is that so?"

"Yes. I'm quite sure."

Catherine regarded him. "If you're so certain, I trust you'll tell him yourself, as I don't wish to be rude to your friend."

"My friend will certainly survive, but I'll speak to him if it will put your mind at ease."

"It will indeed."

"What are you two chatting about? Leaving the rest out." The Duchess of Wesley clucked her tongue at Quin, her eyes darting between the two of them.

"We are discussing a mutual friend and his annoyance," Quin replied.

Catherine swatted him.

"That is not what we were discussing."

The Duchess of Wesley gave a pitying shake to her head. "I tried too hard to teach him manners. I'm afraid it was a failure in some aspects."

"Why, thank you, Mother."

"Seems it's just the truth," his mother replied.

Catherine leaned toward him. "See? Favorite."

Quin speared her with a somewhat sarcastic expression.

"Rude," Catherine returned.

"Good Lord, I'm surrounded," Quin said, looking heavenward.

The string quartet started then, the strains of a cotillion starting up and filling the room with the joyful music. Quin turned to say something to Catherine, but he was distracted by the quite determined stride of Lord Buckeen, heading directly toward them, eyes intent on Catherine.

Quin decided that the dancing was absurdly overrated and was far less satisfied with the evening than he'd been a moment before.

"I believe this is my dance, Lady Catherine." Lord Buckeen bowed and extended his hand.

"Of course," Lady Catherine said sweetly and followed him onto the dance floor.

Quin watched them line up to begin the dance, some emotion dangerously close to jealousy filling him as he watched.

"If you don't wipe that expression off your face, you're going to cause more gossip than you wish to endure." His mother's words were spoken brightly, as if she were discussing a fascinating topic, but Quin noted that it was a blind. She was faking one emotion to cover another, so those seeing them wouldn't suspect.

His mother was quite brilliant.

Quin quickly schooled his features and murmured to his mother, "Thank you."

"Of course. Did you ask her to dance?" his mother asked quickly.

"Yes, she saved me the dinner waltz," he remarked, knowing the significance wouldn't be lost on his mother. "Along with another dance."

"Two?" His mother's lips formed a surprised O. "Am I the last to know about everything? The least you could have done was bring me into your confidence. Last I heard was your firm disinterest." She regarded him. "You're a better liar than you were as a boy. That's not a compliment."

Quin had opened his mouth to reply, but at her last words snapped it shut.

His mother narrowed her eyes.

"I promise you'll be the first to know. We're just…exploring." He put it delicately, knowing the path ahead wasn't exactly going to be easy. The gossip alone would be its own hailstorm. And while he had promised Catherine to make it right, he wanted to do so without the public eye or the scandal that could accompany a hasty proposal. She was his; now he'd woo her with the world watching.

"Just be sure that any…*exploring*…doesn't give me an early grandchild," his mother said curtly.

Quin coughed, trying to swallow his shock and failing. "Mother," he scolded.

"I'm not an idiot." His mother gave him a once-over and regarded him with a warning expression.

"I assure you that is not a current possibility." Quin felt the need to defend his honor, and Catherine's.

"Current possibilities…change. Don't be a simpleton." The Duchess of Wesley said the last words with a delighted tone as she scanned the crowd.

Quin marveled at her ability to play the part. To throw off the scent of gossipmongers. He peeked back to the swirling dancers, finding Catherine and watching her spin and dance.

Deciding he needed a distraction, he sought out Morgan

with the intention of gaining his approval to steal his dance with Catherine for himself. It would serve a twofold purpose, because then he could ask Joan for a dance as well.

Morgan was easy to find and, with only minimal harassment, was convinced to abdicate his dance for Quin's sake. One errand done, Quin turned his attention to gaining a dance from Joan.

Morgan was happy to offer the formal introduction, which was indeed a mere formality since Quin had known of Joan and her antics for years, but they hadn't ever had the pleasure of an introduction.

She was a slight-framed girl, but her fiery-red hair and sparkling green eyes were filled with a determination that made her formidable. He knew this from the many stories Morgan had shared over the years.

He'd much rather take on Morgan any day, rather than Joan.

Where Morgan was diabolical in his approach—which made him quite the asset at the War Office—Joan was methodical, and you could never determine when she'd exact her revenge. But she had righteousness in her favor, for any revenge she gave was justly deserved by her brother.

Quin bowed as he met his friend's sister, noticing the familial resemblance in their demeanor and expression. "A pleasure, Lady Joan."

"And a pleasure for me as well. I've heard so much about you."

"I hope you believe only the good aspects."

"Only if you promise to do the same for all you've heard about me."

"Done," Quin agreed. "And may I have the pleasure of a dance this evening? Or are all your dances taken?"

Joan's eyes narrowed playfully. "Morgan tends to frighten off most gentlemen, though as much as I wish I could disparage him for such a thing, I don't wish for any suitor who is terrified of someone as unthreatening as he is." She shot a challenging glare at her sibling.

"I'll take that as a yes," Quin replied. "How about a reel?"

"Perfect," Joan replied. "Thank you for asking."

"My pleasure." Quin bowed. "I look forward to it."

He pitied the man who tried to court Joan. However, he suspected the more formidable of the two was certainly Joan. It was a sibling relationship that he understood, the fighting and teasing but the underlying loyalty and trust that came from blood. He missed that. But Morgan and Joan had lost a brother too. It seemed that fire had stolen something from everyone.

His ponderings were cut short when he was intercepted by a shorter man walking intently toward him. His clothing was meticulous, too much so. The gentleman's effort to make an impression with his dress was bordering on gaudy, right down to the silver-handled cane.

"Your Grace." The man bowed low, surprising Quin with an unexpected address.

It went against Quin's nature to cut the man, regardless of his faux pas of addressing a duke without a proper introduction. Quin gave a sharp nod and waited for the gentleman in question to continue, but the man paused in his bow as if waiting for Quin to speak first. Quin paused, resenting the attention this uncomfortable situation was attracting. He addressed the man. "I find myself at a disadvantage. You are...?"

The gentleman snapped straight. "Percival Armstrong, Baron Bircham."

Quin offered his hand, studying the man with a renewed interest. So this was Catherine's cousin, the trustee of the estate. *Interesting.* "A pleasure."

"The honor is all mine, Your Grace."

The man bowed again, and Quin clenched his jaw at such officious attention. Quin withdrew his ignored outstretched hand and tucked it in his pocket, feeling awkward.

"I've been told that Lady Catherine has been taken under the wing of your mother, and I wanted to offer my thanks."

Quin nodded. "No thanks are necessary. It is my mother's pleasure to have such a dear friend so often in her company." Quin regarded the man, searching for what his game was.

"Nonetheless, with someone as alone in the world as Lady Catherine, I'm sure she appreciates your friendship."

Ah, so his approach would be to portray her as a weak and foolish female. How...disappointing.

"One is never alone when surrounded by friends. If you'll excuse me, Lord Bircham." As far as Quin was concerned, they had finished with the conversation. There was no need to paint Catherine's situation as pitiful, not when she was anything but. And Quin knew from experience she wouldn't appreciate such pity.

Nor would he.

They had endured more than their share. There was no need to add to what had already been measured out for them. Lord Bircham bowed as Quin left and thankfully didn't follow. Quin made his way back to his mother, knowing that was where Catherine would come when the dance finished. It was quite beneficial to have his mother as her chaperone. After the dance finished, Catherine was led by her partner to his mother's side.

Before the music from one dance settled, the new strains of a reel began. It was Quin's turn to take his leave and find Joan. Had he known the reel was next, he would have kept his place by Morgan, but there was nothing for it now.

He excused himself, giving Catherine a quiet look of affection as he left, and sought out Joan for his promised dance. She was waiting beside her brother in nearly the same position as he had left them.

"I believe this is my dance." Quin bowed and extended his hand.

"It seems it is," Joan offered.

As Quin led her onto the dance floor, he noted the way Morgan abandoned his post and headed toward the north corner of the ballroom. Quin wouldn't have noted his friend's progress were it not for the way Morgan moved seamlessly through the crowd, as if anticipating each person's movements and darting around them without so much as touching the fabric of skirt or jacket. It was impressive, and just as Quin started the reel, he noted that Morgan disappeared behind a large statue. Quin turned his full attention to Joan and began to dance.

As they passed each other in the turn, the movement of the dance added color to her pale skin. Her smile was infectious, and Quin grinned in return. It was a delight to dance with someone just for the pure pleasure. No expectations, no hopes he'd have to thwart. Joan knew he was asking for the benefit of her brother and for the pleasure of a lively partner. Quin enjoyed the dance more than he usually would.

"You're a better dancer than Morgan," Joan commented as they passed each other.

"Oh? I shouldn't think that would be a difficult feat."

"It isn't," she returned with a joking tone.

When they met again, she said, "Thank you. I know you asked because my brother requested it."

"I'm enjoying myself. You clearly got all the dancing talent in the family," Quin replied.

Joan rolled her eyes, then seemed to catch herself in the unladylike response. "Yes, well, as you so eloquently said, it doesn't mean much."

"I meant it as a compliment regardless."

"Then I thank you."

The reel ended, and Quin bowed to Joan. After offering his arm, he started to lead her back to where he'd last seen her brother, only Morgan was nowhere to be found. Odd.

Quin scanned the room, not wanting to leave Joan alone. As he surveyed the crowd, another reel started up. Quin led Joan to the side of the dance floor, keeping them out of the way of the new dancers. As they reached the edge, he turned them to face the dancers and noted that Morgan was lining up with Catherine. Odd, he thought their dance was later, giving him a chance to steal it from Morgan.

Quin's first reaction was irritation, but it soon gave way to concern as he noted the expression on Catherine's face. There wasn't the keen enjoyment that he had expected from a lively dance with a familiar partner. No, it was the anxiety of learning something distasteful.

He admired her as she moved around the dancers, performing the steps automatically, yet every time she came close to Morgan, he would speak to her. The nod of her head gave away her intent listening, and more than once he noted a fierce determination spreading across her features.

Curiosity burning within him, he impatiently waited for the reel to end, never once taking his eyes from the pair.

"Is all well?" Joan asked, whispering softly from beside him.

He shifted his feet so he faced her. "Indeed."

He turned his attention back to Morgan and Catherine.

"You're a terrible liar," Joan said for his ears alone, and Quin flicked his glare to her. "It's the truth." She shrugged. "It's not a bad thing. If you were a good liar, it would mean you had to practice it regularly, and that's not a skill one should need to perfect."

"Unless it's your profession." He arched a brow, then flicked his appraisal to her brother, who was, by profession, a liar of sorts. Only his sort of lies kept people safe, traitors in prison, and information secret.

"That's different. He's honorable."

"Indeed, he is," Quin agreed, then as the music ended, led Joan toward Morgan as he exited the dance floor.

As Quin approached, he raised an eyebrow of query to his friend.

But rather than impart any information, Morgan nodded to

Lady Catherine, thanked her for the dance, and took his sister's hand from where it rested on Quin's forearm. "If you'll excuse us."

As the brother and sister departed, Quin shifted to face Catherine just as the strains of the supper waltz began. The timing couldn't have been better, and Quin held out his hand. Catherine took it and stepped closer. Quin moved in, then back, leading them into the steps as they entered into the swirl of other dancers.

"Are you well?" Quin asked, needing to know the important information first.

"Yes. Quite. Just…irritated," Catherine said in a frustrated tone. "But I will confess that I've been looking forward to this dance all evening, and I won't have it spoiled."

Quin nodded. "I've been anticipating it as well, but I find I'm more concerned with your heart than the dance."

"Ah, when you put it such a way, how can I refuse?"

"I'm hoping you won't," Quin replied. "Is there anything I can do to help? And if you wish not to share whatever Morgan told you, I can respect that as well. If I've learned anything about you, Catherine…" He caressed her name with his voice, as if his words could touch her in ways he couldn't on the full dance floor.

Catherine looked up at him through her lashes, her shoulders relaxing slightly as if releasing some of the weight carried upon them.

"What do you know of an actor by the name of Kean? Because if he's as brilliant as I've heard, I just might need your help."

"Help? Of course. In what way?"

Catherine leaned into his embrace further, but still maintaining propriety. "It seems my cousin is bound and determined to adjust my investments. So I'm going to beat him to it. They probably are outdated, and I'm of age. I would like your assistance in becoming a patroness."

"Patroness…of Kean's?"

"No. Of Drury Lane Theatre."

# Twenty-six

*Happiness and unhappiness are in the heart and spirit of each one of us: If you feel unhappy, then place yourself above that and act so that your happiness does not get to be dependent on anything.*

—*Catherine the Great*

CATHERINE RESISTED THE URGE TO BITE HER LIP AND STUDIED Quin's face as he reacted to her words. It wasn't that women couldn't be patronesses of the arts; it was just that usually they were older and established, not young and single.

But if her sources were correct, the Drury Lane Committee of Management was sinking fast into bankruptcy, and she wasn't about to let the arts fade away in the cold mists of financial ruin. Kean was renowned for his interpretation of Shakespeare. His earlier performance of Shylock in January had given the theater a much-needed boost, but it hadn't been enough. The committee had entered into negotiations to hire him for further performances. Catherine was going to make sure they had the funds to make that happen.

Quin nodded once. "Consider it done." And then he leaned forward, his green eyes sparkling with something she couldn't quite name but felt down to her toes. "What else do you have in mind?"

Such a question had only one answer.

"Anything I want," she whispered with the power of a woman taking control of her destiny.

"I believe that." Quin nodded his approval. "Are there other investments you're considering?"

Catherine looked around them, then met Quin's gaze again. "Yes, but let's save that conversation for later. I'd rather enjoy this moment without distraction."

"I couldn't agree more."

Quin's grip tightened on her waist as he drew her in a fraction of an inch, and his scent enveloped her.

Licking her lips, her eyes darted down to his mouth.

"Don't," Quin whispered.

She glanced up, the words causing a sharp pain of rejection, till she saw the same hunger reflected in his own eyes. Understanding dawned, and her cheeks warmed with a blush.

"I find myself unequal to the task of resisting the temptation you offer, Catherine, and I wouldn't harm your reputation by my lack of self-control," Quin murmured softly.

Their eyes met, and Catherine broke away before she did something rash and daring and utterly scandalous.

Fighting a warm flush at the memory of his touch, she forced herself to be calm. Leave it to the most honorable man in London to make her feel utterly tempted to be shocking.

It was enchanting and ironic, and she adored the dichotomy of it all.

"What devilish intentions are you hiding?" Quin inquired.

Catherine gave her head a slow shake as her lips widened.

"Your expression is utterly terrifying," Quin whispered. "And equally tempting. Why do I feel as if I'm party to whatever plan you're hatching?"

"Who says you're simply a party? Why not the whole reason?" Catherine said flirtatiously.

"Is that the way it works? I feel as if I should be concerned." Quin narrowed his glare in mock suspicion.

"You should be," Catherine replied, hitching a shoulder. "Don't say I didn't warn you."

"I will endeavor to be equal to the task, my lady." Quin bowed, winking as he did so.

"Of that I have no doubts."

"You'll be the death of me…or at least of my self-control," Quin lamented.

"And that is exactly the plan." She gave him a once-over that was not strictly proper and made her way toward the Duchess of Wesley, who was waiting nearby.

She could feel Quin watching her as she retreated, but it wasn't the kind of unnerving sensation that she'd so often felt when people stared after her—judging, pitying, or speaking ill.

It was an enchanting feeling of knowing someone cared.

She wasn't sure how things had progressed this far; she was only thankful that they had.

Catherine's enjoyment of the evening was cut short when the Duchess of Wesley decided to leave the party, claiming a headache. Without a proper chaperone, Catherine decided it was in her best interest to leave as well.

It would have been a sad prospect but for the hope of tomorrow and the promise of Quin calling upon her. If Lord Bircham did make good on his intentions of persuading her of his particular plans for investment, she would need some sort of diversion to look forward to in the afternoon.

When she arrived home, Catherine proceeded to her grandfather's study. She took a seat behind the grand desk, sinking into the soft leather chair. There was work to be done, so she didn't linger in her relaxation. Instead, she leaned forward and withdrew a quill, ink, and linen paper to make a list.

Her first endeavor was with Drury Lane, and she'd contact the financial committee tomorrow to make her formal proposal.

That situated, she moved on to other concepts. If she were to invest in something, she wanted it to matter as well as make profits.

She tapped her fingernail on the wooden desk, then paused as a thought flickered through her mind.

With the anticipated defeat of Napoleon in the War of the Sixth Coalition, what of those left behind by soldier and sailor? Surely, there were orphans. Her investment in the textile industry had proven quite lucrative; she could use some of the profit to be helpful.

An orphanage didn't have to be profitable, just self-sufficient. And perhaps a library. Her eyes widened with the idea of creating a small library in Providence Place and maybe a school for literacy. All her grand ideas flew through her mind and onto paper as she wrote them down.

But she needed more than grand ideas—she needed plans, business plans to present to her solicitor. So withdrawing a clean sheet of paper, she outlined what she needed for a proper proposal.

She was thankful that Quin was surely going to be of assistance as well; with his economic passion, he could outline the areas she was finding ambiguous. It was perfect.

Catherine worked into the night, her thoughts focused with determination as she put her intentions into words. It wasn't until the darkest reaches of the night that she finally set her pen down. She wished she could go over the details with her grandmother, ask for her keen insight and unapologetic directness. But even with the slow progress her grandmother had made, Catherine wouldn't tax her with questions. It was enough to be able to outline the proposal. With a sense of satisfaction, she stood from the desk. The peaceful feeling followed her to her rooms and lulled her to sleep. It kept her at rest till the bright sunlight of midmorning awakened her hours later. With no time to linger in bed, she dressed quickly, broke her fast, checked on her sleeping grandmother, and waited for Quin's arrival, anticipating his presence.

She'd notified Mrs. Burke that she was having a guest and would require her presence. It went against the grain, having her present when she was discussing an all-out coup against the woman's employer. He'd find out soon enough, and Mrs. Burke's presence was unfortunately necessary since Catherine would be in an unmarried gentleman's presence. Regardless of how many times she'd had Quin to herself in the past, it was different now.

The promise of forever hung in the air with that kiss.

Then the waltz.

And she was quite certain there was more to be done on that front.

It was just after noon when Brooks announced Quin's arrival, and Catherine put no effort into hiding her welcoming beam in his direction. His green eyes danced, and Catherine's cheeks heated at her body's response to seeing him. Warm all over, she felt her fingers tingle with the lingering sensation of his hand at her hip during their waltz last night.

"Good afternoon," Quin said by way of greeting.

"Indeed it is. Especially now," she responded, unable to resist her impulsive nature.

Quin bowed. "I assume you have a plan for our time together?" His eyes flicked from her to Mrs. Burke. He gave a nod to the widow.

Catherine replied to his query, "Of course."

"And you say I'm the predictable one, restrained." He inclined his head.

"I said you were not one to find himself in trouble."

Quin arched a brow, his expression challenging and engaging at the same time. "And yet I find myself attracted to it, nonetheless."

"I'll take that as a compliment." Catherine peeked behind her to Mrs. Burke, wondering if she read into the hidden meaning.

The chaperone worked silently on her needlepoint, seeming to ignore them both.

Quin met her amused expression with one of his own. "What's all this?" He gestured to the side table with a neat stack of papers on top.

Catherine moved over to the table and traced a finger over the pile. "These are some of my ideas."

"Some?" Quin's brows arched. "How large would the pile be if it were *most* of your ideas?" he inquired good-naturedly.

"A veritable mountain."

"I suppose I should be thankful you're starting me off small."

"Indeed."

Catherine lifted the stack and began to sort through it. "First of all, I'd like to get your perspective on several things. We spoke last night about Drury Lane, and I still think that's a solid endeavor."

Quin nodded, his brows hooding his eyes as he studied a sheet of paper she'd handed to him. "Do you have any of their quarterly reports? Any financial information?"

"Not yet, but I requested them and they should arrive today."

"Good, good," he murmured as he read the page.

Catherine hesitated, opening her mouth then shutting it as she struggled to decide how to formulate the next question.

Quin's eyes narrowed. "Out with it."

"Am I that transparent?"

"Yes." He nodded once, then turned to the next sheet of paper.

Catherine forced her shoulders to relax. Taking a seat, she gestured to one across from her, inviting Quin to sit as well. "I'd like to invest in a company that you'll certainly recognize. But I don't just want to invest. I want to help with distribution. The East India Trading Company."

He gave an encouraging nod.

"I heard about it last year and dismissed it at the time. It wasn't my place to invest, and my grandmother had only mentioned it in passing after one of her meetings with the solicitor. However, I inquired about it a week or so ago, just on a whim. It's grown consistently and is in need of some assistance to take the next steps. I want to be that help."

"Do you have someone to consult on investments?"

"Yes. My solicitor should have the name already."

Quin nodded. "It's a huge market, and the company's trade

between Britain and China is quite lucrative." He leaned forward. "I've seen a Fellow at the college buy his title from the investment he made a few years ago. If you wish to invest, I'd do it quickly."

"I'll speak to my solicitor today."

Quin gave an approving nod. "Any other companies?"

Catherine frowned. "I want to do something more than just make money. I want to make a difference." She outlined her desire to set up a library, perhaps an orphanage. Both her ideas were met with Quin's enthusiastic approval. Catherine's heart warmed as they continued to discuss options, ideas, and ways to create the business plans to present later.

It was comforting, but more than that, it was fun to have a partner, to have someone she could trust. It was reminiscent of her courtship with Avery, but this was far deeper. With Avery, she shared her interests and ideas; with Quin she shared her soul.

He still hadn't mentioned their kiss or attempted to kiss her again, but some instinct within her said he cared and far more than the way one friend cared for another.

She only wished he'd say the words rather than let his countenance speak for him.

# Twenty-seven

IT WAS AN ACUTE FORM OF TORTURE TO BE IN THE PRESENCE OF Catherine in her element while being unable to taste her enthusiasm, hold her energy, or even trace the outline of her lips. Quin struggled to keep his focus on her words, to impart whatever insight he could offer rather than be lost in the way her presence lit up the parlor. The damnable Mrs. Burke was ever present.

He watched Catherine bend over the desk, scribbling across the page, striking through a line and then rewriting it.

Her handwriting was abominable. He remembered trying to decipher her initial plans on paper. He'd expected the elegant script of a lady, but rather he'd found the hurried cursive of a quick mind. It fit her, somehow. Brilliant in her own right, she had a vision in business he'd rarely seen in gentlemen her age, or older. It was a challenge to keep up with her, and he loved every moment. When he'd explained something she'd not quite understood on her own, her eyes narrowed slightly, and she'd leaned forward, studying the words and committing them to memory.

As a professor, he loved it when his students reacted in such a way. It meant the subject mattered to them. It had found a home in their minds, growing and becoming a live concept that could change, grow, and expand.

He saw that same hunger for understanding in Catherine, but its effect on him was different. In his students, he'd found it satisfying. In Catherine, it was thrilling, erotic, and moved him in ways he didn't know could happen when discussing investments.

It had caught him off guard, the power of his attraction and how it came alive with the simplest of looks, touches, or even topics they discussed. He was contemplating that as she paused in her writing, her hazel gaze a welcome haven for him, a source of peace and desire that were equally powerful.

"I think I have it all written down. Can you think of anything I should add?"

"No," he answered.

Accepting his answer, she turned back to her writing.

He watched as her golden curls draped from the coiffure her maid had twisted into submission, but the few strands of hair caressing her shoulder drew his attention, tempting him to feel the softness they touched with such ease.

That was out of his reach, and even if it weren't, he couldn't touch her in such an intimate way in the presence of Mrs. Burke.

"Finished," Catherine replied. "I'll need to rewrite it all, of course. I was in such a hurry that it's a trifle messy." She frowned.

Quin resisted the urge to agree with her *trifle* remark. He stifled an amused laugh but apparently didn't hide it well enough, as Catherine speared him with a challenging expression.

He lifted a hand in surrender, even if his lips widened too much to appear sincere.

"Very good." Catherine set everything aside. "Now, with that done, I think we deserve tea and cake."

"I couldn't agree more, and then a walk?"

"Charming idea," Catherine replied.

Quin hazarded a glimpse at Mrs. Burke, who watched them unabashedly from her corner perch. No doubt she'd report their intentions to her employer, but hopefully by then it would be too late.

He watched as Catherine smoothed her skirts, frowning as she lifted an ink-smudged hand, then shifted in her seat. The lack of gloves was probably a good idea—better to smudge the inside of the glove rather than the outside. She started toward him, and he prefaced his query cautiously. "Would you like my assistance later today when you meet with your solicitor and cousin?"

He could read the answer in her eyes without her ever voicing the words. It was a welcome and surprising revelation to know someone so well.

"Thank you for your kind offer, but I need to do this myself."

"I understand," Quin replied honestly. How often had he done some difficult thing by himself when he could have asked for assistance from a colleague or even from his family? He respected her strength.

"Thank you for understanding," Catherine replied. "If there's something I've learned about myself in all this, it's that I resent being at anyone's mercy." She paused. "I don't know if this makes sense, but it feels like pity, unwelcome, unsolicited, and yet something you can't avoid either." Her brows knitted as she spoke.

Quin nodded silently. Her words resonated deep within him. Hadn't he felt the same way? He couldn't imagine not having some semblance of control in his own life, especially when he felt the weight of his decisions so powerfully because of their effect on his family, his title, his name.

"It's kind of like a wound," Quin replied after a moment, and Catherine's eyes darted to his.

"A wound?"

"Yes." He leaned forward, resting his elbows on his knees. "A visiting professor, Johann Christian Riel, came to Cambridge from Berlin and gave a lecture. He was raising awareness of the conditions of institutions like asylums, but he touched on some other topics that have stayed with me." Quin paused, his brows puckering as he selected his words. "He made the argument that when we find ourselves in a situation that is not comfortable, we have an instinct—a vital force that compels us to repair our situation."

Catherine regarded him, her hazel eyes flashing with intelligence as she considered his words.

"It was unfair to lose Wes—Avery, for both of us. And there is no sense in it, but we have an instinct, a vital force that compels us forward. It's that strength I see in you that is unrelenting, passionate, determined."

Quin paused, not expecting the pang that assaulted him at his own words. Pain because he still missed his brother, and pain because that same brother had been assured of something Quin wanted…Catherine's affection. He shoved the unwanted reactions away and continued. "And we know what it feels like to be out of control and unable to change something foundational. So we are more highly aware of things that make us feel out of control. Heaven knows I struggled with my title and responsibilities, feeling the weight of every decision." He gave a shiver of remembrance. It was better now; he'd adapted, which led him to his final point. "We adapt, however. And while some people run from those unwanted reactions, Catherine, you rise to meet and challenge them. It's to your credit."

He watched her reaction, unreadable and intense, with interest.

"Mrs. Burke, will you please go to the kitchens and request fresh tea and biscuits?" Catherine turned to the woman in the corner.

Mrs. Burke gave a twitch of her lips as they thinned in what appeared to be irritation, and she set her needlepoint aside. "You can't find a maid to assist you?"

"You're available, are you not?" Catherine replied.

Mrs. Burke gave a huff and stood from her chair near the window. With a prim gait, she exited the room and made a show of leaving the door wide open, her stare spearing them both with a warning.

Quin watched the woman leave, her footsteps fading in the hall. *What an odd duck.* He turned back to Catherine and found she wasn't sitting across from him, but was taking a seat beside him on the sofa.

Her proximity had an immediate effect. Her skirts rustled against his leg, a splash of pale yellow against the black of his breeches. His body tingled with awareness of her, and he reached out to trace the curve of her cheek, allowing his fingers the pleasure of her soft skin.

"Are you going to kiss me or not?" Catherine's words came in a rush. Her cheeks were heightened with color.

He traced his hand from her cheek to the back of her neck, his fingers finding the softness of her hair. He pulled her forward gently, slowly, allowing the anticipation to build. He didn't have much time before Mrs. Burke would return, but he wasn't going to rush this.

Her breath tickled his lips, sending a current of desire coursing through him. He angled his head slightly, covering more of her lips with his own, allowing the barest tip of his tongue to trace the seam of her lips, his body hungry for more of a taste of her.

She leaned into him, melting as she pressed her lips more fully against his, opening her mouth slightly to nibble on his lower lip, and he groaned at the erotic pleasure of it.

If a kiss was this powerful, making love to her would be his undoing.

In the best way possible.

He deepened the kiss, drawing the passion from her like nectar and feeding his own to her. His hands released their light grip on her neck and traced the lines of her back till he spanned her hips, arching his fingers into the swell of her curves, mapping her body, worshiping it with every touch as his tongue darted into her mouth, sampling her with abandon.

Some corner of his mind reminded him of the time, and he slowly eased out of the passionate exchange. He wouldn't damage Catherine's reputation in her own parlor, as much as he'd like to damn the consequences and continue tasting her. With a final kiss, he slowly retreated, his body humming with unfulfilled need.

Not yet.

And it was the *yet* that helped cool his fevered desires. It wasn't a matter of if, simply of when.

And God help him, it was going to be magnificent.

Catherine's eyes were cloudy with passion and her lips bee-stung from his attentions.

Quin roamed her features wondrously, a power burning through him at the adoration he had for her. "Does that answer your question?" he asked, trailing a finger down her cheek and outlining her lips. He couldn't help himself; he kissed her once more, lingering, then once more before forcing himself to retreat again.

"You're far too tempting, and I have too little control. If we're to have any semblance of propriety, you're going to need to stand in the furthest corner of the room," he growled, then gave her a final quick kiss.

"But such an action would require Herculean effort on my part, and far more self-control than I have at the moment as well," Catherine replied with an affection he could feel rather than see as his lips lingered near hers, not touching but nearly.

The sound of footsteps in the hall acted like cold water, and Quin watched with reluctance as Catherine gave a glare toward the door and moved back over to her original seat. Quin noted her rosy and swollen lips and reached out, lifted her teacup, and handed it to her, dipping his chin in a nod.

Understanding dawned in her expression, and she giggled as she lifted the teacup to her lips just as Mrs. Burke came into the room, her expression of sour indifference unchanged. "It will be here directly." She narrowed her eyes at Quin, then returned to her corner of the room and took up her embroidery.

Catherine's back was to the woman, thankfully, and she lowered the teacup and speared Quin with an impish grin.

As a maid brought in the promised biscuits and a fresh pot of tea, he made plans.

Because life was too short to waste time.

He'd learned that lesson last year, and he wasn't going to let it be in vain.

# Twenty-eight

*I sincerely want peace, not because I
lack resources for war, but because I hate
bloodshed.*

—Catherine the Great

"My, my, Lady Catherine, you've done your research,
haven't you? Or rather, had it done for you," Lord Bircham murmured as his eyes narrowed while he regarded her.

Catherine swallowed her nerves and turned her attention to her solicitor, Mr. Sheffield.

"My cousin's intentions are noble, I'm sure, but if I need to invest some of the funds from my estate to diversify, I'd rather select the investments." Catherine had decided that being generous in word to her cousin would be wise, prideful as he seemed.

"I see," Mr. Sheffield remarked. "Your grandmother was already contemplating an investment in the East India Company, so I think that is a good option. As for Drury Lane, I would advise you to find out more information."

"I have a meeting tomorrow, and I'm expecting documentation today," Catherine replied.

"Very good." Mr. Sheffield adjusted his spectacles and continued to read.

Lord Bircham cleared his throat and leaned forward. "I trust you'll give the same attention to my suggestions, Mr. Sheffield."

Mr. Sheffield regarded him. "Of course. After all, I'm pursuing the best interests of the estate, Lord Bircham. Whatever is *best* for the estate is what I'll suggest we investigate."

It wasn't the most powerful setdown, but it got the point across nicely, Catherine thought. She leaned back in her chair, observing the two men. She'd welcomed them into the green salon, choosing that room for the two writing desks along the wall and the view of the sunset as the afternoon waned.

Her mind longed to wander to the earlier events of the day, to Quin's kiss and their walk afterward. Every little smile, secretive wink, or touch of his hand had been glorious, and she'd enjoyed every moment in his company. But she forced her thoughts into submission as Mr. Sheffield began to speak again.

"Before any approval can happen for your philanthropy, there must be a plan for your endeavors, submitted in writing." He turned to her. "However, personally, I welcome such an idea."

Catherine felt a swell of pride at his approval. "Thank you."

"And I do suggest we look into Lord Bircham's company as well."

At this, Catherine deflated slightly. If it was in the best interest for her estate, then fine, but her instinct said it wasn't. And she wasn't sure how to articulate her feeling.

"I see" was all she could manage.

She'd find out more information and fight Lord Bircham's investment choice with hard facts.

As Mr. Sheffield stood to take his leave, she thanked him for his perceptiveness and watched as he disappeared through the door.

Lord Bircham stood but made no move to leave the room. Rather, he nodded to the ever-present Mrs. Burke. "It seems you were planning quite the strategy this morning."

Catherine didn't reply, simply waited for him to continue. "Mrs. Burke said you had a gentleman caller who was quite persuasive in his thoughts. I would suggest you steer clear of such men. They can easily influence someone of delicate sensibilities."

Catherine faltered. "Pardon me?"

She turned to regard Mrs. Burke, who was studiously avoiding her.

"Those ideas were all mine," Catherine asserted. "And Qu—His Grace—assisted only with more financial detail."

"Yes, well, a title doesn't mean—"

"He's a professor of politics and history and has overseen the Wesley dukedom with great success," Catherine interrupted. *Damn politeness.*

"Those who cannot do, teach, dear Catherine."

"Lady Catherine," she corrected, clenching her jaw and daring him to contradict her.

"Lady Catherine." He nodded contritely; however, his expression was anything but.

"I'll be sure to personally check into the companies you've suggested," she said clearly, hoping to assure him and show she wasn't afraid of confrontation. She wasn't about to give him any ideas concerning her "delicate sensibilities" as he'd put it.

"Good. I think you'll be impressed and see things from my perspective."

"Of that, we shall certainly see," Catherine replied, feeling nothing but caution.

"If that is all, I'll take my leave." He headed toward the door more slowly than Catherine would have wished. "Oh, and the next time you send Mrs. Burke on a maid's errand to have time alone with your *friend*, he will gain an unwanted mark on his reputation, and you will on yours. Good evening."

Catherine resisted the urge to growl, stomp, or do some other such nonsense. She had taken a risk earlier, and she would gladly take it again, but it wasn't worth ruining Quin's reputation, or hers.

There had to be another way.

After Lord Bircham left, Catherine turned her attention to Mrs. Burke. The woman was regarding her with an expectant gleam in her eye, as if looking forward to any skirmish Catherine wished to begin.

"And here I thought a chaperone was to protect one's reputation." Catherine clipped the words.

"I can only protect that which I can see, my *lady*." She emphasized the title, arching a brow. "You'd be wise to keep your prospects lower than a duke, regardless. You're reaching too high." She shifted her needlepoint and began stabbing the fabric.

Catherine's brow furrowed with confusion, but then she realized Mrs. Burke didn't know what had transpired the summer before. She opened her mouth to inform the woman, then paused. It wasn't worth it, and she also didn't want to expose herself, or Quin, to speculation. If Mrs. Burke didn't already know that Catherine had been engaged to the former Duke of Wesley, then the woman didn't need to know she was developing tender feelings for the current one. Sometimes privacy was more important than being right.

Catherine nodded, let her feel she'd won. It was of no import to her.

"If that's all?"

Mrs. Burke regarded her coldly. "For now."

Catherine took her leave and, needing to find something familiar, made her way to her grandmother's chambers. The door was slightly ajar, and as she pushed the heavy portal open farther, her heart stuttered with relief and wonder at the sigh that greeted her.

"Grammy?" she exclaimed.

Lady Greatheart was sitting up in bed, feeding herself from a soup tureen upon a bed table that sat across her knees. A soft bread roll completed the small meal.

A tear trailed down Catherine's cheek, and her eyes stung with more as she watched in wonder. Lady Greatheart hesitated, then set the spoon down, offering a weak grin that held more promise than a million words.

For the first time in so long, Catherine had more than just the hope that her grandmother would heal. She had proof, and it was balm to her soul.

"Catherine, come sit." Lady Greatheart's voice was hoarse, as if rusty from not being used, but it was familiar and wrapped around Catherine's heart like a fluffy, warm blanket. Quickly she crossed the room and sat in the chair beside her grandmother, sharing a quick smile of hope with the maid on the other side of the bed.

"She demanded I let her feed herself this afternoon," the maid commented happily.

Lady Greatheart gave a small huff. "I didn't demand," she nearly croaked, but the indignation bled through.

The maid gave a wry expression in response to that.

"Fine, I may have demanded it a bit. But I need to do more. If I'm...well, able to do more." Lady Greatheart gave a dismissive wave with her hand as she spoke, then let her arm fall to the bed as if the movement had been exhausting.

"Little steps... You'll get there."

"It's bloody frustrating," Lady Greatheart retorted, but closed her eyes as she lay back on the propped-up pillows.

"I'm sure it is, but progress is progress, and every step forward is one to be proud of."

Lady Greatheart opened one eye and regarded her granddaughter. "I'm exhausted, but for once, my curiosity is stronger than my need to sleep. What have you been doing? And why did I hear a strange voice in the hall earlier?"

Catherine placed her hand upon her grandmother's, thankful for the warmth that met her. "It's a bit complicated but nothing to worry about."

At this, her grandmother opened both eyes and turned her head to meet Catherine's avoidant answer. "What's complicated?"

Catherine turned from her grandmother to the maid, a question in her expression. Should she give further details? Would worry cause her grandmother to have a setback? They had just had the clearest proof of hope. Catherine didn't want to jeopardize her grandmother's health in any way.

"Out with it, ducky."

Apparently, her grandmother wasn't going to let her wait. Catherine bit her lip and considered how best to inform her grandmother of the changes that had taken place. "In your"—she paused, struggling for a delicate way to phrase it—"lapse of health, Mr. Sheffield contacted the estate's trustee, Lord Bircham—"

"You're telling me the man's still alive?" her grandmother asked with more strength than Catherine would have expected.

Catherine took a moment to regain her thoughts. "Er, his son is. So not the man Grandfather named, but his heir."

"Oh…" Her grandmother gave a weak nod. "That makes more sense." Then as if she finally realized what that meant, she narrowed her eyes. "Trustee of the estate? Just how long have I been up here?"

Catherine was vague, trying to keep many of the details from her grandmother till they were sure she was out of the woods. "A while."

"A *while*," Lady Greatheart repeated. Then apparently realizing she wasn't going to get further information, she exhaled. "Fine. So Bircham is contacted…"

"And he's come to London and brought a respectable chaperone"—Catherine tried not to wince at the words—"who is our guest and is probably who you've heard in the hall."

"I see." Lady Greatheart's eyes darted to the door, then back to Catherine. "That would make sense, but I still don't think it was necessary to involve Bircham. I'll have a chat with Sheffield," she murmured, almost to herself.

"Well, since you're on the mend, I'm sure we'll be back to normal quite soon."

At this, her grandmother agreed, then leaned her head back again while closing her eyes. "Yes."

Catherine caressed her grandmother's hand with her fingers. "Sleep. I'll be back later."

Lady Greatheart nodded, and the maid removed the tray from her lap and set it on the side table.

"I think we've turned the corner, my lady," she said softly.

"Me too."

Catherine regarded her grandmother, her eyes burning with tears again. It had been simply survival, these weeks without her grandmother's voice or wit. And now that she had been given the gift once more, she realized how much she had missed her grandmother, with a bone-deep ache.

She wiped a tear from her cheek, then felt a soft touch at her elbow.

The maid had moved closer and was offering a white handkerchief. "Thank you." The maid was teary-eyed as well.

"We're a pair, you and I." Catherine sniffled, but beamed at the camaraderie.

The maid nodded. "There is much to be grateful for today."

That was the truth. And all the other obstacles of the day paled in comparison with the glory of something as powerful as hope.

# Twenty-nine

*I have no way to defend my borders but to extend them.*

—Catherine the Great

CATHERINE AWOKE THE NEXT DAY WITH A FULL SCHEDULE, AND it wasn't the agenda of a debutante with fittings and parties and walks in the park. No, it was the plan of a woman taking charge of her life. Yesterday, the financial information she'd requested from Drury Lane Theatre had arrived, and she'd looked over it late into the night. With several conclusions drawn, she thought over her questions and plans as she readied for the day. The theater's committee was meeting around noon, a bit early for her taste, but she'd been invited to attend, so she wasn't going to miss it.

After breaking her fast, she spent a few hours in her study, outlining the plan for a small orphanage near the docks in London. It was an industrial area, but plenty of the poorer class lived nearby, and the area was known for its street urchins roaming about. Her heart ached, knowing many had nowhere to be safe, to call home, so it was her first-choice location. Lady Greatheart would approve of the plan; she was always soft-hearted toward the less fortunate. Today Catherine would explore several buildings for the orphanage, but it wasn't somewhere she could go alone.

The request to be escorted there should have been asked of Quin yesterday, but she had been far too distracted by his proximity and the meeting later on with Bircham and Sheffield to have been thinking clearly. She quickly dispatched a missive to the

Duchess of Wesley, for her to inquire if Quin would be available. It was a pity she couldn't contact Quin directly, and with Mrs. Burke already on alert, the rules of propriety had to be followed more closely than usual.

With that completed, Catherine turned her attention to Lord Bircham's suggestion for an investment. The linen paper with all the particulars of the venture rested on her desk under several other sheets, and she withdrew them reluctantly. As she scanned the page, she noted the details of the company. It was industrial, and its financial records for the past two years were promising— that much she had to admit. It dealt in tobacco from the Caribbean but didn't sell locally; rather, it shipped the tobacco to Russia. She hadn't thought of the Russians as needing tobacco, but it certainly could be the case. Reading further, she grudgingly realized the company was a very viable option for investment. With more financial backing, it could fulfill larger orders, and since they were at capacity, they were to the point of turning down new clients.

Catherine set the pages aside and bit her lip. As much as it grated against her nerves, she would likely approve of such an investment. Good Lord, she could nearly hear Lord Bircham crow as he touted some nonsense about her feminine sensibilities. Irritated, she noted the time, then reached for the bell pull.

In a few minutes, the butler entered the study. "How may I be of service, my lady?"

"Please notify Mrs. Burke that we are leaving in a quarter hour. And ready the carriage."

"Of course." Brooks bowed slightly, then went to do her bidding.

Catherine quickly freshened up and, with time to spare, stepped into the coach, nodding a welcome to the already-seated Mrs. Burke. The ride to the theater was a silent one. Catherine didn't exactly wish to enter into conversation with her sour chaperone, and the feeling must have been mutual since Mrs. Burke didn't engage her either. The drive took nearly a half hour from Mayfair to Covent Garden.

The driver pulled up directly in front of the stone building on Catherine Street. She wondered if it was fate or simply ironic that the theater was on her namesake's street, but she pushed the fanciful thoughts aside as she alighted from the carriage.

A white stone portico covered the entrance. She took a moment to regard the large structure with its white columns supporting the portico. A footman waited by the door, opening it wide and bowing a welcome as she approached. Smiling her thanks, she heard Mrs. Burke's footsteps behind her as she made her way into the main entrance of the theater. Wide staircases led upward to the boxes, and a graceful chandelier hung from the ceiling. Its crystals refracted the light from the door and windows. Several other lights brightened the foyer, which led toward the main entrance to the grand stage.

Through the open doors, Catherine could see row upon row of velvet-covered seats, all arching toward the stage at the center, its size hidden by the doorframe.

A man in the theater's livery gestured for her to follow him, and they were led to a smaller staircase. Each step creaked as they ascended, and then the man opened a door on their left, exposing an impressive salon where several other gentlemen were seated and milling about in turn.

"Ah, Lady Catherine." A gentleman with a white beard and kind eyes rose from his seat at the head of a large mahogany table to greet her. "We're so thankful you agreed to come." He bowed to her, then took her offered hand. "I'm Mr. Whitbred, chairman of the committee."

"A pleasure," Catherine replied warmly.

"If you'll have a seat?" He motioned to the long table just beyond the view of the entrance.

She nodded. "Of course, thank you."

"Gentlemen?" the man announced.

The room hushed, and all flocked to their chairs, giving her kind nods of greeting. Her chair was pulled out, and she sat, awaiting the beginning of the meeting. Mrs. Burke took a seat on the perimeter of the room, her disapproving expression never relaxing.

"Lady Catherine, thank you for meeting with us today," the gentleman started. "On behalf of everyone present, I welcome you." He gestured to the table. "Allow me to introduce Mr. Sherman, Sir Teasdale, Mr. Dingam, and Mr. Rafe—all board members of our beloved theater."

"Thank you for your kind invitation," Catherine replied to the gentlemen.

Mr. Whitbred nodded. "I assume you received and looked over the fiscal details in the documents we sent over yesterday?"

"Indeed, I have."

"Before I continue, do you have any questions?"

Catherine swallowed and then nodded. "There are a few particulars I would like to have clarified, Mr. Whitbred."

He signaled for her to continue, his silver brows lifting in an engaging manner.

"I noted that you were experimenting with several actors, most interestingly, Edmund Kean. Do you continue to promote his talents?"

Mr. Whitbred gave a curt nod. "As you know, the theater has struggled financially, and it was only in January with Kean playing Shylock in *The Merchant of Venice* that we made any headway. We wish to continue on this path."

"Very good. What plays do you propose for him?"

"I'm glad you asked, Lady Catherine. In fact, why don't you follow me? Gentlemen?" He gestured to the table and then made his way to the door. A man beside her pulled back her chair, and she followed them all down the small stair and into the main entrance, casting a quick look behind to see Mrs. Burke following a few paces back. Mr. Whitbred turned and led them all into the main floor of the theater. "Sit wherever you wish," he instructed, and then took a seat near the stage.

Catherine cast a look to Mrs. Burke, who seemed oddly uncomfortable, and then took a seat near the front with Mr. Whitbred, nodding her approval when Mrs. Burke sat beside her.

"We have asked Kean to perform a small sample of an upcoming performance. I trust that an experience of his acting will speak volumes more than a description can." He gave a signal to the stage boy who had appeared to the left. A moment later, the lights dimmed, and Catherine gasped as a figure walked onto the stage.

He was dressed in red velvet with ermine fur covering the edges of the fabric. A kingly crown sat upon his head, but it was the gait with which he walked that was fascinating. Rather than proudly strutting onto the stage as his costume suggested he might, the character limped or hobbled with each step, his body contorted. As the light illuminated his features, a stern determination lit his expression, and with a voice that rent the very air of the theater with its power, he began.

> *"Why, I, in this weak piping time of peace*
> *Have no delight to pass away the time,*
> *Unless to see my shadow in the sun*
> *And descant on mine own deformity.*
> *And therefore, since I cannot prove a lover,*
> *To entertain these fair well-spoken days,*
> *I am determined to prove a villain*
> *And hate the idle pleasures of these days."*

Catherine watched spellbound as Edmund Kean spun part of the opening monologue of Shakespeare's *Richard III*. When he finished the scene, he bowed, straightened, and walked from the stage.

Catherine stood with the rest of the committee and applauded. Mr. Whitbred moved closer and leaned in, a look of deep satisfaction on his face. "I'll have my solicitor contact you regarding the financial details." She held out her gloved hand. "That performance was brilliant. See to it that he has more than just one upcoming performance."

Mr. Whitbred clasped her hand. "Done."

Catherine couldn't restrain her excitement as she released his hand, even though she could sense Mrs. Burke's disapproval at her offering a gentleman a handshake. Ignoring her chaperone's surely baleful glare, she spoke once more to Mr. Whitbred. "And I want to reserve a box for the season."

"For you, anything, Lady Catherine."

She knew the box would probably come at a dear price, but she wasn't going to miss a performance, not if she could help it.

Her business complete, she took leave of the theater, skin still prickling with gooseflesh over the rendition of King Richard's speech. Mrs. Burke followed her exit, a silent sentry of misery behind her.

As they entered the carriage, Catherine expected the widow to have at least something to say regarding the performance. "Well, did you enjoy that?" she asked after no compliment was forthcoming. Catherine righted herself as the carriage moved forward, jerking her slightly backward.

Mrs. Burke's eyebrows drew into lines of disapproval as she glared at her. "It's not my idea of pleasure to watch a man flounce about pretending to be a king."

The words surprised Catherine. Was this woman unable to find beauty in even the most fascinating arts such as theater? And for the first time, Catherine wondered if perhaps something had happened in Mrs. Burke's past that had destroyed the woman's ability to find joy in, well, anything.

That was a pity.

*Haven't I suffered?* she thought. *Haven't I known the acute sense of loss? Haven't I felt fear of the unknown regarding a loved one's fate? Yet I moved forward, still open to life and its beauty, regardless of pain's price.* It was a choice. She chose to focus on the beauty, and it wasn't easy.

But it was always worth it.

"I'm sorry you feel that way," Catherine replied.

The West End of London passed by the window of the carriage, and rather than put energy into a one-sided conversation, Catherine thought over the remainder of the day's appointments.

When they finally returned home, she inquired whether she'd had a reply from the Duchess of Wesley regarding Quin's availability for the afternoon.

"My lady, this came for you while you were out." Brooks held out a silver tray with a familiar seal on the envelope.

"Thank you." Catherine dismissed Mrs. Burke, took the missive into the study, and shut the door, not wanting her chaperone's prying eyes on her.

She sat behind the desk, withdrew a letter opener from the side drawer, and slit open the missive.

The note came not from the Duchess of Wesley but from Quin, accepting her request for his company.

She looked at the clock, considering how much time she had before Quin would arrive. Deciding she had time for tea, she rang for a maid and ordered refreshment, and after a moment's deliberation, she invited Mrs. Burke to partake as well. Unfortunately, she would still need Mrs. Burke to accompany her this afternoon, especially with Quin present. Maybe she'd be lucky and the incorrigible woman would hold her tongue in the presence of a duke. Silence from the woman would be a welcome boon.

Mrs. Burke arrived around the same time as the tea.

And as if her thoughts had conjured him, Quin's arrival was announced a few minutes later. Brooks showed him into the study.

His green eyes regarded her warmly, highlighted by the dark-emerald color of his cravat and matching coat. Long and lean, he moved with a powerful grace that reminded her of their dance and built anticipation for their next.

Catherine rose to greet him, and as she approached, she held out her hand, her face heating with understanding as he grasped her fingers and kissed the back of them slowly, intentionally, causing heat to prickle her skin up her arm and travel into her spine, sending tingles of desire through her limbs. He regarded her openly, communicating more than what he could say with propriety, and Catherine couldn't resist the devilish impulse to lick her lips, then bite her lower one, gratified when his eyes went smoky with desire.

Let him burn along with her.

"A pleasure to see you," Quin murmured softly, his eyes roaming over her features like a kiss.

"You as well." She could have said his name, or more properly *Your Grace*, but her throat caught as he slowly released her hand only to twine his fingers with hers scandalously, lingering in every touch.

She arched her brow at his subtle yet shocking behavior. He winked back unrepentantly.

"This is going to be a very long day…" she taunted softly.

"An acute form of torture for sure," he replied. "I look forward to every moment."

Catherine looked down as her face heated, and she beamed at his open flirtation. Gathering her scattered wits, she replied, "So do I."

# Thirty

IT WAS SURPRISING HOW ONE COULD BE DRIVEN MAD WITH desire by the most innocent of touches. Quin's afternoon with Catherine had been a devilish mix of need and restraint, a push and pull that nearly had him coming apart at the seams. Holding her while they waltzed hadn't been nearly enough to satiate his intense desire and had only served to make him far hungrier. He had bided his time, waiting for the perfect way to make their arrangement public, but he was growing more impatient by the minute.

They had spent hours touring buildings that could host children and caretakers for an orphanage.

Catherine's queries and perceptions about the buildings, as well as the operations of the potential orphanage, gave Quin a deeper understanding into how her mind worked, and more importantly how it affected her heart and actions. So many people would say the right words and feel pity, but that wouldn't produce any action. But Catherine? She spoke best by her actions, and he loved her all the more for it.

He'd come to admit that it wasn't just fascination with her or even deep friendship or something as shallow as lust. It was love—real, abiding, feverish, and consuming in its purest form. When he dreamed at night, he welcomed the fantasies, planning for when they could be not a dream but his reality. But certain obstacles had to be overcome first.

His greatest concern was that his attachment to Catherine might be construed by some as her own mercenary attempt at his title. Unsure how he could address such a heresy, he had approached his mother regarding the topic earlier that day.

The Duchess of Wesley had given a knowing nod at his words.

But she was expected at a luncheon soon, so they had postponed their conversation till later in the evening. Quin was certain that the long afternoon of reflection his mother could do on the subject would be both helpful and detrimental. Helpful because she'd likely come up with a grand solution, and detrimental because she'd never let him hear the end of it. Though that conclusion could be drawn regardless.

Quin regarded Catherine as they made their way back to her residence after evaluating the buildings.

"Have you made progress?" Quin asked, swaying with the movement of the carriage over the uneven streets.

Catherine turned from her study of the passing scenery. "Not as much as I'd hoped. I spent this morning at the theater. Good mercy, Quin, I can't wait till the next performance. I have a box now, you know." She blushed, and Quin's mind immediately went to all the delightful touches and flirtations they could experiment with in a secluded box.

"I can't wait."

"I didn't say you were invited."

He chuckled. "Turns out I don't need your invitation. I have my own box." He shrugged indifferently.

Catherine gave him a mock glare. "I won't bother you with it then."

"I could invite you," he returned.

"It's a bit much for us each to have a box." She all but rolled her eyes, and then, apparently realizing how her words could be taken, she cast a furtive query at Mrs. Burke.

Quin ignored the chaperone and whatever disapproval she wished to convey with her expression and leaned forward. "It is a bit much. We'll have to share. Think you can manage that?"

he challenged, implying so much more than sharing a box at the theater.

Like sharing his name. Because as man and wife, they wouldn't need two separate boxes but one. Catherine's words had implied as much, and Quin wasn't about to let her get away with such an implication without pouncing on it.

Catherine regarded him flirtatiously. "I find I can share when motivated."

Quin remarked with a pleased tone, "Challenge accepted." He crossed his arms and pressed back against the carriage seat.

Mrs. Burke huffed loudly beside him, and he turned to see her disapproval in the thin line of her lips. But being a duke had its benefits; he knew she wouldn't dare reprimand him.

He turned again to Catherine. Certainly, he had no doubt Mrs. Burke would chastise her later, but Catherine could hold her own. Hadn't he seen it so many times before? It was one of the many aspects of her character that he loved.

She was more than just a lady. She was a great lady, in action and in word.

She was his own Catherine the Great.

"You know…" He leaned forward again. "You're doing your name quite the service."

Catherine frowned. "How so?"

"Catherine the Great." He spoke with intention. "Patroness of the arts, philanthropist. Decisive, strong, a powerful leader in history—"

"I'm nothing of the sort." She all but snorted as she regarded him playfully.

"Oh?" he inquired. "You're providing the funds for the theater to continue, you're setting up an orphanage, and I know of few people who would dare cross you."

"You have no such problem," she returned.

"I know you quite well, and I can remember several times I've had my own setdowns from your mouth," he reminded her.

She twisted her lips. "You give me too much credit."

"You perhaps do not give yourself enough."

She gave an inarticulate groan. "Well, I do not have several lovers, nor have I been married to an emperor."

"Perhaps that isn't a similarity you need to replicate," Quin corrected. "You were engaged to a duke." As he spoke, he realized the words didn't bring the pain they once had. It was a portion of her past and a portion of his. Nothing could change that, nor should it. Wes was loved by them both, and while a jealous part of Quin wanted all of Catherine's affection for himself, he also realized it was quite poetic that they had both lost and found love together.

Catherine's scrutiny softened. "It was a lifetime ago." She then boldly reached across the carriage and touched his hand. "And it led me to you."

Propriety be damned, Quin wanted nothing more than to pull her forward by that delicate hand and kiss her senseless in the carriage before God and the devil (Mrs. Burke), but at that moment, the carriage came to a stop in front of the Greatheart residence. Reluctantly, Quin gave a disappointed half smile to Catherine, and rather than kiss her with his lips, he chose to do it with his words. "Indeed, it did, and I'm ever so thankful."

Mrs. Burke grumbled something as the footman opened the door.

Quin released Catherine's hand and alighted from the carriage, then held out his hand to assist her.

"Are you engaged for the remainder of the afternoon?" he asked as Catherine stepped from the carriage.

She turned to answer him. "What did you have in mind?"

Quin could think of several things, but none of them could be done under the watchful eye of Mrs. Burke. *Pity, that.* If only he could find a way to get Catherine away from the old crone.

"Why don't you pay a call at Wesley House? My mother would certainly love to see you."

Catherine inclined her head, clearly catching on to his ploy. "When?"

Quin shrugged. "Now?"

"Impatient, are you?"

"I blame you."

At this, she rolled her eyes, earning a huff of disapproval from Mrs. Burke, who was waiting beside her. Catherine ignored her and nodded. Quin said, "We can take my curricle. It's proper enough since it's open and will fit the two of us perfectly."

Catherine turned to Mrs. Burke. "You're dismissed."

With a haughty look, the dour chaperone disappeared into the house.

Catherine's amusement broke through and Quin released his pent-up humor as well, joining in her mirth. The curricle was soon brought forth, and he held out his hand to help Catherine step into the large-wheeled, two-seated frame. She moved over to the right on the bench seat, and he followed her in, then settled beside her.

Her leg pressed tightly against his, following the length with her own, the heat from her kindling to the flame already burning bright within him. The footman handed up the ribbons, and Quin gripped them in hand as he gave a snap across the horses' backs, commanding the matched bays to move.

The curricle rolled forward, and as they passed through the gate onto the street, Catherine relaxed her tense shoulders.

"It's like tasting freedom." She leaned into the slight breeze.

"She is rather like a tyrant," Quin agreed, referring to Mrs. Burke. "At least I can give you a respite from her watchful eyes by trading it for the curious observation of all of London's speculation as we ride through the streets together." He waved a hand as they passed a few ladies on a stroll, punctuating his point.

"I'm thankful." Catherine closed her eyes as she raised her face to the sunshine. "And thank you for coming today."

"I wouldn't have missed it," he said truthfully. "If you need assistance with the orphanage, I'm happy to help, but if you'd rather do it on your own, I understand."

"I have the generalities figured out. It's the details. And I'd like your assistance, so thank you for offering." She turned to him.

"Rather than just telling you?"

"Yes, exactly."

They rode in comfortable silence as they rounded the bend and then made the short trek to Wesley House. As Quin pulled into the semicircular drive, the footmen came forward to hold the horses and help Catherine alight.

He followed, and soon he was leading her to the entrance. "Is my mother at home?" he inquired of the butler.

"Not yet, Your Grace. Shall I have her find you when she arrives?"

Quin could feel Catherine's attention on his back. "Yes, we'll take tea in the ivory parlor in the meantime." As he led Catherine to the sitting room, he was careful to keep the door to the parlor wide open.

He gestured for her to take a seat. She did so, then leaned forward slightly. "You knew your mother wasn't home."

Quin shrugged. "Is that so terrible?"

"No. Not at all."

Quin's chest swelled with joy at her words. "And I'd be happy to show you the library once we finish tea, just in case you need more books." He waggled a brow daringly, hinting at their first kiss.

"You know…" She lowered her chin. "You're full of brilliant ideas today."

"Just today?"

She shrugged. "A gentleman's sense of self can be ever so fragile." She grinned unrepentantly at her flirtatious barb.

"Is that the way you wish to play it? Very well, you've been warned." He nodded at the maid as she set down a tea service on the table between them.

He turned to Catherine as she poured their tea, noting the way her eyes narrowed in challenge. It was fun to spar with her; she never ceased to come armed to a battle of wits.

Quin lifted his teacup in salute to Catherine. "You're silent, which I find terrifying. What devious plans are you hatching?"

"None I will share before they are ready, but you'll know"—she took a dainty sip of tea, her face a mask of innocence—"when you encounter them."

"You'll not fool me," Quin replied.

"Challenge accepted," she promised, returning his earlier words.

They finished their tea, and after Quin set his cup on the table, he stood, offering his hand to her. "Care to escape to the library?"

"Right now, anywhere is an escape!" Catherine stated with delight.

Quin led her from the salon and down the hall to the library, his heart pounding with anticipation. The salon was far more frequented by servants, leaving no place to steal a moment alone. But the library... He had a new appreciation for its size and shelving. Who would have thought a library could be the ideal location for tasting love? Of course, it was amusing that the place where he'd always found solace would also be where he first found love. Life was nothing if not ironic at times. The fates truly had a sense of humor.

He opened the door wide for Catherine and resisted the urge to close it after they entered. He wouldn't risk Catherine's reputation in that way.

"Did you ever finish those books you borrowed?" Quin inquired as Catherine walked ahead of him, her fingers brushing the spines of the tomes lining the wall as if touching the books allowed her a momentary escape.

He understood the sentiment.

"Not all of them. I've been a little preoccupied." She looked over her shoulder. "But I will."

He quickened his steps and came up behind her. He reached out, grasped her hand, and led her to the left behind a small border of shelves that made a small alcove. He nodded to the shelf at eye level and gently caressed the spine of a reddish leather-bound book with gold lettering. *Gulliver's Travels.* "This one is my favorite."

Catherine turned her full attention to the shelves, her gloved fingers skimming the spines as she read through the titles. "You like Byron?"

"He's a fascinating individual," Quin commented. Catherine had turned her back to him as she continued. Her head angled just enough to expose the curve of her neck, and Quin couldn't look away. It called to him like a siren on the seas. Reaching out, he swept a stray curl from her shoulder. He hesitated when she froze then slowly rotated her head to meet his gaze. The hazel of her eyes was endless as her lips bent upward.

It wasn't a wide and playful expression.

No. It was the kind of small tip of her bow-curved lips that had invited him to touch her in his dreams. It was the sultry whisper of daring similar to a fine brandy and just as intoxicating. She arched her neck ever so slightly. She had removed a book, and as she placed it back in its slot, Quin traced his hand down her spine to her hip and pulled her backward, meeting her halfway with a step forward. The scent of roses flooded his senses as he bent his nose to the tender curve below her ear and placed a lingering kiss there, his body humming with energy. Her soft curves pressed into his hard planes, and the effect had his blood pounding hot through his veins.

She whispered his name.

He caressed his lips against her soft skin, savoring the moment.

It wasn't often that one's dream became a reality.

And he wasn't going to rush.

# Thirty-one

*If I may venture to be frank, I would say about
myself that I was every inch a gentleman.*

—Catherine the Great

CATHERINE STRUGGLED TO KEEP HER BREATHING EVEN.
Wantonly, she pressed back into Quin's strength, his hand at her
hip like a brand as his fingers moved across her waist, then moved
forward, covering her belly and pulling her in toward him. It was
comforting yet deliriously erotic as she felt every line of his form
against hers. His lips were wicked against her skin, making her
needy and frantic for more than just a tender kiss.

Yet she didn't want any part of this to rush forward.

It was still new.

Delicate.

Catherine wanted to savor every nuance. She murmured his
name, tasting it on her lips. She bit down, suppressing a groan
of pleasure as Quin's other hand gripped her hip insistently, then
inched up her side, grazing the edge of her breast and causing her
to gasp at the pleasure of it.

"Not yet," he said softly against her neck.

She was about to make what would assuredly have been an
incoherent reply, but he twisted her hips, guiding her to turn
and face him, and before she could formulate the words, he was
devouring her lips with a kiss.

The power of it pinioned her back against the bookcase, his lips
nearly assaulting hers with a need that rocked her. Pressing in to

him, she tasted his desire on his lips and matched his power with her own as she ran her fingers up his arms and wove them though his hair, twisting her fingers around the strands, holding him captive in her arms.

He groaned against her lips and ran his fingers down her sides, spanning her hips, his fingers arching into her curves.

She pushed closer in toward him, needing to feel more of his body against hers, if that were possible. Yet it wasn't enough. Instinctively, she knew he could be closer, and she was hungry for it—greedy for whatever pleasure that could give. Heart racing, she melted into his embrace, gasping as his lips left hers and trailed down her jawline, nipping and tasting her skin. His kiss reached the hollow of her throat, and his hand arched upward from her waist, curving over the swell of her breast. His fingers traced over her sensitive flesh. She gasped, her body nearly combusting at the pleasure of his touch, however light. Even through her clothing, his hands were hot against her, creating so much pleasure that she gave a soft cry.

Quin's groan pierced her blissful haze, ragged and hot. His lips scorched her neck as he trailed kisses lower. His other hand reached behind her, pulling her closer in to him as he pressed a kiss to the curve of her breast just above her dress.

Catherine's gasp came in ragged pants as she gave herself over to the pleasure. He made her body sing with each touch, as if he were a master and she the instrument. His hand at her breast slowly released and retreated back to her hips, gripping her with almost punishing force. "Not yet," he whispered, his voice raw.

Catherine opened her eyes and met his eyes, lost in the green depths that swirled with passion. "Not yet?"

She swallowed, her throat dry. Her tongue darted out to lick her lips, her body reacting powerfully to the way Quin watched her movement with a hunger she echoed.

She'd never wanted anything as badly as she'd wanted him to

continue, to bring her to the fullness of the pleasure he tormented her with so mercilessly.

"But why?" she asked in a soft voice.

He kissed her, pulling back slightly and tugging on her lip playfully before returning to ravage her mouth. Abruptly, he pushed her away and answered her with fierce power in his expression. "Because I'm not going to take you in my library behind dusty old books, hurried and wondering if someone is going to walk in." His voice was rough, barely restrained as he ground out the words.

His hold on her gentled as he trailed his fingers from her shoulder to her fingers, twining them with his own. He lifted her hand to his lips, kissing it tenderly. His eyes closed, as if he was using the moment to master himself once more. As he lowered her hand, he opened his eyes to meet hers. Passion, restraint, and love swirled in their depths, beckoning her to get lost in them. With his other hand, he reached up and traced the outline of her jaw, rubbing a thumb over her lower lip. He leaned in, and she met him halfway.

Using their laced fingers as a tether, she pulled him close and lost herself in the scent, touch, and nearness of him. His kiss was soft, lingering, and sweet—achingly sweet. It touched her heart in a way she couldn't have anticipated. Soft breath fanned her lips as he withdrew only to cover her once more with a fresh kiss at a new angle. Lips tingling, she pressed in to him, squeezing his hand and nibbling playfully on his lower lip, unable to suppress the pure joy she felt.

"Your smile is my Achilles' heel. I swear it will be my undoing if you persist," Quin whispered against her curved lips. "There's nothing more beautiful, more provoking and disarming. It tempts me to be less of a gentleman, yet reminds me you deserve so much more." He kissed her again, lingering at her lips as if they were his air, water, and life.

Or maybe that was how it was for her. Maybe his kiss was her air, her water and life. It certainly felt that way. She wasn't able to think of anything but him: his kiss, his touch, and the near madness of wanting more. His words washed over her, settling in her heart and warming her from the inside out. With a soft flick of his tongue, he caressed her mouth with his own, rendering her senseless. Yet a moment later he withdrew slowly, and she followed him, seeking his kiss.

And then the words came in a soft verbal caress against her lips. "Marry me."

Her eyes flew open, and her countenance surely answered his question before she could. "Ah, is this the official proposal?"

Quin bent his head to the side, regarding her with a dangerous gleam in his eyes. "I'm happy to convince you, but yes, it is. You've been mine since the moment I kissed you in my waking dreams, but…" He boldly moved a hand up from its place on her hip and grasped her breast, his finger softly rounding its hard tip once more. "You deserve more than an understanding because I took your kisses. You deserve more… Will you have me?"

He caressed the soft sphere of her breast through the fabric of her dress. Gasping, she closed her eyes with the ecstasy of it. "That's not fair. I can't think when you touch me like that."

"All's fair in love and war."

Catherine swallowed. "You never said you love me." Her heart stuttered at the bold words, regarding him with the first sense of insecurity she'd felt since being in his arms. "Does that imply that it's war?" Her soft voice held none of the teasing she'd intended; rather, she just pressed herself against him, needy for more.

He chuckled once, the vibrations of it echoing through his chest and against her hands placed around his neck. "There's certainly a war going on, but not with you. It's within me." He rubbed his nose against hers. "It's reminding myself of what I said a moment ago about not taking you in the library. And believe me, it's a bloody war inside me because there's nothing I want more than you."

She closed her eyes, soaking in his voice.

"Catherine." He moaned her name, resting his head against hers as his heartbeat slowed a little. She could feel his heart pounding against hers, which echoed with its own fevered rhythm.

"I loved you before I even knew how to name it," he confessed. "And I've loved you more each passing day since. I dream of you, Catherine. I burn for you…"

Catherine's heart swelled at the way his voice rang with passion. His words consumed her like his kiss, and she felt her heart swell with such happiness she wondered how she'd bear it.

"Marry me." His fierce gaze burned through her with welcome heat.

Catherine kept her eyes downcast as she wondered at the beauty of the moment. "Yes." She met his intense expression with her heart in her eyes.

He kissed her then, hungry and joyful. She grinned against his lips, unable to restrain her joy. He pulled back and caressed her face.

"You haven't asked." She arched a brow, feeling playful, almost drunk with happiness.

"Asked what?" he inquired.

"If I love you." She tipped her chin upward flirtatiously.

"You do." He shrugged, confident.

She arched a brow. "You're so certain."

"Indeed, I am." He tapped her nose with his finger. "But you took longer."

At this, she narrowed her eyes, but then she sobered slightly. "There were…obstacles. And I wouldn't wish you to think I was after your title. So I regarded you as forbidden in my heart."

Quin nodded. "I had to overcome a variant of the same obstacle."

Catherine hesitated, and then as if he'd noted the way she seemed to debate about speaking, he nodded for her to continue.

Inhaling deeply, she pushed aside her trepidation. "I was engaged to your brother and I… That is… You need to know…" She struggled with expressing herself correctly. "I *loved* him." She hazarded a peek up to Quin. "But I *love* you. It's different, and I'm not sure how I can explain, but…"

Quin's finger touched her lips as she struggled for the right words. "I'm not jealous…much," he replied, a hint of chagrin coloring his tone.

Catherine gave a soft giggle at his playful confession.

"But, Catherine, I understand. I loved my brother too. And it was that loyalty to him that led me to you. We can be thankful rather than trying to explain it. Sometimes God brings things about in mysterious ways."

Catherine nodded, then leaned forward to kiss him, needing to feel his lips against hers, the power of his love feeding her soul. "I love you," she whispered. "I *love* you. And I can't imagine spending my life with anyone else."

She could taste his joy as he kissed her with the deep happiness that echoed in her own heart. With a final lingering kiss, he released her. A loose curl caressed her cheek, and he smoothed it behind her ear, his eyes alight with a wild abandon that set her heart to pounding.

"When?" she inquired. "How long till we can be married?"

Quin marveled. "Never before have I been so thankful for your impatient nature."

She swatted him playfully.

"There will be scandal if we marry too soon—"

At this, she gave her eyes an indelicate roll. "There will be scandal regardless. Consider the circumstances…"

"A very persuasive argument." He bobbed his head in agreement. "Then I shall see about going to Doctors' Commons to procure a special license."

Catherine couldn't restrain her joy, showing far too many teeth in her smile to be proper, but it couldn't be helped; she was too happy for anything but wild displays of joy.

Quin's answering grin filled her heart to overflowing. She pulled back for a moment, studying him. "Wait. What do you mean I took longer?"

He took a step back, then as if he couldn't stand the distance, reached out and grasped her hand. As if he needed to touch her.

"Exactly that." He shrugged, tugging her out from their little alcove in the library. He paused and tucked several strands of wayward curls behind her ears and caressed the outline of her bodice and then tugged it straighter, all while clearly impressed with his handiwork.

"How are you so certain?" Catherine asked, following his example and adjusting his cravat for him, careful not to wrinkle the neckcloth further. She bit her lip, realizing belatedly she had been quite aggressive with her hands. She smoothed the rather well-loved hair to the side and back of his head, trying to replicate his earlier tidiness.

"Is it a lost cause?" he asked, as if not caring a fig that he looked nearly accosted.

"I never thought of myself as quite so aggressive." Catherine's cheeks heated with a blush as she attempted in vain to smooth the damage.

Quin's robust merriment echoed in the library. Catherine covered his mouth with her fingers, and he reached up and grasped her hands, moving them so he could speak. "I'll be waylaid by you any day, love."

She gave up on trying to fix his disheveled appearance. "Do I look any better?"

"Somewhat. But I was rather careful." His lips were pressed together as if he was trying to restrain his amusement.

"Are you amused?"

"No," he replied, then couldn't deny it any longer. "Yes. Yes, but not because I'm making fun. Rather because it gives me so much pleasure to know I drove you to unawareness. You have no idea what that does to me." He murmured the last words and seared her lips with a kiss that left her burning from the inside out.

"Well, then, I suppose I can look past it this once," she said eagerly.

"How magnanimous of you." He earned a swat from Catherine before leading her toward the library's entrance.

"Oh! Finally. I was searching for you." The Duchess of Wesley bustled into the room just as they rounded the shelf between them and the door. She was thankfully at a distance so that Catherine had a moment to adjust her expression and calm her reaction.

Quin shot her a brief glance, widening his eyes slightly as if communicating that they'd ended their private moment none too early.

"Yes, how can we help you, Mother?" Quin asked.

"Well, I was told you want to speak to *me*." She cocked her head to the side as if evaluating them, her eyes narrowing slightly.

"Yes, we need to ask you about a very important upcoming event." Quin's expression turned quite serious, and Catherine wondered just what he was going to tell his mother. At first, she thought he was going to tell her about their engagement, but his expression made her hesitate. As the thought flickered through her mind, she noted the way his lips twitched as if he was restraining his real emotions.

"I see. Well, carry on." The Duchess of Wesley's voice was slightly suspicious, and Catherine noted the way she studied the two of them, back and forth as if trying to ascertain what Quin was referring to before he spoke the words.

"First, I have to admit something that is very difficult for me." Quin placed his hand over his heart.

The Duchess of Wesley's suspicious expression deepened as she arched a brow. "Heaven only knows what that will be."

"You were right." He nodded soberly, though Catherine could see his lips were pinched from holding in his amusement.

At this confession, the Duchess of Wesley frowned in confusion. She recovered quickly and then agreed. "Well, that's not surprising."

"I thought you'd feel that way," he answered, his tone full of humor.

"About what in particular am I right?" she inquired.

Catherine turned to Quin, her heart full as she awaited his answer. "I love her. And Lady Catherine Greatheart has agreed to be my duchess."

The Duchess of Wesley studied the two of them, and then hurried forward with wide arms. "I knew it!" She rushed toward them, grasped their intertwined hands, and squeezed tightly. "I knew it. I knew it from that first dinner when you were here and Quin couldn't keep his eyes from you," she gushed. "You were meant to be a part of our family, my love."

She lowered her eyes, but Catherine thought she saw the shine of tears brimming.

"You know what it is to lose someone you love." She turned her attention to her soon-to-be daughter-in-law, confirming Catherine's earlier observation about her teary eyes.

Hot tears prickled Catherine's eyes as well as she listened intently to the Duchess of Wesley.

"I never weep." She sniffed, wiping a tear. "But I will say that loss can teach more about love and gratitude than anything else I know of, and that is a blessing you bring. I know you cared for Avery"—the Duchess of Wesley took a calming sniff—"and I'm thankful you care for Quin."

Catherine was going to interject that she *loved* Quin, but the Duchess of Wesley wasn't done, so Catherine waited.

"The day I lost Avery…I also lost you, or so I thought. I was so thrilled to have a daughter-in-law. Sons are all well and good." She waved her hand in Quin's direction. "But I was looking forward to having you in the family as well. And now"—she hitched a shoulder—"I get to keep you too." She turned to Quin and cupped his chin in her hand. "I love you, Son. You've made a good choice."

"I think she's taking the news well." Quin turned to Catherine as his mother released her hold on his chin.

"At least we don't have to talk her into it," Catherine answered.

"So, a wedding!" The Duchess of Wesley stepped back, clapping her hands and then touching her lips as if holding back all the things she wished to say at once, trying to discern which was most important.

"We were thinking a special—"

"*Don't* you say 'special license,'" the Duchess of Wesley warned, her brows raised high on her forehead.

"License," Quin finished.

"What is your suggestion, Your Grace?" Catherine asked.

The Duchess of Wesley began to pace. "There will be talk. After all, you are marrying the brother of the man you were engaged to…"

Catherine wondered just how many times that very phrase was going to be circulated before they heard the end of it. If that was the price to pay, she'd happily pay it, but it did grate against her nerves, true as it might be. It implied she was marrying Quin for reasons other than love.

"Let me think," the Duchess of Wesley said. "Have you said anything to anyone else?"

Quin smirked. "It's quite recent."

The Duchess of Wesley nodded. "Let's keep it quiet for a day or two till I figure out the details and what will be best. Do you mind?"

Quin turned to Catherine.

"I would like to speak to my grandmother," she said.

"Oh, dear, of course! I'm talking about announcing it to the world. Maybe wait on that."

"In that case, I can be patient for a few days, if you think it will help."

"Well, it will help me consider the angles. It's a tricky situation, and I wish to give you the best start with the least amount of gossip. Of course, people will talk, but let's keep it to a minimum, you know?"

Catherine nodded. She honestly didn't care what people thought, but she did care about Quin and the Duchess of Wesley, and if they could make the news less scandalous, it would be a benefit for all of them.

"Good, very good. Catherine, I'll call on you tomorrow, and I'll bring Quin so you won't need your nasty chaperone hovering and listening in."

"Lovely," Catherine answered from the heart.

"And you..." The Duchess of Wesley turned to Quin. "Take her home, make sure all is well, and come back. We have much to discuss and organize."

Quin nodded, his expression utterly unrepentant.

The Duchess of Wesley tapped her lips, thinking. Then, "I'll bid you good afternoon, sweet Catherine. I'm ever so happy." She spoke grandly, then bustled out of the room, calling for the butler and a maid.

"And so it begins," Quin murmured. He turned to Catherine. "Are you at peace with what my mother suggested, truly? Because you know I will kidnap you and take you to Gretna Green tonight if you wish." He pulled her in tight against him, kissing her lips softly.

"Is that an option?" she asked playfully, then leaned into his kiss.

"It's a very viable option."

Catherine kissed him for a moment. "No, let's make this as scandal-free as possible. I keep thinking of my grandmother. She wouldn't wish for any more talk. It will only be to our benefit and to our children's too. No questions asked."

Quin sobered, studying her eyes. "Say that again."

"What part?" Catherine teased.

"Our children! Good Lord, Catherine. I can't go there. But I want a little girl who looks like you, and we shall name her Trouble."

Catherine swatted at him. "We shall not name here anything like that."

"A nickname then." He kissed her.

Catherine pushed away. "Then hurry up and let's get this figured out so we can start on that…" She nibbled his lip.

"I'm tempted to start right now, but if I do, I won't let you out of my sight ever again, so that might not be conducive to our plans."

"Pity, that," Catherine said, baiting him. "Take me home. I need to tell my grandmother. She will be quite pleased. She's always liked you."

Quin studied her with a fiery regard, but he took a step back as if needing the distance to cool his body.

"If I must."

"Thankfully, it's only temporary."

"If I have anything to say about it, *very* temporary."

# Thirty-two

*For to tempt and to be tempted are things very nearly allied... Whenever feeling has anything to do in the matter, no sooner is it excited than we have already gone vastly farther than we are aware of.*

—*Catherine the Great*

CATHERINE PEEKED INTO HER GRANDMOTHER'S ROOM, HER heart soaring at the welcome sight. The evening sun was beaming into the room with a gold and orange hue that illuminated her grandmother's form sitting in the chair and holding a small teacup in her petite hands.

"Ducky?"

Catherine couldn't restrain the tears that spilled down her cheeks at the sound of the woman's voice calling her pet name. "Yes," she blubbered, sniffing back the tears.

"Don't be like that. I'm well, see?" Lady Greatheart gave a somewhat shaky gesture to herself, and then sipped her tea.

"I'm so glad." Catherine stepped into the room and approached her grandmother, taking a seat beside her. "You're improving so much." It seemed as if every time she saw her, she lost her composure, but it was just so powerfully relieving to see her grandmother, to hear her voice.

"I'm too stubborn to die. God doesn't want me yet. He knows He has to deal with me in heaven forever, so He's biding His time till I get there," her grandmother answered with a hint of her usual pluck.

Catherine reached out and grasped her free hand, holding it gently and savoring the touch, letting it feed her soul.

"So, how was your afternoon?" Lady Greatheart asked, her tone still weak but growing stronger by the day.

Catherine noted that while she was stouter, her grandmother still looked tired. Her ordinarily bright eyes were dull from fatigue, and her usually impeccable posture was still hunched, but her spirit? That was fully back and with a vengeance.

"My afternoon was…eventful," Catherine answered honestly, considering all she'd actually done that day, especially the highlight of Quin's proposal.

"Oh?" This apparently piqued her grandmother's curiosity because she set down her teacup on the side table and turned fully to her granddaughter.

"Indeed." Catherine debated telling her grandmother the best news first or lead into it.

Yet as she considered her options, she had the sobering thought of how short life could be and she decided to start with the most important news.

"Well, you have another reason to be here a little longer," Catherine answered as she traced the lines of her grandmother's hand.

"Oh? Do I need another reason?" her grandmother asked.

"No, but I rather think you'll like this reason." Catherine hazarded a peek at her grandmother, who was studying her.

"Did Quin finally come up to scratch?"

"While I'm sure he would appreciate your sentiment, he didn't need much of a fire lit under him. And yes, he did propose." Catherine couldn't restrain her reaction any longer as her grandmother perked up with understanding.

"Good Lord! Well, that is good news! I always liked the boy. He's been lost on you for a while now. I wondered if he'd ever get around to telling you." She shook her head. "So that's my additional reason to keep alive and kicking?"

"Well, I was thinking specifically about seeing your great-grandchildren, but there are really about a million reasons."

Lady Greatheart's expression narrowed. "And just when can I expect these grandchildren…"

"Good mercy." Catherine rolled her eyes. "Not yet."

"Good, it's always the quiet ones you have to watch out for," her grandmother muttered.

"Pardon?"

"Quin…it wouldn't surprise me…and honestly I don't put much more faith in you either. Anticipating your vows does rather complicate things—"

"Grandmother!" Catherine interjected.

"What? It's true."

Catherine stuttered, unsure what to say.

"Never you mind, ducky. Do you love him?"

Catherine's answering look spoke for her.

"Whew, yes. You should marry quickly. Just to keep from the larger scandal of grandbabies before their time." She gave an enthusiastic little clap.

"I love him so much." Catherine's eyes burned with the power of it as a tear trailed down her cheek. "It's so strong, sometimes I can hardly handle it."

Lady Greatheart reached out and grasped Catherine's cheek. "I'm glad you're not settling for anything less."

Catherine leaned into her grandmother's warm hand. "The Duchess of Wesley is coming tomorrow to discuss the details. She was quite pleased as well."

"I can only imagine. She lost more than a son. She lost you, too, in a way."

"She said something like that."

"And now she has you back. She's going to be a force to be reckoned with. That woman is one of my favorites." Her grandmother nodded as if emphasizing her words. "I'm glad she will address the details. I would, but I know my limits, and they are short right now, ducky."

As if validating her words, Lady Greatheart closed her eyes and relaxed back against the chair.

"I'll help you get to your bed. Where's your maid?"

"Poor dear, she's barely left my side. I gave her an hour to herself. She'll be here soon."

"Well, let's move you." Catherine helped her grandmother stand and then supported her as they took the slow steps to her bed.

"Ah." Lady Greatheart exhaled softly as she lay into her pillow. "I wish I wasn't so tired all the bloody time."

Catherine bit her lip with amusement at her grandmother's vulgar word and tucked her into the bedcovers. "Sleep. I'll be back in the morning."

"I love you, and I'm so happy for you."

Catherine cupped her grandmother's cheek and kissed it. "I love you more."

Catherine tiptoed from the room, and as she opened the door, she startled, noticing Mrs. Burke walking down the hall at a hurried pace.

"Good evening!" Catherine called, curious why her chaperone was so close to Lady Greatheart's room.

"Good evening," Mrs. Burke answered with a quick curtsy, then continued on her way and disappeared down the stairs.

Frowning, Catherine watched her retreat. Her stomach rumbled slightly, reminding her of the time, and she headed to her rooms. It had been a lovely, busy, and glorious day. She wanted to bask in her own private thoughts and joy.

As she arrived at her room, she bid her maid help her change into a more comfortable day dress and ordered her dinner brought up. Tomorrow was another busy day; she'd be meeting with Bircham regarding his investment idea and then would host the Duchess of Wesley and Quin to plan her wedding.

The rest of the evening, her smile never left her face.

And as she finally fell into a dream-filled sleep, that same glow of happiness echoed the soul-deep joy that she'd found.

And it was enough.

It was more.

It was everything.

And it lingered through her morning ministrations and through breakfast. Even the presence of Mrs. Burke in the parlor as Catherine awaited the arrival of Lord Bircham couldn't dampen her joy. The silent sentinel had actually smiled at her over her needlepoint.

It was truly a day when miracles could happen, Catherine thought. The maid brought in a tea service, and Catherine poured for herself, then offered tea to Mrs. Burke.

"No, thank you," the woman replied, her lips twitching.

It was curious, seeing her joyful twice in one morning. Catherine turned to her own teacup and wondered just what had happened in the past day to lift Mrs. Burke's spirits so much.

Brooks entered the parlor then, bowing and announcing the arrival of Lord Bircham.

Catherine nodded her welcome. "Tea?" she offered, watching as the gentleman strode in, silver-tipped cane in hand.

"Good afternoon, yes. I thank you." He set his cane to the side of the sofa and took a seat, giving an acknowledging nod to Mrs. Burke.

Catherine poured Lord Bircham a cup of tea and then took her seat again, picking up her own teacup once more. "I had the opportunity to review the investment you suggested."

She watched his reaction as she spoke the words. He took a sip of his tea, then nodded to her, waiting. "And?"

Catherine set her cup in its saucer and regarded her cousin. "It seems a viable option." Then she added, "Thank you for suggesting it."

Lord Bircham opened his mouth, paused, then continued, "I'm pleased you approve."

"How did you hear of it?"

Lord Bircham set his cup aside as well, then leaned forward slightly. "I have a friend from Eton who started the company. I've been investing in it for years, and it's given me a great return. I wanted to invite you to have the same benefit."

Catherine nodded. "I didn't realize you were so connected with the company."

"I thought it unnecessary information. My personal investment doesn't affect the company much."

"But I still would have liked to know."

"Would that have changed your mind? Or your research?" Lord Bircham asked, as he lifted his teacup.

Catherine answered, "No." He had a point.

"Besides, I–I don't feel we have started off well. Your suspicions are understandable." He sipped his tea. "By my way of thinking, if you knew of my personal investment, you'd be less likely to approve of it yourself, based solely on the knowledge that I approved."

"That's a rather spiteful accusation," Catherine warned, but she also silently agreed with his words.

"Is it wrong?" he asked.

Catherine debated how to address the question. She had been frank from the beginning, so she decided to continue with that same honesty. "No. You're absolutely right. I'm hesitant to admit such a thing to you since you've made it abundantly clear you think little of my intelligence and opinion."

Lord Bircham paused in setting down his cup and regarded her for a moment before finishing his task. "I see."

"Do you?" Catherine remarked, arching a brow.

Lord Bircham had the good sense to appear abashed. "You're correct, and I...have been mistaken. You've proven yourself wise and discerning. True, it's more than I anticipated, but I'm not so boorish that I can't amend my opinion."

Catherine regarded him, testing his expression for authenticity. Seeing nothing that left her suspicions of his ulterior motive, she nodded. "Thank you."

He nodded.

Mrs. Burke passed by as she walked to the door of the parlor, offering a soft excuse as she ducked out into the hall and closing the door behind her.

"Strange," Catherine muttered, then turned to Lord Bircham.

"She has a good heart. You'd do better to give her a chance," he remarked.

"Lord Bircham, you'll find I take advice far better when it's solicited or offered without a condescending pitch." Catherine's ire was rising.

He nodded. "Very well. Good Lord, I've never met a more opinionated lady," he stated. "Mrs. Burke is a fine chaperone and far kinder than you seem to think. It might be in your best interest to give her a chance." He waved his hand as if tossing the words to the middle of the sparring ring, offering them for criticism.

"Thank you," Catherine replied. "I will admit that she has been oddly friendly this morning. I'm not sure why…"

Brooks knocked on the door and then opened it, casting a warning expression to Lord Bircham as he did so. "My lady, His Grace and the Duchess of Wesley have arrived and wish to speak to you. They say it's urgent." He regarded Lord Bircham with distrust, clearly wondering if he was divulging too much information.

Catherine frowned, then turned to Lord Bircham. "If you don't mind, I believe we'll conclude our meeting."

"Of course, I understand." He stood.

"And Brooks, please show them in," Catherine requested.

The butler disappeared.

Lord Bircham lifted his cane and bowed. "It's my hope that

whatever urgent business needs to be discussed isn't anything too serious. If you need my assistance, you know where to find me." He paused, then bit his lip with suppressed humor. "I believe that now that we understand each other, you will have less hesitation in the future."

Catherine smiled in return, but was preoccupied with whatever news was forthcoming from Quin and the Duchess of Wesley. "Of course."

"Good day." He started toward the door, bowing to the Duchess of Wesley and Quin as they started to enter.

"You bastard!" Quin swore in a low voice, and before Lord Bircham could question the epithet, Quin reared back and gave a roundhouse punch to Bircham's gut, dropping the man to the floor.

"Quin!" Catherine rushed forward, wondering what could have happened to create such a reaction in Quin.

"Leave him," the Duchess of Wesley murmured softly, coming to stand beside Catherine.

"Which one?" Catherine asked, taking a step forward.

"Both." The Duchess of Wesley shook her head, and Catherine turned to regard her, studying her expression for the first time. Wide eyes and tension lined the woman's expression.

"What in the bloody—" Lord Bircham started.

"Don't pretend—" Quin's words were stalled by the kick he swiftly dispatched to Bircham's gut as he tried to stand.

Catherine moved forward, not wanting to see Quin brought to the constable for accosting another peer of the realm. "Quin, what is going on?" she asked, entreating him with her tone.

Quin flicked his attention to her, his expression fierce, then lowered his focus to the floor. "You tell her." Quin nudged the man on the floor with his boot. "Tell her what you've done."

Catherine turned her attention to Lord Bircham. "Explain yourself."

Lord Bircham coughed, reaching up to wipe the corner of his mouth and smearing blood across his chin. "Good God, man. What is the meaning of this?"

Quin scoffed at the question, his lips twisting in disgust. "I'll ask once more—"

"Stop, please." Bircham lifted his hands in surrender, not moving to stand, clearly afraid that any sudden movement would set off the quite-furious duke standing over him.

"Explain." Quin bit out the word, his tone as cutting as a shard of glass.

Lord Bircham's eyes were wide as he seemed to debate what course of action to take. He was saved by the entrance of Brooks.

To the butler's credit, he looked dubiously at the lord on the floor and gave his full attention to Catherine. "My lady, did you give Mrs. Burke permission to travel back to Cambridge?"

Catherine frowned. "Mrs. Burke has left London?"

Brooks nodded.

"Are you certain?"

"Yes, in a hackney coach just a half hour ago. A footman just reported assisting her into the coach. I was attending to other duties and didn't see her leave. Once I was aware, I came to you directly."

"And she was leaving for Cambridge?" Quin asked Brooks, his words deathly smooth.

"That is what the footman overheard, Your Grace." The butler bowed as he spoke, offering deference to the duke's high rank.

"Bloody hell." Quin rubbed the back of his neck as he swore. He concentrated on the floor for several seconds and then fixed his stare on Bircham. "I may have been mistaken."

Bircham gave him a wary expression.

"Why would she leave?" Catherine asked, turning to the Duchess of Wesley, who had been oddly silent through the whole exchange.

"I think I know," she replied, meeting her son's gaze.

Catherine looked from one to the other. "And?"

"I think we had best sit down," Quin clipped, then turned to Lord Bircham, offering him a hand. "I believe I'm going to owe you an apology, unless you knew she was abandoning ship."

"Mrs. Burke?" Bircham inquired, then took Quin's outstretched hand tentatively.

Quin nodded and helped the gentleman to stand.

"No, I didn't give her leave to go home, if that's what you're asking." Bircham tugged on his coat and cuffs, adjusting himself, though it was a lost cause. The man's once-crisp white shirt was wrinkled and splattered with blood.

"What is the meaning of all this?" Catherine asked, hoping to find some answers. It was madness.

Quin motioned to his mother, and the Duchess of Wesley took a seat, then began. "This morning I had an early caller, wishing me congratulations on your engagement."

Catherine frowned. "Why is that a problem? I know we were going to wait to tell—"

"Engagement to Lord Bircham," the Duchess of Wesley answered.

Catherine's blood went cold, then hot as she turned angry eyes to Lord Bircham, who suddenly was clearly not bloody enough for her taste.

"What?" Lord Bircham finished dusting off a sleeve and regarded the Duchess of Wesley with open confusion.

"We assumed you put forth the information, but the rather sudden disappearance of Mrs. Burke is very suspect," Quin said. "Based on the information we were given, you can understand my righteous frustration toward you."

Lord Bircham paused. "I see." Then, as if deciding to pardon Quin's behavior, he relaxed his shoulders slightly. "No. I didn't say anything of the sort. It was a thought at first, but it's quite clear that

Lady Catherine and I do not see eye to eye on…well, anything." He gave a slight shrug, then seemed to wince at the movement.

"Why—… How?" Catherine questioned, stunned.

"It's worse," the Duchess of Wesley continued with chilling calm. "Lady Kirkham revealed the news and said that it was a marriage that was…required. Saying the chaperone hired by Lord Bircham hadn't been diligent, leaving the two of you alone…"

"So the London *ton* thinks Lord Bircham compromised me," Catherine replied, her tone lifeless.

And to think a few hours ago she'd been wondering what kind of scandal it would cause to marry the brother of her deceased fiancé. That seemed small in comparison to being compromised by a man she could hardly stand.

"What do we do?" Catherine asked, turning imploring eyes to Quin, then to the Duchess of Wesley.

"Well…first, you…" He turned to Lord Bircham. "Are you going to set the record straight?"

Lord Bircham nodded. "I'm not sure how much it will help, but I'll do what I can."

"It's true. Often the scandalous news is believed, regardless of how inaccurate." The Duchess of Wesley frowned. "Thankfully, for now it's just a rumor. With Mrs. Burke gone, there will be great speculation about the claim's validity. That's our best ally right now."

Catherine's body tingled with the stress of it all. She turned to Quin. "I'm marrying you." She spoke the words with a conviction that was stronger than her fear, and some of the tension melted away.

"Damn right you are," Quin agreed. Then as if coming to some conclusion, he strode forward and grasped Catherine's waist, pulling her close as his lips seared hers, surprising her with a passionate kiss that melted what remained of the tension left in her heart. She wrapped her arms around his neck and snuggled into his embrace, kissing him back with all the love in her heart, needing to feel him close, reminding her very being that she belonged to him, and he to her.

Quin released her slowly, then pulled back. "If anyone asks, I'm the one who did the compromising." He touched her face softly, then turned to Lord Bircham. "Understood?"

"I don't think such information will be necessary, especially with Mrs. Burke missing, but if so, I'll be sure to tell others what I've…seen," he added, clearly uncomfortable. "Though I do have one question."

The Duchess of Wesley motioned for him to continue. Quin slowly released his tight hold on Catherine's waist and pivoted her so that they could both face Lord Bircham.

"Go on," Quin encouraged.

"The question is why?" Lord Bircham frowned, his slightly bloody lip swollen from Quin's assault. "Why would Mrs. Burke spread such a rumor? Motive, we're missing a motive. Not that I want to add anything to incriminate myself, but honestly, I'm the only one who would benefit by such an alliance, minus the fact that I'd be at constant war with Lady Catherine." He gave her a nod of honesty, as if asking her to disregard what could be otherwise insulting.

"No offense taken," Catherine said, lifting a hand.

"Thank you," Lord Bircham replied. "But you see what I'm asking?" He turned his attention to Quin.

"Indeed." Quin's hold tightened slightly on her waist, but Catherine wanted more answers. "How did you find Mrs. Burke? How do you know of her?"

Lord Bircham revealed an interesting fact. "She is my aunt, my mother's twin sister."

The Duchess of Wesley nodded. "I see, so an alliance between you and Lady Catherine could benefit her if you are her benefactor…"

Lord Bircham addressed the statement. "If I were her sole means of support, that would be true, but while she isn't wealthy, her husband left her more than enough." He seemed ashamed of the last part, as if unwilling to admit such a truth. "Her late husband was in trade and did well enough."

Catherine watched as Quin frowned. "Hmm, something's missing. Some detail we don't have."

"It would seem so, but in any case we need to take action to fix this," the Duchess of Wesley insisted. "We have the word of a lord against the word of a missing chaperone, but we need more."

"She went back to Cambridge?" Catherine pondered, her mind formulating a plan.

"Yes," Brooks confirmed, and Catherine suppressed a gasp of surprise. She'd forgotten he hadn't left the room.

"Thank you," she answered. "If we're missing a piece of the puzzle, then maybe it's there."

"You're not going to Cambridge," Quin said in a tight voice.

Catherine focused her attention on him, arching a brow. "If unraveling the mystery means I can marry you without further scandal, I think that travel to Cambridge would be desirable."

"Take Morgan and Joan," the Duchess of Wesley interjected.

Quin shot his mother a glare.

"Don't give me that look. She can't very well go with you— or him." She jabbed a thumb in Lord Bircham's direction. "If she leaves with you, it will look like she's running off to avoid him, and that will only feed the fire."

Quin thought it over.

"As much as it goes against the grain, I do see your logic. And while I might balk at a lady taking on such an activity, I think you'll agree with me when I say that Lady Catherine isn't the sort to back down from anything," Lord Bircham said in deference to Catherine.

"Is that a compliment?" Catherine asked.

"If you wish to take it as one, be my guest."

Facing Catherine, Quin studied her for a moment. "I don't like the plan, but if there's anything to be found in Cambridge that will help unwind the problem, Morgan can find it. Joan's presence will keep you respectable as you travel, and continuing with what seems like natural travel plans with friends will lend inauthenticity to the gossip, especially if Bircham and I remain in London." He cast a confirming peek at Bircham, who showed his agreement.

"I'll remain in London, and better yet, let us be seen at White's together. I'll congratulate you on your engagement." Lord Bircham paused. "You are, in fact, promised to one another, correct?"

"Yes," Quin answered directly.

"Then celebration is in order."

The Duchess of Wesley agreed. "This just might work. And if it works well, we might not need to know all the reasons..."

"I want to know," Catherine insisted. "Mrs. Burke has had a plan from the beginning. I'm sure of it. I don't want that hanging over me as I move forward."

"Agreed." Quin addressed Lord Bircham: "I apologize for my earlier behavior. You've been of great assistance in this current situation. Thank you."

Lord Bircham lifted a hand. "I can overlook it, given the information you had and your engagement to Lady Catherine."

"Much obliged." After the two men clasped hands, Quin returned his attention to Catherine. "Just when I have the full expectation of spending time with you, travel takes you away. I must say, I've never harbored ill feelings for my home—"

"Your home! That will be splendid!" the Duchess of Wesley interrupted, clapping her hands.

"Pardon?" Quin inquired.

"Lady Catherine will stay in your town house in Cambridge. It will lend truth to the story."

Quin gave his approval. "I see. Brilliant. And if I cannot be there with you, it does soothe me slightly to know you'll be in my house."

"If you'll excuse me, it seems as if there is a working plan, and I wish to clean up." Lord Bircham grasped his cane. "You will, of course, know where to find me if you need further information or assistance."

"Yes, thank you," Catherine said.

Quin inclined his head with approval, and Lord Bircham bowed as he departed, giving a wary glance to Brooks, who watched him carefully then followed him.

Catherine turned to Quin. "Well, this is not how I was expecting today to proceed."

Quin agreed heartily. "Nor I."

"At least we have a plan, and it should work fine. We're catching it early, and that's what matters," the Duchess of Wesley said. "You carried yourself quite well, Quin," his mother added, then turned her focus to Catherine. "I was concerned a fistfight wouldn't be the end, and he'd demand satisfaction."

Catherine was alarmed. Duels were illegal, even for a duke.

"It didn't come to that." Quin squeezed her waist. "Nothing is going to stop me from marrying you." His expression was as fierce as his tone.

Catherine's insides melted, and she pressed in to his side. "There's always Gretna Green," she said temptingly.

"Heavens, that's just what we need right now." The Duchess of Wesley gave an indelicate roll of her eyes. Apparently, the stress of the situation had negated the need for ladylike behavior.

Quin stifled his entertained reaction to his mother's theatrics, then looked at Catherine. She drank it in, smiling even as she knew the road ahead wasn't going to be easy.

Nothing worth fighting for was easy.

Her future with Quin was worth it.

# Thirty-three

QUIN'S HEARTBEAT HAD FINALLY CALMED TO A SLOWER, MORE rational pace as the minutes stretched on. Lord Bircham's departure had further soothed his tension, and he kept his attention on Catherine.

As much as he wanted to disregard the opinion of other peers of the realm, it was in Catherine's best interest to not enter into marriage with black marks that would make her the object of gossip for years ahead.

He loved her too much to put her through that because he was impatient. She was worth the wait. Even if every moment was torture. He'd been burning for her for months. He'd burn for longer if he must. Love was like that. He'd read about it, heard about it, and even seen it in his parents' relationship, but he'd never expected to experience it himself.

"Quin?" Catherine's voice broke through his reverie. She made him happy, complete, whole.

Her soft regard was like a warm blanket, soothing his soul. "Good Lord, I love you," she whispered. "Don't stop looking at me like that, ever. When I'm older than my grandmother, still look at me that way."

"I promise," Quin responded, then kissed her forehead gently.

"Will you come with me to my grandmother's room? I told her yesterday."

Quin nodded. "If you think she's well enough for a visit, then of course."

Catherine's answer warmed him. "If you'll excuse me, I'll go and check on her first."

"I'll be here."

Catherine excused herself and left the room.

"I can't tell you the joy I have watching the two of you," his mother said as he caught the last glimpse of Catherine disappearing down the hall.

Quin turned to his mother.

"Truly, it fills my heart. I… That is, there was just so much sorrow. You understand. I didn't see any hope. You were so broken." The Duchess of Wesley spoke with a trembling voice. "And I wasn't much better. I'm sure Catherine also was hurting so deeply. Isn't it lovely how the pain that surrounded us all actually ended up bringing us together to heal?"

"It's quite amazing," Quin agreed. "I've thought of it that way as well."

The Duchess of Wesley lifted a shoulder in a half shrug. "I know they say that time heals, but I don't think that's true. I think relationships heal people."

"Look at you, getting wise in your old age," Quin replied, touched by his mother's words.

"Wise and sentimental. Good mercy, I never thought I'd be a watering pot, but the past two days have proven me a ninny."

"With good reason. They've been mostly happy tears. I think you deserve a few of those after all the heartbroken tears you've shed in the past years." Quin moved to stand beside his mother. He grasped her hands and pressed them against his heart.

"Thank you." She released his grasp and withdrew a hanky.

A maid walked into the room as his mother was dabbing her eyes and bid them to follow her to Lady Greatheart's room.

Quin offered his arm to his mother, and they followed the maid down the hall and up the stairs to where Catherine waited beside the door.

Catherine smiled and then led them into the room. Quin noted how Lady Greatheart sat in a high-backed chair beside the fire, her posture perfect and an expectant air lighting up her features. She looked thinner, her frame slight, but her expression was just as fierce as he remembered.

"Lady Greatheart." He bowed and went to stand beside Catherine. "I would like to ask for your granddaughter's hand in marriage."

"It's about time." Lady Greatheart's voice was raspy but no less strong than he remembered. "Took you long enough. How much work did it take?" This final question was directed at his mother.

"It took some arranging, but he came to the sticking point," the Duchess of Wesley answered, her tone amused.

"Figured," Lady Greatheart said, mostly to herself. "Well, Catherine's of age and I certainly give my blessing."

"Thank you." Quin bowed.

"So, when is the wedding? I'm not in my best form, but I'll be there. I'm already sick to death of these four walls." Lady Greatheart glared at the offending plaster and then regarded Quin expectantly.

He cast a questioning peek to Catherine, wondering how much of their current situation she wished to divulge to her grandmother. Certainly, she was on the mend, but perhaps Catherine didn't want to give her all the particulars of their current predicament.

"There are a few details to figure out," Catherine answered hesitantly.

"I'm thinking there's more than a few," Lady Greatheart remarked with mirth, then sobered. "Wait. What are you not telling me? Ducky…" She gave a warning in her tone as she studied her granddaughter.

"There's a bit of a situation, but we have a solution." The Duchess of Wesley stepped forward.

"What sort of situation?" Lady Greatheart's suspicion raked over all three of them. Despite the tension of the atmosphere, Quin bit his tongue to keep his amusement in check. He'd seen that same expression on Catherine's face, and he no longer wondered where she'd learned it.

"What are you smiling about?" Lady Greatheart speared him with a glare.

"Just noticing the familial resemblance," Quin replied.

"Oh, speaking of familial resemblance," Lady Greatheart interjected as if just remembering something she wished to say earlier. "Catherine, you said that Lord Bircham brought a chaperone for you, correct?"

"Yes." Catherine frowned at Quin and then turned back to her grandmother. "What of her?"

"I figured out why she sounded so familiar," Lady Greatheart said. "She sounds just like the late Lord Bircham's wife, nasty woman. I never liked her. That voice grated on my nerves." She gave a delicate shiver. "I only met her a few times, but it was enough."

Catherine's eyes widened. "Well, this is actually his aunt. Apparently, his mother is a twin and he brought Mrs. Burke to be my chaperone."

"I see. That explains the similarity of the voice. That was a curious situation. They are family and all, but I never approved. Desperation causes people to do strange things."

"But Grandfather named them the trustee of the estate. Why would he do that if you didn't get along?"

"He was a safe option since we thought they couldn't have children." Lady Greatheart waved her hand in the air. "But that's enough of this right now. No need for a lesson on the odder branches of your family tree, ducky—"

"What do you mean they couldn't have children? Clearly, they had Lord Bircham…" Quin took a slight step toward Lady Greatheart, his mind doing some quick calculations and wondering.

His mother leaned forward. He could see her movement from the corner of his eye. Some sense of premonition hinted that they were about to uncover the missing piece of the puzzle.

Lady Greatheart continued, "Well, it was all kept quiet. I never approved. It's a twisted thing, if you ask my opinion. Your grandfather understood why they did what they did. An heir is important, but I still didn't approve of the lengths they took. But desperation sometimes makes you adopt certain circumstances as extenuating." She exhaled slowly. "Lady Bircham couldn't have children. She had a fever when she was young, and it left her barren. But they didn't know this till she was married, of course. But her sister..."

"No..." Quin swore softly.

"Like I said, desperation can lead to some strange actions. The sisters were identical to everyone but those closest to them. I don't know if Lady Bircham asked her sister or if it was Lord Bircham who had an affair...but the child was carried by the sister, not the wife. But of course no one knew that. The sister was living with them since their parents were deceased, so anyone visiting would just assume the pregnant sister was the lady of the house." She shrugged. "Stranger things have happened, I'm sure, but I haven't heard of many."

Quin froze, giving a fruitless effort to processing the onslaught of information. So that would make Mrs. Burke the mother of Lord Bircham.

"But if they were so careful to hide the truth, how did you find out?" Catherine asked, her tone shocked.

Lady Greatheart replied, "One of my great friends had grown up with the twins. She could always tell them apart by the freckle under one of their earlobes. If you weren't looking for it, you wouldn't see it. Few knew of it, but on one of the rare visits I paid with my husband to Cambridge, we visited their estate and I, curious as I was, tried to determine which twin was which based on the freckle. I was confused because the pregnant one was the one with the freckle, not as I had expected. I thought I'd remembered incorrectly. However, when I came back and spoke with my friend, she turned ashen. She was the one who figured out what had happened."

"Good Lord," the Duchess of Wesley muttered.

Quin frowned. "So Mrs. Burke—Wait, she had to marry later, then?"

"Yes, she married an older tradesman, but she never had another child. And the sisters became estranged after the whole sordid mess."

"I'm not sure what to think of this," Catherine murmured.

"Me either," the Duchess of Wesley commented. "And I've heard some strange things. I think this is the winner."

"So you'll see why I was hesitant to have her in my home." Lady Greatheart shifted as if the thought made her uncomfortable. "But enough of that! I mean it this time. We have happy news to discuss!" She clapped enthusiastically.

Quin turned to Lady Greatheart. "Indeed, and we will tell you as soon as we have a date selected." He needed to talk to Catherine, but he didn't want to alarm her grandmother. This revelation was astounding. "We don't wish to tire you, so we'll take our leave and come back once we know more. Thank you for your blessing." *And so much more*, Quin added in his thoughts as he bowed to Lady Greatheart.

"You're welcome. Take care of her. She's the best out there."

"I will, and I agree." Quin smiled at Catherine.

Catherine turned to her grandmother. "I'll be back later, Grammy." She kissed her grandmother's cheek.

The Duchess of Wesley bid her goodbye as well, and they all moved into the hall. Quin exchanged a wide-eyed expression with Catherine and then his mother, but by silent agreement, they didn't speak but all took the stairs to the parlor where Catherine closed the doors behind them.

"Never would I ever—"

"Nor I," the Duchess of Wesley added, shivering slightly.

"But we do have some understanding… Now we need one thing."

Catherine regarded Quin, her intelligent eyes flashing. "Motive. And that's exactly what I'm going to find in Cambridge."

Quin nodded. "Unless we find it sooner. I'm not a gambling man, but I'd wager on this…" He paused briefly. "Lord Bircham has no idea."

# Thirty-four

*Bad news travels faster than good.*

—*Catherine the Great*

CATHERINE WAS IMPRESSED BY THE SPEED WITH WHICH THE Duchess of Wesley had flown into action after their startling revelation. Lady Joan and Lord Penderdale—Morgan—were quickly contacted and agreed to accompany Catherine to Cambridge. It had all been decided in less than a day, and before she had a moment to do anything but give a quick affectionate hand squeeze to Quin given their audience, he helped her into the carriage, gave his friend a nod, and then stepped back, disappearing from view as they departed for Cambridge.

"What do you expect to find?" Morgan asked, comfortably swaying with the movement of the carriage.

The Duchess of Wesley had informed them of the current situation, and Catherine was curious what perception Morgan had. "I have no idea, but there has to be a reason. Don't you think?"

Lady Joan gave an indelicate lament.

Her brother studied her, and she gave a shrug and answered, "If there's one thing I've learned from this one's escapades with the War Office—"

"Which I constantly regret sharing any details about," her brother interrupted.

"Hush, you didn't tell me anything sensitive," she scolded, then turned back to Catherine. "As I was saying..." She shot a glare to her brother, then turned brightly to Catherine. "If there's one thing I've learned about human nature, it's that a reason isn't always necessary for action. It's common but not required. People often don't know their own hearts anyway. There may be motive, but she might not even be able to articulate it."

Catherine nodded.

"Besides," Morgan added, "motive is helpful but doesn't excuse her past actions. The goal... Let us focus on the goal."

"To have her set the record straight but also make sure she doesn't have further plans to wreak havoc on my family," Catherine stated, turning her attention to the window.

And honestly, the last part was more concerning than the first. With Mrs. Burke gone, the gossip could be managed without her recanting, if necessary, but if she were malignant enough to want to undermine Catherine's reputation, she might try something else. And Catherine wasn't about to live with that threat over her head.

"I must say, I've heard some interesting stories over the course of my work with the War Office, and this one regarding the parentage of Lord Bircham surprised me—not an easy feat, that."

Catherine and Morgan shared a look of understanding.

Joan shifted slightly as she spoke. "So, the plan is to locate her with the sleuthing skills possessed by my brother, and then what? Confront her?"

"In simple terms, yes. But I find such things usually are not that simple."

Catherine frowned. "That is what I'm afraid of."

Morgan replied, "It's nothing I cannot manage, my lady." He gave a slight head bow. "But I am disappointed in myself for not uncovering this truth earlier regarding his birth." His brows knitted together. "I did quite a bit of research—"

"On Bircham?" Catherine asked.

"Yes," he answered, then continued slowly as if admitting something he was unsure she was aware of. "Quin asked me to check into him. I'm assuming you guessed as much."

Catherine arched a brow. "I wasn't certain, but it does not surprise me."

Morgan replied with the tone of imparting a great secret. "He was gone on you before he knew it—Quin, that is. I tried to tell him to offer for you right away. His attachment to you was clear to anyone but himself."

Catherine's heart warmed at the picture Morgan painted with his words. "It was a process, for both of us."

"Love is never without obstacles," Joan said sagely.

"Listen to you." Morgan nodded in approval. He turned to Catherine. "You'd be interested to know how my sister has been spending her spare time." He gave Joan a half-indulgent shrug.

"He doesn't entirely approve, but there's not much he can do without openly threatening me, and I have far too much information for that to be wise." Joan arched her brows challengingly at her brother as she spoke. She paid him no heed, simply spoke in a forthright manner to her companion. "I'm a bit of a bluestocking and have been working with a few ladies to bring awareness to the situation of women in London."

Catherine addressed her young friend. "Truly?"

Joan nodded. "I believe that men and women are created equal, yet society doesn't treat them that way."

"That's quite forward-thinking." Catherine was curious what had started a gently bred lady on such a path.

"You're kind. Most people call me something much different when they learn my sentiments." Joan spoke with a dry tone. "I've studied Mary Wollstonecraft's works and find them inspiring, but I have my own opinions. That's the goal, is it not? To learn, grow, and then think for oneself?"

Catherine approved. "I can see we are going to be wonderful friends."

"You don't think ill of my radical beliefs?" Joan asked, casting a furtive look to her brother.

Catherine waved a hand dismissively. "No, you have passion, and that is sorely lacking in our world." She touched Joan on the shoulder. "Tell me more."

The carriage rumbled on, the time moving far more swiftly than Catherine would have thought. Joan's discernment and education were impressive, and they spoke at length regarding possible plans for the future.

Joan wasn't active only in the movement for the expansion of ladies' rights, but also for improving the conditions for women and children in the poorer regions of London. Upon learning that Catherine was in the middle of drawing up plans for an orphanage, Joan quickly asked to be a part, and the rest of the journey was completed with the making of plans and exchange of ideas.

Morgan listened politely, adding his thoughts, perceptions, and humor. The tension that had surrounded Catherine at the beginning of the journey melted away slowly, and as they arrived on the outskirts of Cambridge, she was nearly feeling peaceful.

A feat for sure, given her previous strain.

"Ah, home," Morgan said with a reverent tone, his attention fixed on the passing buildings from the carriage window.

"He's attached to this place," Joan said, smiling. "He's never really at rest in London."

"It's too loud, and I know…too much about the people there," Morgan agreed softly. "Too many motives, intentions, and responsibilities." He turned to his sister. "I don't mean you, of course."

"Of course." Joan beamed at Catherine. "I'm the easiest part of your life."

At this, Morgan gave her a sarcastic look.

"What?" Joan feigned innocence.

"It's far simpler here," Morgan said as he turned back toward the window. "This is where it all started, you know."

"What started?" Catherine asked, watching the scenery as well.

"The brotherhood." Morgan smiled. "It's not as impressive

as it sounds, but it's been a lifeline for us with all that happened, you know." He shrugged, but his words were heavy, even for their soft tone.

"The fire." Catherine's heart pinched at the mention of the event that had changed all their lives.

"Before, it was all so…planned out? We were friends at school, and that friendship turned into a brotherhood."

"How?" Catherine had never actually heard the story, simply knew the three friends were close.

Morgan relaxed into the squabs. "It began when Rowles's mother started to get ill. His father had died the year before, and he was very protective of his mother. There was some cause for alarm at how she was acting, and then one day Rowles received a missive from London and left immediately for home. We didn't find out till he returned that his mother had, er, walked around London in her nightdress."

"In daylight?" Catherine asked, her tone shocked.

"Yes. There had been whispers of her staying out of society and acting oddly, but when she made such a public spectacle, news of course spread like wildfire. We were attending Cambridge school at the time, all of us at various colleges. We were meeting after schooling for a pint of beer when some other students arrived at the pub and started to taunt Rowles."

Catherine listened intently.

"Well, Rowles was fully aware of what had happened. He'd just returned from London that day after situating his mother with a nurse to care for her. Let us just say he was low on sleep and patience."

"I can't blame him," Joan said.

Morgan continued, "Quin tried to defuse the situation. He stood and asked the gentlemen to stop and take their business elsewhere."

Catherine smiled. That was so like Quin. Taking control,

protecting, and the first to step up when the situation required. It was one of the many aspects of his character she loved.

"Did they leave?" Joan asked. "I haven't heard the full story either," she confided to Catherine.

"No. They got louder, and so I stepped in, but before I could—"

"Shed blood?" his sister asked knowingly.

He gave her a placating expression. "I only shed blood if necessary." He turned to Catherine to continue the story. "Rowles stood up and started a brawl that got us kicked out of the pub for good." He let out a low whistle. "Let's just say we all were nursing black eyes and sore fists for the next few days." He appeared as if the memory was a good rather than painful one.

"Only men would find joy in fisticuffs." Joan nudged her brother playfully with her elbow.

Morgan winked at his sister and then continued. "We knew it wouldn't be the last time something like that would happen, and that evening as we were all seeing out of one good eye, we made a pact." He hitched a shoulder. "I don't think we put much weight into it. There was no contract in blood or even a charter written up."

"What? No blood? How does this even count, then?" Joan asked with a hint of irony.

"Minx," her brother taunted lovingly. "But we promised we'd have each other's backs. We'd been friends for ages, and our brothers were friends as well. Our families had known each other for generations. It only seemed right to continue that association. Little did we know it would be so pivotal a few years later," Morgan continued. "We all made it through school, then loved Cambridge so much we decided to stay and teach, each in our separate delegations. So of course we all attended different colleges. The school is divided up into disciplines, and each study has its own college," he explained. "But they are all in Cambridge, dispersed throughout the city, and we lived uneventful, predictable lives as we taught and studied."

"You sound like it was quite idyllic, yet you work for the War Office?" Catherine asked, curious how that came into play.

"Yes, that's a whole new story, and I'm afraid we don't have time for it right now. See? That's Quin's residence." No sooner had he said the words than the carriage rolled to a stop before a stone building a city block long. Stoops all led to similar doors, dividing up the building into different residences.

"Ah, I see." Catherine waited as the door opened.

Morgan stepped out first, Joan followed, and Catherine disembarked last, taking in the sight of Quin's home, the place where he felt most at peace. She promised in her heart that the next time she saw it, it would be with him, and she'd watch the peace spread over his face as he came back to the place that he called home above all other places.

Morgan took the steps quickly and knocked on the door. A butler answered promptly, his expression bright with recognition as he welcomed them inside.

Catherine let out a small sigh.

It had been a wonderfully distracting carriage ride.

But it was time to start unwinding the truth.

The sooner she found it, the sooner she could return home.

Because she was finding that home was really where the heart was.

And she'd left hers with Quin.

# Thirty-five

QUIN TAPPED HIS FINGER ON THE PILE OF DOCUMENTS ON THE side of his desk, his mind working as he listened to the sound of approaching footsteps. His butler showed in the invited guest, and Quin stood, his chair making a scraping sound on the polished hardwood floor as he did so.

"Lord Bircham, thank you for agreeing to meet with me." Quin extended his hand and winced as he noted the purple bruising around the man's left eye and red jawline. "Again, I apologize for my earlier behavior," he added, thinking it necessary. He had a feeling that the news he was about to impart to Lord Bircham would hurt far more than a facer.

"It's understandable, given the circumstances." Lord Bircham accepted Quin's hand, gave it a solid shake, and then sat when Quin gestured to a chair across from his desk.

"Brandy?" Quin offered.

"Yes, thank you." Bircham set that ever-present silver cane to the side.

Quin nodded and then walked to the table and poured them each a crystal goblet of fine brandy. He handed the glass to Bircham and then took his seat once more. "There's some information I believe you should be aware of," Quin started, then took a sip of his brandy. It was smooth and the heat was a welcome burn in his throat.

Bircham nodded and took a sip as well, his eyes closing for a moment in appreciation. "And what is that?"

Quin set his brandy to the side and folded his hands on his

desk. "It would seem there was some information my betrothed's grandmother had."

Bircham nodded.

"Lord Bircham, can you tell me about your mother and father?" Quin asked, testing the waters to see if perhaps the man had any inclination regarding his parentage.

Lord Bircham frowned. "My mother is—was—Lady Bircham, twin sister to Mrs. Burke, of which you're aware. And my father was Percival Armstrong, the fourth Baron Bircham. The title has been in our family for five generations, and my mother was the daughter of a local baron. It's rather traditional, I believe." He took another sip of brandy, then regarded Quin. "Why do you ask?"

Quin looked down to his hands. Information like this shouldn't come from a relatively unknown person, but there was nothing for it, so he soldiered on. "There was a situation between your mother and her sister," Quin started.

Lord Bircham nodded. "Continue."

"The wife of Lord Bircham was unable to have children." Quin waited, gauging Bircham's reaction.

The man frowned but nodded for him to continue. "And so," Quin went on, "that put your father in a difficult place."

"What are you saying, Your Grace?" Lord Bircham asked with sudden menace.

Quin hesitated. This wasn't going well. In trying to be gentle, he was drawing out the story too long. "Mrs. Burke is your mother, Lord Bircham. And the reason this is known is because Lord and Lady Greatheart visited your family while they were expecting..."

The air whooshed out of Lord Bircham's lungs in a loud gasp. He stood abruptly, the brandy splashing from the glass in his haste. "What are you saying?"

Quin speared him with a sharp look. "Mrs. Burke is your mother and therefore may have had more motivation to spread gossip about Catherine and you. And I'm asking a question because of it.

What did you have to gain that such an alliance would benefit you so greatly that she would go to such lengths?"

Bircham's answering glare wasn't much of a help, but after several moments of silence, his expression transitioned to one of more sorrow than anger. "Are you certain? How could it possibly be certain? They were nearly identical except for—"

"The freckle under the ear," Quin finished, knowing it would be the only detail that could prove the story's validity.

"Good God," the man gasped, then as if his legs couldn't hold him, he sank back into the chair, the remainder of the brandy sloshing in the glass.

"Here." Quin rose and went to the side table, bringing back the decanter and refilling the poor man's goblet. Lord Bircham nodded his thanks and then drank a long swallow.

"I, that is, they never…"

"I didn't think they had. But that does leave us to believe that Mrs. Burke was motivated as more than a mere widowed relative."

"Indeed," he agreed. "But why?"

Quin groaned. "I was hoping you'd know the answer to that."

Lord Bircham exhaled slowly, then ran a hand down his face, staring ahead but his gaze unfocused. "It's difficult to grasp, you understand."

Quin nodded.

"Why would my father…"

"You said it yourself. Generations have held the title…" Quin answered gently. "Imagine trying to resign yourself to the fact that it ends with you."

Lord Bircham closed his eyes. "He wasn't one to admit defeat or failure." He opened his eyes. "So he found a way around it."

"It would seem."

"But why would my…his wife, my aunt—Good Lord, what a bloody mess this is." Bircham gave a humorless snigger. "What a cocked-up bloody disaster this is. Damn."

"I'm not sure. Maybe she wasn't one to admit failure either?" Quin answered the lingering implied question.

Lord Bircham was shaking his head. "I'm sure so many things will make more sense now, though I'll admit I had no suspicions."

He let out a slow snort, his focus on the floor as he shook his head slowly, then paused, and did it again as if carrying on a conversation in his mind. "Would you be so kind as to allow me some time to think? I understand that this has implications for you and Lady Catherine. But I don't think that I'm currently much help."

Quin nodded. "Of course. I understand. Please call upon me when you've had some time to think."

"I will," Lord Bircham said automatically, then rose and departed.

Quin stood when the gentleman started to leave, then sank back into his chair with relief that the hardest part was over. Pity welled up within him for the man—pity he knew would be unwelcome but was present nonetheless. He couldn't imagine believing one thing for an entire life and then being told it was a lie.

Lies were the very devil.

Quin wiped his hand down his face, then gripping his chin, he reclined back in his seat, thinking.

Looking at the clock, he realized that Catherine would be at Cambridge by this time, viewing his home, settling into her room. It was acute torture to have her there without him. At least she wasn't alone. Morgan would watch over her like a guardian angel, and hopefully this would all be behind them soon so he could take her to Cambridge himself, show her what he loved about the place he called home, and have the privacy such a place afforded.

His body burned with the need for it; his heart ached as well. He turned to the clock once more and did a quick calculation before rising from his desk and striding to the door.

Doctors' Commons would close at three, and it was almost

two. If he traveled there directly, he could procure a special license and have it on hand.

He'd dealt with people's pity after his brother died. He'd dealt with expectations and responsibilities that he wasn't prepared for. He'd dealt with falling in love and fighting his own heart's voice. He could bloody well deal with people's gossip for a few months. A fierce determination lifted his lips as he called for his gelding to be saddled. In short order, he was making his way down the street.

One day at a time, he was getting closer.

To healing.

To growing.

And to calling Catherine his own.

# Thirty-six

*You philosophers are lucky men. You write on paper, and paper is patient. Unfortunate Empress that I am, I write on the susceptible skins of living beings.*

—Catherine the Great

CATHERINE JUMPED AS JOAN PLACED A HAND ON HER KNEE.

"All will be well," Joan said softly.

Realizing she had been bouncing her toes and acting quite fidgety, Catherine gave Joan an apologetic look. "Pardon me, I'm not usually this anxious. It's just that—" She moaned.

They had been waiting nearly two hours. Tea had come, gone, then been brought back as they waited for Morgan to return with any news regarding the whereabouts of Mrs. Burke. Catherine had wanted to accompany him, but Morgan had kindly reminded her that he was going to be much quicker without her assistance.

*Waiting* was far more difficult than *doing*.

"He's very good at his job," Joan assured her. "Almost too good. His faith in his own skill is disturbing." She gave a small smirk.

"I'm certain he is. I'm just not accustomed to being idle."

"Ah yes, I've heard stories regarding all your endeavors, not only the orphanage we spoke about on the way here," Joan said. "It caused quite a stir when you gave funding to the theater. I think everyone will attend because they are so curious now what could have made you take such a risk."

"No risk, no reward. And honestly, it is quite amazing. You'll love Kean."

"I cannot wait." Joan gave her a wistful expression. "I love the theater."

"I do as well, but this is something more... I don't know how to describe it." Catherine pursed her lips. "It's a feeling, an engagement—rather, an emotional investment into what's happening before you—as if it were happening to you, and—" She paused, her face heated.

"I understand," Joan said.

Catherine considered her for a moment. "Indeed, you do." Catherine regarded Joan, wondering if there was more than met the eye to this bold young woman.

They all had their secrets.

What were Joan's?

Before she could inquire, the sound of purposeful footsteps sounded in the hall, and Catherine stood expectantly.

Joan followed suit, and within moments, Morgan strode into the room, his expression bright with success. "Good afternoon, ladies." He bowed smartly and then smiled when he saw the tea service. "Exactly what I need."

"Allow me," Catherine offered, eager for him to tell them of the afternoon's events. Surely, he had information.

"Thank you." He took a seat. "I found Mrs. Burke, and while I didn't talk to her, I think that tomorrow it would be wise for you to accompany me to where she is staying. You certainly have questions you'll wish to ask, and I believe it is best done by the person offended."

"Thank heavens," Joan said in a relieved tone.

Catherine handed him a teacup and speared him with a questioning gaze. "Why not today?"

Morgan took a sip. "Pardon?"

"Why not leave for where she is staying directly? Confront her, get it over and done with. I'm sure she'll..." Catherine paused.

"Well, she might not feel guilty, but certainly she has some guilt. She left London quite suddenly."

"Because she didn't want to get caught," Morgan said.

"No." Catherine took her seat once more. "If she didn't want to get caught, she wouldn't have returned to the very first place someone would look for her."

Morgan frowned. "Maybe she didn't think anyone would search for her?"

At this, Joan twisted her lips impatiently. "Regardless, the question stands. Why not today?"

Catherine turned to him expectantly.

Morgan yawned. "Because I laid some groundwork, and I want to wait for a day."

Catherine frowned. "What does that mean?"

Joan answered, her expression disapproving. "It means he went about finding information in a way that would get back to her, cause a little fear, seem like a veiled threat or two…"

"Ah…" Catherine turned back to Morgan. "I see."

Morgan nodded once, unrepentant. "People are far more persuadable when under duress."

"Remind me never to be on your bad side." Catherine smirked, entertained by her friend's methods. "Blackmail is always helpful to have in one's arsenal. Don't you agree?" she asked. "If we can find out what motivated her, we can always reverse it."

"I like the way you think." Morgan nodded approvingly.

"You two are dangerous together," Joan observed, but her tone was amused.

"You might have to be quick on your feet once you find the motive," Morgan warned.

"I've been known to have a quick wit." Catherine bit her lip. It wasn't one of her finer qualities when provoked. But she was determined to end this. "Tomorrow, then." She nodded, picking up her teacup.

"Morning," Morgan added.

Catherine grinned over her cup. "Lovely. The sooner the better."

The rest of the evening went by slowly. Dinner was served in a small dining room where Catherine could easily picture Quin sitting with the paper to the side of his plate, silence his happy companion. So much about the house reminded her of him; it was as painful as it was comforting. She missed him acutely, as if half of her heart was tethered to London.

After dinner, they had all agreed to seek their rooms earlier than usual. The previous day of travel had been taxing, and Catherine hadn't quite recovered yet. After she said her good nights, she slipped down the corridor. The flickering candlelight illuminated the hallway, and Catherine twisted the brass knob to open the door to the room she'd been given. It was a guest room, cozy and welcoming, but she wondered just where Quin's rooms were located—and how long it would be till she found out for herself.

A warm and cheery fire danced in the hearth as she settled in the bed. As her head touched the pillow, she drew the coverlet over herself.

Sleep finally found her, and soon it was morning.

Expectation made her shake off her sleep quickly, and with eagerness she dressed for the day. Upon arriving downstairs, Catherine found Joan and Morgan already at the breakfast table.

They had decided on a midmorning visit, and as the time finally arrived, Catherine found her heart pounding not only with anticipation but also with anger. She had no affection for Mrs. Burke; the lady had done nothing but make Catherine's life difficult. As the carriage rolled down the streets of Cambridge, taking a smaller side street before halting before a home similar to Quin's, Catherine resolved to see this through to whatever end.

They alighted from the carriage, and Morgan and Joan led the way to the large wooden door, using the wide brass knocker to announce their presence. An older butler answered the door, his gray eyes narrowing slightly as he asked for Morgan's card. Before the butler could turn down the hall with the offered rectangle bearing Morgan's title, a familiar voice spoke. "Let them in, Jarrod. I'm expecting them."

Mrs. Burke appeared behind the butler. "Come in." She met Catherine's wary gaze with a disinterested one of her own and then led them to a parlor.

The butler took stock of them but apparently decided there was no threat and disappeared down the hall in the opposite direction.

Catherine noted the simple furnishings placed about the house. When her grandmother said Mrs. Burke had married a tradesman, she'd assumed he had been wealthy. Even Lord Bircham had said her fortune was great.

But that was perhaps a misunderstanding.

"Tea?" Mrs. Burke offered as they entered a long, narrow parlor with sparse furnishings. The rug lying under the small table that would likely hold the tea service was faded. Clearly once colorful, the age of the rug left it dull and lifeless. The furniture was clean, but the polish was faded as if it had been wiped off with the dust from so many years of use. The windows were small and framed by drapes that had seen better days, all drawing a picture that Catherine hadn't been expecting.

"Tea, Mary," Mrs. Burke barked at the young maid waiting in the room. The servant nodded and disappeared out into the hall to do her mistress's bidding. Catherine shared a glance with Joan, who widened her eyes slightly in return.

"Please, sit." Mrs. Burke selected a wing-backed chair and gestured them toward the sofa, its green stripes nearly gray with age. Catherine took a seat beside Joan, and Morgan chose a wooden chair across from them.

"Mrs. Burke, thank you for seeing us," Morgan started, his voice genial.

Mrs. Burke huffed slightly, her eyes taking on an irritated

expression. "You need to know, your threats yesterday are not why you are here, Lord Penderdale," she said in an almost haughty tone.

"Oh?" he asked, his expression and tone unconcerned. In fact, Catherine thought he almost sounded amused and jovial, as if this type of situation brought him delight.

She gave a shudder. This certainly was not her idea of a pleasant morning.

"No. I expected you'd come here eventually. It took longer than I anticipated," Mrs. Burke replied testily.

Morgan shrugged and leaned back in his chair, completely at ease. "Then I apologize for our tardiness. Clearly you have something on your mind?"

Catherine's eyes darted from Mrs. Burke to Morgan and back, studying each expression and nuance.

Mrs. Burke narrowed her eyes at Morgan, as if to scold his insolent behavior, and turned her attention to Catherine. "You will marry Lord Bircham."

It was Catherine's turn to be amused. Odd how such a shift could happen. "I think not."

"You'll find no one better, and since you've been compromised—"

"I was no such thing," Catherine replied, her tone taking on a hard edge at the woman's bold accusation. "And you'd be wise to watch your words."

"It's nothing but the truth. I left you alone and—"

"On purpose. With intent to ruin my reputation and force an alliance. Why?" Catherine demanded.

From the corner of her eye, she saw Morgan shift forward. "You might as well set the record straight. Lord Bircham refused to risk the ire of the Duke of Wesley."

"Ah yes, your *friend*." Mrs. Burke said the word as if it had less than honorable connotations.

"My betrothed," Catherine added, watching as the smug expression on Mrs. Burke's face froze, then shifted to skepticism. "You offended the wrong people, Mrs. Burke. And thankfully, your intentions didn't get very far. The Duchess of Wesley has already set the record straight, and you'll find that your reputation is the one in question." Catherine laid out the words carefully, watching the older woman's reaction.

"In fact," Catherine continued, "I think the real threat is the effect this whole situation is having on Lord Bircham's reputation."

Mrs. Burke swallowed, her expression hard but her earlier confidence ebbing.

Catherine moved forward. "Yes, the way you put forth the news made it sound as if he were taking advantage of my situation and finances, not very gentlemanly. Some would say he was dishonorable, even."

Mrs. Burke's lips pursed. "I said nothing of the sort, but that you practically begged him, that it was necessary because of your actions—" She broke off abruptly.

This admission of guilt was what they needed. And with witnesses.

Catherine leaned back in her chair. "Ah, so you admit it."

"I never said I didn't," Mrs. Burke shot back.

"You need to recant your words," Morgan added into the conversation, his voice nearly startling Catherine because her focus had been so intent on Mrs. Burke.

"No," Mrs. Burke replied flatly. "Whatever gossip surrounds Lord Bircham will be forgotten once he marries you."

"He's not going to—" Catherine began.

At the same time, Morgan said, "What did you say?"

Mrs. Burke looked between the two of them, as if deciding who to answer first. It was then that Catherine realized something. She was enjoying this.

As angry and agitated as she was, Mrs. Burke was thriving on the drama of it all, the conflict. In some twisted way, it fed her soul. Revulsion swirled in Catherine's stomach.

"It doesn't matter what you said, because here is the truth." Catherine's voice was soft, but her words held a swordlike edge. She had reached the end of her patience. No rationalization. Nothing was going to get to this woman but her own weapons.

With a calculated and measured approach, Catherine stood slowly and walked toward Mrs. Burke.

The woman watched her.

"It would be a shame..." Catherine started and then circled Mrs. Burke's chair like a hawk circling a mouse in a field, "if word were to get out regarding Lord Bircham's birth."

The silence that followed spoke louder than words. "You see, my grandmother is doing quite well, thank the Lord. And she noticed something very distinct about you, Mrs. Burke."

Catherine moved to stand in front of Mrs. Burke's chair and gave her a frown. When there was no answer, she continued, "She explained how Lady Bircham had been unable to bear children. Such a pity." Catherine exhaled. "Yet how fortuitous that her twin sister...nearly identical...should not have the same problem. And what luck that she was residing with Lord and Lady Bircham."

Morgan arched a brow and nodded, as if encouraging Catherine to continue.

Her confidence growing, Catherine slowed as she circled the chair once more, then bent down to eye level with Mrs. Burke and spoke softly. "But someone saw a solution, didn't he? Because you *could* have a child...and he needed one. But not just any child, one who could be presented as legitimate, an *heir*." She lingered for a moment and then stood upright, continuing her slow circle.

"So you switched with your sister, and anyone visiting would assume the sister in a delicate condition was the twin married to the late Lord Bircham."

At this, Mrs. Burke turned hateful eyes to her. "You have no proof. We were identical, such a story could never be believed because it couldn't be proven one way or the other. You're grasping at straws."

It was then that Catherine lowered her chin, a predatory expression spreading across her lips. "There's a spot of proof..." She pointed to the freckle just below Mrs. Burke's ear. "You are Lord Bircham's mother."

Mrs. Burke flinched.

"Don't worry. He knows the truth now," Catherine added as a parting swing.

At this, Mrs. Burke's control snapped, and she stood, her voice shrill. "You witch!"

"Now, there's no need for name-calling."

Catherine spun at the sound of Quin's voice, her heart hammering with relief, joy, and surprise. Lord Bircham stood beside Quin, a fading bruise circling his eye and adding a rather pirate-like effect to the usually impeccable gentleman.

Mrs. Burke stilled, her gaze darting from Lord Bircham to Quin to Catherine and back, as if the rest of her was paralyzed.

"So where are we in the conversation? Clearly, we're late," Quin added with some levity as he crossed the room to stand beside Catherine.

His warm hands circled her waist and pulled her close, then he placed a tender kiss to her head. "I missed you," he murmured.

Catherine closed her eyes and melted in to him, her earlier tension dissolving like sugar in tea. As if just thinking of tea had conjured it up, the maid brought in the service and apparently sensing the tension in the room placed it quickly on the table and left with alacrity.

"Well, it would seem there needs to be some clarification." Lord Bircham approached Mrs. Burke, his expression cool. "Because I for one would like to know the truth."

He took a seat and motioned for Mrs. Burke to do the same.

"From the beginning, if you please. You owe me that at least."

# Thirty-seven

THEY HAD RIDDEN THROUGH THE NIGHT, LEAVING THE EVE-
ning before in order to get to Cambridge as quickly as possible.
Once Lord Bircham had reconciled himself to it, he had come to
the conclusion that he needed to talk to Mrs. Burke directly, and
given the rumors, he felt it necessary to have Quin accompany him
should Catherine be present at any point.

Quickly agreeing, Quin had made the necessary arrangements
and, sooner than he had hoped, relished the expectation of seeing
Catherine. He had missed her, like his very soul was hungry for
her presence. When they arrived at Mrs. Burke's residence, Lord
Bircham had been given the familial access to the home, and the
butler hadn't hesitated to conduct them to Mrs. Burke.

Quin hadn't heard much, but it appeared as if Catherine had hit
a nerve, given the resounding epithet thrown at her. It had been a
struggle not to hurl his own insult at the older woman, but he had
been able to see by Catherine's expression that she was holding her
own. He knew that she was quite capable of delivering a proper
setdown when needed. Some women wanted a knight in shining
armor to protect them. But Catherine fought her own battles and
did it well. So, with a squeeze, he'd held her waist with his arm and
drawn her in close, giving her room to be herself while reminding
her he would stand beside her always. Because some day she'd do
the same for him.

"From the beginning, please." Lord Bircham waved to Mrs.
Burke and then nodded to Quin.

Mrs. Burke had nearly shriveled at the sight of her son, as if all the bluster and bravado were sucked from her body at the understanding that he knew the truth.

"I'm not sure. That is, it's all hearsay—"

"Please, do not toy with me." He gave a frustrated groan.

And then Mrs. Burke crumpled into the chair, her head in her hands, and began to spill out the truth.

Quin listened in silence, noting that the details of the story were the same as what Lady Greatheart had said, save one difference.

"I wanted a child, and I knew my prospects for marriage were small. We didn't have much of a dowry, and it was only luck that my sister married before our parents died." She added, "And to a lord, no less."

Lord Bircham nodded.

"So when it was discovered that Sara couldn't bear children, Lord Bircham became distant, and it broke her heart. He began drinking more heavily, and then one night I was in my bedroom reading and…" Her gaze darted to the floor. "I don't know if he realized it wasn't Sara or if he was too drunk to care. But you can guess what happened."

"He forced you?" Lord Bircham asked coldly.

Mrs. Burke met his cool regard. "The first time."

Quin felt more than heard Catherine's intake of breath.

"My sister didn't find out till I was increasing, and she never forgave me. Once I delivered you, I was asked to leave." Mrs. Burke released a snort. "Lord Bircham no longer had a use for me. He had a son. And my sister couldn't look at me…so I had no reason to stay either. I married a tradesman, and he was kind to me." Mrs. Burke spoke softly, the usually harsh edge to her tone absent. "But I never forgot you." She turned tear-filled eyes toward Lord Bircham, her son. "So when my sister and brother-in-law passed…" She winced. "I did my best to care for you."

Lord Bircham's shoulders slumped, as if the conversation defeated him. "I won't ever understand…" His voice trailed off.

"But why? All the past doesn't excuse your mistreatment of Lady Catherine or its consequent effect on my honor as a gentleman."

Mrs. Burke nodded. "Well, you had a title from your father, and you had the love of a mother from my sister. What was there left for me to give you?" She gave a humorless cackle, sounding bitter. "I had no inheritance, and your father started gambling all yours away before he died. You built it back, but it was merely a shadow of what it was before…so I thought…"

"You haven't answered my question," Lord Bircham said, but his tone was gentler.

"I didn't have a fortune of my own to give you, but I could give you another's…" She slid a glimpse to Catherine. "One with deep coffers, connections, and a respectability that heightened your position in society."

Quin's hold on her tightened, and she pressed snugly in to him. Mrs. Burke shrugged. "It was the only thing I could do for you. I couldn't tell you the truth—God knows I still don't want anyone to know it—and I couldn't give you a title. You already had that. And I couldn't even give you my affection. It was too hard. I couldn't bear it. So I did what I could…"

"Damn the consequences," Morgan added, reminding Quin of his presence.

Joan turned to her brother and nodded.

"Given the circumstances, I believe you owe Lady Catherine and His Grace an apology," Lord Bircham insisted, his tone formal.

Mrs. Burke nodded once and then turned to Catherine, meeting her gaze. "My apologies, Lady Catherine. I'll be sure to retract my earlier statements."

"Thank you," Catherine said somberly.

"I think perhaps we should allow them some time alone." Morgan stood and looked back and forth between Mrs. Burke and Lord Bircham.

"Agreed." Quin turned to Catherine, who nodded her assent.

The four of them made their farewells and left, the tension remaining behind in the room that had held so many secrets and revealed so many truths.

Quin assisted Catherine into the carriage, then waited for Morgan and Joan to enter as well before rapping on the roof to signal the coachman to move.

"Well, that was certainly interesting," Morgan said with mirth. "Brava, Lady Catherine. Remind *me* never to be *your* adversary."

Catherine's face melted into a relieved expression. "I was just so frustrated and angry that I went with my instincts, and they proved correct."

"They usually do," Joan added.

Quin grasped Catherine's hand.

She squeezed it, meeting his gaze with a warm one of her own.

"I've seen her in action. I have no doubt that it was quite an uneven match."

Morgan snickered. "Mrs. Burke didn't have a chance."

Catherine swatted at Quin. "I'm not so terrible."

"I never said you were. I mean it as a compliment."

At this, she turned her face heavenward. "What am I to do with you?"

Quin could think of several things, none for the ears of their companions, so he settled for a roguish grin. Catherine's blush enticed him further, and he forced his gaze away, needing to calm his already-burning blood.

"Well, it would seem as if the crisis has been averted," Morgan added. "And now are we to leave for London?" He said the last part as a lament, as if returning to London were a duty and punishment.

"Don't sound so happy about it," Joan said with dry sarcasm. "I do have a party I need to attend, plus there's a meeting at the library—"

"I know, I remember you telling me. We'll be there. It's not worth the pain of your harassment if I forget something."

"You poor henpecked thing," Joan said with even heavier sarcasm.

"Ah, siblings," Quin remarked with amusement.

Morgan gave him a dirty look, then caved. "Yes, we will return to London. Which means—"

"We will remain here," Quin answered.

Morgan's eyebrows rose, and Joan let out a gasp.

Catherine's chin tilted upward expectantly.

"I have one request before you leave for London." Quin leaned forward. "Will you witness our wedding?"

# Thirty-eight

*Men make love more intensely at twenty, but*
*make love better, however, at thirty.*

—*Catherine the Great*

IF SOMEONE HAD ASKED CATHERINE HOW SHE EXPECTED THE
day would proceed, she wouldn't have said that it would end with
a wedding planned for the next day.

They stayed up playing cards, enjoying the cozy atmosphere
of Quin's lodgings, with the promise of tomorrow sweetening the
very air. When it was time to retire, Quin gave her the barest kiss,
as if not trusting himself to do anything more.

"I love you." He'd avowed the words against her waiting lips
and then withdrew as she pursued another kiss. "Tomorrow," he'd
promised and then disappeared down the hall.

Sleep was elusive that night, her heart fluttering with every
remembrance that tomorrow would be the day she took Quin's
name. Delight, anticipation, and desire ripped through her by
turns, causing her to toss and turn in bed. When the moon was
high in the night sky, she drifted to sleep.

As directed, her maid bid her wake early, and with only the
pale light of dawn streaming through her window, Catherine
rose to prepare for the day. Her wedding day. The maid brushed
her hair thoroughly, her scalp tingling with each stroke. With a
frown of concentration, the maid began to twist, braid, and pin
Catherine's hair.

The one evening dress Catherine brought had been hung up

the night before, and once her hair was finished, she approached the gown, fingering the soft muslin.

As the maid buttoned up the back of the dress, the oval mirror of the guest room where she was sleeping was more than adequate to reveal the fruits of the morning labor on Catherine's hair. Her thoughts drifted to Quin. No doubt he was dressing for the event, just as she was.

Joan and Morgan were either readying themselves or waiting down in the parlor. Yesterday Morgan had been sent out to procure a minister and a chapel. He had departed with a wide smirk, after uttering a quick word to Quin.

Catherine wasn't sure what they were planning, but as long as it meant she was marrying Quin, she didn't care.

It was almost a year ago that she'd met Avery—Quin's older brother. Who would have guessed that the introduction would have led her here? She mourned Avery's death, but it was more now. She mourned him not only as someone she'd loved, but as Quin's brother as well, sharing Quin's pain with him, not just carrying her own. And in that, her burden felt lighter. Grief lessened the more it was shared with others.

Studying her reflection in the mirror, she realized that while her appearance hadn't altered much, her heart had gone through a transformation. She was older and wiser in heart, far beyond what one year could do in age, but she was grateful for it. Each step had led her to Quin.

And him to her.

The only damper on the morning was the intense wish for her grandmother to attend. A pinch in her heart made her eyes moist with unshed tears at the thought. But even in her improved condition, a wedding would be a stretch for her grandmother to attend. Catherine consoled herself knowing that even if the wedding were in London, her grandmother's health couldn't be hazarded by attending.

"My lady, you're finished," the maid said.

Catherine's golden locks were twisted into a simple yet elegant braid that met in a cascade of curls on the top of her head. The effect was almost angelic. She studied her reflection further and noted the way her pink muslin dress flowed down her body in a feminine fashion, adding to the effect.

"Thank you."

"An honor." The maid dipped a curtsy and left.

Pleased, Catherine slowly turned toward her closed door. As she reached for the handle, a knock sounded, startling her.

She twisted the knob and opened the door, then gasped with joy. "Hello." She spoke softly.

The moment was too reverent for a loud greeting. It was as if the very air muted all other sound as she met Quin's warm expression. Wordlessly, he raised his hand and trailed a finger down her jawline, smoothing his thumb across her lower lip, his gaze drinking her in. She felt beautiful down to her toes, cherished and loved, and all of it without a word. And she wondered if he'd been loving her wordlessly for much longer than she'd realized.

Because love wasn't simply the word. It was the action that gave the word life. It started in the heart and came out in the hands, the eyes, and was dearer because of the intensity that went beyond the word itself.

It was a way of living. No longer for self, but for someone else. Catherine loved Quin with a depth that was consuming. And she knew he loved her the same.

His thumb paused on her lip, and then he placed a single sweet and lingering kiss where his thumb had been. The feel of his lips sent shivers down her back and made her toes curl. "I love you." He whispered the words across her lips, sealing them there.

"I love you." She mouthed the words back, her eyes tightly shut with the power of her emotions.

"Marry me?" he murmured against her lips, then kissed her softly before retreating.

"Now?" she asked playfully.

"Right now," he answered.

He offered his arm, and she took it. He led her down the hall and to the stairs. Catherine met the approving looks of Morgan and Joan, who were waiting for them.

Quin helped Catherine climb into the carriage, and then waved as Morgan and Joan took a hackney coach. The horses started off, and Catherine reached across the space between them to hold Quin's hand. Words were too small for the moment, so she beamed, unable to restrain her joy. Quin's smile was just as broad as they passed through the streets before pausing in front of a great green lawn leading up to a white church with spires reaching to the sky.

"King's College Chapel," Quin said as she studied the building. "Built during the Wars of the Roses and several decades after." Quin alighted from the carriage and offered his hand to assist her. She took the step down onto the cobbled street and then observed the larger view of the building. Intricate stained-glass windows decorated the front of the structure, arches and spires reaching heavenward alongside the beautiful glass.

"Well, I think this even lovelier than St. James's," Catherine murmured as they approached the arched entrance.

Quin nodded to Morgan and Joan, who had just arrived. "It is impressive. I had Morgan inquire after an old friend who is the former chaplain. He agreed to marry us, and I, thankfully, had the insight to procure a special license before I left London..." He gave a devious smirk. "Just in case."

"Just in case," Catherine repeated, smiling.

Quin lifted her hand and kissed it as they walked through the entrance, passing into the impossibly tall chapel.

Catherine gasped as she took in the stained-glass windows that flanked either side of the center aisle of the chapel, depicting scenes from the Bible and Christ's crucifixion. The large room was illuminated in a soft rose color from the light filtering through the windowpanes, which made it seem cozy and romantic. The pillars rose from the floor to the ceiling, holding up a fan pattern in the plaster or stone. She couldn't quite decide which, because the height put them too far away, but the pattern was beautiful, captivating her. The wooden pews lined the aisle as they walked forward, and an older gentleman rose from the first pew, his arms wide in welcoming them.

"Ah, Your Grace," the man greeted Quin. "It is a blessing to see you again, old friend. It's been some time. And on such a happy occasion! Shall we begin?"

"By all means." Quin led his bride to the altar.

Catherine peeked behind her to see Morgan and Joan following her entrance so they could stand beside them during the vows. She turned back toward the chaplain but heard footsteps and looked back toward the entrance.

"What in the—" Quin whispered softly, turning toward the entrance as well. Other people whom Catherine didn't recognize filed into the building, all nodding to Quin as if honoring him.

The chaplain gave a wink to Quin. "You didn't think I could keep a secret, did you?"

"I can't believe—"

"We all miss you." The chaplain held up a hand. "We understand you have a duty and responsibility, but that doesn't mean we don't miss your presence. You're a good friend, Quinton. We honor you in this way."

Quin nodded with an awed expression and turned to Catherine. "My fellow professors of the economics department and various others."

Catherine nodded. "How kind of them."

"Now, without further ado!" The chaplain opened the wedding service.

Catherine vowed her heart endlessly to Quin.

He promised the same, and before long they were declared husband and wife.

Quin grinned wolfishly as the chaplain announced that he could kiss the bride, and Catherine melted into his arms willingly, not caring that the kiss was performed in front of several notable Fellows of Cambridge University.

All that mattered was that she was Quin's.

And he was hers.

# Thirty-nine

THE CUSTOMARY WEDDING BREAKFAST WAS TO FOLLOW, AND based on the activity of the house when they'd departed for the chapel, the staff was making their best efforts to please. Quin extended the invitation to the Fellows who had attended his wedding. He still could hardly fathom that they had attended, or that the chaplain had invited them. It was a sprinkling of sugar on an already delightful event, and he'd been moved by their kindness. Colleagues he had worked with for years, all taking time to offer their congratulations, meant more than he was able to articulate.

It was a piece of who he was. Matching up with who he had grown to be, the past and the present together.

Catherine's hand nestled within his as they sat at the table, the hum of conversation fading into the background as his eyes met hers, finding home as so much more than a place. It was a person. Which was saying a lot, since Cambridge had always been where he felt most himself, most at peace.

He lifted her hand gently and bowed, closing his eyes as he inhaled the sweet scent of rosewater. He felt the slow burn of need for her that consumed him. Kindling caught fire quickly but burned out just as fast. His need for her was more like the smoldering embers that flared and glowed, burning hot and consistent.

As if sensing his thoughts, her face flushed a pretty pink, making him feel hot and needy. But they had still one more course of food before he could sweep her from the dining hall and into his bedroom.

Morgan stood, the movement catching Quin's attention and providing a much-needed distraction.

"I'd like to offer a toast." Morgan lifted his wineglass.

Everyone turned toward him, raising their glasses.

"Quin, you and I have quite a history. Many here can testify to it."

There were a few chuckles from those who knew Morgan and Quin best.

"Never in all my life have I seen you as happy, contented, and, dare I say, bested—" More mirth, and this time Quin joined in. Catherine gave his arm a squeeze. "But as your longtime friend, it is my greatest honor to lift my glass to celebrate your marriage to such a lovely lady." Morgan nodded in Catherine's direction and everyone cried, "Hear, hear!"

Quin reached for his wine as Catherine did, and they clinked their glasses together.

"Now, as my wedding gift, because I tend to be more of the last-minute type fellow..." Morgan began.

Quin tore his attention from Catherine and back to his friend, who winked at him.

"I'm going to say good night and encourage you all to do the same."

Quin was torn between wanting to thank his friend profusely and to berate him for playing the poor host when he wasn't even in his own home. But gratitude won out as the guests at the table provided a few knowing chortles and slowly, one by one, offered their congratulations and then bid them a good evening.

Morgan waited till the last guest left, then offered his arm to Joan and approached Quin and Catherine, who had moved to the doorway, making it more convenient to bid the guests good night and thank you.

"Well, that was easier than I thought it was going to be," Morgan said to Quin, offering his hand.

"I can't believe you did that," Quin admitted, bemused and shaking his friend's hand.

"Yes, you can," Morgan replied, then slapped Quin's back. "Congratulations, my friend. You've done quite well for yourself."

"If you imply that I'm marrying above my touch, you're entirely correct."

Morgan sniggered. "Indeed, but I think she didn't get the raw end of the deal. There are few better than you, Quinton Errington." Morgan nodded, his expression sober as he gave a final nod and then led Joan through the open door.

"My greatest good wishes." Joan gave a quick squeeze to Catherine's hand. "I'll see you in London."

"Yes, indeed, and soon I'm sure," Catherine replied. She and Quin watched their friends enter a hackney coach headed for the inn where they had reserved a night's stay to give the newlyweds some privacy.

Quin was thankful for his friend's foresight, and it benefited them as well since the inn was just beyond Cambridge and would give them a head start back to London in the morning.

Quin turned and lowered his attention to Catherine's hand resting on his arm. Her delicate gloves were stark white against the black of his coat. As he grasped her hand within his, he smoothed his thumb over the soft kid leather of the glove, traced her first finger to the tip, and then pinched the top, tugging lightly. He moved to the next finger and repeated the process till the glove was loose and he slipped it off, tucking it into a pocket of his coat. The warmth of her hand melted into his, and he grasped her fingertips, then laced his fingers through hers.

Their eyes met, and the hazel of her irises made small rings around her pupils as her hunger reflected in their depths. Without looking away, he lifted her hand to his lips, kissing each finger one by one.

Her pink lips parted, her gasping became ragged, betraying the effect of his kisses.

As Quin kissed her last finger, he rubbed his lips softly against her knuckles. "I love you," he whispered.

"I love you," she answered, the words barely more than a gasp.

He lowered her hand from his lips and tucked it against his chest before leading her toward the stairs. Catherine followed, the air crackling with the kind of tension that made his body pulse with desire. He guided her into his room, amusement tugging on his lips. He paused for a moment as Catherine lingered beside him.

"Whenever I imagined you with me, it was always here. I just realized it."

Catherine's hand pulled away from where he had tucked it into his chest, and she splayed her fingers across his shoulder, her warmth radiating through her fingertips and echoing in his body as if blowing on embers, causing them to glow.

Quin turned to face her, shutting the door behind them without breaking eye contact. He took a small step toward her, closing the distance that no longer needed to separate them.

Ever again.

The need to touch Catherine was overwhelming. He reached up and traced the line below her jaw, encouraging her nearer. He rested his head against hers. His panting was ragged, echoing hers as he memorized the moment, then lowered his lips to hers.

Her lips were soft and demanding as she pressed in to him, her perfect curves a siren call for his eager body that he couldn't deny any more than he could deny himself air. His kiss was hungry, and he first nibbled her lower lip, then devoured it, tangling his tongue with hers, waltzing, making love with his mouth. It wasn't enough, and he trailed his kiss from her lips to her jawline, licking the curve just beside her ear and then nibbling down below her earlobe, feasting on her soft whimpers of pleasure. It was his undoing, her surrender.

She was a fierce ally.

A devoted friend.

Every inch the great force of nature her namesake claimed to be. And she was his.

And more important, he was hers. Utterly.

"I love you," he whispered, worshiping with his voice as his lips captured hers once more. "I adore every inch of you, body and soul."

"Quin." Her voice was breathless, adding to his already delirious need to claim her. "I love you... I love you, I love—"

He silenced her vows with a searing kiss, then lifted her into his arms to carry her to their bed.

Fulfilling every promise to worship her body with the reverence she deserved.

# Epilogue

*The title of Queen rang sweet to my ears, child though I was... This idea of a crown began running in my head then like a tune, and has been running a lot in it ever since.*

—*Catherine the Great*

HER GRACE CATHERINE, NÉE GREATHEART, DUCHESS OF Wesley, was less than pleased with her grandmother, who had insisted upon leaving her sickroom and attending the celebration ball that the Dowager Duchess of Wesley had asserted must be given to present the newlyweds.

Since arriving back in London, they had learned that Quin's mother's efforts to curb the gossip surrounding Lord Bircham and Catherine had been successful, especially with Mrs. Burke having abandoned London before she had done a thorough job in spreading the news.

Lord Bircham had written Quin, stating that he was certain that his mother, Mrs. Burke, had no intentions of creating further trouble for them, and he was staying in Cambridge to make sure of it.

Now the only loose end was the formal part to announce and celebrate Catherine's scandalous and romantic wedding to His Grace the Duke of Wesley. The gossip had spread like wildfire, so every invitation the former Duchess of Wesley dispatched had been accepted eagerly.

Catherine was waiting for the maid to finish the final details of her hair when there was a knock on her door. It was strange, having her own room with a bed that she never slept in, but it was convenient to have a rather large closet all to herself, so she'd accepted the trade, though she did spend most of her time in the rooms designated as Quin's. Her lips dimpled at the corners, holding in her amusement as she bid the person knocking to enter.

Quin's beloved face lit up as she met his gaze, love radiating like the warmth from a fire. "I have something for you." His expression turned playful.

The maid stepped back, gave a quick curtsy, and left the room.

"Oh? And what is that?" Catherine stood and faced her husband, and unable to resist, she rose onto her tiptoes and kissed him softly, then a bit more hungrily, unable ever to get enough of him.

"If you continue on that path, love, we won't make it to the party." Quin's panting was ragged.

"I love that you can't resist me." Catherine spoke softly, seductively.

"Love, it goes both ways."

Catherine's cheeks heated with a mild warmth as she followed his line of thought. She had nearly accosted him in his study earlier. She had an ink stain on her wrist, just covered by her glove, from when he'd lifted her onto the desk. Her wrist had pressed into a freshly signed document, leaving her with Quin's name on her skin.

"You said you had something for me?" Catherine changed the subject. Her body was hungry for his, and they didn't have the time to spare at the moment.

But anticipation never hurt either.

"You have a one-track mind," Quin goaded.

"Are you complaining?" she asked, feigning a pout.

"Not at all. I find it exceedingly pleasant."

Catherine giggled. "That's what I thought."

Quin pecked her on the cheek as if anything more would be too tempting, but he couldn't resist touching her either. "Here." He held out a hand and then opened it, palm down, dropping a pendant on a gold chain.

The candlelight reflected in the sapphire and diamond oval, delicate and lovely. "Allow me," Quin whispered reverently.

Catherine turned, facing the mirror as Quin stood behind her and fastened the circle of alternating stones around her neck. "It was my grandmother's and has always been passed down to the Duchess of Wesley. It was yours to wear the moment you married me, but I wanted to wait to give it to you tonight. I hope you don't mind."

"It's lovely." Catherine admired it, then met his eyes in the reflection. "Thank you."

He kissed her shoulder, and her eyes fluttered closed. Another knock sounded on the door. "Ducky?"

Catherine chuckled and gave an apologetic smirk when Quin opened the door.

Lady Greatheart faltered as she saw Quin's face rather than her granddaughter's. "I swear, it's a bloody miracle you're not in confinement already."

"It's been one month." Catherine all but rolled her eyes.

Her grandmother speared her with a look. "Since you've been married, I know. But you two, the way you carry on. It's… impressive." She gave a low titter. "I'm not worried about great-grandchildren, that's for sure. I'll have more than I can count."

Catherine gave a wry chuckle to Quin.

"I'm doing my best, Lady Greatheart."

"I'm painfully aware, young man. Now, we're all waiting for you, so if you don't mind joining your company…" she badgered.

"Of course." Quin offered her his arm.

"Good for you, at least you can take your eyes off your wife long enough to see to your duty." She snickered as she took his arm. "However, please don't lead me into a wall or something. Newlyweds can be easily distracted." She gestured to the door and smiled unapologetically.

They walked down the hall and descended the stairway to the main floor and the foyer from where they'd enter the ballroom to meet their waiting guests.

Lady Greatheart paused and turned to Catherine, touching her face lightly. Then she gave an approving smile and walked into the room.

"'I beg you, take courage. The brave soul can mend even disaster,'" Catherine murmured.

Quin paused and regarded her. "Catherine the Great."

"Well, since you've compared me to her, I thought I should know who she was…and I thought the quote was fitting."

Quin nodded approvingly. "A brave soul can not only mend disaster but make it into something beautiful. And that, dear Catherine, is what we've done. What started as disaster has become something that will bring life. And it took a brave soul. Yours."

What can I say? We saved each other." Catherine answered.

"Isn't that how it should be?"

"In all the best stories, it is." She agreed.

"Ah, sweet Catherine…I can say with definite honesty that in all of my study of history, my favorite story is ours."

"It is a bit romantic, isn't it?"

"It's more than romantic, it's great."

"Like me?" Catherine asked with an impish grin.

"Exactly like you. My personal Catherine the Great. Long live the empress of my heart."

Don't miss book one in The Duke's Estates, the
brand-new captivating Regency romance series
from esteemed author Jane Ashford:

# THE DUKE

## WHO LOVED ME

Available now from
Sourcebooks Casablanca

# One

THREE DAYS AFTER HE INHERITED THE TITLE DUKE OF Tereford, James Cantrell set off to visit the ducal town house just off London's Berkeley Square. He walked from his rooms, as the distance was short and the April day pleasant. He hoped to make this first encounter cordially brief and be off riding before the sunlight faded.

He had just entered the square when a shouted greeting turned his head. Henry Deeping was approaching, an unknown young man beside him.

"Have you met my friend Cantrell?" Henry asked his companion when they reached James. "Sorry. Tereford, I should say. He's just become a duke. Stephan Kandler, meet the newest peer of the realm as well as the handsomest man in London."

As they exchanged bows James silently cursed whatever idiot had saddled him with that label. He'd inherited his powerful frame, black hair, and blue eyes from his father. It was nothing to do with him. "That's nonsense," he said.

"Yes, Your Grace." Henry's teasing tone had changed recently. It held the slightest trace of envy.

James had heard it from others since he'd come into his inheritance. His cronies were young men who shared his interest in sport, met while boxing or fencing, on the hunting field, or perhaps clipping a wafer at Manton's shooting gallery, where Henry Deeping had an uncanny ability. They were generally not plump in the pocket. Some lived on allowances from their fathers and would inherit as James had; others would have a moderate income all their lives. All of them preferred vigorous activity to smoky gaming hells or drunken revels.

They'd been more or less equals. But now circumstances had pulled James away, into the peerage and wealth, and he was feeling the distance. One old man's death, and his life was changed. Which was particularly hard with Henry. They'd known each since they were uneasy twelve-year-olds arriving at school.

"We're headed over to Manton's if you'd care to come," Henry said. He sounded repentant.

"I can't just now," James replied. He didn't want to mention that he was headed to Tereford House. It was just another measure of the distance from Henry. He saw that Henry noticed the vagueness of his reply.

"Another time perhaps," said Henry's companion in a Germanic accent.

James gave a noncommittal reply, wondering where Henry had met the fellow. His friend was considering the diplomatic corps as a means to make his way in the world. Perhaps this Kandler had something to do with that.

They separated. James walked across the square and into the narrow street containing Tereford House.

The massive stone building, of no particular architectural distinction, loomed over the cobbles. Its walls showed signs of neglect, and the windows on the upper floors were all shuttered. There was no funerary hatchment above the door. Owing to the eccentricities of his great-uncle, the recently deceased sixth duke, James had never been inside. His every approach had been rebuffed.

He walked up to the door and plied the tarnished knocker. When that brought no response, he rapped on the door with the knob of his cane. He had sent word ahead, of course, and expected a better reception than this. At last the door opened, and he strolled inside—to be immediately assailed by a wave of stale mustiness. The odor was heavy rather than sharp, but it insinuated itself into the nostrils like an unwanted guest. James suspected that it would swiftly permeate his clothes and hair. His dark brows drew together. The atmosphere in the dim entryway, with closed doors on each side and at the back next to a curving stair, was oppressive. It seemed almost threatening.

One older female servant stood before him. She dropped a curtsy. "Your Grace," she said, as if the phrase was unfamiliar.

"Where is the rest of the staff?" They really ought to have lined up to receive him. He had given them a time for his visit.

"There's only me. Your Grace."

"What?"

"Keys is there." She pointed to a small side table. A ring of old-fashioned keys lay on it.

James noticed a small portmanteau sitting at her feet.

She followed his eyes. "I'll be going then. Your Grace." Before James could reply, she picked up the case and marched through the still-open front door.

Her footsteps faded, leaving behind a dismal silence. The smell seemed to crowd closer, pressing on him. The light dimmed briefly as a carriage passed outside. James suppressed a desire to flee. He had a pleasant set of rooms in Hill Street where he had, for some years, been living a life that suited him quite well. He might own this house now, but that didn't mean he had to live here. Or perhaps he did. A duke had duties. It occurred to him that the servant might have walked off with some valuable items. He shrugged. Her bag had been too small to contain much.

He walked over to the closed door on the right and turned the knob. The door opened a few inches and then hit some sort of obstacle. He pushed harder. It remained stuck. James had to put his shoulder to the panels and shove with the strength developed in Gentleman Jackson's boxing saloon before it gave way, with a crash of some largish object falling inside. He forced his way through but managed only one step before he was brought up short, his jaw dropping. The chamber—a well-proportioned parlor with high ceilings and elaborate moldings—was stuffed to bursting with a mad jumble of objects. Furniture of varying eras teetered in haphazard stacks—sofas, chairs, tables, cabinets. Paintings and other ornaments were pushed into every available crevice. Folds and swathes of fabric that might have been draperies or bedclothes drooped over the mass, which towered far above his head. There was no room to move. "Good God!" The stale odor was much worse here, and a scurrying sound did not bode well.

James backed hastily out. He thought of the shuttered rooms on the upper floors. Were they all...? But perhaps only this one was a mare's nest. He walked across the entryway and tried the door on the left. It concealed a larger room in the same wretched condition. His heart, which had not been precisely singing, sank. He'd assumed that his new position would require a good deal of tedious effort, but he hadn't expected chaos.

The click of footsteps approached from outside. The front door was still open, and now a fashionably dressed young lady walked through it. She was accompanied by a maid and a footman. The latter started to shut the door behind them. "Don't," commanded James. The young servant shied like a nervous horse.

"What is that smell?" the lady inquired, putting a gloved hand to her nose.

"What are you doing here?" James asked the bane of his existence.

"You mentioned that you were going to look over the house today."

"And in what way is this your concern?"

"I was so curious. There are all sorts of rumors about this place. No one has been inside for years." She went over to one of the parlor doors and peered around it. "Oh!" She crossed to look into the other side. "Good heavens!"

"Indeed."

"Well, this is going to be a great deal of work." She smiled. "You won't like that."

"You have no idea what I..." James had to stop, because he knew that she had a very good idea.

"I know more about your affairs than you do," she added.

It was nearly true. Once, it certainly had been. That admission took him back thirteen years to his first meeting with Cecelia Vainsmede. He'd been just fifteen, recently orphaned, and in the midst of a blazing row with his new trustee. Blazing on his side, at any rate. Nigel Vainsmede had been pained and evasive and clearly just wishing James would go away. They'd fallen into one of their infuriating bouts of pushing in and fending off, insisting and eluding. James had understood by that time that his trustee might agree to a point simply to be rid of him, but he would never carry through with any action. Vainsmede would forget—willfully, it seemed to James. Insultingly.

And then a small blond girl had marched into her father's library and ordered them to stop at once. Even at nine years old, Cecelia had been a determined character with a glare far beyond her years. James had been surprised into silence. Vainsmede had actually looked grateful. And on that day they had established the routine that allowed them to function for the next ten years—speaking to each other only through Cecelia. James would approach her with "Please tell your father." And she would manage the matter, whatever it was. James didn't have to plead, which he hated, and Nigel Vainsmede didn't have to do anything at all, which was his main hope in life as far as James could tell.

James and Cecelia had worked together all through their youth. Cecelia was not a friend, and not family, but some indefinable other sort of close connection. And she did know a great deal about him. More than he knew about her. Although he had observed, along with the rest of the *haut ton*, that she had grown up to be a very pretty young lady. Today in a walking dress of sprig muslin and a straw bonnet decorated with matching blue ribbons, she was lithely lovely. Her hair was less golden than it had been at nine but far better cut. She had the face of a renaissance Madonna except for the rather too lush lips. And her luminous blue eyes missed very little, as he had cause to know. Not that any of this was relevant at the moment. "Your father has not been my trustee for three years," James pointed out.

"And you have done nothing much since then."

He would have denied it, but what did it matter? Instead he said, "I never could understand why my father appointed *your* father as my trustee."

"It was odd," she said.

"They were just barely friends, I would say."

"Hardly that," she replied. "Papa was astonished when he heard."

"As was I." James remembered the bewildered outrage of his fifteen-year-old self when told that he would be under the thumb of a stranger until he reached the age of twenty-five. "And, begging your pardon, but your father is hardly a pattern card of wisdom."

"No. He is indolent and self-centered. Almost as much as you are."

"Why, Miss Vainsmede!" He rarely called her that. They had dropped formalities and begun using first names when she was twelve. "I am not the least indolent."

She hid a smile. "Only if you count various forms of sport. Which I do not. I have thought about the trusteeship, however. From what I've learned of your father—I did not know him of course—I think he preferred to be in charge."

A crack of laughter escaped James. "Preferred! An extreme understatement. He had the soul of an autocrat and the temper of a frustrated tyrant."

She frowned at him. "Yes. Well. Having heard something of that, I came to the conclusion that your father chose mine because he was confident Papa would do nothing in particular."

"What?"

"I think that your father disliked the idea of not being…present to oversee your upbringing, and he couldn't bear the idea of anyone *doing* anything about that."

James frowned as he worked through this convoluted sentence.

"And so he chose my father because he was confident Papa wouldn't…bestir himself and try to make changes in the arrangements."

Surprise kept James silent for a long moment. "You know that is the best theory I have heard. It might even be right."

"You needn't sound so astonished," Cecelia replied. "I often have quite good ideas."

"What a crackbrained notion!"

"I beg your pardon?"

"My father's, not yours." James shook his head. "You think he drove me nearly to distraction just to fend off change?"

"If he had lived…" she began.

"Oh, that would have been far worse. A never-ending battle of wills."

"You don't know that. I was often annoyed with my father when I was younger, but we get along well now."

"Because he lets you be as scandalous as you please, Cecelia."

"Oh nonsense."

James raised one dark brow.

"I *wish* I could learn to do that," exclaimed his pretty visitor. "You are said to have the most killing sneer in the *ton*, you know."

He was not going to tell her that he had spent much of a

summer before the mirror when he was sixteen perfecting the gesture.

"And it was *not* scandalous for me to attend one ball without a chaperone. I was surrounded by friends and acquaintances. What could happen to me in such a crowd?" She shook her head. "At any rate, I am quite on the shelf at twenty-two. So it doesn't matter."

"Don't be stupid." James knew, from the laments of young gentleman acquaintances, that Cecelia had refused several offers. She was anything but "on the shelf."

"I am never stupid," she replied coldly.

He was about to make an acid retort when he recalled that Cecelia was a positive glutton for work. She'd also learned a great deal about estate management and business as her father pushed tasks off on her, his only offspring. She'd come to manage much of Vainsmede's affairs as well as the trust. Indeed, she'd taken to it as James never had. He thought of the challenge confronting him. Could he cajole her into taking some of it on?

She'd gone to open the door at the rear of the entryway. "There is just barely room to edge along the hall here," she said. "Why would anyone keep all these newspapers? There must be years of them. Do you suppose the whole house is like this?"

"I have a sinking feeling that it may be worse. The sole servant ran off as if she was conscious of her failure."

"One servant couldn't care for such a large house even if it hadn't been…"

"A rubbish collection? I think Uncle Percival must have actually been mad. People called him eccentric, but this is…" James peered down the cluttered hallway. "No wonder he refused all my visits."

"Did you try to visit him?" Cecelia asked.

"Of course."

"Huh."

"Is that so surprising?" asked James.

"Well, yes, because you don't care for anyone but yourself."

"Don't start up this old refrain."

"It's the truth."

"More a matter of opinion and definition," James replied.

She waved this aside. "You will have to do better now that you are the head of your family."

"A meaningless label. I shall have to bring some order." He grimaced at the stacks of newspapers. "But no more than that."

"A great deal more," said Cecelia. "You have a duty…"

"As Uncle Percival did?" James gestured at their surroundings.

"His failure is all the more reason for you to shoulder your responsibilities."

"I don't think so."

Cecelia put her hands on her hips, just as she had done at nine years old. "Under our system the bulk of the money and all of the property in the great families passes to one man, in this case you. You are obliged to manage it for the good of the whole." She looked doubtful suddenly. "If there is any money."

"There is," he replied. This had been a continual sore point during the years of the trust. And after, in fact. His father had not left a fortune. "Quite a bit of it seemingly. I had a visit from a rather sour banker. Uncle Percival was a miser as well as a…" James gestured at the mess. "A connoisseur of detritus. But if you think I will tolerate the whining of indigent relatives, you are deluded." He had made do when he was far from wealthy. Others could follow suit.

"You must take care of your people."

She was interrupted by a rustle of newsprint. "I daresay there are rats," James said.

"Do you think to frighten me? You never could."

This was true. And he had really tried a few times in his youth.

"I am consumed by morbid curiosity," Cecelia added as she slipped down the hall. James followed. Her attendants came straggling after, the maid looking uneasy at the thought of rodents.

They found other rooms as jumbled as the first two. Indeed, the muddle seemed to worsen toward the rear of the house. "Is that a spinning wheel?" Cecelia exclaimed at one point. "Why would a duke want such a thing?"

"It appears he was unable to resist acquiring any object that he came across," replied James.

"But where would he come across a spinning wheel?"

"In a tenant's cottage?"

"Do you suppose he bought it from them?"

"I have no idea." James pushed aside a hanging swag of cloth. Dust billowed out and set them all coughing. He stifled a curse.

At last they came into what might have been a library. James thought he could see bookshelves behind the piles of refuse. There was a desk, he realized, with a chair pulled up to it. He hadn't noticed at first because it was buried under mountains of documents. At one side sat a large wicker basket brimming with correspondence.

Cecelia picked up a sheaf of pages from the desk, glanced over it, and set it down again. She rummaged in the basket. "These are all letters," she said.

"Wonderful."

"May I?"

James gestured his permission, and she opened one from the top. "Oh, this is bad. Your cousin Elvira needs help."

"I have no knowledge of a cousin Elvira."

"Oh, I suppose she must have been your uncle Percival's cousin. She sounds rather desperate."

"Well, that is the point of a begging letter, is it not? The effect is diminished if one doesn't sound desperate."

"Yes, but James…"

"My God, do you suppose they're all like that?" The basket was as long as his arm and nearly as deep. It was mounded with correspondence.

Cecelia dug deeper. "They all seem to be personal letters. Just thrown in here. I suppose they go back for months."

"Years," James guessed. Dust lay over them, as it did everything here.

"You must read them."

"I don't think so. For once I approve of Uncle Percival's methods. I would say throw them in the fire, if lighting a fire in this place wasn't an act of madness."

"Have you no family feeling?"

"None. You read them if you're so interested."

She shuffled through the upper layer. "Here's one from your grandmother."

"Which one?"

"Lady Wilton."

"Oh no."

Cecelia opened the sheet and read. "She seems to have misplaced an earl."

"What?"

"A long-lost heir has gone missing."

"Who? No, never mind. I don't care." The enormity of the task facing him descended on James, looming like the piles of objects leaning over his head. He looked up. One wrong move, and all that would fall about his ears. He wanted none of it.

A flicker of movement diverted him. A rat had emerged from a crevice between a gilded chair leg and a hideous outsized vase. The creature stared down at him, insolent, seeming to know that it was well out of reach. "Wonderful," murmured James.

Cecelia looked up. "What?"

He started to point out the animal, to make her jump, then bit back the words as an idea recurred. He, and her father, had taken advantage of her energetic capabilities over the years. He knew it. He was fairly certain she knew it. Her father had probably never noticed. But Cecelia hadn't minded. She'd said once that the things she'd learned and done had given her a more interesting life than most young ladies were allowed. Might his current plight not intrigue her? So instead of mentioning the rodent, he offered his most charming smile. "Perhaps you would like to have that basket," he suggested. "It must be full of compelling stories."

Her blue eyes glinted as if she understood exactly what he was up to. "No, James. This mare's nest is all yours. I think, actually, that you deserve it."

"How can you say so?"

"It is like those old Greek stories, where the thing one tries hardest to avoid fatefully descends."

"Thing?" said James, gazing at the looming piles of *things*.

"You loathe organizational tasks. And this one is monumental."

"You have always been the most annoying girl," said James.

"Oh, I shall enjoy watching you dig out." Cecelia turned away. "My curiosity is satisfied. I'll be on my way."

"It isn't like you to avoid work."

She looked over her shoulder at him. "*Your* work. And as you've pointed out, our…collaboration ended three years ago. We will call this visit a final farewell to those days."

She edged her way out, leaving James in his wreck of an inheritance. He was conscious of a sharp pang of regret. He put it down to resentment over her refusal to help him.

---

Thinking of James's plight as she sat in her drawing room later that day, Cecelia couldn't help smiling. James liked order, and he didn't care for hard work. That house really did seem like fate descending on him like a striking hawk. Was it what he deserved? It was certainly amusing.

She became conscious of an impulse, like a nagging itch, to set things in order. The letters, in particular, tugged at her. She couldn't help wondering about the people who had written and their troubles. But she resisted. Her long association with James was over. There were reasons to keep her distance. She'd given in to curiosity today, but that must be the end.

"Tereford will manage," she said, ostensibly to the other occupant of the drawing room, but mostly to herself.

"Mmm," replied her aunt, Miss Valeria Vainsmede.

Cecelia had told her the story of the jumbled town house, but as usual her supposed chaperone had scarcely listened. Like Cecelia's father, her Aunt Valeria cared for nothing outside her own chosen sphere. "I sometimes wonder about my grandparents," Cecelia murmured. These Vainsmede progenitors, who had died before she was born, had produced a pair of plump, blond offspring with almost no interest in other people.

"You wouldn't have liked them," replied Aunt Valeria. One never knew when she would pick up on a remark and respond, sometimes after hours of silence. It was disconcerting. She was bent over a small pasteboard box. It undoubtedly contained a bee, because nothing else would hold her attention so completely. A notebook, quill, and inkpot sat beside it.

"You think not?" asked Cecelia.

"No one did."

"Why?"

"They were not likable," said her aunt.

"In what way?"

"In the way of a parasitic wasp pushing into the hive."

Cecelia stared at her aunt, who had not looked up from whatever she was doing, and wondered how anyone could describe their parents in such a disparaging tone. Aunt Valeria might have been speaking of total strangers. Whom she despised.

She felt a sudden flash of pain. How she missed her mother! Mama had been the polar opposite of the Vainsmedes. Warm and affectionate and prone to joking, she'd even brought Papa out of his self-absorption now and then and made their family feel—-familial. She'd made him laugh. And she'd filled Cecelia's days with love. Her absence was a great icy void that would never be filled.

Cecelia took a deep breath. And another. These grievous moments were rare now. They'd gradually lessened in the years since Mama died when she was twelve, leaving her in the care of her distracted father. She'd found ways to move on, of course. But she would never forget that day, and feeling so desperately alone.

Until James had come to see her. He'd stepped into this very drawing room so quietly that she knew nothing until he spoke her name. Her aunt had not yet arrived; her father was with his books. She was wildly startled when he said, "Cecelia."

She'd lashed out, expecting some heartless complaint about his financial affairs. But James had sat down beside her on the sofa and taken her hand and told her how sorry he was. That nineteen-year-old sprig of fashion and aspiring sportsman, who'd often taunted her, had praised her mother in the kindest way and acknowledged how much she would be missed. Most particularly by Cecelia, of course. After a moment of incredulity, she'd burst into tears, thrown herself upon him, and sobbed on his shoulder. He'd tolerated the outburst as her father would not. He'd tried, clumsily, to comfort her, and Cecelia had seen that there was more to him than she'd understood.

A footman came in and announced visitors. Cecelia put the past aside. Aunt Valeria responded with a martyred sigh.

Four young ladies filed into the room, and Cecelia stood to greet them. She'd been expecting only one, Miss Harriet Finch, whose mother had been a school friend of her mama. Mrs. Finch had written asking for advice and aid with her daughter's debut, and Cecelia had volunteered to help Miss Harriet acquire a bit of town polish. Now she seemed to be welcoming the whole upper level of a girls' school, judging from the outmoded wardrobes and dowdy haircuts. "Hello," she said.

The most conventionally pretty of the group, with red-blond hair, green eyes, a pointed chin beneath a broad forehead, and a beautiful figure, stepped forward. "How do you do?" she said. "I am Harriet Finch."

According to the gossips, she was a considerable heiress. Quite a spate of inheritances lately, Cecelia thought, though she supposed people were always dying.

"And these are Miss Ada Grandison, Miss Sarah Moran, and Miss Charlotte Deeping," the girl went on. She pointed as she gave their names.

"I see," said Cecelia.

"They are my friends." Miss Finch spoke as if they were a set of china that mustn't on any account be broken up.

"May I present my aunt, Miss Vainsmede," said Cecelia.

Aunt Valeria pointed to one ear and spoke in a loud toneless voice. "Very deaf. Sorry." She returned to her box and notepad, putting her back to their visitors.

Cecelia hid a sigh. Her aunt could hear as well as anyone, but she insisted on telling society that she could not. It must have been an open secret, because the servants were well aware of her true state. But the ruse allowed Aunt Valeria to play her part as chaperone without making any effort to participate in society. Cecelia had once taxed her with feigning what others found a sad affliction. Her aunt had informed her that she actually did not hear people who nattered on about nothing. "My mind rejects their silly yapping," she'd declared. "It turns to a sort of humming in my brain, and then I begin to think of something interesting instead." Cecelia gestured toward a sofa. "Do sit down," she said to her guests.

The girls sat in a row facing her. They didn't fold their hands, but it felt as if they had. They looked hopeful and slightly apprehensive. Cecelia examined them, trying to remember which was which.

Miss Ada Grandison had heavy, authoritative eyebrows. They dominated smooth brown hair, brown eyes, a straight nose, and full lips.

Miss Sarah Moran, the shortest of the four, was a smiling round little person with sandy hair, a turned-up nose, and sparkling light blue eyes. It was too bad her pale brows and eyelashes washed her out.

The last, Miss Charlotte Deeping, was the tallest, with black hair, pale skin, and a sharp dark gaze. She looked spiky. "I thought you didn't have a chaperone," she said to Cecelia, confirming this impression.

"What made you think that?"

"We heard you went to a ball on your own."

"I met my party there," Cecelia replied, which was nearly true. She had attached herself to friends as soon as she arrived. That solitary venture had perhaps been a misjudgment. But it was a very minor scandal, more of an eccentricity, she told herself. She was impatient with the rules now that she was in her fourth season. "My aunt has lived with us since my mother died," she told her visitors.

"I thought it must be a hum," replied Miss Deeping. "It seems we are to be stifled to death here in London."

Cecelia could sympathize. Because her father paid no attention and her aunt did not care, her situation was unusual. She'd been the mistress of the house for nine years, and manager of the Vainsmede properties for even longer. Her father left everything to her, too lazy to be bothered. Indeed Cecelia sometimes wondered how she ever came to be in the first place, as Papa cared for nothing but rich meals and reading. She supposed her maternal grandmother had simply informed him that he was being married and then sent someone to drag him from his library to the church on the day. But no, he had cared for Mama. She must believe that.

"Every circumstance is different," said Miss Moran.

She was one who liked to smooth things over, Cecelia noted.

"And Miss Vainsmede is older than…" Miss Moran blushed and bit her lip as if afraid she'd given offense.

"Three years older than you," Cecelia acknowledged. "Do you all want my advice?"

"We must have new clothes and haircuts," said Miss Grandison. The others nodded.

"We're new to London and fashionable society, where you are well established," said Miss Finch. "My mother says we would be wise to heed an expert."

"Which doesn't precisely answer my question," said Cecelia. "Do you wish to hear my opinions?"

They looked at each other, engaged in a brief silent communication, and then all nodded. The exchange demonstrated a solid friendship, which Cecelia envied. Many of her friends had married and did not come to town for the season. She missed them. "Very well," she began. "I think you, Miss Moran, would do well to darken your brows and lashes. It would draw attention to your lovely eyes."

The girl looked shocked. "Wouldn't that be dreadfully *fast*?"

"A little daring perhaps," said Cecelia. "But no one will know if you do it before your entry into society."

"Don't be missish, Sarah," said Miss Deeping.

Cecelia wondered if she was a bully. "You should wear ruffles," she said to her. She suspected that this suggestion would not be taken well, and it was not.

"Ruffles," repeated the dark girl in a tone of deep revulsion.

"To soften the lines of your frame."

"Disguise my lamentable lack of a figure you mean."

Cecelia did not contradict her. Nor did she evade the glare that came with these words. They either wanted her advice or they didn't. She didn't know them well enough to care which it was to be.

"You haven't mentioned my eyebrows," said Miss Grandison, frowning.

"You appear to use them to good effect."

Miss Grandison was surprised into a laugh.

"And I?" asked Miss Finch. There seemed to be an undertone of resentment or bitterness in her voice. Odd since she had the least to fear from society, considering her inheritance.

"New clothes and a haircut," Cecelia replied. "We could call on my modiste tomorrow if you like."

The appointment was agreed on.

"Oh, I hope this season goes well," said Miss Moran.

"There will be another next year," Cecelia said. She heard the trace of boredom in her voice and rejected it. She was not one of those languishing women who claimed to be overcome by ennui.

"I shan't be here. It was always to be only one season for me." Miss Moran clasped her hands together. "So I intend to enjoy it *immensely*."

# Acknowledgments

I have so much to be thankful for, and so many people to thank. A book doesn't write itself, and it isn't finished with "the end." I'm so grateful for my Heavenly Father who has blessed me with this love for reading and writing, and for my family who make it possible to carve out the time to write, especially my hubby. And my editors, God bless you, every one of you. I'd be lost, LOST without you. Each minute you spend sharpening my words and making them stronger, better, clearer, I'm grateful for all that you do. And Deb, thank you for pushing me to be a stronger storyteller. All in all, I'm thankful for a job I love! Huzzah!

# About the Author

Kristin Vayden has published more than a dozen titles with Blue Tulip Publishing, *New York Times* bestselling author Rachel Van Dyken's publishing company. Kristin's inspiration for the romance she writes comes from her tall, dark, and handsome husband with killer blue eyes. With five children to chase, she is never at a loss for someone to kiss, something to cook, or some mess to clean, but she loves every moment of it! Life is full—of blessings and adventure. Needless to say, she's a big fan of coffee and wine…and living in Washington, she's within walking distance of both.

Follow her on Facebook: facebook.com/kristinvaydenauthor
Instagram: @kristinkatjoyce